SPECTER!

BOOKS BY BILL PRONZINI

NOVELS
Scattershot
Masques
Hoodwink
Labyrinth
Blowback
Games
Snowbound
Undercurrent
The Vanished
Panic!
The Snatch
The Stalker

COLLABORATIVE NOVELS
The Cambodia File (with Jack Anderson)
Prose Bowl (with Barry N. Malzberg)
Night Screams (with Barry N. Malzberg)
Twospot (with Collin Wilcox)
Acts of Mercy (with Barry N. Malzberg)
The Running of Beasts (with Barry N. Malzberg)

NONFICTION
Gun in Cheek

ANTHOLOGIES
The Arbor House Treasury of Mystery and Suspense (with
    Barry N. Malzberg and Martin H. Greenberg)
The Arbor House Treasury of Horror and the Supernatural
    (with Barry N. Malzberg and Martin H. Greenberg)
Creature!
The Arbor House Necropolis
Mummy!
Voodoo!
Werewolf!
The Edgar Winners
Bug-Eyed Monsters (with Barry N. Malzberg)
Shared Tomorrows (with Barry N. Malzberg)
The End of Summer: Science Fiction of the 50s (with Barry N.
    Malzberg)
Midnight Specials
Dark Sins, Dark Dreams (with Barry N. Malzberg)
Tricks & Treats (with Joe Gores)

SPECTER!

A CHRESTOMATHY OF
"SPOOKERY"

Edited by
Bill Pronzini

ARBOR HOUSE
New York

ACKNOWLEDGMENTS

This page constitutes an extension of the copyright page.

THE PANELLED ROOM, by August Derleth.
Copyright © 1933 by *The Westminster Magazine*; copyright © 1941, 1969 by August Derleth. Reprinted by permission of Arkham House Publishers, Inc., Sauk City, WI. 53583.

THE SKULL OF THE MARQUIS DE SADE, by Robert Bloch.
Copyright © 1945 by Weird Tales, Inc. First published in *Weird Tales*. Reprinted by permission of Scott Meredith Literary Agency, Inc., 845 Third Avenue, New York, N.Y. 10022.

SILVER SPECTRE, by Jon L. Breen.
Copyright © 1980 by Davis Publications, Inc. First published in *Alfred Hitchcock's Mystery Magazine*. Reprinted by permission of the author.

DEATHLOVE, by Bill Pronzini.
Copyright © 1978 by Charles L. Grant. First published in *Shadows*. Reprinted by permission of the author.

FISH NIGHT, by Joe R. Lansdale.
Copyright © 1982 by Joe R. Lansdale. An original story published by permission of the author.

DUST TO DUST, by Marcia Muller.
Copyright © 1982 by Marcia Muller. An original story published by permission of the author.

CHAINED, by Barry N. Malzberg.
Copyright © 1982 by Barry N. Malzberg. An original story published by permission of the author.

NIGHT-SIDE, by Joyce Carol Oates.
Copyright © 1977 by Joyce Carol Oates. Reprinted by permission of the author.

CONTENTS

INTRODUCTION

THIS HOUSE IS HAUNTED.

The people who live in this remote countryside have sworn it to you. According to them, evil men built the house a century ago, and eventually died there under mysterious circumstances, and now their malefic spirits prowl the crumbling rooms. You have also been told that everyone who has sought to dwell in the house has fled in terror after only a few days' occupancy; and that some of the foolish thrill-seekers who have spent a night there have never been seen or heard from again. Don't set foot inside those rotting walls, the locals have warned you, especially not if you're alone. Stay away. If you value your life—stay away!

This house is haunted.

Perhaps it is, but you remain skeptical. Ghost-hunting is your hobby; you've spent nights in a dozen other supposedly haunted houses, with little to show in the way of supernatural or paranormal activity. You anticipate more of the same here. It's not that you disbelieve in ghosts *per se*; no, what you disbelieve in is the notion of evil spirits, of phantoms

9

and specters, bent on reaching out from beyond the veil to harm the living.

You stand on the weed-choked lane leading to the house, your hands full of the provisions you've carried from the car: camera with infrared lens, portable tape recorder, flashlight, kerosene lantern, blankets, food and coffee to help see you through the night's vigil. The night itself is warm, redolent of approaching summer; and yet, curiously, no birds sing, no insects buzz or hum. There are no sounds at all except for your own quiet breathing—an odd, almost preternatural hush.

The moon is three-quarters full in the black-velvet sky, and in its glow the house is clearly visible. Once it was a simple country-style Victorian; now it is only a decaying hulk, its roof partially collapsed, nearly all of its windows shattered, and great gaps in its boarding. Coarse grass, creepers, wild rose bushes and wisteria vines rise up in the thick profusion to conceal part of the front porch, so that you have the impression the house is slowly sinking into the earth. Giant oaks grow on both sides, casting grotesque shadows, their branches bent away from the ruins as if shunning them.

A vague chill touches your neck as you survey the house and grounds, as you listen to the absence of sound. The place is eerie, all right, particularly at night; no wonder the superstitious locals believe it is inhabited by malevolent spirits. But you are not prone to flights of dark fancy; you are a pragmatist, and the unknown holds little terror for you. You smile at the looming shapes ahead, shrug, and then proceed up the lane.

Once a fence surrounded the house, but it long ago collapsed; your shoes clump on the remains of the gate hidden in the high grass. No one has been here in a long time: the grass is untrampled, the bushes and vines grow so thickly that you are forced to blaze your own path to the porch.

Thorns scratch your arms. Something tugs at your foot, but you know it's only a creeper; you don't even bother to look down as you wrench loose from it.

The porch stairs are rotting, and before you ascend you make certain they will support your weight. The front door stands open, canted at a drunken angle from one hinge; you move to the threshold, set your provisions down, and switch on the flashlight. When you play the beam inside you see more or less what you expected to find: an empty foyer with a sagging staircase at the rear and two empty rooms opening on either side; floors littered with broken boards and pieces of plaster and shards of broken glass; walls pocked with holes, here and there showing fragments of ancient wallpaper like strips of peeling skin; a haze of spiderwebs, the tattered remnants of once-elegant portières.

You step inside, wrinkling your nose at the strong smell of decay, and pause to listen. There is nothing to hear, not even the expected scurrying of rats; the breathless night-hush envelops the interior of the house as well. Then you carry everything inside the parlor, set it down near the marble-fronted fireplace where there is not quite so much debris. And once you've lit the lantern and spread out your blanket, you loop the camera around your neck and set off to explore the rest of the house.

Downstairs first—sitting room, dining room, back parlor, kitchen, pantry, crude toilet. The flash beam shows you that each is empty except for debris and a few pieces of splintered furniture in the kitchen. You return to the foyer, carefully climb the dilapidated stairs to the second floor. Three bedrooms, an upstairs sitting room, another toilet—all as empty as the rooms downstairs. The window in one of the bedrooms is boarded up and the walls and floor bear a series of stains; but the stains are so old and faded that you can't tell what might have spilled or splashed there.

Back in the downstairs parlor, you set up the tape recorder

and then make yourself comfortable on the blanket with a cup of coffee. Now you're ready for the long night's wait.

The hours pass slowly and in silence. There are no rattling chains, no eerie wails, no ghostly manifestations of any kind. No sounds at all other than the creaking of old joints. You become convinced that nothing is going to happen; boredom sets in and you have to fight off drowsiness.

You're pouring the last cup of coffee, long past midnight, when you hear the thump.

It comes suddenly, from overhead—a single loud noise, as if something heavy had dropped on the floor directly above. You scramble to your feet, scoop up the lantern, and then stand poised. But not for flight; a bump in the night does not make you afraid. You stand poised to listen for other sounds.

You hear only silence.

It was probably a falling board or chunk of plaster, you think. But your curiosity has been piqued; you take the lantern out to the stairs, climb to the second floor. The room directly above the front parlor, you realize as you near it, is the bedroom with the faded stains on the walls and floor.

In the doorway you pause and extend the lantern into the room. The flickering light reveals the same emptiness as before. But what made the thump? You step inside, move to the center of the room. Then you see it: a piece of plaster must have worked itself loose from the ceiling, lying near the boarded-up window.

You chuckle softly. Nothing here to be concerned about; no spooks or specters or anything else. You chuckle again, then say what you're thinking aloud: "Nothing here at all."

"Except us," a voice behind you says.

And the bedroom door slams shut . . .

But are there *really* such things as ghosts?

There is no easy answer to that question. It all depends

on whether one believes, or at least does not disbelieve, in the supernatural; and on whether or not one requires cold hard proof of the existence of disembodied souls, denizens of what spiritualists call the "Other Side." For despite the efforts of a variety of psychical research organizations, and the claims of any number of individual investigators, no such proof has yet been found.

Until the latter half of the nineteenth century, the existence of spooks and specters, and of other forms of psychic phenomena, was either accepted without question or scoffed at as superstitious nonsense; there was no organized scientific study of such matters. In the 1870s and 1880s, F.W.H. Meyers in this country, and the Society for Psychical Research (founded in 1882) in England, initiated critical investigation into a wide range of paranormal activity. Their pioneering contributions are negligible, but they led to important studies in the 1930s which legitimized parapsychology as a viable field of scientific research.

These studies, in the areas of extrasensory perception and psychokinesis (the movement of an object not in contact with the body generating the force) were conducted in the Parapsychology Laboratory at Duke University, under the direction of famed psychologist J.B. Rhine. The results obtained in many individual experiments and in the research as a whole, based on statistics and the laws of probability, could not be attributed to chance. The scientific validity of both ESP and psychokinesis was therefore proven, at least to the satisfaction of most observers.

Dr. Rhine retired from Duke University in 1965 to continue his research with the privately endowed Foundation for Research on the Nature of Man. Since then, parapsychology has become established at other universities—The University of Virginia now has a division of parapsychology—and has become a credit course at several institutions. Independent research centers have grown in number as well, among them

14   SPECTER!

the American Society for Psychical Research based in New York City, and the Parapsychological Association, an international organization founded in 1957 by scientists and scholars actively working in the field, which was later granted affiliation status by the American Society for the Advancement of Science. Researches at these universities and by independent groups have led to the partial acceptance of such other psychic phenomena as precognition (previous knowledge of future events), retrocognition (knowledge of past events and past lives), clairvoyance (the power of discerning objects or happenings not evident to the normal senses), clairaudience (the audible hearing of sounds without the use of one's ears), and psychometry (subjective knowledge drawn from contact with objects belonging to or used by some other person).

But parapsychologists still have been unable to prove or disprove the existence of ghosts. Nor have the dwindling number of proponents of spiritualism been able to prove it, despite a vast amount of contrary claims. The spiritualist movement, a major part of which involves the use of trance mediums and seances to contact and communicate with those on the Other Side, enjoyed considerable popularity during the period 1900–1930, and was championed by such luminaries as the creator of Sherlock Holmes, Sir Arthur Conan Doyle; but spiritualism has fallen into disfavor and disrepute because of the number of charlatans and criminals who have used it to bilk the unwary, and because few people in this more sophisticated technological age are willing to accept the validity of such phenomena as apports (movement of objects by supernormal means, at times from great distances and through locked doors and stone walls), automatic writing (messages written on paper or chalkboards by someone on the Other Side), spirit guides (an excarnate, or former mortal, who serves as a go-between for a medium and ghostly entities and who relays messages), bilocation (the transporation of the astral body, or spirit, from the physical body to a distant place), ectoplasm (the emanation from a medium which apparently produces motion in distant objects without physical contact), or xenoglossis (the talk of entranced mediums in languages with which they are not familiar in their conscious state).

Be this as it may, proof or no proof, ghosts *may* still exist, of course. As Dr. Rhine has written, "No one knows what thought is. Nobody knows how consciousness is produced. There isn't even a theory." The human brain has been operated on countless times, without the life force, the soul, ever being seen or its presence scientifically proven. Yet we know it's there—a force, an energy. A ghost can be a manifestation of that same force or energy; it can be there without our seeing it, or being able to prove we've seen it.

And just as there are good and evil souls in the human animal, there can be good and evil ghosts. When an evil person dies there is no reason to believe that his spirit will undergo any magical transformation and become good; spooks and specters are the same personalities they were in this life. Given the opportunity, the wicked ones are bound to continue doing what they did while they lived on this side: giving pain, destroying life.

What sort of opportunity? Mediums have long believed that when you delve into the unknown to seek spirits, you should be extra careful; for if the spirits you're after are evil, you're liable to find a great deal more than you bargained for.

In the realm of the supernatural, you almost always attract what you seek . . .

The first nonfiction work on psychic phenomena was F.W.H. Meyers' *Human Personality and Its Survival of Bodily Death* (circa 1900)—a comprehensive study for its time, but heavily outdated in light of what has been learned during the past eighty years. Dr. J.B. Rhine's *The Reach of the Mind* (1947) and *Parapsychology, Frontier Science of the Mind* (1957) are both excellent accounts of his research work at Duke University and of his theories on the paranormal.

Perhaps the best account of the spiritualist movement is Conan Doyle's exhaustive two-volume *History of Spiritualism* (1926). He also wrote a number of other books on the subject, having become a zealous convert following the death of his eldest son in World War I; among these are *The Vital Message* (1919), *Spiritualism and Rationalism* (1920), *Psychic Experiences* (1925), and *The Edge of the Unknown* (1930).

There have been a large number of nonfiction works devoted to spectral sightings and encounters, many of them well-documented "case histories." The most accomplished writer in this area is probably James Reynolds, whose prose has been called "magical" and "eerie"; his books include *Ghosts in American Houses* (1954), *Ghosts in Irish Houses* (1955), and *More Ghosts in Irish Houses* (1956). Two other writers of note are veteran ghost-hunters Susy Smith and Hans Holzer. Smith, who is also a medium, has produced several provocative works, among them *Prominent American Ghosts* (1967), *Haunted Houses for the Millions* (1967), and *Ghosts Around the World* (1970). Holzer's many titles include *The Ghost Hunter* (1965), *Lively Ghosts of Ireland* (1967), and *Yankee Ghosts* (1966).

Other unusual books of this genre are Danton Walker's *I Believe in Ghosts* (revised edition, 1969), which recounts the spectral experiences of such celebrities as Noel Coward, Burl Ives, Mae West and Ida Lupino; N.M.W. Stirling's *Ghosts Vivisected* (1958), an "impartial inquiry into the manners, habits, mentality, motives and physical construction" of ghosts; and *Great Ghosts of the West* (1971) by actor Richard Webb (who portrayed Captain Midnight on television)—a collection of "true" ghost stories from the Mojave Desert, the High Sierras and other California locales. Two books on the poltergeist are also worth reading: *Haunted People* (1951) by

Hereward Carrington and Nandor Fodor, a historical study of this mischievous phenomenon noted for banging on walls, throwing things, and making objects appear and disappear; and *This House is Haunted* (1980), a documentation of the activities of a single poltergeist by another experienced investigator of the paranormal, Guy Lyon Playfair.

One other important nonfiction catergory is that of critical studies of the fictional tale of the supernatural and its writers. For the broad historical overview, the best of these works is the brief but incisive *Supernatural Horror in Literature*, by the man whom many consider to be the grand master of the macabre, H.P. Lovecraft. First published in 1927, this study was reprinted by Dover Books in 1973. A valuable book on the English ghost story, particularly those from the Edwardian and Victorian periods, is Jack Sullivan's *Elegant Nightmares* (1978). J. Sheridan LeFanu, M.R. James, Algernon Blackwood, W.F. Harvey, Arthur Machen, H.R. Wakefield, and E.F. Benson are among the writers whose work is examined in depth in this volume.

It has been said that the ideal form for the fictional tale of spooks and specters is the short story. This may well be true, but some of the finest and most memorable excursions into the supernatural have been novels and plays. Shakespeare's *Hamlet*, for instance. Theophile Gautier's *Spirite: A Fantasy* (1877), George Sand's *The Naiad; A Ghost Story* (1892), Henry James' *The Turn of the Screw* (1898). And such contemporary novels as Shirley Jackson's *The Haunting of Hill House* (1959), Robert Marasco's *Burnt Offerings* (1973), Stephen King's *The Shining* (1977), and Peter Straub's *Ghost Story* (1979).

The first anthology of stories of the supernatural, the anonymously edited *Ghost Stories*, appeared in England in 1823; the first American anthology, *Modern Ghosts*, was published in 1890. Dozens of other spectral anthologies, as well as numerous single-author collections, have appeared during

18   SPECTER!

the twentieth century. Among the best of the former are
the three-volume *The Ghost Book*, edited by Cynthia Asquith
(1927), *The Supernatural Omnibus*, edited by Montague Summers (1931), and *Famous Ghost Stories*, edited by Bennett
Cerf (1944); among the best of the collections are M.R.
James' *Ghost Stories of an Antiquary*, Oliver Onions' *Widdershins*
(1911), *The Best Ghost Stories of J. Sheridan LeFanu* (1964),
The Best Ghost Stories of Algernon Blackwood (1964), and *The
Ghost Stories of Edith Wharton* (1973).

The pick of the crop among ghostly films seems to be
those adapted from novels or short stories. In this writer's
opinion, the finest is *The Haunting* (1963), starring Julie
Harris and Claire Bloom and based on Shirley Jackson's *The
Haunting of Hill House*—an intelligent film which derives its
eerie effects by leaving a good deal unexplained, such as
what goes crashing and banging along the corridors of the
haunted house. Other noteworthy movies, much less subtle
but no less effective in their depiction of the more terrifying
aspects of the supernatural, are *The Skull* (1965), featuring
Peter Cushing and based on Robert Bloch's story "The Skull
of the Marquis de Sade" (which appears in these pages);
The Legend of Hell House (1973), based on Richard Matheson's
novel *Hell House* and starring Pamela Franklin and Roddy
McDowall; *The Shining* (1980), with Jack Nicholson (some
of whose facial contortions are unintentionally hilarious)
and Shelley Duvall, based on the Stephen King novel; and
Peter Straub's *Ghost Story* (1981), starring Fred Astaire and
Melvyn Douglas.

There have been several ghost-comedies that are worth
watching when they turn up on the Late Show: *Topper* (1937),
starring Cary Grant, Roland Young, and Constance Bennett,
and its two sequels, *Topper Takes a Trip* (1938) and *Topper
Returns* (1941)—all based on characters created by Thorne
Smith; *Hold that Ghost* (1942), the best and most restrained
of the Abbott and Costello farces; *The Canterville Ghost* (1944),

from the Oscar Wilde story (which also appears in these pages) and featuring Charles Laughton and Margaret O'Brien; and *The Ghost and Mrs. Muir* (1947), with Rex Harrison and Gene Tierney.

Anthologies of ghost stories tend to reprint overly familiar rather than little known tales, and eschew the use of original material. That is not the case with *Specter!* In the pages of this chrestomathy, you'll find such seldom-reprinted classics as Poe's "Berenice," Dickens' "The Story of the Bagman's Uncle," O. Henry's "The Furnished Room," M.R. James' "Lost Hearts," Bram Stoker's "The Judge's House," Oliver Onions' "Phantas," W.F. Harvey's "On the Moors," and Oscar Wilde's "The Canterville Ghost"; uncommon popular tales by August Derleth ("The Panelled Room"), Robert Bloch ("The Skull of the Marquis de Sade"), Jon L. Breen ("Silver Spectre"), and Bill Pronzini ("Deathlove"); originals by Joe R. Lansdale ("Fish Night"), Marcia Muller ("Dust to Dust"), and Barry N. Malzberg ("Chained"); and a neoclassic, "Night-Side," by Joyce Carol Oates.

These sixteen stories offer a wide variety of spectral entertainment, from pure wonder to pure comedy to pure horror—a little something for everyone. Once you begin reading, it won't take you long to get into the proper spirit.

Just don't let an *im*proper spirit get into you . . .

Remember: Evil is all around us, not only in this world but on the Other Side. The shades of evil excarnates are waiting there for an opportunity to return—waiting to work their malefic powers on the unsuspecting.

So beware as you travel the supernatural byways in the pages ahead.

You almost always attract what you seek . . .

Bill Pronzini
San Francisco, California
March, 1982

PART I

CLASSIC STORIES

BERENICE
by
EDGAR ALLAN POE

The narrator of "Berenice," like the protagonists of so many Poe stories, is quite mad. But the question here is: What drove Egaeus over the edge into psychotic lunacy? Was it merely an idée fixe, born in a mind slowly collapsing of its own accord? Or was it, in fact, an encounter with the supernatural?

The answer is for you to judge. But whether the specter in this little-known Poe tale is real or imagined, the consequences of Egaeus's madness are inescapably monstrous. And so is the horror which permeates these pages—the horror of both the known and the unknown . . .

Edgar Allan Poe (1809–1849) wrote so devastatingly of mental aberration because, at least in the last years of his life, madness was a specter with which he himself was plagued. Nevertheless, the bulk of his work—verse and epic poetry, essays, sketches, short stories, literary criticism— is of such quality that it has earned him a place of high rank in American literature. He published his first book, Tamerlane and Other Poems, *in 1827, and was a major force in the development of the short story as a distinct literary form in*

*the 1830s and 1840s. He was also the father of the detective story
as we know it today, having written the first tale of this type,
"Murders in the Rue Morgue," in 1841. His deteriorating mental
condition, compounded by alcohol and perhaps drug abuse, was the
cause of his premature death in Baltimore in 1849.*

DICEBANT MIHI SODALES, SI SEPULCHRUM AMICAE VIS-
ITAREM, CURAS MEAS ALIQUANTULUM FORE LEVATAS.

Ebn Zaiat

MISERY IS MANIFOLD. THE WRETCHEDNESS OF EARTH IS
multiform. Overreaching the wide horizon as the rainbow,
its hues are as various as the hues of that arch,—as distinct
too, yet as intimately blended. Overreaching the wide horizon
as the rainbow! How is it that from beauty I have derived
a type of unloveliness?—from the covenant of peace a simile
of sorrow? But as, in ethics, evil is a consequence of good,
so, in fact, out of joy is sorrow born. Either the memory of
past bliss is the anguish of to-day, or the agonies which *are*
have their origin in the ecstasies which *might have been.*

My baptismal name is Egaeus; that of my family I will not
mention. Yet there are no towers in the land more time-
honoured than my gloomy, grey hereditary halls. Our line
has been called a race of visionaries; and in many striking
particulars—in the character of the family mansion—in the
frescoes of the chief saloon—in the tapestries of the dor-
mitories—in the chiselling of some buttresses in the armoury—
but more especially in the gallery of antique paintings—in
the fashion of the library chamber—and, lastly, in the very
peculiar nature of the library's contents, there is more than
sufficient evidence to warrant the belief.

The recollections of my earlier years are connected with
that chamber, and with its volumes—of which latter I will

say no more. Here died my mother. Herein was I born. But it is mere idleness to say that I had not lived before—that the soul had no previous existence. You deny it?—let us not argue the matter. Convinced myself, I seek not to convince. There is, however, a remembrance of aerial forms—of spiritual and meaning eyes—of sounds, musical yet sad—a remembrance which will not be excluded; a memory like a shadow, vague, variable, indefinite, unsteady; and like a shadow, too, in the impossibility of my getting rid of it while the sunlight of my reason shall exist.

In that chamber was I born. Thus awaking from the long night of what seemed, but was not, nonentity, at once into the very regions of fairy-land—into a palace of imagination—into the wild dominions of monastic thought and erudition—it is not singular that I gazed around me with a startled and ardent eye—that I loitered away my boyhood in books, and dissipated my youth in reverie; but it *is* singular that as years rolled away, and the noon of manhood found me still in the mansion of my father—it is wonderful what stagnation there fell upon the springs of my life—wonderful how total an inversion took place in the character of my commonest thought. The realities of the world affected me as visions, and as visions only, while the wild ideas of the land of dreams became, in turn—not the material of my everyday existence—but in very deed that existence utterly and solely in itself.

Berenice and I were cousins, and we grew up together in my paternal halls. Yet differently we grew—I ill of health, and buried in gloom—she agile, graceful, and overflowing with energy; hers the ramble on the hillside—mine the studies of the cloister—I living within my own heart, and addicted body and soul to the most intense and painful meditation—she roaming carelessly through life with no thought of the shadows in her path, or the silent flight of the raven-winged hours. Berenice!—I call upon her name—Berenice!—and

from the grey ruins of memory a thousand tumultuous recollections are startled at the sound! Ah! vividly is her image
before me now, as in the early days of her light-heartedness
and joy! Oh! gorgeous yet fantastic beauty! Oh! sylph amid
the shrubberies of Arnheim! Oh! Naiad among its foundations!—and then—then all is mystery and terror, and a
tale which should not be told. Disease—a fatal disease—fell
like the simoom upon her frame, and, even while I gazed
upon her, the spirit of change swept over her, pervading
her mind, her habits, and her character, and, in a manner
the most subtle and terrible, disturbing even the identity of
her person! Alas! the destroyer came and went, and the
victim—where was she? I knew her not—or knew her no
longer as Berenice.

Among the numerous train of maladies superinduced by
that fatal and primary one which effected a revolution of
so horrible a kind in the moral and physical being of my
cousin, may be mentioned as the most distressing and ob-
stinate in its nature, a species of epilepsy not unfrequently
terminating in *trance* itself—trance very nearly resembling
positive dissolution, and from which her manner of recovery
was, in most instances, startlingly abrupt. In the meantime
my own disease—for I have been told that I should call it
by no other appellation—my own disease, then, grew rapidly
upon me, and assumed finally a monomaniac character of
a novel and extraordinary form—hourly and momentarily
gaining vigour—and at length obtaining over me the most
incomprehensible ascendancy. This monomania, if I must
so term it, consisted in a morbid irritability of those properties
of the mind in metaphysical science termed the *attentive*. It
is more than probable that I am not understood; but I fear,
indeed, that it is in no manner possible to convey to the
mind of the merely general reader, an adequate idea of that
nervous *intensity of interest* with which, in my case, the powers
of meditation (not to speak technically) busied and buried

themselves, in the contemplation of even the most ordinary objects of the universe.

To muse for long unwearied hours with my attention riveted to some frivolous device on the margin, or in the typography of a book; to become absorbed for the better part of a summer's day in quaint shadow falling aslant upon the tapestry, or upon the door; to lose myself for an entire night in watching the steady flame of a lamp, or the embers of a fire; to dream away whole days over the perfume of a flower; to repeat monotonously some common word, until the sound, by dint of frequent repetition, ceased to convey any idea whatever to the mind; to lose all sense of motion or physical existence, by means of absolute bodily quiescence long and obstinately persevered in—such were a few of the most common and least pernicious vagaries induced by a condition of the mental faculties, not, indeed, altogether unparalleled, but certainly bidding defiance to anything like analysis or explanation.

Yet let me not be misapprehended. The undue, earnest, and morbid attention thus excited by objects in their own nature frivolous, must not be confounded in character with that ruminating propensity common to all mankind, and more especially indulged in by persons of ardent imagination. It was not even, as might be at first supposed, an extreme condition, or exaggeration of such propensity, but primarily and essentially distinct and different. In the one instance, the dreamer, or enthusiast, being interested by an object usually *not* frivolous, imperceptibly loses sight of this object in a wilderness of deductions and suggestions issuing there-from, until, at the conclusion of a day-dream *often replete with luxury*, he finds the *incitamentum* or first cause of his musings entirely vanished and forgotten. In my case the primary object was *invariably frivolous*, although assuming, through the medium of my distempered vision, a refracted and unreal importance. Few deductions, if any, were made;

and those few pertinaciously returning in upon the original object as a centre. The meditations were *never* pleasurable; and, at the termination of the reverie, the first cause, so far from being out of sight, had attained that supernaturally exaggerated interest which was the prevailing feature of the disease. In a word, the powers of mind more particularly exercised were, with me, as I have said before, the *attentive*, and are, with the day-dreamer, the *speculative*.

My books, at this epoch, if they did not actually serve to irritate the disorder, partook, it will be perceived, largely, in their imaginative and inconsequential nature, of the characteristic qualities of the disorder itself. I well remember, among others, the treatise of the noble Italian Coelius Secundus Curio, *De Amplitudine Beati Regni Dei*; St. Austin's great work, *The City of God*; and Tertullian, *De Carne Christi*, in which the paradoxical sentence: *"Mortuus est Dei filius; credible est quia ineptum est: et sepultus resurrexit; certum est quia impossibile est,"* occupied my undivided time, for many weeks of laborious and fruitless investigation.

Thus it will appear that, shaken from its balance only by trivial things, my reason bore resemblance to that ocean-crag spoken of by Ptolemy Hephestion, which, steadily resisting the attacks of human violence, and the fiercer fury of the waters and the winds, trembled only to the touch of the flower called Asphodel. And although, to a careless thinker, it might appear a matter beyond doubt, that the alteration produced by her unhappy malady, in the *moral* condition of Berenice, would afford me many objects for the exercise of that intense and abnormal meditation whose nature I have been at some trouble in explaining, yet such was not in any degree the case. In the lucid intervals of my infirmity, her calamity, indeed, gave me pain, and, taking deeply to heart that total wreck of her fair and gentle life, I did not fail to ponder frequently and bitterly upon the wonder-working means by which so strange a revolution had been so suddenly brought to pass. But these reflections partook not of the idiosyncrasy of my disease, and were such as would have occured, under similar circumstances, to the ordinary mass of mankind. True to its own character, my disorder revelled in the less important but more startling changes wrought in the *physical* frame of Berenice—in the singular and most appalling distortion of her personal identity.

During the brightest days of her unparalleled beauty, most surely I had never loved her. In the strange anomaly of my existence, feelings with me *had never been* of the heart, and my passions *always were* of the mind. Through the grey of the early morning—among the trellised shadows of the forest at noonday—and in the silence of my library at night, she had flitted by my eyes, and I had seen her—not as the living and breathing Berenice, but as the Berenice of a dream—not as a being of the earth, earthy, but as the abstraction of such a being—not as a thing to admire, but to analyse—not as an object of love, but as the theme of the most abstruse although desultory speculation. And *now*—now I shuddered in her presence, and grew pale at her approach; yet bitterly lamenting her fallen and desolate condition, I called to mind that she had loved me long, and, in an evil moment, I spoke to her of marriage.

And at length the period of our nuptials was aproaching, when, upon an afternoon on the winter of the year,—one of those unseasonably warm, calm, and misty days which are the nurse of the beautiful Halcyon[1]—I sat (and sat, as I thought, alone) in the inner apartment of the library. But uplifting my eyes I saw that Berenice stood before me.

Was it my own excited imagination—or the misty influence of the atmosphere—or the uncertain twilight of the cham-

---

[1]For as Jove, during the winter season, gives twice seven days of warmth, men have called this clement and temperate time the nurse of the beautiful Halcyon.—SIMONIDES.

ber—or the grey draperies which fell around her figure—
that caused in it so vacillating and indistinct an outline? I
could not tell. She spoke no word, and I—not for worlds
could I have uttered a syllable. An icy chill ran through my
frame; a sense of insufferable anxiety oppressed me; a con-
suming curiosity pervaded my soul; and sinking back upon
the chair, I remained for some time breathless and motionless,
with my eyes riveted upon her person. Alas! its emaciation
was excessive, and not one vestige of the former being lurked
in any single line of the contour. My burning glances at
length fell upon the face.

The forehead was high, and very pale, and singularly
placid; and the once jetty hair fell partially over it, and
overshadowed the hollow temples with innumerable ringlets
now a vivid yellow, and jarring discordantly, in their fantastic
character, with the reigning melancholy of the countenance.
The eyes were lifeless, and lustreless, and seemingly pupil-
less, and I shrank involuntarily from their glassy stare to
the contemplation of the thin and shrunken lips. They parted;
and in a smile of peculiar meaning, *the teeth* of the changed
Berenice disclosed themselves slowly to my view. Would to
God that I had never beheld them or that, having done so,
I had died!

The shutting of a door disturbed me, and, looking up, I
found that my cousin had departed from the chamber. But
from the disordered chamber of my brain, had not, alas!
departed, and would not be driven away, the white and
ghastly *spectrum* of the teeth. Not a speck on their surface—
not a shade on their enamel—not an indenture in their
edges—but what that period of her smile had sufficed to
brand in upon my memory. I saw them *now* even more
unequivocally than I beheld them *then*. The teeth!—the
teeth!—they were here, and there, and everywhere, and
visibly and palpably before me; long, narrow, and excessively

white, with pale lips writhing about them, as in the very moment of their first terrible development. Then came the full fury of my *monomania*, and I struggled in vain against its strange and irresistible influence. In the multiplied objects of the external world I had no thoughts but for the teeth. For these I longed with a phrenzied desire. All other matters and all different interests became absorbed in their single contemplation. They—they alone were present to the mental eye, and they, in their sole individuality, became the essence of my mental life. I held them in every light. I turned them in every attitude. I surveyed their characteristics. I dwelt upon their peculiarities. I pondered upon their conformation. I mused upon the alteration in their nature. I shuddered as I assigned to them in imagination a sensitive and sentient power, and even when unassisted by the lips, a capability of moral expression. Of Mad'selle Sallé it has been well said, *"que tous ses pas étaient des sentiments,"* and of Berenice I more seriously believed *que toutes ses dents étaient des idées. Des idées!*— ah here was the idiotic thought that destroyed me! *Des idées!*— ah *therefore* it was that I coveted them so madly! I felt that their possession could alone ever restore me to peace, in giving me back to reason.

And the evening closed in upon me thus—and then the darkness came, and tarried, and went—and the day again dawned—and the mists of a second night were now gathering around—and still I sat motionless in that solitary room; and still I sat buried in meditation, and still the *phantasma* of the teeth maintained its terrible ascendency as, with the most vivid and hideous distinctness, it floated about amid the changing lights and shadows of the chamber. At length there broke in upon my dreams a cry as of horror and dismay; and thereunto, after a pause, succeeded the sound of troubled voices, intermingled with many low moanings of sorrow, or of pain. I arose from my seat and, throwing open one of the doors of the library, saw standing out in the ante-chamber a servant maiden, all in tears, who told me that Berenice was—no more. She had been seized with epilepsy in the early morning, and now, at the closing in of the night, the grave was ready for its tenant, and all the preparations for the burial were completed.

I found myself sitting in the library, and again sitting there alone. It seemed that I had newly awakened from a confused and excited dream. I knew that it was now midnight, and I was well aware that since the setting of the sun Berenice had been interred. But of that dreary period which intervened I had no positive—at least no definite comprehension. Yet its memory was replete with horror—horror more horrible from being vague, and terror more terrible from ambiguity. It was a fearful page in the record of my existence, written all over with dim, and hideous, and unintelligible recollections. I strived to decipher them, but in vain; while ever and anon, like the spirit of a departed sound, the shrill and piercing shriek of a female voice seemed to be ringing in my ears. I had done a deed—what was it? I asked myself the question aloud, and the whispering echoes of the chamber answered me, *"what was it?"*

On the table beside me burned a lamp, and near it lay a little box. It was of no remarkable character, and I had seen it frequently before, for it was the property of the family physician; but how came it *there*, upon my table, and why did I shudder in regarding it? These things were in no manner to be accounted for, and my eyes at length dropped to the open pages of a book, and to a sentence underscored therein. The words were the singular but simple ones of the poet Ebn Zaiat, *"Dicebant mihi sodales si sepulchrum amicae visitarem, curas meas aliquantulum fore levatas."* Why then, as I perused them, did the hairs of my head erect themselves on end, and the blood of my body become congealed within my veins?

There came a light tap at the library door, and pale as the tenant of a tomb, a menial entered upon tiptoe. His looks were wild with terror, and he spoke to me in a voice tremulous, husky, and very low. What said he?—some broken sentences I heard. He told of a wild cry disturbing the silence of the night—of the gathering together of the household—of a search in the direction of the sound;—and then his tones grew thrillingly distinct as he whispered me of a violated grave—of a disfigured body enshrouded, yet still breathing, still palpitating, still *alive!*

He pointed to my garments;—they were muddy and clotted with gore. I spoke not, and he took me gently by the hand;—it was indented with the impress of human nails. He directed my attention to some object against the wall;—I looked at it for some minutes;—it was a spade. With a shriek I bounded to the table, and grasped the box that lay upon it. But I could not force it open; and in my tremor it slipped from my hands, and fell heavily, and burst into pieces; and from it, with a rattling sound, there rolled out some instruments of dental surgery, intermingled with thirty-two small, white, and ivory-looking substances that were scattered to and fro about the floor.

THE STORY OF THE BAGMAN'S UNCLE
by
CHARLES DICKENS

Those who know the work of Charles Dickens only through such relatively grim novels as David Copperfield, Bleak House, *and* A Tale of Two Cities, *are in for a surprise when they read "The Story of the Bagman's Uncle." It is not a dark tale of ghostly doings but rather a good-humored—and in places very funny—one. The bagman's uncle, in fact, may be one of the great unsung comic characters of nineteenth-century fiction.*

His adventures, on a night when he successfully undertakes to outdrink a Scotchman of prodigious capacity, are strange as well as lighthearted, swashbuckling and amorous. To lay not one but two ghosts, and to win the love of a spectral lady in the bargain, is a feat of no small worth for any man, drunk or sober.

The novels of Charles Dickens (1812–1870) are well known, but the fact that he also wrote a number of "popular fictions" (of which "The Story of the Bagman's Uncle" is one example) for a variety of British weekly periodicals in the mid-1800s, has not been as widely publicized. He wrote these stories to supplement his income and help finance a wide range of extra-literary interests—charitable

34

organizations, social reform, travels in Europe and America, a
theatrical company. Inasmuch as they reflect his storytelling mastery,
his insight and complex use of symbolism, as well as his fascination
with the psychological and the supernatural, they are an important
part of the Dickens canon.

"MY UNCLE, GENTLEMEN," SAID THE BAGMAN, "WAS ONE OF
the merriest, pleasantest, cleverest fellows that ever lived. I
wish you had known him, gentlemen. On second thoughts,
gentlemen, I *don't* wish you had known him; for if you had,
you would have been all by this time, in the ordinary course
of nature, if not dead, at all events so near it as to have
taken to stopping at home and giving up company, which
would have deprived me of the inestimable pleasure of addressing you at this moment. Gentlemen, I wish your fathers
and mothers had known my uncle. They would have been
amazingly fond of him, especially your respectable mothers;
I know they would. If any two of his numerous virtues
predominated over the many that adorned his character, I
should say they were his mixed punch and his after-supper
song. Excuse my dwelling on these melancholy recollections
of departed worth; you won't see a man like my uncle every
day in the week.

"I have always considered it a great point in my uncle's
character, gentlemen, that he was the intimate friend and
companion of Tom Smart, of the great house of Bilson and
Slum, Cateaton Street, City. My uncle collected for Tiggin
and Welps, but for a long time he went pretty near the same
journey as Tom; and the very first night they met, my uncle
took a fancy for Tom, and Tom took a fancy for my uncle.
They made a bet of a new hat, before they had known each
other half an hour, who should brew the best quart of punch
and drink it the quickest. My uncle was judged to have won

the making, but Tom Smart beat him in the drinking by about half a salt-spoonful. They took another quart apiece to drink each other's health in, and were stanch friends ever afterwards. There's a destiny in these things, gentlemen; we can't help it.

"In personal appearance my uncle was a trifle stouter than the middle size; he was a thought stouter, too, than the ordinary run of people, and perhaps his face might be a shade redder. He had the jolliest face you ever saw, gentlemen—something like Punch, with a handsomer nose and chin; his eyes were always twinkling and sparkling with good-humour; and a smile—not one of your unmeaning wooden grins, but a real, merry, hearty, good-tempered smile—was perpetually on his countenance. He was pitched out of his gig once, and knocked, head first, against a milestone. There he lay, stunned, and so cut about the face with some gravel which had been heaped up alongside it, that, to use my uncle's own strong expression, if his mother could have revisited the earth, she wouldn't have known him. Indeed, when I come to think of the matter, gentlemen, I feel pretty sure she wouldn't; for she died when my uncle was two years and seven months old, and I think it's very likely that, even without the gravel, his top-boots would have puzzled the good lady not a little, to say nothing of his jolly red face. However, there he lay, and I have heard my uncle say, many a time, that the man said who picked him up that he was smiling as merrily as if he had tumbled out for a treat, and that after they had bled him, the first faint glimmerings of returning animation were his jumping up in bed, bursting out into a loud laugh, kissing the young woman who held the basin, and demanding a mutton chop and a pickled walnut instantly. He was very fond of pickled walnuts, gentlemen. He said he always found that, taken without vinegar, they relished the beer.

"My uncle's great journey was in the fall of the leaf, at

which time he collected debts and took orders in the north; going from London to Edinburgh, from Edinburgh to Glasgow, from Glasgow back to Edinburgh, and thence to London by the smack. You are to understand that his second visit to Edinburgh was for his own pleasure. He used to go back for a week, just to look up his old friends; and what with breakfasting with this one, lunching with that, dining with a third, and supping with another, a pretty tight week he used to make of it. I don't know whether any of you, gentlemen, ever partook of a real substantial hospitable Scotch breakfast, and then went out to a slight lunch of a bushel of oysters, a dozen or so of bottled ale, and a noggin or two of whisky to close up with. If you ever did, you will agree with me that it requires a pretty strong head to go out to dinner and supper afterwards.

"But bless your hearts and eyebrows, all this sort of thing was nothing to my uncle! He was so well seasoned that it was mere child's play. I have heard him say that he could see the Dundee people out any day, and walk home afterwards without staggering; and yet the Dundee people have as strong heads and as strong punch, gentlemen, as you are likely to meet with between the poles. I have heard of a Glasgow man and a Dundee man drinking against each other for fifteen hours at a sitting. They were both suffocated, as nearly as could be ascertained, at the same moment, but with this trifling exception, gentlemen, they were not a bit the worse for it.

"One night, within four-and-twenty hours of the time when he had settled to take shipping for London, my uncle supped at the house of a very old friend of his, a Bailie Mac-something and four syllables after it, who lived in the old town of Edinburgh. There were the Bailie's wife, and the Bailie's three daughters, and the Bailie's grown-up son, and three or four stout, bushy-eyebrowed, canty old Scotch fellows, that the Bailie had got together to do honour to my uncle, and help to make merry. It was a glorious supper. There were kippered salmon, and Finnan Haddocks, and a lamb's head, and a haggis—a celebrated Scotch dish, gentlemen, which my uncle used to say always looked to him, when it came to table, very much like a Cupid's stomach—and a great many other things besides that I forget the names of, but very good things notwithstanding. The lassies were pretty and agreeable, the Bailie's wife one of the best creatures that ever lived, and my uncle in thoroughly good cue. The consequence of which was that the young ladies tittered and giggled, and the old lady laughed out loud, and the Bailie and the other old fellows roared till they were red in the face the whole mortal time. I don't quite recollect how many tumblers of whisky toddy each man drank after supper, but this I know, that about one o'clock in the morning the Bailie's grown-up son became insensible while attempting the first verse of 'Willie brewed a peck of maut'; and he having been, for half an hour before, the only other man visible above the mahogany, it occurred to my uncle that it was almost time to think about going, especially as drinking had set in at seven o'clock, in order that he might get home at a decent hour. But thinking it might not be quite polite to go just then, my uncle voted himself into the chair, mixed another glass, rose to propose his own health, addressed himself in a neat and complimentary speech, and drank the toast with great enthusiasm. Still nobody woke; so my uncle took a little drop more—neat this time, to prevent the toddy disagreeing with him—and laying violent hands on his hat, sallied forth into the street.

"It was a wild, gusty night when my uncle closed the Bailie's door, and settling his hat firmly on his head to prevent the wind from taking it, thrust his hands into his pockets, and looking upwards, took a short survey of the state of the weather. The clouds were drifting over the moon at their giddiest speed—at one time wholly obscuring her; at another suffering her to burst forth in full splendour and shed her light on all the objects around; anon driving over her again with increased velocity, and shrouding everything in darkness. 'Really, this won't do,' said my uncle, addressing himself to the weather, as if he felt himself personally offended. 'This is not at all the kind of thing for my voyage. It will not do at any price,' said my uncle, very impressively. Having repeated this several times, he recovered his balance with some difficulty—for he was rather giddy with looking up into the sky so long—and walked merrily on.

"The Bailie's house was in the Canongate, and my uncle was going to the other end of Leith Walk, rather better than a mile's journey. On either side of him there shot up against the dark sky tall, gaunt, straggling houses, with time-stained fronts, and windows that seemed to have shared the lot of eyes in mortals, and to have grown dim and sunken with age. Six, seven, eight stories high were the houses—story piled above story, as children build with cards—throwing their dark shadows over the roughly-paved road, and making the dark night darker. A few oil lamps were scattered at long distances, but they only served to mark the dirty entrance to some narrow close, or to show where a common stair communicated, by steep and intricate windings, with the various flats above. Glancing at all these things with the air of a man who had seen them too often before to think them worthy of much notice now, my uncle walked up the middle of the street, with a thumb in each waistcoat pocket, indulging from time to time in various snatches of song, chanted forth with such goodwill and spirit that the quiet, honest folk started from their first sleep, and lay trembling in bed till the sound died away in the distance; when, satisfying themselves that it was only some drunken ne'er-do-weel finding his way home, they covered themselves up warm and fell asleep again.

"I am particular in describing how my uncle walked up

the middle of the street with his thumbs in his waistcoat pockets, gentlemen, because, as he often used to say (and with great reason too), there is nothing at all extraordinary in this story, unless you distinctly understand at the beginning that he was not by any means of a marvellous or romantic turn.

"Gentlemen, my uncle walked on with his thumbs in his waistcoat pockets, taking the middle of the street to himself, and singing, now a verse of a love song, and then a verse of a drinking one; and when he was tired of both, whistling melodiously until he reached the North Bridge, which at this point connects the old and new towns of Edinburgh. Here he stopped for a minute to look at the strange, irregular clusters of lights, piled one above the other, and twinkling afar off so high in the air that they looked like stars, gleaming from the castle walls on the one side, and the Calton Hill on the other, as if they illuminated veritable castles in the air; while the old, picturesque town slept heavily on, in gloom and darkness below, its palace and chapel of Holyrood, guarded day and night, as a friend of my uncle's used to say, by old Arthur's Seat, towering, surly and dark, like some gruff genius, over the ancient city he has watched so long. I say, gentlemen, my uncle stopped here for a minute to look about him, and then, paying a compliment to the weather, which had a little cleared up, though the moon was sinking, walked on again as royally as before, keeping the middle of the road with great dignity, and looking as if he should very much like to meet with somebody who would dispute possession of it with him. There was nobody at all disposed to contest the point, as it happened, and so on he went, with his thumbs in his waistcoat pockets, like a lamb.

"When my uncle reached the end of Leith Walk, he had to cross a pretty large piece of waste ground, which separated him from a short street which he had to turn down to go direct to his lodging. Now, in this piece of waste ground

there was at that time an enclosure belonging to some wheelwright, who contracted with the Post-office for the purchase
of old, worn-out mail-coaches; and my uncle, being very
fond of coaches, old, young, or middle-aged, all at once
took it into his head to step out of his road for no other
purpose than to peep between the palings at these mails—
about a dozen of which he remembered to have been seen
crowded together in a very forlorn and dismantled state
inside. My uncle was a very enthusiastic, emphatic sort of
person, gentlemen; so, finding that he could not obtain a
good peep between the palings, he got over them, and sitting
himself quietly down on an old axle-tree, began to contemplate
the mail-coaches with a deal of gravity.

"There might be a dozen of them, or there might be
more—my uncle was never quite certain on this point, and
being a man of very scrupulous veracity about numbers,
didn't like to say—but there they stood, all huddled together
in the most desolate condition imaginable. The doors had
been torn from their hinges, and removed; the linings had
been stripped off, only a shred hanging here and there by
a rusty nail; the lamps were gone, the poles had long since
vanished, the ironwork was rusty, the paint worn away; the
wind whistled through the chinks in the bare woodwork and
the rain, which had collected on the roofs, fell, drop by
drop, into the insides with a hollow and melancholy sound.
They were the decaying skeletons of departed mails, and
in that lonely place, at that time of night, they looked chill
and dismal.

"My uncle rested his head upon his hands, and thought
of the busy, bustling people who had rattled about years
before in the old coaches, and were now as silent and changed;
he thought of the numbers of people to whom one of those
crazy, mouldering vehicles had borne, night after night, for
many years and through all weathers, the anxiously-expected
intelligence, the eagerly looked-for remittance, the promised

assurance of health and safety, the sudden announcement of sickness and death. The merchant, the lover, the wife, the widow, the mother, the school-boy, the very child who tottered to the door at the postman's knock—how had they all looked forward to the arrival of the old coach. And where were they all now?

"Gentlemen, my uncle used to *say* that he thought all this at the time, but I rather suspect he learned it out of some book afterwards; for he distinctly stated that he fell into a kind of doze as he sat on the old axle-tree, looking at the decayed mail-coaches, and that he was suddenly awakened by some deep church bell striking two. Now, my uncle was never a fast thinker; and if he had thought all these things, I am quite certain it would have taken him till full half-past two o'clock, at the very least. I am, therefore, decidedly of opinion, gentlemen, that my uncle fell into the kind of doze without having thought about anything at all.

"Be this as it may, a church bell struck two. My uncle woke, rubbed his eyes, and jumped up in astonishment.

"In one instant after the clock struck two the whole of this deserted and quiet spot had become a scene of most extraordinary life and animation. The mail-coach doors were on their hinges, the lining was replaced, the ironwork was as good as new, the paint was restored, the lamps were alight, cushions and greatcoats were on every coach-box, porters were thrusting parcels into every boot, guards were stowing away letter-bags, hostlers were dashing pails of water against the renovated wheels, numbers of men were rushing about, fixing poles into every coach; passengers arrived, portmanteaus were handed up, horses were put to; and, in short, it was perfectly clear that every mail there was to be off directly. Gentlemen, my uncle opened his eyes so wide at all this that to the very last moment of his life he used to wonder how it fell out that he had ever been able to shut 'em again.

" 'Now, then!' said a voice, as my uncle felt a hand on his shoulder, 'you're booked for one inside. You'd better get in.'

" '*I* booked!' said my uncle, turning round.

" 'Yes, certainly.'

"My uncle, gentlemen, could say nothing, he was so very much astonished. The queerest thing of all was, that although there was such a crowd of persons, and although fresh faces were pouring in every moment, there was no telling where they came from. They seemed to start up, in some strange manner, from the ground or the air, and disappear in the same way. When a porter had put his luggage in the coach and received his fare, he turned round and was gone; and before my uncle had well begun to wonder what had become of him, half a dozen fresh ones started up, and staggered along under the weight of parcels which seemed big enough to crush them. The passengers were all dressed so oddly too: large, broad-skirted laced coats, with great cuffs and no collars; and wigs, gentlemen—great formal wigs, with a tie behind. My uncle could make nothing of it.

" 'Now, *are* you going to get in?' said the person who had addressed my uncle before. He was dressed as a mail guard, with a wig on his head and most enormous cuffs to his coat, and had a lantern in one hand and a huge blunderbuss in the other, which he was going to stow away in his little arm-chest. '*Are* you going to get in, Jack Martin?' said the guard, holding the lantern to my uncle's face.

" 'Hallo!' said my uncle, falling back a step or two. 'That's familiar!'

" 'It's so on the way-bill,' replied the guard.

" 'Isn't there a "Mister" before it?' said my uncle. For he felt, gentlemen, that for a guard he didn't know to call him Jack Martin was a liberty which the Post-office wouldn't have sanctioned if they had known it.

" 'No, there is not,' rejoined the guard, coolly.

" 'Is the fare paid?' inquired my uncle.

" 'Of course it is,' rejoined the guard.

" 'It is, is it?' said my uncle. 'Then here goes! Which coach?'

" 'This,' said the guard, pointing to an old-fashioned Edinburgh and London Mail, which had the steps down and the door open. 'Stop! Here are the other passengers; let them get in first.'

"As the guard spoke, there all at once appeared, right in front of my uncle, a young gentleman in a powdered wig, and a sky-blue coat trimmed with silver, made very full and broad in the skirts, which were lined with buckram. Tiggin and Welps were in the printed calico and waistcoat-piece line, gentlemen, so my uncle knew all the materials at once. He wore knee breeches, and a kind of leggings rolled up over his silk stocking, and shoes with buckles; he had ruffles at his wrists, a three-cornered hat on his head, and a long taper sword by his side. The flaps of his waistcoat came half-way down his thighs, and the ends of his cravat reached to his waist. He stalked gravely to the coach door, pulled off his hat, and held it above his head at arm's length, cocking his little finger in the air at the same time, as some affected people do when they take a cup of tea. Then he drew his feet together, and made a low grave bow, and then put out his left hand. My uncle was just going to step forward and shake it heartily, when he perceived that these attentions were directed, not towards him, but to a young lady who just then appeared at the foot of the steps, attired in an old-fashioned green velvet dress with a long waist and stomacher. She had no bonnet on her head, gentlemen, which was muffled in a black silk hood; but she looked round for an instant as she prepared to get into the coach, and such a beautiful face as she discovered my uncle had never seen— not even in a picture. She got into the coach, holding up her dress with one hand; and, as my uncle always said with a round oath when he told the story, he wouldn't have believed it possible that legs and feet could have been brought to such a state of perfection unless he had seen them with his own eyes.

"But in this one glimpse of the beautiful face my uncle saw that the young lady had cast an imploring looking upon him and that she appeared terrified and distressed. He noticed, too, that the young fellow in the powdered wig, notwithstanding his show of gallantry, which was all very fine and grand, clasped her tight by the wrist when she got in, and followed himself immediately afterwards. An uncommonly ill-looking fellow, in a close brown wig and a plum-coloured suit, wearing a very large sword, and boots up to his hips, belonged to the party; and when he sat himself down next to the young lady, who shrunk into a corner at his approach, my uncle was confirmed in his original impression that something dark and mysterious was going forward, or, as he always said to himself, that 'there was a screw loose somewhere.' It's quite surprising how quickly he made up his mind to help the lady at any peril, if she needed help.

" 'Death and lightning!' exclaimed the young gentleman, laying his hand upon his sword as my uncle entered the coach.

" 'Blood and thunder!' roared the other gentleman. With this he whipped his sword out, and made a lunge at my uncle without further ceremony. My uncle had no weapon about him, but with great dexterity he snatched the ill-looking gentleman's three-cornered hat from his head, and receiving the point of his sword right throught the crown, squeezed the sides together, and held it tight.

" 'Pink him behind!' cried the ill-looking gentleman to his companion, as he struggled to regain his sword.

" 'He had better not,' cried my uncle, displaying the heel of one of his shoes in a threatening manner. 'I'll kick his brains out, if he has any, or fracture his skull if he hasn't.'

Exerting all his strength at this moment, my uncle wrench-
ed the ill-looking man's sword from his grasp, and flung it
clean out of the coach window, upon which the younger
gentleman vociferated 'Death and lightning!' again, and
laid his hand upon the hilt of his sword in a very fierce
manner, but didn't draw it. Perhaps, gentlemen, as my uncle
used to say with a smile—perhaps he was afraid of alarming
the lady.

" 'Now, gentlemen,' said my uncle, taking his seat deliberately, 'I don't want to have any death, with or without
lightning, in a lady's presence, and we have had quite blood
and thundering enough for one journey; so, if you please,
we'll sit in our places like quiet insides.—Here, guard, pick
up that genleman's carving-knife.'

"As quickly as my uncle said the words, the guard appeared
at the coach window with the gentleman's sword in his hand.
He held up his lantern, and looked earnestly in my uncle's
face as he handed it in; when by its light my uncle saw, to
his great surprise, that an immense crowd of mail-coach
guards swarmed round the window, every one of whom had
his eyes earnestly fixed upon him too. He had never seen
such a sea of white faces, and red bodies, and earnest eyes,
in all his born days.

" 'This is the strangest sort of thing I ever had anything
to do with,' thought my uncle. 'Allow me to return you your
hat, sir.'

"The ill-looking gentleman received his three-cornered
hat in silence, looked at the hole in the middle with an
inquiring air, and finally stuck it on the top of his wig with
a solemnity the effect of which was a trifle impaired by his
sneezing violently at the moment and jerking it off again.

" 'All right!' cried the guard with the lantern, mounting
into his little seat behind. Away they went. My uncle peeped
out of the coach window as they emerged from the yard,
and observed that the other mails, with coachmen, guards,

horses, and passengers complete, were driving round and round in circles, at a slow trot of about five miles an hour. My uncle burnt with indignation, gentlemen. As a commercial man, he felt that the mail bags were not to be trifled with, and he resolved to memorialize the Post-office on the subject the very instant he reached London.

"At present, however, his thoughts were occupied with the young lady who sat in the farthest corner of the coach, with her face muffled closely in her hood—the gentleman with the sky-blue coat sitting opposite to her, and the other man in the plum-coloured suit by her side, and both watching her intently. If she so much as rustled the folds of her hood, he could hear the ill-looking man clap his hand upon his sword, and could tell by the other's breathing (it was so dark he couldn't see his face) that he was looking as big as if he were going to devour her at a mouthful. This roused my uncle more and more and he resolved, come what come might, to see the end of it. He had a great admiration for bright eyes, and sweet faces, and pretty legs and feet; in short, he was fond of the whole sex. It runs in our family, gentlemen. So am I.

"Many were the devices which my uncle practised to attract the lady's attention, or at all events to engage the mysterious gentlemen in conversation. They were all in vain; the gentlemen wouldn't talk, and the lady didn't dare. He thrust his head out of the coach window at intervals, and bawled out to know why they didn't go faster? But he called till he was hoarse; nobody paid the least attention to him. He leaned back in the coach, and thought of the beautiful face and the feet and legs. This answered better; it whiled away the time, and kept him from wondering where he was going, and how it was that he found himself in such an odd situation. Not that this would have worried him much anyway; he was a mighty free-and-easy, roving, devil-may-care sort of person, was my uncle, gentlemen.

"All of a sudden the coach stopped. 'Hallo!' said my uncle, 'what's in the wind now?'

" 'Alight here,' said the guard, letting down the steps.

" 'Here!' cried my uncle.

" 'Here,' rejoined the guard.

" 'I'll do nothing of the sort,' said my uncle.

" 'Very well, then, stop where you are,' said the guard.

" 'I will,' said my uncle.

" 'Do,' said the guard.

"The other passengers had regarded this colloquy with great attention, and finding that my uncle was determined not to alight, the younger man squeezed past him, to hand the lady out. At this moment the ill-looking man was inspecting the hole in the crown of his three-cornered hat. As the young lady brushed past, she dropped one of her gloves into my uncle's hand, and softly whispered, with her lips so close to his face that he felt her warm breath on his nose, the single word, 'Help!' Gentlemen, my uncle leaped out of the coach at once, with such violence that it rocked on the springs again.

" 'Oh! you've thought better of it, have you?' said the guard when he saw my uncle standing on the ground.

"My uncle looked at the guard for a few seconds, in some doubt whether it wouldn't be better to wrench his blunderbuss from him, fire it in the face of the man with the big sword, knock the rest of the company over the head with the stock, snatch up the young lady, and go off in the smoke. On second thoughts, however, he abandoned this plan, as being a shade too melodramatic in the execution, and followed the two mysterious men, who, keeping the lady between them, were now entering an old house in front of which the coach had stopped. They turned into the passage, and my uncle followed.

"Of all the ruinous and desolate places my uncle had ever beheld, this was the most so. It looked as if it had once been

THE STORY OF THE BAGMAN'S UNCLE

a large house of entertainment; but the roof had fallen in in many places, and the stairs were steep, rugged, and broken. There was a huge fireplace in the room into which they walked, and the chimney was blackened with smoke; but no warm blaze lighted it up now. The white feathery dust of burnt wood was still strewed over the hearth, but the stove was cold, and all was dark and gloomy.

" 'Well,' said my uncle, as he looked about him, 'a mail travelling at the rate of six miles and a half an hour, and stopping for an indefinite time at such a hole as this, is rather an irregular sort of proceeding, I fancy. This shall be made known. I'll write to the papers.'

"My uncle said this in a pretty loud voice, and in an open, unreserved sort of manner, with the view of engaging the two strangers in conversation if he could. But neither of them took any more notice of him than whispering to each other, and scowling at him as they did so. The lady was at the farther end of the room, and once she ventured to wave her hand, as if beseeching my uncle's assistance.

"At length the two strangers advanced a little, and the conversation began in earnest.

" 'You don't know this is a private room, I suppose, fellow?' said the gentleman in sky-blue.

" 'No, I do not, fellow,' rejoined my uncle. 'Only, if this is a private room specially ordered for the occasion, I should think the public room must be a *very* comfortable one.' With this my uncle sat himself down in a high-backed chair, and took such an accurate measure of the gentlemen with his eyes, that Tiggin and Welps could have supplied him with printed calico for a suit, and not an inch too much or too little, from that estimate alone.

" 'Quit this room,' said both the men together, grasping their swords.

" 'Eh?' said my uncle, not at all appearing to comprehend their meaning.

" 'Quit the room, or you are a dead man,' said the ill-looking fellow with the large sword, drawing it at the same time and flourishing it in the air.

" 'Down with him!' cried the gentleman in sky-blue, drawing his sword also, and falling back two or three yards—'down with him!' The lady gave a loud scream.

"Now my uncle was always remarkable for great boldness and great presence of mind. All the time that he had appeared so indifferent to what was going on, he had been looking slyly about for some missile or weapon of defence, and at the very instant when the swords were drawn, he espied, standing in the chimney corner, an old basket-hilted rapier in a rusty scabbard. At one bound my uncle caught it in his hand, drew it, flourished it gallantly above his head, called aloud to the lady to keep out of the way, hurled the chair at the man in sky-blue, and the scabbard at the man in plum-colour, and taking advantage of the confusion, fell upon them both, pell-mell.

"Gentlemen, there is an old story—none the worse for being true—regarding a fine young Irish gentleman, who being asked if he could play the fiddle, replied he had no doubt he could, but he couldn't exactly say for certain, because he had never tried. This is not inapplicable to my uncle and his fencing. He had never had a sword in his hand before except once, when he played Richard the Third at a private theatre; upon which occasion it was arranged with Richmond that he was to be run through from behind, without showing fight at all. But here he was, cutting and slashing with two experienced swordsmen—thrusting and guarding, and poking and slicing, and acquitting himself in the most manful and dexterous manner possible, although up to that time he had never been aware that he had the least notion of the science. It only shows how true the old saying is, that a man never knows what he can do till he tries, gentlemen.

"The noise of the combat was terrific—each of the three

combatants swearing like troopers, and their swords clashing with as much noise as if all the knives and steels in Newport market were rattling together at the same time. When it was at its very height, the lady (to encourage my uncle, most probably) withdrew her hood entirely from her face, and disclosed a countenance of such dazzling beauty that he would have fought against fifty men, to win one smile from it, and die. He had done wonders before, but now he began to powder away like a raving mad giant.

"At this very moment the gentleman in sky-blue, turning round and seeing the young lady with her face uncovered, vented an exclamation of rage and jealousy, and turning his weapon against her beautiful bosom, pointed a thrust at her heart, which caused my uncle to utter a cry of apprehension that made the building ring. The lady stepped lightly aside, and snatching the young man's sword from his hand before he had recovered his balance, drove him to the wall, and running it through him and the panelling, up to the very hilt, pinned him there, hard and fast. It was a splendid example. My uncle, with a loud shout of triumph and a strength that was irresistible, made his adversary retreat in the same direction, and plunging the old rapier into the very centre of a large red flower in the pattern of his waistcoat, nailed him beside his friend. There they both stood, gentlemen, jerking their arms and legs about in agony, like the toy-shop figures that are moved by a piece of pack-thread. My uncle always said afterwards that this was one of the surest means he knew of for disposing of an enemy; but it was liable to one objection on the ground of expense, inasmuch as it involved the loss of a sword for every man disabled.

" 'The mail, the mail!' cried the lady, running up to my uncle and throwing her beautiful arms round his neck; 'we may yet escape.'

" '*May!*' cried my uncle; 'why, my dear, there's nobody

else to kill, is there?' My uncle was rather disappointed, gentlemen; for he thought a little quiet bit of love-making would be agreeable after the slaughtering, if it were only to change the subject.

" 'We have not an instant to lose here,' said the young lady. 'He' (pointing to the young gentleman in sky-blue) 'is the only son of the powerful Marquess of Filletoville.'

" 'Well, then my dear, I'm afraid he'll never come to the title,' said my uncle, looking coolly at the young gentleman as he stood fixed up against the wall, in the cockchafter fashion I have described. 'You have cut off the entail, my love.'

" 'I have been torn from my home and friends by these villains,' her features glowing with indignation. 'That wretch would have married me by violence in another hour.'

" 'Confound his impudence!' said my uncle, bestowing a very contemptuous look on the dying heir of Filletoville.

" 'As you may guess from what you have seen,' said the young lady, 'the party were prepared to murder me if I appealed to anyone for assistance. If their accomplices find us here, we are lost. Two minutes hence may be too late. The mail!' With these words, overpowered by her feelings, and the exertion of sticking the young Marquess of Filletoville, she sunk into my uncle's arms. My uncle caught her up, and bore her to the house-door. There stood the mail, with four long-tailed, flowing-maned, black horses, ready harnessed; but no coachman, no guard, no hostler even, at the horses' heads.

"Gentlemen, I hope I do no injustice to my uncle's memory when I express my opinion, that although he was a bachelor, he *had* held some ladies in his arms before this time; I believe, indeed, that he had rather a habit of kissing barmaids; and I know that in one or two instances he had been seen by credible witnesses to hug a landlady in a very perceptible manner. I mention the circumstance to show what a very uncommon sort of person this beautiful young lady must have been to have affected my uncle in the way she did; he used to say that as her long, dark hair trailed over his arm, and her beautiful dark eyes fixed themselves upon his face when she recovered, he felt so strange and nervous that his legs trembled beneath him. But who can look in a sweet, soft pair of dark eyes without feeling queer? *I* can't, gentlemen. I am afraid to look at some eyes I know, and that's the truth of it.

" 'You will never leave me,' murmured the young lady.

" 'Never,' said my uncle. And he meant it too.

" 'My dear preserver!' exclaimed the young lady—'my dear, kind, brave preserver!'

" 'Don't,' said my uncle, interrupting her.

" 'Why?' inquired the young lady.

" 'Because your mouth looks so beautiful when you speak,' rejoined my uncle, 'that I am afraid I shall be rude enough to kiss it.'

"The young lady put up her hand as if to caution my uncle not to do so, and said—no, she didn't say anything— she smiled. When you are looking at a pair of the most delicious lips in the world, and see them gently break into a roguish smile—if you are very near them, and nobody else by—you cannot better testify your admiration of their beautiful form and colour than by kissing them at once. My uncle did so, and I honour him for it.

" 'Hark!' cried the young lady, starting: 'the noise of wheels and horses!'

" 'So it is,' said my uncle, listening. He had a good ear for wheels and tramping of hoofs; but there appeared to be so many horses and carriages rattling towards them from a distance, that it was impossible to form a guess at their number. The sound was like that of fifty brakes, with six blood cattle in each.

" 'We are pursued!' cried the young lady, clasping her

hands. 'We are pursued. I have no hope but in you!'

"There was such an expression of terror in her beautiful face that my uncle made up his mind at once. He lifted her into the coach, told her not to be frightened, pressed his lips to hers once more, and then advising her to draw up the window to keep the cold air out, mounted the box.

" 'Stay, love,' cried the young lady.

" 'What's the matter?' said my uncle, from the coach-box.

" 'I want to speak to you,' said the young lady, 'only a word—only one word, dearest.'

" 'Must I get down?' inquired my uncle. The lady made no answer, but she smiled again. Such a smile, gentlemen! it beat the other one all to nothing. My uncle descended from his perch in a twinkling.

" 'What is it, my dear?' said my uncle, looking in at the coach window. The lady happened to bend forward at the same time, and my uncle thought she looked more beautiful than she had done yet. He was very close to her just then, gentlemen, so he really ought to know.

" 'What is it, my dear?' said my uncle.

" 'Will you never love any one but me—never marry any one beside?' said the young lady.

"My uncle swore a great oath that he never would marry anybody else, and the young lady drew in her head and pulled up the window. He jumped upon the box, squared his elbows, adjusted the ribbons, seized the whip which lay on the roof, gave one flick to the off leader, and away went the four long-tailed, flowing-maned black horses, at fifteen good English miles an hour, with the old mail-coach behind them. Whew! how they tore along!

"The noise behind grew louder. The faster the old mail went, the faster came the pursuers—men, horses, dogs were leagued in the pursuit. The noise was frightful, but above all rose the voice of the young lady, urging my uncle on, and shrieking: 'Faster! faster!'

"They whirled past the dark trees as feathers would be swept before a hurricane. Houses, gates, churches, haystacks, objects of every kind they shot by, with a velocity and noise like roaring waters suddenly let loose. Still the noise of pursuit grew louder, and still my uncle could hear the young lady wildly screaming: 'Faster! faster!'

"My uncle plied whip and rein, and the horses flew onward till they were white with foam; and yet the noise behind increased, and yet the young lady cried: 'Faster! faster!' My uncle gave a loud stamp on the boot in the energy of the moment, and—found that it was grey morning, and he was sitting in the wheelwright's yard, on the box of an old Edinburgh mail, shivering with the cold and wet, and stamping his feet to warm them! He got down, and looked eagerly inside for the beautiful young lady. Alas! there was neither door nor seat to the coach; it was a mere shell.

"Of course my uncle knew very well that there was some mystery in the matter, and that everything had passed exactly as he used to relate it. He remained stanch to the great oath he had sworn to the beautiful young lady—refusing several eligible landladies on her account, and dying a bachelor at last. He always said what a curious thing it was that he should have found out, by such a mere accident as his clambering over the palings, that the ghosts of mail-coaches and horses, guards, coachmen, and passengers were in the habit of making journeys every night. He used to add that he believed he was the only living person who had ever been taken as a passenger on one of these excursions. And I think he was right, gentlemen—at least I never heard of any other."

THE FURNISHED ROOM
by
O. HENRY

O. Henry's tales of the "Four Million," the inhabitants of New York City just after the turn of the century, were the most popular of this celebrated American short-story writer's work, and remain so today. They deal not with the wealthy class of that era, but with ordinary people—the shopgirls, the saloon denizens, the grifters, the "transients in abode, transients in heart and mind." Some of these New York stories are humorous in tone; others are steeped in pathos. And all carry the distinctive O. Henry touch, as well as the distinctive O. Henry surprise ending.

"The Furnished Room" is one of his finest stories of the "Four Million"—a tale of love and heartache and tragedy . . . and yes, the supernatural. No one who has read it is likely to forget it. Or to feel moved, and perhaps chilled, by its final revelation.

William Sydney Porter (1862–1910) was born in Greensboro, North Carolina, migrated to Texas in 1882, and followed a varied career as a cowboy, journalist, and bank teller in Austin from 1891 to 1894. In 1898 he was tried and convicted of embezzlement committed during his years as a bank teller and subsequently served three years in an Ohio penitentiary. He began writing short stories for the popular magazines while in prison, adopting the pen name of O. Henry to conceal the fact of his incarceration, and on his release moved to New York City, where the bulk of his stories were written. Among his most memorable collections are The Four Million *(1906),* The Gentle Grafter *(1908),* The Voice of the City *(1908), and* Whirligigs *(1910). A prodigious drinker, as were many writers before and after him, he died of cirrhosis of the liver in his native state.*

RESTLESS, SHIFTING, FUGACIOUS AS TIME IS A CERTAIN VAST bulk of the population of the red brick district of the lower West Side. Homeless, they have a hundred homes. They flit from furnished room to furnished room, transients forever—transients in abode, transients in heart and mind. They sing "Home Sweet Home" in ragtime; they carry their *lares et penates* in a bandbox; their vine is entwined about a picture hat; a rubber plant is their fig tree.

Hence the houses of this district, having had a thousand dwellers, should have a thousand tales to tell, mostly dull ones, no doubt; but it would be strange if there could not be found a ghost or two in the wake of all these vagrant guests.

One evening after dark a young man prowled among these crumbling red mansions, ringing their bells. At the twelfth he rested his lean hand-baggage upon the step and wiped the dust from his hatband and forehead. The bell sounded faint and far away in some remote, hollow depths.

To the door of this, the twelfth house whose bell he had rung, came a housekeeper who made him think of an unwholesome, surfeited worm that had eaten its nut to a hollow shell and now sought to fill the vacancy with edible lodgers.

He asked if there was a room to let.

"Come in," said the housekeeper. Her voice came from her throat; her throat seemed lined with fur. "I have the third-floor-back, vacant since a week back. Should you wish to look at it?"

The young man followed her up the stairs. A faint light from no particular source mitigated the shadows of the halls. They trod noiselessly upon a stair carpet that its own loom would have forsworn. It seemed to have become vegetable; to have degenerated in that rank, sunless air to lush lichen or spreading moss that grew in patches to the stair-case and was viscid under the foot like organic matter. At each turn of the stairs were vacant niches in the wall. Perhaps plants had once been set within them. If so they had died in that foul and tainted air. It may be that statues of the saints had stood there, but it was not difficult to conceive that imps and devils had dragged them forth in the darkness and down to the unholy depths of some furnished pit below.

"This is the room," said the housekeeper, from her furry throat. "It's a nice room. It ain't often vacant. I had some most elegant people in it last summer—no trouble at all, and paid in advance to the minute. The water's at the end of the hall. Sprowls and Mooney kept it three months. They done a vaudeville sketch. Miss B'retta Sprowls—you may have heard of her—Oh, that was just the stage names—right there over the dresser is where the marriage certificate hung, framed. The gas is here, and you see there is plenty of closet room. It's a room everybody likes. It never stays idle long."

"Do you have many theatrical people rooming here?" asked the young man.

"They comes and goes. A good proportion of my lodgers is connected with the theatres. Yes, sir, this is the theatrical district. Actor people never stays long anywhere. I get my share. Yes, they comes and they goes."

He engaged the room, paying for a week in advance. He

was tired, he said, and would take possession at once. He counted out the money. The room had been made ready, she said, even to towels and water. As the housekeeper moved away he put, for the thousandth time, the question that he carried at the end of his tongue.

"A young girl—Miss Vashner—Miss Eloise Vashner—do you remember such a one among your lodgers? She would be singing on the stage, most likely. A fair girl, of medium height and slender, with reddish, gold hair and a dark mole near her left eyebrow."

"No, I don't remember the name. Them stage people has names they change as often as their rooms. They comes and they goes. No, I don't call that one to mind."

No. Always no. Five months of ceaseless interrogation and the inevitable negative. So much time spent by day in questioning managers, agents, schools and choruses; by night among the audiences of theatres from all-star casts down to music halls so low that he dreaded to find what he most hoped for. He who had loved her best had tried to find her. He was sure that since her disappearance from home this great, water-girt city held her somewhere, but it was like a monstrous quicksand, shifting its particles constantly, with no foundation, its upper granules of to-day buried to-morrow in ooze and slime.

The furnished room received its latest guest with a first glow of pseudo-hospitality, a hectic, haggard, perfunctory welcome like the specious smile of a demirep. The sophistical comfort came in reflected gleams from the decayed furniture, the ragged brocade upholstery of a couch and two chairs, a foot-wide cheap pier glass between the two windows, from one or two gilt picture frames and a brass bedstead in a corner.

The guest reclined, inert, upon a chair, while the room, confused in speech as though it were an apartment in Babel, tried to discourse to him of its divers tenantry.

A polychromatic rug like some brillant-flowered, rectangular, tropical islet lay surrounded by a billowy sea of soiled matting. Upon the gay-papered wall were those pictures that pursue the homeless one from house to house—The Huguenot Lovers, The First Quarrel, The Wedding Breakfast, Psyche at the Fountain. The mantel's chastely severe outline was ingloriously veiled behind some pert drapery drawn rakishly askew like the sashes of the Amazonian ballet. Upon it was some desolate flotsam cast aside by the room's marooned when a lucky sail had borne them to a fresh port—a trifling vase or two, pictures of actresses, a medicine bottle, some stray cards out of a deck.

One by one, as the characters of a cryptograph become explicit, the little signs left by the furnished room's procession of guests developed a significance. The threadbare space in the rug in front of the dresser told that lovely women had marched in the throng. The tiny fingerprints on the wall spoke of little prisoners trying to feel their way to sun and air. A splattered stain, raying like the shadow of a bursting bomb, witnessed where a hurled glass or bottle had splintered with its contents against the wall. Across the pier glass had been scrawled with a diamond in staggering letters the name "Marie." It seemed that the succession of dwellers in the furnished room had turned in fury—perhaps tempted beyond forbearance by its garish coldness—and wreaked upon it their passions. The furniture was chipped and bruised; the couch, distorted by bursting springs, seemed a horrible monster that had been slain during the stress of some grotesque convulsion. Some more potent upheaval had cloven a great slice from the marble mantel. Each plank in the floor owned its particular cant and shriek as from a separate and individual agony. It seemed incredible that all this malice and injury had been wrought upon the room by those who had called it for a time their home; and yet it may have been the cheated home instinct surviving blindly, the resentful rage at false household gods that had kindled their wrath. A hut that is our own we can sweep and adorn and cherish.

The young tenant in the chair allowed these thoughts to file, soft-shod, through his mind, while there drifted into the room furnished sounds and furnished scents. He heard in one room a tittering and incontinent, slack laughter; in others the monologue of a scold, a rattling of dice, a lullaby, and one crying dully; above him a banjo tinkled with spirit. Doors banged somewhere; the elevated trains roared intermittently; a cat yowled miserably upon a back fence. And he breathed the breath of the house—a dank savor rather than a smell—a cold, musty effluvium as from underground vaults mingled with the reeking exhalations of linoleum and mildewed and rotten woodwork.

Then suddenly, as he rested there, the room was filled with the strong, sweet odor of mignonette. I came as upon a single buffet of wind with such sureness and fragrance and emphasis that it almost seemed a living visitant. And the man cried aloud: "What, dear?" as if he had been called, and sprang up and faced about. The rich odor clung to him and wrapped him around. He reached out his arms for it, all his senses for the time confused and commingled. How could one be peremptorily called by an odor? Surely it must have been a sound. But, was it not the sound that had touched, that had caressed him?

"She has been in this room," he cried, and he sprang to wrest from it a token, for he knew he would recognize the smallest thing that had belonged to her or that she had touched. This enveloping scent of mignonette, the odor that she had loved and made her own—whence came it?

The room had been but carelessly set in order. Scattered upon the flimsy dresser scarf were half a dozen hairpins—those discreet, indistinguishable friends of womankind, feminine of gender, infinite mood and uncommunicative of tense. These he ignored, conscious of their triumphant lack of identity. Ransacking the drawers of the dresser he came upon a discarded, tiny, ragged hankerchief. He pressed it to his face. It was racy and insolent with heliotrope; he hurled it to the floor. In another drawer he found odd buttons, a theatre programme, a pawnbroker's card, two lost marshmallows, a book on the divination of dreams. In the last was a woman's black satin hair bow, which halted him, poised between ice and fire. But the black satin hair bow also is femininity's demure, impersonal common ornament and tells no tales.

And then he traversed the room like a hound on the scent, skimming the walls, considering the corners of the bulging matting on his hands and knees, rummaging mantel and tables, the curtains and hangings, the drunken cabinet in the corner, for a visible sign, unable to perceive that she was there beside, around, against, within, above him, clinging to him, wooing him, calling him so poignantly through the finer senses that even his grosser ones became cognizant of the call. Once again he answered loudly: "Yes, dear!" and turned, wild-eyed, to gaze on vacancy, for he could not yet discern form and color and love and outstretched arms in the odor of mignonette. Oh, God! whence that odor, and since when have odors had a voice to call? Thus he groped.

He burrowed in crevices and corners, and found corks and cigarettes. These he passed in passive contempt. But once he found in a fold of the matting a half-smoked cigar, and this he ground beneath his heel with a green and trenchant oath. He sifted the room from end to end. He found dreary and ignoble small records of many a peripatetic tenant; but of her whom he sought, and who may have lodged there, and whose spirit seemed to hover there, he found no trace.

And then he thought of the housekeeper.

He ran from the haunted room downstairs and to a door that showed a crack of light. She came out to his knock. He smothered his excitement as best he could.

"Will you tell me, madam," he besought her, "who occupied the room I have before I came?"

"Yes, sir. I can tell you again. 'Twas Sprowls and Mooney, as I said. Miss B'retta Sprowls it was in the theatres, but Missis Mooney she was. My house it well known for respectability. The marriage certificate hung, framed, on a nail over—"

"What kind of a lady was Miss Sprowls—in looks, I mean?"

"Why, black-haired, sir, short, and stout, with a comical face. They left a week ago Tuesday."

"And before they occupied it?"

"Why, there was a single gentleman connected with the draying business. He left owing me a week. Before him was Missis Crowder and her two children, that stayed four months; and back of them was old Mr. Doyle, whose sons paid for him. He kept the room six months. That goes back a year, sir, and further I do not remember."

He thanked her and crept back to his room. The room was dead. The essence that had vivified it was gone. The perfume of mignonette had departed, In its place was the old, stale odor of mouldy house furniture, of atmosphere in storage.

The ebbing of his hope drained his faith. He sat staring at the yellow, swinging gaslight. Soon he walked to the bed and began to tear the sheets into strips. With the blade of his knife he drove them tightly into every crevice around windows and door. When all was snug and taut he turned out the light, turned the gas full on again and laid himself gratefully upon the bed.

It was Mrs. McCool's night to go with the can for beer. So she fetched it and sat with Mrs. Purdy in one of those subterranean retreats where housekeepers foregather and the worm dieth seldom.

"I rented out my third-floor-back this evening," said Mrs.

Purdy, across a fine circle a foam. "A young man took it. He went up to bed two hours ago."

"Now, did ye, Mrs. Purdy, ma'am?" said Mrs. McCool, with intense admiration. "You do be a wonder for rentin' rooms of that kind. And did ye tell him, then?" she concluded in a husky whisper laden with mystery.

"Rooms," said Mrs. Purdy, in her furriest tones, "are furnished for to rent. I did not tell him, Mrs. McCool."

" 'Tis right ye are, ma'am; 'tis by renting rooms we kape alive. Ye have the rale sense for business, ma'am. There be many people will rayjict the rentin' of a room if they be tould a suicide has been after dyin' in the bed of it."

"As you say, we has our living to be making," remarked Mrs. Purdy.

"Yis, ma'am; 'tis true. 'Tis just one wake ago this day I helped ye lay out the third-floor-back. A pretty slip of a colleen she was to be killin' herself wid the gas—a swate little face she had, Mrs. Purdy, ma'am."

"She'd a-been called handsome, as you say," said Mrs. Purdy, assenting but critical, "but for that mole she had a'growin' by her left eyebrow. Do fill up your glass again, Mrs. McCool."

LOST HEARTS
by
M.R. JAMES

It has been said the M.R. James wrote a greater number of consistently fine ghost stories than any other author; that he was as important to the development of this genre as was Sir Arthur Conan Doyle to the development of the detective story. This is not an overstatement, as anyone who has read such classic and oft-anthologized works as "Casting the Runes," "Oh, Whistle and I'll Come to You, My Lad," "The Ash Tree," and "The Treasure of Abbot Thomas" can attest.

The present selection, "Lost Hearts," is probably not as familiar as the above-mentioned stories—but it should be. An account of a bizarre series of events in 1811 and 1812, it is comparable to "The Ash Tree" in its evocation of sheer horror; and the faint of heart will certainly find it . . . unsettling.

Montague Rhodes James (1862–1936) was a Medieval European scholar and perhaps the world's greatest authority on medieval manuscripts. But there was another side to the man: He was an omnivorous reader of detective fiction, an authority on minor Victorian fiction, an admirer and translator of the work of Hans Christian Andersen, and an aficionado of stories of the supernatural. Not a prolific writer, he produced only four books of spectral tales: Ghost Stories of an Antiquary *(1904)*, More Ghost Stories of an Antiquary *(1911)*, A Thin Ghost and Others *(1919), and* A Warning for the Curious *(1926). Each volume stands as a classic, and should be sought out and read by anyone with an abiding interest in macabre fiction.*

IT WAS, AS FAR AS I CAN ASCERTAIN, IN SEPTEMBER OF THE year 1811 that a post-chaise drew up before the door of Aswarby Hall, in the heart of Lincolnshire. The little boy who was the only passenger in the chaise, and who jumped out as soon as it had stopped, looked about him with the keenest curiosity during the short interval that elapsed between the ringing of the bell and the opening of the hall door. He saw a tall, square, red-brick house, built in the reign of Anne; a stone-pillared porch had been added in the purer classical style of 1790; the windows of the house were many, tall and narrow, with small panes and thick white woodwork. A pediment, pierced with a round window, crowned the front. There were wings to right and left, connected by curious glazed galleries, supported by colonnades, with the central block. These wings plainly contained the stables and offices of the house. Each was surmounted by an ornamental cupola with a gilded vane.

An evening light shone on the building, making the windowpanes glow like so many fires. Away from the Hall in front stretched a flat park studded with oaks and fringed with firs, which stood out against the sky. The clock in the church-tower, buried in trees on the edge of the park, only its golden weathercock catching the light, was striking six, and the sound came gently beating down the wind. It was altogether a pleasant impression, though tinged with the sort of melancholy appropriate to an evening in early autumn, that was conveyed to the mind of the boy who was standing in the porch waiting for the door to open to him.

The post-chaise had brought him from Warwickshire, where, some six months before, he had been left an orphan. Now, owing to the generous offer of his elderly cousin, Mr. Abney, he had come to live at Aswarby. The offer was unexpected, because all who knew anything of Mr. Abney looked upon him as a somewhat austere recluse, into whose steady-going household the advent of a small boy would import a new and, it seemed, incongruous element. The truth is that very little was known of Mr. Abney's pursuits or temper. The Professor of Greek at Cambridge had been heard to say that no one knew more of the religious beliefs of the later pagans that did the owner of Aswarby. Certainly his library contained all the then available books bearing on the Mysteries, the Orphic poems, the worship of Mithras, and the Neo-Platonists. In the marble-paved hall stood a fine group of Mithras slaying a bull, which had been imported from the Levant at great expense by the owner. He had contributed a description of it to the *Gentleman's Magazine*, and he had written a remarkable series of articles in the *Critical Museum* on the superstitions of the Romans of the Lower Empire. He was looked upon, in fine, as a man wrapped up in his books, and it was a matter of great surprise among his neighbours that he should even have heard of his orphan cousin, Stephen Elliott, much more that he should have volunteered to make him an inmate of Aswarby Hall.

Whatever may have been expected by his neighbours, it is certain that Mr. Abney—the tall, the thin, the austere—seemed inclined to give his young cousin a kindly reception. The moment the front door was opened he darted out of his study, rubbing his hands with delight.

"How are you, my boy?—how are you? How old are you?" said he—"that is, you are not too much tired, I hope, by your journey to eat your supper?"

"No, thank you, sir," said Master Elliott. "I am pretty well."

"That's a good lad," said Mr. Abney. "And how old are you, my boy?"

It seemed a little odd that he should have asked the question twice in the first two minutes of their acquaintance.

"I'm twelve years old next birthday, sir," said Stephen.

"And when is your birthday, my dear boy? Eleventh of September, eh? That's well—that's very well. Nearly a year hence, isn't it? I like—ha, ha!—I like to get these things down in my book. Sure it's twelve? Certain?"

"Yes, quite sure, sir."

"Well, well! Take him to Mrs. Bunch's room, Parkes, and let him have his tea—supper—whatever it is."

"Yes, sir," answered the staid Mr. Parkes; and conducted Stephen to the lower region.

Mrs. Bunch was the most comfortable and human person whom Stephen had as yet met in Aswarby. She made him completely at home; they were great friends in a quarter of an hour: and great friends they remained. Mrs. Bunch had been born in the neighbourhood some fifty-five years before the date of Stephen's arrival, and her residence at the Hall was of twenty years' standing. Consequently, if anyone knew the ins and outs of the house and the district, Mrs. Bunch knew them; and she was by no means disinclined to communicate her information.

Certainly there were plenty of things about the Hall and the Hall gardens which Stephen, who was of an adventurous and inquiring turn, was anxious to have explained to him. "Who built the temple at the end of the laurel walk? Who was the old man whose picture hung on the staircase, sitting at a table, with a skull under his hand?" These and many similar points were cleared up by the resources of Mrs. Bunch's powerful intellect. There were others, however, of which the explanations furnished were less satisfactory.

One November evening Stephen was sitting by the fire in the housekeeper's room reflecting on his surroundings.

"Is Mr. Abney a good man, and will he go to heaven?" he suddenly asked, with the peculiar confidence which children possess in the ability of their elders to settle these questions, the decision of which is believed to be reserved for other tribunals.

"Good?—bless the child!" said Mrs. Bunch. "Master's as kind a soul as ever I see! Didn't I never tell you of the little boy as he took in out of the street, as you may say, this seven years back? and the little girl, two years after I first come here?"

"No. Do tell me all about them, Mrs. Bunch—now this minute!"

"Well," said Mrs. Bunch, "the little girl I don't seem to recollect so much about. I know master brought her back with him from his walk one day, and give orders to Mrs. Ellis, as was housekeeper then, as she should be took every care with. And the pore child hadn't no one belonging to her—she told me so her own self—and here she lived with us a matter of three weeks it might be; and then, whether she were somethink of a gipsy in her in her blood or what not, but one morning she out of her bed afore any of us had opened a eye, and neither track nor yet trace of her have I set eyes on since. Master was wonderful put about, and had all the ponds dragged; but it's my belief she was had away by them gipsies, for there was singing round the house for as much as an hour the night she went, and Parkes, he declare as he heard them a-calling in the woods all that afternoon. Dear, dear! a hodd child she was, so silent in her ways and all, but I was wonderful taken up with her, so domesticated she was—surprising."

"And what about the little boy?" said Stephen.

"Ah, that pore boy!" sighed Mrs. Bunch. "He were a foreigner—Jevanny he called hisself—and he come a-tweaking his 'urdy-gurdy round and about the drive one winter day, and master 'ad him in that minute, and ast all about where he came from, and how old he was, and how he made his way, and where was his relatives, and all as kind as heart could wish. But it went the same way with him. They're a hunruly lot, them foreign nations, I do suppose, and he was off one fine morning just the same as the girl. Why he went and what he done was our question for as much as a year after; for he never took his 'urdy-gurdy, and there it lays on the shelf."

The remainder of the evening was spent by Stephen in miscellaneous cross-examination of Mrs. Bunch and in efforts to extract a tune from the hurdy-gurdy.

That night he had a curious dream. At the end of the passage at the top of the house, in which his bedroom was situated, there was an old disused bathroom. It was kept locked, but the upper half of the door was glazed, and, since the muslin curtains which used to hang there had long been gone, you could look in and see the lead-lined bath affixed to the wall on the right hand, with its head towards the window.

On the night of which I am speaking, Stephen Elliott found himself, as he thought, looking through the glazed door. The moon was shining through the window, and he was gazing at a figure which lay in the bath.

His description of what he saw reminds me of what I once beheld myself in the famous vaults of St. Michan's Church in Dublin, which possess the horrid property of preserving corpses from decay for centuries. A figure inexpressibly thin and pathetic, of a dusty leaden colour, enveloped in a shroud-like garment, the thin lips crooked into a faint and dreadful smile, the hands pressed tightly over the region of the heart.

As he looked upon it, a distant, almost inaudible moan seemed to issue from its lips, and the arms began to stir. The terror of the sight forced Stephen backwards, and he awoke to the fact that he was indeed standing on the cold boarded floor of the passage in the full light of the moon. With a courage which I do not think can be common among boys of his age, he went to the door of the bathroom to ascertain if the figure of his dream were really there. It was not, and he went back to bed.

Mrs. Bunch was much impressed next morning by his story, and went so far as to replace the muslin curtain over the glazed door of the bathroom. Mr. Abney, moreover, to whom he confided his experiences at breakfast, was greatly interested, and made notes of the matter in what he called "his book."

The spring equinox was approaching, as Mr. Abney frequently reminded his cousin, adding that this had been always considered by the ancients to be a critical time for the young: that Stephen would do well to take care of himself, and to shut his bedroom window at night; and that Censorinus had some valuable remarks on the subject. Two incidents that occurred about this time made an impression upon Stephen's mind.

The first was after an unusually uneasy and oppressed night that he had passed—though he could not recall any particular dream that he had had.

The following evening Mrs. Bunch was occupying herself in mending his nightgown.

"Gracious me, Master Stephen!" she broke forth rather irritably, "how do you manage to tear your nightdress all to flinders this way? Look here, sir, what trouble you do give to poor servants that have to darn and mend after you!"

There was indeed a most destructive and apparently wanton series of slits or scorings in the garment, which would undoubtedly require a skilful needle to make good. They were confined to the left side of the chest—long, parallel slits, about six inches in length, some of them not quite piercing the texture of the linen. Stephen could only express his entire ignorance of their origin: he was sure they were not there the night before.

"But," he said, "Mrs. Bunch, they are just the same as the scratches on the outside of my bedroom door; and I'm sure I never had anything to do with making *them*."

Mrs. Bunch gazed at him open-mouthed, then snatched up a candle, departed hastily from the room, and was heard making her way upstairs. In a few minutes she came down.

"Well," she said, "Master Stephen, it's a funny thing to me how them marks and scratches can 'a' come there—too high up for any cat or dog to 'ave made 'em, much less a rat: for all the world like a Chinaman's fingernails, as my uncle in the tea-trade used to tell us of when we was girls together. I wouldn't say nothing to master, not if I was you, Master Stephen, my dear; and just turn the key of the door when you go to your bed."

"I always do, Mrs. Bunch, as soon as I've said my prayers."

"Ah, that's a good child: always say your prayers, and then no one can't hurt you."

Herewith Mrs. Bunch addressed herself to mending the injured nightgown, with intervals of meditation, until bed-time. This was on a Friday night in March, 1812.

On the following evening the usual duet of Stephen and Mrs. Bunch was augmented by the sudden arrival of Mr. Parkes, the butler, who as a rule kept himself rather *to* himself in his own pantry. He did not see that Stephen was there: he was, moreover, flustered, and less slow of speech than was his wont.

"Master may get up his own wine, if he likes, of an evening," was his first remark. "Either I do it in the daytime or not at all, Mrs. Bunch. I don't know what it may be: very like it's the rats, or the wind got into the cellars; but I'm not so young as I was, and I can't go through with it as I have done."

"Well, Mr. Parkes, you know it is a surprising place for the rats, is the Hall."

"I'm not denying that, Mrs. Bunch; and, to be sure, many a time I've heard the tale from the men in the shipyards about the rat that could speak. I never laid no confidence in that before; but to-night, if I'd demeaned myself to lay my ear to the door of the further bin, I could pretty much have heard what they was saying."

"Oh, there, Mr. Parkes, I've no patience with your fancies! Rats talking in the wine-cellar indeed!"

"Well, Mrs. Bunch, I've no wish to argue with you: all I say is, if you choose to go to the far bin, and lay your ear to the door, you may prove my words this minute."

"What nonsense you do talk, Mr. Parkes—not fit for children to listen to! Why, you'll be frightening Master Stephen there out of his wits."

"What! Master Stephen?" said Parkes, awaking to the consciousness of the boy's presence. "Master Stephen knows well enough when I'm a-playing a joke with you, Mrs. Bunch."

In fact, Master Stephen knew much too well to suppose that Mr. Parkes had in the first instance intended a joke. He was interested, not altogether pleasantly, in the situation; but all his questions were unsuccessful in inducing the butler to give any more detailed account of his experiences in the wine-cellar.

We have now arrived at March 24, 1812. It was a day of curious experiences for Stephen: a windy, noisy day, which filled the house and the gardens with a restless impression. As Stephen stood by the fence of the grounds, and looked out into the park, he felt as if an endless procession of unseen people were sweeping past him on the wind, borne on resistlessly and aimlessly, vainly striving to stop themselves, to catch at something that might arrest their flight and bring them once again into contact with the living world of which they had formed a part. After luncheon that day Mr. Abney said:

"Stephen, my boy, do you think you could manage to come to me to-night as late as eleven o'clock in my study? I shall be busy until that time, and I wish to show you something connected with your future life which it is most important that you should know. You are not to mention this matter to Mrs. Bunch nor to anyone else in the house; and you had better go to your room at the usual time."

Here was a new excitement added to life: Stephen eagerly grasped at the opportunity of sitting up till eleven o'clock. He looked in at the library door on his way upstairs that evening, and saw a brazier, which he had often noticed in the corner of the room, moved out before the fire; an old silver-gilt cup stood on the table, filled with red wine, and some written sheets of paper lay near it. Mr. Abney was sprinkling some incense on the brazier from a round silver box as Stephen passed, but did not seem to notice his step.

The wind had fallen, and there was a still night and a full moon. At about ten o'clock Stephen was standing at the open window of his bedroom, looking out over the country. Still as the night was, the mysterious population of the distant moonlit woods was not yet lulled to rest. From time to time strange cries as of lost and despairing wanderers sounded from across the mere. They might be the notes of owls or water-birds, yet they did not quite resemble either sound. Were not they coming nearer? Now they sounded from the nearer side of the water, and in a few moments they seemed to be floating about among the shrubberies. Then they ceased; but just as Stephen was thinking of shutting the window and resuming his reading of *Robinson Crusoe,* he caught sight of two figures standing on the gravelled terrace that ran along the garden side of the Hall—the figures of a boy and girl, as it seemed; they stood side by side, looking up at the windows. Something in the form of the girl recalled irresistibly his dream of the figure in the bath. The boy inspired him with more acute fear.

Whilst the girl stood still, half smiling, with her hands clasped over her heart, the boy, a thin shape, with black hair and ragged clothing, raised his arms in the air with an appearance of menace and of unappeasable hunger and longing. The moon shone upon his almost transparent hands, and Stephen saw that the nails were fearfully long and that the light shone through them. As he stood with his arms thus raised, he disclosed a terrifying spectacle. On the left side of his chest there opened a black and gaping rent; and there fell upon Stephen's brain, rather that upon his ear, the impression of one of those hungry and desolate cries that he had heard resounding over the woods of Aswarby all that evening. In another moment this dreadful pair had moved swiftly and noiselessly over the dry gravel, and he saw them no more.

Inexpressibly fightened as he was, he determined to take his candle and go down to Mr. Abney's study, for the hour appointed for their meeting was near at hand. The study or library opened out of the front hall on one side, and Stephen, urged on by his terrors, did not take long in getting there. To effect an entrance was not so easy. The door was not locked, he felt sure, for the key was on the outside of it as usual. His repeated knocks produced no answer. Mr. Abney was engaged: he was speaking. What! why did he try to cry out? and why was the cry choked in his throat? Had he, too, seen the mysterious children? But now everything was quiet, and the door yielded to Stephen's terrified and frantic pushing.

On the table in Mr. Abney's study certain papers were found which explained the situation to Stephen Elliott when he was of an age to understand them. The most important sentences were as follows:

"It was a belief very strongly and generally held by the ancients—of whose wisdom in these matters I have had such experience as induces me to place confidence in their assertions—that by enacting certain processes, which to us moderns have something of a barbaric complexion, a very remarkable enlightenment of the spirtual faculties in man may be attained: that, for example, by absorbing the personalities of a certain number of his fellow-creatures, an individual may gain a complete ascendancy over those orders of spiritual beings which control the elemental forces of our universe.

"It is recorded of Simon Magus that he was able to fly in the air, to become invisible, or to assume any form he pleased, by the agency of the soul of a boy whom, to use the libellous phrase employed by the author of the *Clementine Recognitions,* he had 'murdered.' I find it set down, moreover, with considerable detail in the writing of Hermes Trismegistus, that similar happy results may be produced by the absorption of the heart of not less than three human beings below the age of twenty-one years. To the testing of the truth of this receipt I have devoted the greater part of the last twenty years, selecting as the *corpora vilia* of my experiment such persons as could conveniently be removed without occasioning a sensible gap in society. The first step I effected by the removal of one Phoebe Stanley, a girl of gipsy extraction, on March 24, 1792. The second, by the removal of a wandering Italian lad, named Giovanni Paoli, on the night of March 23, 1805. The final 'victim'—to employ a word repugnant in the highest degree to my feelings—must be my cousin, Stephen Elliott. His day must be this March 24, 1812.

"The best means of effecting the required absorption is to remove the heart from the *living* subject, to reduce it to ashes, and to mingle them with about a pint of some red wine, preferably port. The remains of the first two subjects, at least, it will be well to conceal: a disused bathroom or wine-cellar will be found convenient for such a purpose. Some annoyance may be experienced from the psychic portion of the subjects, which popular language dignifies with the name of ghosts. But the man of philosophic temperament—to whom alone the experiment is appropriate—will be little prone to attach importance to the feeble efforts of these beings to wreak their vengeance on him. I contemplate with the liveliest satisfaction the enlarged and emancipated existence which the experiment, if successful, will confer on me; not only placing me beyond the reach of human justice (so-called), but eliminating to a great extent the prospect of death itself."

Mr. Abney was found in his chair, his head thrown back, his face stamped with an expression of rage, fright, and mortal pain. In his left side was a terrible lacerated wound, exposing the heart. There was no blood on his hands, and a long knife that lay on the table perfectly clean. A savage wild-cat might have inflicted the injuries. The window of the study was open, and it was the opinion of the coroner that Mr. Abney had met his death by the agency of some wild creature. But Stephen Elliott's study of the papers I have quoted led him to a very different conclusion.

THE JUDGE'S HOUSE
by
BRAM STOKER

Spooks and specters can be pretty frightening, as we've already seen, but there are a lot of other things in this world that can terrrify us. Take rats, for instance. Nasty creatures, rats, with their evil eyes and sharp teeth and insatiable hunger. Any house populated by both rats and ghosts is a house that just about everybody would gladly shun. Not Malcolm Malcolmson, though; he wasn't afraid of anything natural or supernatural. That was why he went ahead and moved into "The Judge's House" all by himself.

You can move in, too, and live there for a time with Malcolm and the other nonhuman inhabitants. But before you do, you'd better not make the same mistake he made, lest the same thing happen to you that happens to him. You'd better not ignore the old landlady's warning that "Bogies is rats, and rats is bogies . . ."

Dublin-born Bram Stoker (1845–1912) spent most of his adult life associated with British actor Sir Henry Irving in the management of London's Lyceum Theatre, and wrote sparingly as a result. His classic vampire novel, Dracula, *caused an immediate stir when it first appeared in 1897; with the possible exception of Mary Shelley's*

Frankenstein, *no other book has had such a lasting impact on the fantasy/horror genre. Stoker also authored three lesser known novels of the weird and the wonderful:* The Mystery of the Sea *(1902),* The Jewel of Seven Stars *(1903), and* The Lair of the White Worm *(1909). The only collection of his macabre stories,* Dracula's Guest, *was published posthumously in 1914.*

WHEN THE TIME FOR HIS EXAMINATION DREW NEAR MALCOLM Malcolmson made up his mind to go somewhere to read by himself. He feared the attractions of the seaside, and also he feared completely rural isolation, for of old he knew its charms, and so he determined to find some unpretentious little town where there would be nothing to distract him. He refrained from asking suggestions from any of his friends, for he argued that each would recommend some place of which he had knowledge, and where he had already acquaintances. As Malcolmson wished to avoid friends he had no wish to encumber himself with the attention of friends' friends, and so he determined to look out for a place for himself. He packed a portmanteau with some clothes and all the books he required, and then took ticket for the first name on the local time-table which he did not know.

When at the end of three hours' journey he alighted at Benchurch, he felt satisfied that he had so far obliterated his tracks as to be sure of having a peaceful opportunity of pursuing his studies. He went straight to the one inn which the sleepy little place contained, and put up for the night. Benchurch was a market town, and once in three weeks was crowded to excess, but for the remainder of the twenty-one days it was as attractive as a desert. Malcolmson looked around the day after his arrival to try to find quarters more isolated than even so quiet an inn as "The Good Traveller" afforded. There was only one place which took his fancy, and it certainly satisfied his wildest ideas regarding quiet; in fact, quiet was not the proper word to apply to it—desolation was the only term conveying any suitable idea of its isolation. It was an old rambling, heavy-built house of the Jacobean style, with heavy gables and windows, unusually small, and set higher than was customary in such houses, and was surrounded with a high brick wall massively built. Indeed, on examination, it looked more like a fortified house than an ordinary dwelling. But all these things pleased Malcolmson. "Here," he thought, "is the very spot I have been looking for, and if I can only get opportunity of using it I shall be happy." His joy was increased when he realised beyond doubt that it was not at present inhabited.

From the post-office he got the name of the agent, who was rarely surprised at the application to rent a part of the old house. Mr. Carnford, the local lawyer and agent, was a genial old gentleman, and frankly confessed his delight at anyone being willing to live in the house.

"To tell you the truth," said he, "I should be only too happy, on behalf of the owners, to let anyone have the house rent free for a term of years if only to accustom the people here to see it inhabited. It has been so long empty that some kind of absurd prejudice has grown up about it, and this can be best put down by its occupation—if only," he added with a sly glance at Malcolmson, "by a scholar like yourself, who wants its quiet for a time."

Malcolmson thought it needless to ask the agent about the "absurd prejudice"; he knew he would get more information, if he should require it, on that subject from other quarters. He paid his three months' rent, got a receipt, and the name of an old woman who would probably undertake to "do" for him, and came away with the keys in his pocket. He then went to the landlady of the inn, who was a cheerful and most kindly person, and asked her advice as to such stores and provisions as he would be likely to require. She

threw up her hands in amazement when he told her where
he was going to settle himself.

"Not in the Judge's House!" she said, and grew pale as
she spoke. He explained the locality of the house, saying
that he did not know its name. When he had finished she
answered:

"Aye, sure enough—sure enough the very place! It is the
Judge's House sure enough." He asked her to tell him about
the place, why so called, and what there was against it. She
told him that it was so called locally because it had been
many years before—how long she could not say, as she herself
was from another part of the country, but she thought it
must have been a hundred years or more—the abode of a
judge who was held in great terror on account of his harsh
sentences and his hostility to prisoners at Assizes. As to what
there was against the house itself she could not tell. She had
often asked, but no one could inform her; but there was a
general feeling that there was *something*, and for her own
part she would not take all the money in Drinkwater's Bank
and stay in the house an hour by herself. Then she apologised
to Malcolmson for her disturbing talk.

"It is too bad of me, sir, and you—and a young gentleman,
too—if you will pardon me saying it, going to live there all
alone. If you were my boy—and you'll excuse me for saying
it—you wouldn't sleep there a night, not if I had to go there
myself and pull the big alarm bell that's on the roof!" The
good creature was so manifestly in earnest, and was so kindly
in her intentions, that Malcolmson, although amused, was
touched. He told her kindly how much he appreciated her
interest in him, and added:

"But, my dear Mrs. Witham, indeed you need not be
concerned about me! A man who is reading for the Math-
ematical Tripos has too much to think of to be disturbed
by any of these mysterious "somethings," and his work is of
too exact and prosaic a kind to allow of his having any corner

in his mind for mysteries of any kind. Harmonical Progression, Permutations and Combinations, and Elliptic Functions have sufficient mysteries for me!" Mrs. Witham kindly undertook to see after his commissions, and he went himself to look for the old woman who had been recommended to him. When he returned to the Judge's House with her, after an interval of a couple of hours, he found Mrs. Witham herself waiting with several men and boys carrying parcels, and an upholsterer's man with a bed in a cart, for she said, though tables and chairs might be all very well, a bed that hadn't been aired for mayhap fifty years was not proper for young bones to lie on. She was evidently curious to see the inside of the house; and although manifestly so afraid of the "somethings" that at the slightest sound she clutched on to Malcolmson, whom she never left for a moment, went over the whole place.

After his examination of the house, Malcolmson decided to take up his abode in the great dining-room, which was big enough to serve for all of his requirements; and Mrs. Witham, with the aid of the charwoman, Mrs. Dempster, proceeded to arrange matters. When the hampers were brought in and unpacked, Malcolmson saw that with much kind forethought she had sent from her own kitchen sufficient provisions to last a few days. Before going she expressed all sorts of kind wishes; and at the door turned and said:

"And perhaps, sir, as the room is big and draughty it might be well to have one of those big screens put round your bed at night—though, truth to tell, I would die myself if I were to be so shut in with all kinds of—of 'things,' that put their heads round the sides, or over the top, and look on me!" The image which she had called up was too much for her nerves, and she fled incontinently.

Mrs. Dempster sniffed in a superior manner as the landlady disappeared, and remarked that for her own part she wasn't afraid of all the bogies in the kingdom.

"I'll tell you what it is, sir," she said; "bogies is all kinds and sorts of things—except bogies! Rats and mice, and beetles; and creaky doors, and loose slates, and broken panes, and stiff drawer handles, that stay out when you pull them and then fall down in the middle of the night. Look at the wainscot of the room! It is old—hundreds of years old! Do you think there's no rats and beetles there! And do you imagine, sir, that you won't see none of them! Rats is bogies, I tell you, and bogies is rats; and don't you get to think anything else!"

"Mrs. Dempster," said Malcolmson gravely, making her a polite bow, "you know more than a Senior Wrangler! And let me say, that, as a mark of esteem for your indubitable soundness of head and heart, I shall, when I go, give you possession of this house, and let you stay here by yourself for the last two months of my tenancy, for four weeks will serve my purpose."

"Thank you kindly, sir!" she answered, "but I couldn't sleep away from home a night. I am in Greenhow's Charity, and if I slept a night away from my rooms I should lose all I have got to live on. The rules is very strict; and there's too many watching for a vacancy for me to run any risks in the matter. Only for that, sir, I'd gladly come here and attend on you altogether during your stay."

"My good woman," said Malcolmson hastily, "I have come here on purpose to obtain solitude; and believe me that I am grateful to the late Greenhow for having so organized his admirable charity—whatever it is—that I am perforce denied the opportunity of suffering from such a form of temptation! Saint Anthony himself could not be more rigid on the point!"

The old woman laughed harshly. "Ah, you young gentlemen," she said, "you don't fear for naught; and belike you'll get all the solitude you want here." She set to work with her cleaning; and by nightfall, when Malcolmson returned from his walk—he always had one of his books to study as he walked—he found the room swept and tidied, a fire burning in the old hearth, the lamp lit, and the table spread for supper with Mrs. Witham's excellent fare. "This is comfort, indeed," he said, as he rubbed his hands.

When he had finished his supper, and lifted the tray to the other end of the great oak dining-table, he got out his books again, put fresh wood on the fire, trimmed his lamp, and set himself down to a spell of real hard work. He went on without pause till about eleven o'clock, when he knocked off for a bit to fix his fire and lamp, and to make himself a cup of tea. He had always been a tea-drinker, and during his college life had sat late at work and had taken tea late. The rest was a great luxury to him, and he enjoyed it with a sense of delicious, voluptuous ease. The renewed fire leaped and sparkled, and threw quaint shadows through the great old room; and as he sipped his hot tea he revelled in the sense of isolation from his kind. Then it was that he began to notice for the first time what a noise the rats were making.

"Surely," he thought, "they cannot have been at it all the time I was reading. Had they been, I must have noticed it!" Presently, when the noise increased, he satisfied himself that it was really new. It was evident that at first the rats had been frightened at the presence of a stranger, and the light of fire and lamp; but that as the time went on they had grown bolder and were now disporting themselves as was their wont.

How busy they were! and hark to the strange noises! Up and down behind the old wainscot, over the ceiling and under the floor they raced, and gnawed, and scratched! Malcolmson smiled to himself as he recalled to mind the saying of Mrs. Dempster, "Bogies is rats, and rats is bogies!" The tea began to have its effect of intellectual and nervous stimulus, he saw with joy another long spell of work to be done before the night was past, and in the sense of security which it gave him, he allowed himself the luxury of a good look around the room. He took his lamp in one hand, and went all around, wondering that so quaint and beautiful an old house had been so long neglected. The carving of the oak on the panels of the wainscot was fine, and on and round the doors and windows it was beautiful and of rare merit. There were some old pictures on the walls, but they were coated so thick with dust and dirt that he could not distinguish any detail of them, though he held his lamp as high as he could over his head. Here and there as he went round he saw some crack or hole blocked for a moment by the face of a rat with its bright eyes glittering in the light, but in an instant it was gone, and a squeak and a scamper followed.

The thing that most struck him, however, was the rope of the great alarm bell on the roof, which hung down in a corner of the room on the right-hand side of the fireplace. He pulled up close to the hearth a great high-backed carved oak chair, and sat down to his last cup of tea. When this was done he made up the fire, and went back to his work, sitting at the corner of the table, having the fire to his left. For a while the rats disturbed him somewhat with their perpetual scampering, but he got accustomed to the noise as one does to the ticking of a clock or to the roar of moving water; and he became so immersed in his work that everything in the world, except the problem which he was trying to solve, passed away from him.

He suddenly looked up, his problem was still unsolved, and there was in the air that sense of the hour before the dawn, which is so dread to doubtful life. The noise of the rats had ceased. Indeed it seemed to him that it must have ceased but lately and that it was the sudden cessation which had disturbed him. The fire had fallen low, but still it threw out a deep red glow. As he looked he started in spite of his *sang froid*.

There on the great high-backed carved oak chair by the

right side of the fireplace sat an enormous rat, steadily glaring at him with baleful eyes. He made a motion to it as though to hunt it away, but it did not stir. Then he made the motion of throwing something. Still it did not stir, but showed its great white teeth angrily, and its cruel eyes shone in the lamplight with an added vindictiveness.

Malcolmson felt amazed, and seizing the poker from the hearth ran at it to kill it. Before, however, he could strike it, the rat, with a squeak that sounded like the concentration of hate, jumped upon the floor, and, running up the rope of the alarm bell, disappeared in the darkness beyond the range of the green-shaded lamp. Instantly, strange to say, the noisy scampering of rats in the wainscot began again.

By this time Malcolmson's mind was quite off the problem; and as a shrill cock-crow outside told him of the approach of morning, he went to bed and to sleep.

He slept so sound that he was not even waked by Mrs. Dempster coming in to make up his room. It was only when she had tidied up the place and got his breakfast ready and tapped on the screen which closed in his bed that he woke. He was a little tired still after his night's hard work, but a strong cup of tea soon freshened him up, and, taking his book, he went out for his morning walk, bringing with him a few sandwiches lest he should not care to return till dinner time. He found a quiet walk between high elms some way outside the town, and here he spent the greater part of the day studying his Laplace. On his return he looked in to see Mrs. Witham and to thank her for her kindness. When she saw him coming through the diamond-paned bay-window of her sanctum she came out to meet him and asked him in. She looked at him searchingly and shook her head as she said:

"You must not overdo it, sir. You are paler this morning than you should be. Too late hours and too hard work on the brain isn't good for any man! But tell me, sir, how did you pass the night? Well, I hope? But, my heart! sir, I was glad when Mrs. Dempster told me this morning that you were all right and sleeping sound when she went in."

"Oh, I was all right," he answered, smiling, "the 'somethings' didn't worry me as yet. Only the rats; and they had a circus, I tell you, all over the place. There was one wicked looking old devil that sat up on my own chair by the fire, and wouldn't go till I took the poker to him, and then he ran up the rope of the alarm bell and got to somewhere up the wall or the ceiling—I couldn't see where, it was so dark."

"Mercy on us," said Mrs. Witham, "an old devil, and sitting on a chair by the fireside! Take care, sir! take care! There's many a true word spoken in jest."

"How do you mean? 'Pon my word I don't understand."

"An old devil! The old devil, perhaps. There! sir, you needn't laugh," for Malcolmson had broken into a hearty peal. "You young folks thinks it easy to laugh at things that makes older ones shudder. Never mind, sir! never mind! Please God, you'll laugh all the time. It's what I wish you myself!" and the good lady beamed all over in sympathy with his enjoyment, her fears gone for a moment.

"Oh, forgive me!" said Malcolmson presently. "Don't think me rude; but the idea was too much for me—that the old devil himself was on the chair last night!" And at the thought he laughed again. Then he went home to dinner.

This evening the scampering of the rats began earlier; indeed it had been going on before his arrival, and only ceased whilst his presence by its freshness disturbed them. After dinner he sat by the fire for a while and had a smoke; and then, having cleared his table, began to work as before. To-night the rats disturbed him more than they had done on the previous night. How they scampered up and down and under and over! How they squeaked, and scratched, and gnawed! How they, getting bolder by degrees, came to the mouths of their holes and to the chinks and cracks and crannies in the wainscoting till their eyes shone like tiny lamps as the firelight rose and fell. But to him, now doubtless accustomed to them, their eyes were not wicked; only their playfulness touched him. Sometimes the boldest of them made sallies out on the floor or along the mouldings of the wainscot. Now and again as they disturbed him Malcolmson made a sound to frighten them, smiting the table with his hand or giving a fierce "Hsh, hsh," so that they fled straightway to their holes.

And so the early part of the night wore on; and despite the noise Malcolmson got more and more immersed in his work.

All at once he stopped, as on the previous night, being overcome by a sudden sense of silence. There was not the faintest sound of gnaw, or scratch, or squeak. The silence was as of the grave. He remembered the odd occurrence of the previous night, and instinctively he looked at the chair standing close by the fireside. And then a very odd sensation thrilled through him.

There, on the great old high-backed carved oak chair beside the fireplace sat the same enormous rat, steadily glaring at him with baleful eyes.

Instinctively he took the nearest thing to his hand, a book of logarithms, and flung it at it. The book was badly aimed and the rat did not stir, so again the poker performance of the previous night was repeated; and again the rat, being closely pursued, fled up the rope of the alarm bell. Strangely too, the departure of this rat was instantly followed by the renewal of the noise made by the general rat community. On this occasion, as on the previous one, Malcolmson could not see at what part of the room the rat disappeared, for the green shade of his lamp left the upper part of the room in darkness, and the fire had burned low.

On looking at his watch he found it was close on midnight; and, not sorry for the *divertissement*, he made up his fire and made himself his nightly pot of tea. He had got through a good spell of work, and thought himself entitled to a cigarette; and so he sat on the great carved oak chair before the fire and enjoyed it. Whilst smoking he began to think that he would like to know where the rat disappeared to, for he had certain ideas for the morrow not entirely disconnected with a rat-trap. Accordingly he lit another lamp and placed it so that it would shine well into the right-hand corner of the wall by the fireplace. Then he got all the books he had with him, and placed them handy to throw at the vermin. Finally he lifted the rope of the alarm bell and placed the end of it on the table, fixing the extreme end under the lamp. As he handled it he could not help noticing how pliable it was, especially for so strong a rope, and one not in use. "You could hang a man with it," he thought to himself. When his preparations were made he looked around, and said complacently:

"There now, my friend, I think we shall learn something of you this time!" He began his work again, and though as before somewhat disturbed at first by the noise of the rats, soon lost himself in his propositions and problems.

Again he was called to his immediate surroundings suddenly. This time it might not have been the sudden silence only which took his attention; there was a slight movement of the rope, and the lamp moved. Without stirring, he looked to see if his pile of books was within range, and then cast his eye along the rope. As he looked he saw the great rat drop from the rope on the oak armchair and sit there glaring at him. He raised a book in his right hand, and taking careful aim, flung it at the rat. The latter, with a quick movement, sprang aside and dodged the missile. He then took another book, and a third, and flung them one after another at the rat, but each time unsuccessfully. At last, as he stood with a book poised in his hand to throw, the rat squeaked and seemed afraid. This made Malcolmson more than ever eager to strike, and the book flew and struck the rat a resounding blow. It gave a terrified squeak, and turning on its pursuer a look of terrible malevolence, ran up the chair-back and made a great jump to the rope of the alarm bell and it ran up it like lightning. The lamp rocked under the sudden strain, but it was a heavy one and did not topple over. Malcolmson kept his eyes on the rat, and saw it by the light of the second lamp leap to a moulding of the wainscot and disappear through a hole in one of the great pictures which hung on the wall, obscured and invisible through its coating of dirt and dust.

"I shall look up my friend's habitation in the morning," said the student, as he went over to collect his books. "The third picture from the fireplace; I shall not forget." He picked up the books one by one, commenting on them as he lifted them. "*Conic Sections* he does not mind, nor *Cycloidal Oscillations*, nor the *Principia*, nor *Quaternions*, nor *Thermodynamics*. Now for the book that fetched him!" Malcolmson took it up and looked at it. As he did so he started, and a sudden pallor overspread his face. He looked round uneasily and shivered slightly, as he murmured to himself:

"The Bible my mother gave me! What an odd coincidence." He sat down to work again, and the rats in the wainscot renewed their gambols. They did not disturb him, however; somehow their presence gave him a sense of companionship. But he could not attend to his work, and after striving to master the subject on which he was engaged gave it up in despair, and went to bed as the first streak of dawn stole in through the eastern window.

He slept heavily but uneasily, and dreamed much; and when Mrs. Dempster woke him late in the morning he seemed ill at ease, and for a few minutes did not seem to realise exactly where he was. His first request rather surprised the servant.

"Mrs. Dempster, when I am out to-day I wish you would

get the steps and dust or wash those pictures—specially that one the third from the fireplace—I want to see what they are."

Late in the afternoon Malcolmson worked at his books in the shaded walk, and the cheerfulness of the previous day came back to him as the day wore on, and he found that his reading was progressing well. He had worked out to a satisfactory conclusion all the problems which had as yet baffled him, and it was in a state of jubilation that he paid a visit to Mrs. Witham at "The Good Traveller." He found a stranger in the cosy sitting-room with the landlady, who was introduced to him as Dr. Thornhill. She was not quite at ease, and this, combined with the Doctor's plunging at once into a series of questions, made Malcolmson come to the conclusion that his presence was not an accident, so without preliminary he said:

"Dr. Thornhill, I shall with pleasure answer you any question you may choose to ask me if you will answer me one question first."

The Doctor seemed surprised, but he smiled and answered at once. "Done! What is it?"

"Did Mrs. Witham ask you to come here and see me and advise me?"

Dr. Thornhill for a moment was taken aback, and Mrs. Witham got fiery red and turned away; but the doctor was a frank and ready man, and he answered at once and openly:

"She did: but she didn't intend you to know it. I suppose it was my clumsy haste that made you suspect. She told me that she did not like the idea of your being in that house all by yourself, and that she thought you took too much strong tea. In fact, she wants me to advise you if possible to give up the tea and the very late hours. I was a keen student in my time, so I suppose I may take the liberty of a college man, and without offence, advise you not quite as a stranger."

Malcolmson with a bright smile held out his hand. "Shake! as they say in America," he said. "I must thank you for your kindness and Mrs. Witham too, and your kindness deserves a return on my part. I promise to take no more strong tea— no tea at all till you let me—and I shall go to bed to-night at one o'clock at latest. Will that do?"

"Capital," said the Doctor. "Now tell us all that you noticed in the old house," and so Malcolmson then and there told in minute detail all that had happened in the last two nights. He was interrupted every now and then by some exclamation from Mrs. Witham, till finally when he told of the episode of the Bible the landlady's pent-up emotions found vent in a shriek; and it was not till a stiff glass of brandy and water had been administered that she grew composed again. Dr. Thornhill listened with a face of growing gravity, and when the narrative was complete and Mrs. Witham had been restored he asked:

"The rat always went up the rope of the alarm bell?"

"Always."

"I suppose you know," said the Doctor after a pause, "what the rope is?"

"No!"

"It is," said the Doctor slowly, "the very rope which the hangman used for all the victims of the Judge's judicial rancour!" Here he was interrupted by another scream from Mrs. Witham, and steps had to be taken for her recovery. Malcolmson having looked at his watch, and found that it was close to his dinner hour, had gone home before her complete recovery.

When Mrs. Witham was herself again she almost assailed the Doctor with angry questions as to what he meant by putting such horrible ideas into the poor young man's mind. "He has quite enough there already to upset him," she added. Dr. Thornhill replied:

"My dear madam, I had a distinct purpose in it! I wanted

to draw his attention to the bell rope, and to fix it there. It may be that he is in a highly overwrought state, and has been studying too much, although I am bound to say that he seems as sound and healthy a young man, mentally and bodily, as ever I saw—but then the rats—and that suggestion of the devil." The doctor shook his head and went on. "I would have offered to go and stay the first night with him but I felt sure it would have been a cause of offence. He may get in the night some strange fright or hallucination; and if he does I want him to pull that rope. All alone as he is it will give us warning, and we may reach him in time to be of service. I shall be sitting up pretty late to-night and shall keep my ears open. Do not be alarmed if Benchurch gets a surprise before morning."

"Oh, Doctor, what do you mean?"

"I mean this; that possibly—nay, more probably—we shall hear the great alarm bell from the Judge's House to-night," and the Doctor made about as effective an exit as could be thought of.

When Malcolmson arrived home he found that it was a little after his usual time, and Mrs. Dempster had gone away—the rules of Greenhow's Charity were not to be neglected. He was glad to see that the place was bright and tidy with a cheerful fire and a well-trimmed lamp. The evening was colder than might have been expected in April, and a heavy wind was blowing with such rapid-increasing strength that there was every promise of a storm during the night. For a few minutes after his entrance the noise of the rats ceased; but so soon as they became accustomed to his presence they began again. He was glad to hear them, for he felt once more the feeling of companionship in their noise, and his mind ran back to the strange fact that they only ceased to manifest themselves when that other—the great rat with the baleful eyes—came upon the scene. The reading-lamp only was lit and its green shade kept the ceiling and the upper part of the room in darkness, so that the cheerful light from the hearth spreading over the floor and shining on the white cloth laid over the end of the table was warm and cheery. Malcolmson sat down to his dinner with a good appetite and a buoyant spirit. After his dinner and a cigarette he sat steadily down to work, determined not to let anything disturb him, for he remembered his promise to the doctor, and made up his mind to make the best of the time at his disposal.

For an hour or so he worked all right, and then his thoughts began to wander from his books. The actual circumstances around him, the calls on his physical attention, and his nervous susceptibility were not to be denied. By this time the wind had become a gale, and the gale a storm. The old house, solid though it was, seemed to shake to its foundations, and the storm roared and raged through its many chimneys and its queer old gables, producing strange, unearthly sounds in the empty rooms and corridors. Even the great alarm bell on the roof must have felt the force of the wind, for the rope rose and fell slightly, as though the bell were moved a little from time to time, and the limber rope fell on the oak floor with a hard and hollow sound.

As Malcolmson listened to it he bethought himself of the doctor's words, "It is the rope which the hangman used for the victims of the Judge's judicial rancour," and he went over to the corner of the fireplace and took it in his hand to look at it. There seemed a sort of deadly interest in it, and as he stood there he lost himself for a moment in speculation as to who these victims were, and the grim wish of the Judge to have such a ghastly relic ever under his eyes. As he stood there the swaying of the bell on the roof still lifted the rope now and again; but presently there came a new sensation—a sort of tremor in the rope, as though something was moving along it.

Looking up instinctively Malcolmson saw the great rat

coming slowly down towards him, glaring at him steadily. He dropped the rope and started back with a muttered curse, and the rat turning ran up the rope again and disappeared, and at the same instant Malcolmson became conscious that the noise of the rats, which had ceased for a while, began again.

All this set him thinking, and it occurred to him that he had not investigated the lair of the rat or looked at the pictures, as he had intended. He lit the other lamp without the shade, and, holding it up, went and stood opposite the third picture from the fireplace on the right-hand side where he had seen the rat disappear on the previous night.

At the first glance he started back so suddenly that he almost dropped the lamp, and a deadly pallor overspread his face. His knees shook, and heavy drops of sweat came on his forehead, and he trembled like an aspen. But he was young and plucky, and pulled himself together, and after the pause of a few seconds stepped forward again, raised the lamp, and examined the picture which had been dusted and washed, and now stood out clearly.

It was of a judge dressed in his robes of scarlet and ermine. His face was strong and merciless, evil, crafty, and vindictive, with a sensual mouth, hooked nose of ruddy colour, and shaped like the beak of a bird of prey. The rest of the face was of a cadaverous colour. The eyes were of peculiar brilliance and with a terribly malignant expression. As he looked at them, Malcolmson grew cold, for he saw there the very counterpart of the eyes of the great rat. The lamp almost fell from his hand, he saw the rat with its baleful eyes peering out through the hole in the corner of the picture, and noted the sudden cessation of the noise of the other rats. However, he pulled himself together, and went on with his examination of the picture.

The Judge was seated in a great high-backed carved oak chair, on the right-hand side of a great stone fireplace where, in the corner, a rope hung down from the ceiling, its end lying coiled on the floor. With a feeling of something like horror, Malcolmson recognised the scene of the room as it stood, and gazed around him in an awe-struck manner as though he expected to find some strange presence behind him. Then he looked over to the corner of the fireplace— and with a loud cry he let the lamp fall from his hand.

There, in the Judge's arm-chair, with the rope hanging behind, sat the rat with the Judge's baleful eyes, now intensified and with a fiendish leer. Save for the howling of the storm without there was silence.

The fallen lamp recalled Malcolmson to himself. Fortunately, it was of metal, and so the oil was not spilt. However, the practical need of attending to it settled at once his nervous apprehensions. When he had turned it out, he wiped his brow and thought for a moment.

"This will not do," he said to himself. "If I go on like this I shall become a crazy fool. This must stop! I promised the Doctor I would not take tea. Faith, he was pretty right! My nerves must have been getting into a queer state. Funny I did not notice it. I never felt better in my life. However, it is all right now, and I shall not be such a fool again."

Then he mixed himself a good stiff glass of brandy and water and resolutely sat down to his work.

It was nearly an hour when he looked up from his book, disturbed by the sudden stillness. Without, the wind howled and roared louder than ever, and the rain drove in sheets against the windows, beating like hail on the glass; but within there was no sound whatever save the echo of the wind as it roared in the great chimney, and now and then a hiss as a few raindrops found their way down the chimney in a lull of the storm. The fire had fallen low and had ceased to flame, though it threw out a red glow. Malcolmson listened attentively, and presently heard a thin, squeaking noise, very faint. It came from the corner of the room where the rope hung down, and he thought it was the creaking of the rope on the floor as the swaying of the bell raised and lowered it. Looking up, however, he saw in the dim light the great rat clinging to the rope and gnawing it. The rope was already nearly gnawed through—he could see the lighter colour where the strands were laid bare. As he looked the job was completed, and the severed end of the rope fell clattering on the oaken floor, whilst for an instant the great rat remained like a knob or tassel at the end of the rope, which now began to sway to and fro. Malcolmson felt for a moment another pang of terror as he thought that now the possibility of calling the outer world to his assistance was cut off, but an intense anger took its place, and seizing the book he was reading he hurled it at the rat. The blow was well aimed, but before the missile could reach it the rat dropped off and struck the floor with a soft thud. Malcolmson instantly rushed over towards it, but it darted away and disappeared in the darkness of the shadows of the room. Malcolmson felt that his work was over for the night, and determined then and there to vary the monotony of the proceedings by a hunt for the rat, and took off the green shade of the lamp so as to insure a wider spreading light. As he did so the gloom of the upper part of the room was relieved, and in the new flood of light, great by comparison with the previous darkness, the pictures on the wall stood out boldly. From where he stood, Malcolmson saw right opposite to him the third picture on the wall from the right of the fireplace. He rubbed his eyes in surprise, and then a great fear began to come upon him.

In the centre of the picture was a great irregular patch of brown canvas, as fresh as when it was stretched on the frame. The background was as before, with chair and chimney-corner and rope, but the figure of the Judge had disappeared.

Malcolmson, almost in a chill of horror, turned slowly

round, and then he began to shake and tremble like a man in a palsy. His strength seemed to have left him, and he was incapable of action or movement, hardly even of thought. He could only see and hear.

There, on the great high-backed carved oak chair sat the Judge in his robes of scarlet and ermine, with his baleful eyes glaring vindictively, and a smile of triumph on the resolute, cruel mouth, as he lifted with his hands a *black cap*. Malcolmson felt as if the blood was running from his heart, as one does in moments of prolonged suspense. There was a singing in his ears. Without, he could hear the roar and howl of the tempest, and through it, swept on the storm, came the striking of midnight by the great chimes in the market place. He stood for a space of time that seemed to him endless, still as a statue and with wide-open, horror-struck eyes, breathless. As the clock struck, so the smile of triumph on the Judge's face intensified, and at the last stroke of midnight he placed the black cap on his head.

Slowly and deliberately the Judge rose from his chair and picked up the piece of the rope of the alarm bell which lay on the floor, drew it through his hands as if he enjoyed its touch, and then deliberately began to knot one end of it, fashioning it into a noose. This he tightened and tested with his foot, pulling hard at it till he was satisfied and then making a running noose of it, which he held in his hand. Then he began to move along the table on the opposite side to Malcolmson, keeping his eyes on him until he had passed him, when with a quick movement he stood in front of the door. Malcolmson then began to feel that he was trapped, and tried to think of what he should do. There was some fascination in the Judge's eyes, which he never took off him, and he had, perforce, to look. He saw the Judge approach— still keeping between him and the door—and raise the noose and throw it towards him as if to entangle him. With a great effort he made a quick movement to one side, and saw the rope fall beside him, and heard it strike the oaken floor. Again the Judge raised the noose and tried to ensnare him, ever keeping his baleful eyes fixed on him, and each time by a mighty effort the student just managed to evade it. So this went on for many times, the Judge seeming never discouraged nor discomposed at failure, but playing as a cat does with a mouse. At last in despair, which had reached its climax, Malcolmson cast a quick glance round him. The lamp seemed to have blazed up, and there was a fairly good light in the room. At the many rat-holes and in the chinks and crannies of the wainscot he saw the rats' eyes; and this aspect, that was purely physical, gave him a gleam of comfort. He looked around and saw that the rope of the great alarm bell was laden with rats. Every inch of it was covered with them, and more and more were pouring through the small circular hole in the ceiling whence it emerged, so that with their weight the bell was beginning to sway.

Hark! it had swayed till the clapper had touched the bell. The sound was but a tiny one, but the bell was only beginning to sway, and it would increase.

At the sound the Judge, who had been keeping his eyes fixed on Malcolmson, looked up, and a scowl of diabolical anger overspread his face. His eyes fairly glowed like hot coals, and he stamped his foot with a sound that seemed to make the house shake. A dreadful peal of thunder broke overhead as he raised the rope again, whilst the rats kept running up and down the rope as though working against time. This time, instead of throwing it, he drew close to his victim, and held open the noose as he approached. As he came closer there seemed something paralysing in his very presence, and Malcolmson stood rigid as a corpse. He felt the Judge's icy fingers touch his throat as he adjusted the rope. The noose tightened—tightened. Then the Judge, taking the rigid form of the student in his arms, carried him over and placed him standing in the oak chair, and

PHANTAS
by
Oliver Onions

There have been tales of ghost ships ever since men set forth to sail the seven seas. The most famous, of course, is the legend of the Flying Dutchman—*the rotting hulk doomed to sail the misty seas forever with its crew of lost souls. But other ghost ships may also be found on those same misty waters, steered not by the hands of the damned but by the dark winds of the supernatural.*

You'll find one such ship in "Phantas"—a specter unlike any other in macabre fiction. The voyage you're about to take with her is one of the eeriest you'll ever embark on; and the surprise waiting at its end may chill the marrow in your bones . . .

Oliver Onions (1873–1961) disliked what he called "the groans and clankings of the grosser spook"; as a result his spectral stories are more subtle, if no less hair-raising in their effects, than most in the genre. A perfect example is his oft-anthologized "The Beckoning Fair One," which such writers as H. P. Lovecraft and Algernon Blackwood considered to be the finest ghost story in the English language. A slow, careful craftsman, Onions (his real name, although he legally changed it to George Oliver early in life because of

merciless teasing) wrote his first novel, The Compleat Bachelor
*(1901), at the urging of Gillette Burgess; a number of others followed.
His first collection of supernatural stories,* Widdershins, *was published in 1911; two others,* Ghosts in Daylight *and* The Painted
Face, *appeared in 1924 and 1929 respectively.* The Collected
Ghost Stories of Oliver Onions, *first published in England in
1935, was reprinted in this country by Dover Books in 1971.*

*For, barring all pother,
With this, or the other,
Still Britons are Lords of the Main.*
THE CHAPTER OF ADMIRALS

AS ABEL KEELING LAY ON THE GALLEON'S DECK, HELD FROM
rolling down it only by his own weight and the sun-blackened
hand that lay outstretched upon the planks, his gaze wandered, but ever returned to the bell that hung, jammed with
the dangerous heel-over of the vessel, in the small ornamental
belfry immediately abaft the mainmast. The bell was of cast
bronze, with half-obliterated bosses upon it that had been
the heads of cherubs; but wind and salt spray had given it
a thick incrustation of bright, beautiful, lichenous green. It
was this colour that Abel Keeling's eyes liked.

For wherever else on the galleon his eyes rested they
found only whiteness—the whiteness of the extreme eld.
There were slightly varying degrees in her whiteness; here
she was of a white that glistened like salt-granules, there of
a greyish chalky white, and again her whiteness had the
yellowish cast of decay; but everywhere it was the mild,
disquieting whiteness of materials out of which the life had
departed. Her cordage was bleached as old straw is bleached,
and half her ropes kept their shape little more firmly than

the ash of a string keeps its shape after the fire has passed; her pallid timbers were white and clean as bones found in sand; and even the wild frankincense with which (for lack of tar, at her last touching of land) she had been pitched had dried to a pale hard gum that sparkled like quartz in her open seams. The sun was yet so pale a buckler of silver through the still white mists that not a cord or timber cast a shadow; and only Abel Keeling's face and hands were black, carked and cinder-black from exposure to his pitiless rays.

The galleon was the *Mary of the Tower*, and she had a frightful list to starboard. So canted was she that her mainyard dipped one of its steel sickles into the glassy water, and, had her foremast remained, or more than the broken stump of her bonaventure mizzen, she must have turned over completely. Many days ago they had stripped the mainyard of its course, and had passed the sail under the *Mary*'s bottom, in the hope that it would stop the leak. This it had partly done as long as the galleon had continued to guide one way; then, without coming about, she had begun to glide the other, the ropes had parted, and she had dragged the sail after her, leaving a broad barnish on the silver sea.

For it was broadside that the galleon glided, almost imperceptibly, ever sucking down. She glided as if a loadstone drew her, and, at first, Abel Keeling had thought it was a loadstone, pulling at her iron, drawing her through the pearly mists that lay like face-cloths to the water and hid at a short distance the tarnish left by the sail. But later he had known that it was no loadstone drawing at her iron. The motion was due—must be due—to the absolute deadness of the calm in that silent, sinister, three-miles-broad waterway. With the eye of his mind he saw that loadstone now as he lay against a gun-truck, all but toppling down the deck. Soon that would happen again which had happened for five days past. He would hear again the chattering of the monkeys and the screaming of parrots, the mat of green and yellow weeds would creep in towards the *Mary* over the quicksilver sea, and once more the sheer wall of rock would rise, and the men would run. . . .

But no; the men would not run this time to drop the fenders. There were no men left to do so, unless Bligh was still alive. Perhaps Bligh was still alive. He had walked halfway down the quarter-deck steps a little before the sudden nightfall of the day before, had then fallen and lain for a minute (dead, Abel Keeling had supposed, watching him from his place by the gun-truck), and had then got up again and tottered forward to the forecastle, his tall figure swaying and his long arms waving. Abel Keeling had not seen him since. Most likely, he had died in the forecastle during the night. If he had not been dead he would have come aft again for water. . . .

At the remembrance of the water Abel Keeling lifted his head. The strands of lean muscle about his emaciated mouth worked, and he made a little pressure of his sun-blackened hands on the deck, as if to verify its steepness and his own balance. The mainmast was some seven or eight yards away. . . . He put one stiff leg under him and began, seated as he was, to make shuffling movements down the slope.

To the mainmast, near the belfry, was affixed his contrivance for catching water. It consisted of a collar of rope set lower at one side than at the other (but that had been before the mast had steeved so many degrees away from the zenith), and tallowed beneath. The mists lingered later in that gully of a strait than they did on the open ocean, and the collar of rope served as a collector for the dews that condensed on the masts. The drops fell into a small earthen pipkin placed on the deck beneath it.

Abel Keeling reached the pipkin and looked into it. It was nearly a third full of fresh water. Good. If Bligh, the mate, was dead, so much the more water for Abel Keeling, master of the *Mary of the Tower*. He dipped two fingers into the pipkin and put them into his mouth. This he did several times. He did not dare to raise the pipkin to his black and broken lips for dread of a remembered agony, he could not have told how many days ago, when a devil had whispered to him, and he had gulped down the contents of the pipkin in the morning, and for the rest of the day had gone waterless. . . . Again he moistened his fingers and sucked them; then he lay sprawling against the mast, idly watching the drops of water as they fell.

It was odd how the drops formed. Slowly they collected at the edge of the tallowed collar, trembled in their fullness for an instant, and fell, another beginning the process instantly. It amused Abel Keeling to watch them. Why (he wondered) were all the drops the same size? What cause and compulsion did they obey that they never varied, and what frail tenuity held the little globules intact? It must be due to some Cause. . . . He remembered that the aromatic gum of the wild frankincense with which they had parcelled the seams had hung on the buckets in great sluggish gouts, obedient to a different compulsion; oil was different again, and so were juices and balsams. Only quicksilver (perhaps the heavy and motionless sea put him in mind of quicksilver) seemed obedient to no law. . . . Why was it so?

Bligh, of course, would have had his explanation: it was the Hand of God. That sufficed for Bligh, who had gone forward the evening before, and whom Abel Keeling now seemed vaguely and as at a distance to remember as the deep-voiced fanatic who had sung his hymns as, man by man, he had committed the bodies of the ship's company to the deep. Bligh was that sort of man; accepted things without question; was content to take things as they were and be ready with the fenders when the wall of rock rose out of the opalescent mists. Bligh, too, like the waterdrops, had his Law, that was his and nobody else's. . . .

There floated down from some rotten rope up aloft a flake of scurf, that settled in the pipkin. Abel Keeling watched it dully as it settled towards the pipkin's rim. When presently again he dipped his fingers into the vessel the water ran into a little vortex, drawing the flake with it. The water settled again; and again the minute flake determined towards the rim and adhered there, as if the rim had power to draw it. . . .

It was exactly so that the galleon was gliding towards the wall of rock, the yellow and green weeds, and the monkeys and parrots. Put out into mid-water again (while there had been men to put her out) she had glided to the other wall. One force drew the chip in the pipkin and the ship over the tranced sea. It was the Hand of God said Bligh. . . .

Abel Keeling, his mind now noting minute things and now clouded with torpor, did not at first hear a voice that was quakingly lifted up over by the forecastle—a voice that drew nearer, to an accompaniment of swirling water.

> *O Thou, that Jonas in the fish*
> *Three days didst keep from pain,*
> *Which was a figure of Thy death*
> *And rising up again—*

It was Bligh, singing one of his hymns:

> *O Thou, that Noah keptst from flood*
> *And Abram, day by day,*
> *As he along through Egypt passed*
> *Didst guide him in the way—*

The voice ceased, leaving the pious period uncompleted. Bligh was alive, at any rate. . . . Abel Keeling resumed his fitful musing.

Yes, that was the Law of Bligh's life, to call things the

Hand of God; but Abel Keeling's Law was different; no better, no worse, only different. The Hand of God, that drew chips and galleons, must work by some method; and Abel Keeling's eyes were dully on the pipkin again as if he sought the method there. . . .

Then conscious thought left him for a space, and when he resumed it was without obvious connection.

Oars, of course, were the thing. With oars, men could laugh at calms. Oars, that only pinnaces and galliasses now used, had had their advantages. But oars (which was to say a method, for you could say if you liked that the Hand of God grasped the oar-loom, as the Breath of God filled the sail)—oars were antiquated, belonged to the past, and meant a throwing-over of all that was good and new and a return to fine lines, a battle-formation abreast to give effect to the shock of the ram, and a day or two at sea and then to port again for provisions. Oars . . . no. Abel Keeling was one of the new men, the men who swore by the line-ahead, the broadside fire of sakers and demi-cannon, and weeks and months without a landfall. Perhaps one day the wits of such men as he would devise a craft, not oar-driven (because oars could not penetrate into the remote seas of the world)—not sail-driven (because men who trusted to sails found themselves in an airless, three-mile strait, suspended motionless between cloud and water, ever gliding to a wall of rock)—but a ship . . . a ship. . . .

> To Noah and his sons with him
> God spake, and thus said He:
> A cov'nant set I up with you
> And your posterity—

It was Bligh again, wandering somewhere in the waist. Abel Keeling's mind was once more a blank. Then slowly,

slowly, as the water drops collected on the collar of rope, his thought took shape again.

A galliasse? No, not a galliasse. The galliasse made shift to be two things, and was neither. This ship, that the hand of man should one day make for the Hand of God to manage, should be a ship that should take and conserve the force of the wind, take it and store it as she stored her victuals; at rest when she wished, going ahead when she wished; turning the forces of both of calm and storm against themselves. For, of course, her force must be wind—stored wind—a bag of winds, as the children's tale had it—wind probably directed upon the water astern, driving it away and urging forward the ship, acting by reaction. She would have a windchamber, into which wind would be pumped with pumps. . . . Bligh would call that equally the Hand of God, this driving force of the ship of the future that Abel Keeling dimly fore-shadowed as he lay between the mainmast and the belfry, turning his eyes now and then from the ashy white timbers to the vivid green bronze-rust of the bell above him. . . .

Bligh's face, liver-coloured with the sun and ravaged from inwards by the faith that consumed him, appeared at the head of the quarter-deck steps. His voice beat uncontrolledly out.

> *And in the earth there is no place*
> *Of refuge to be found,*
> *Nor in the deep and water-course*
> *That passeth under ground—*

II

BLIGH'S EYES WERE LIDDED, AS IF IN CONTEMPLATION OF HIS inner ecstasy. His head was thrown back, and his brows worked up and down tormentedly. His wide mouth remained open as his hymn was suddenly interrupted on the long-drawn note. From somewhere in the shimmering mists the note was taken up, and there drummed and rang and reverberated through the strait a windy, hoarse, and dismal bellow, alarming and sustained. A tremor rang through Bligh. Moving like a sightless man, he stumbled forward from the head of the quarter-deck steps, and Abel Keeling was aware of his gaunt figure behind him, taller for the steepness of the deck. As that vast empty sound died away, Bligh laughed in his mania.

"Lord, hath the grave's wide mouth a tongue to praise Thee? Lo, again—"

Again the cavernous sound possessed the air, louder and nearer. Through it came another sound, a slow throb, throb—throb, throb—Again the sounds ceased.

"Even Leviathan lifted up his voice in praise!" Bligh sobbed.

Abel Keeling did not raise his head. There had returned to him the memory of that day when, before the morning mists had lifted from the strait, he had emptied the pipkin of the water that was his allowance until night should fall again. During that agony of thirst he had seen shapes and heard sounds with other than his mortal eyes and ears, and even in the moments that had alternated with his lightness, when he had known these to be hallucinations, they had come again. He had heard the bells on a Sunday in his own Kentish home, the calling of children at play, the unconcerned singing of men at their daily labour, and the laughter and gossip of the women as they had spread the linen on the hedge or distributed bread upon the platters. These voices had rung in his brain, interrupted now and then by the groans of Bligh and of two other men who had been alive then. Some of the voices he had heard had been silent on earth this many a long year, but Abel Keeling, thirst-tortured, had heard them, even as he was now hearing that vacant moaning with the intermittent throbbing that filled the strait with alarm. . . .

"Praise Him, praise Him, praise Him!" Bligh was calling deliriously.

Then a bell seemed to sound in Abel Keeling's ears, and, as if something in the mechanism of his brain had slipped, another picture rose in his fancy—the scene when the *Mary of the Tower* had put out, to a bravery of swinging bells and shrill fifes and valiant trumpets. She had not been a leper-white galleon then. The scrollwork on her prow had twinkled with gilding; her belfry and stern-galleries and elaborate lanterns had flashed in the sun with gold; and her fighting-tops and the warpavesse about her waist had been gay with painted coats and scutcheons. To her sails had been stitched gaudy ramping lions of scarlet say, and from her main-yard, now dipping in the water, had hung the broad two-tailed pennant with the Virgin and Child embroidered upon it. . . .

Then suddenly a voice about him seemed to be saying, *"And a half-seven—and a half-seven—"* and in a twink the picture in Abel Keeling's brain changed again. He was at home again, instructing his son, young Abel, in the casting of the lead from the skiff they had pulled out of the harbour.

"And a half-seven!" the boy seemed to be calling.

Abel Keeling's blackened lips muttered: "Excellently well cast, Abel, excellently well cast!"

"And a half-seven—and a half-seven—seven—seven—"

"Ah," Abel Keeling murmured, "that last was not a clear cast—give me the line—thus it should go . . . ay, so. . . . Soon you shall sail the seas with me in the *Mary of the Tower.* You are already perfect in the stars and the motions of the planets; to-morrow I will instruct you in the use of the backstaff. . . ."

For a minute or two he continued to mutter; then he dozed. When again he came to semi-consciousness it was once more to the sound of bells, at first faint, then louder, and finally becoming a noisy clamour immediately above his head. It was Bligh. Bligh, in a fresh attack of delirium, had seized the bell-lanyard and was ringing the bell insanely. The cord broke in his fingers, but he thrust at the bell with his hand, and again called aloud.

"Upon a harp and an instrument of ten strings . . . let Heaven and Earth praise Thy Name! . . ."

He continued to call aloud, and to beat on the bronze-rusted bell.

"Ship ahoy! What ship's that?"

One would have said that a veritable hail had come out of the mists; but Abel Keeling knew those hails that came out of the mists. They came from ships which were not there. "Ay, ay, keep a good look-out, and have a care to your lode-manage," he muttered again to his son. . . .

But, as sometimes a sleeper sits up in his dream, or rises from his couch and walks, so all of a sudden Abel Keeling found himself on his hands and knees on the deck, looking back over his shoulder. In some deep-seated region of his consciousness he was dimly aware that the cant of the deck had become more perilous, but his brain received the intelligence and forgot it again. He was looking out into the bright and baffling mists. The buckler of the sun was of a more ardent silver; the sea below it was lost in brilliant evaporation; and between them, suspended in the haze, no more substantial than the vague darknesses that float before dazzled eyes, a pyramidal phantom-shape hung. Abel Keeling passed his hand over his eyes, but when he removed it the shape was still there, gliding slowly towards the *Mary's* quarter. Its form changed as he watched it. The spirit-grey shape that had been a pyramid seemed to dissolve into four upright members, slightly graduated in tallness, that nearest the *Mary's* stern the tallest and that to the left the lowest. It might have been the shadow of the gigantic set of reed-pipes on which that vacant mournful note had been sounded.

As he looked, with fooled eyes, again his ears became fooled:

"*Ahoy there! What ship's that? Are you a ship? . . . Here, give me that trumpet—*" Then a metallic barking. "*Ahoy there! What the devil are you? Didn't you ring a bell? Ring it again, or blow a blast or something, and go dead slow!*"

All this came, as it were, indistinctly, and through a sort of high singing in Abel Keeling's own ears. Then he fancied a short bewildered laugh, followed by a colloquy from somewhere between sea and sky.

"*Here, Ward just pinch me, will you? Tell me what you see there. I want to know if I am awake.*"

"*See where?*"

"*There, on the starboard bow. (Stop that ventilating fan; I can't hear myself think.) See anything? Don't tell me it's that damned Dutchman—don't pitch me that old Vanderdecken tale—give me an easy one first, something about a sea-serpent. . . . You did hear that bell, didn't you?*"

"*Shut up a minute—listen—*"

Again Bligh's voice was lifted up.

> *This is the cov'nant that I make:*
> *From henceforth nevermore*
> *Will I again the world destroy*
> *With water, as before.*

Bligh's voice died away again in Abel Keeling's ears.

"*Oh—my—fat—Aunt—Julia!*" the voice that seemed to come from between the sea and sky sounded again. Then it spoke more loudly. "*I say,*" it began with careful politeness, "*if you are a ship, do you mind telling us where the masquerade is to be? Our wireless is out of order, and we hadn't heard of it. . . . Oh, you do see it, Ward, don't you? . . . Please, please tell us what the hell you are!*"

Again Abel Keeling had moved as a sleep-walker moves.

He had raised himself up by the belfry timbers, and Bligh had sunk in a heap on the deck. Abel Keeling's movement overturned the pipkin, which raced the little trickle of its contents down the deck and lodged where the still and brimming sea made, as it were, a chain with the carved balustrade of the quarter-deck—one link a still gleaming edge, then a dark baluster, and then another gleaming link. For one moment only Abel Keeling found himself noticing that that which had driven Bligh aft had been the rising of the water in the waist as the galleon settled by the head—the waist was now entirely submerged; then once more he was absorbed in his dream, its voices, and its shape in the mist, which had again taken the form of a pyramid before his eyeballs.

"Of course," a voice seemed to be complaining anew, and still through that confused dinning in Abel Keeling's ears, *"we can't turn a four-inch on it. . . . And, of course, Ward, I don't believe in 'em. D'you hear, Ward? I don't believe in 'em, I say. . . . Shall we call down to old A.B.? This might interest His Scientific Skippership. . . ."*

"Oh, lower a boat and pull out to it—into it—over it—through it—"

"Look at our chaps crowded on the barbette yonder. They've seen it. Better not give an order you know won't be obeyed. . . ."

Abel Keeling, cramped against the antique belfry, had begun to find his dream interesting. For, though he did not know her build, that mirage was in the shape of a ship. No doubt it was projected from his brooding on ships of half an hour before; and that was odd. . . . But perhaps, after all, it was not very odd. He knew that she did not really exist; only the appearance of her existed; but things had to exist like that before they really existed. Before the *Mary of the Tower* had existed she had been a shape in some man's imagination; before that, some dreamer had dreamed the form of a ship with oars; and before that, far away in the dawn and infancy of the world, some seer had seen in a

vision the raft before man had ventured to push out over
the water on his two planks. And since this shape that rode
before Abel Keeling's eyes was a shape in his, Abel Keeling's
dream, he, Abel Keeling, was the master of it. His own
brooding brain had contrived her, and she was launched
upon the illimitable ocean of his own mind. . . .

> *And I will not unmindful be*
> *Of this, My cov'nant, passed*
> *Twixt Me and you and every flesh*
> *Whiles that the world should last,*

sang Bligh, rapt. . . .

But as a dreamer, even in his dreams, will scratch upon
the wall by his couch some key or word to put him in mind
of his vision on the morrow when it has left him, so Abel
Keeling found himself seeking some sign to be a proof to
those to whom no vision is vouchsafed. Even Bligh sought
that—could not be silent in his bliss, but lay on the deck
there, uttering great passionate Amens and praising his
Maker, as he said, upon an harp and an instrument of ten
strings. So with Abel Keeling. It would be the Amen of his
life to have praised God, not upon a harp, but upon a ship
that should carry her own power, that should store wind or
its equivalent as she stored her victuals, that should be something wrested from the chaos of uninvention and ordered
and disciplined and subordinated to Abel Keeling's will. . . .
And there she was, that ship-shaped thing of spirit-grey,
with the four pipes that resembled a phantom organ now
broadside and of equal length. And the ghost-crew of that
ship were speaking again. . . .

The interrupted silver chain by the quarterdeck balustrade
had now become continuous, and the balusters made a her-
ring-bone over their own motionless reflections. The spilt
water from the pipkin had dried, and the pipkin was not

to be seen. Abel Keeling stood beside the mast, erect as God made man to go. With his leathery hand he smote upon the bell. He waited for the space of a minute, and then cried:

"Ahoy! . . . Ship ahoy! . . . What ship's that?"

III

WE ARE NOT CONSCIOUS IN A DREAM THAT WE ARE PLAYING a game the beginning and end of which are in ourselves. In this dream of Abel Keeling's a voice replied:

"*Hallo, it's found its tongue. . . . Ahoy there! What are you?*"

Loudly and in a clear voice, Abel Keeling called: "Are you a ship?"

With a nervous giggle the answer came:

"*We are a ship, aren't we, Ward? I hardly feel sure. . . . Yes, of course, we're a ship. No question about us. The question is what the dickens you are.*"

Not all the words these voices used were intelligible to Abel Keeling, and he knew not what it was in the tone of these last words that reminded him of the honour due to the *Mary of the Tower*. Blister-white and at the end of her life as she was, Abel Keeling was still jealous of her dignity; the voice had a youngish ring; and it was not fitting that young chins should be wagged about his galleon. He spoke curtly.

"You that spoke—are you the master of that ship?"

"*Officer of the watch,*" the words floated back; "*the captain's below.*"

"Then send for him. It is with masters that masters hold speech," Abel Keeling replied.

He could see two shapes, flat and without relief, standing on a high narrow structure with rails. One of them gave a low whistle, and seemed to be fanning his face; but the other rumbled something into a sort of funnel. Presently two shapes became three. There was a murmuring, as of a consultation, and then suddenly a new voice spoke. At its thrill and tone a sudden tremor ran through Abel Keeling's frame. He wondered what response it was that that voice found in the forgotten recesses of his memory. . . .

"*Ahoy!*" seemed to call this new yet faintly remembered voice. "*What's all this about? Listen. We're His Majesty's destroyer* Seapink, *out of Devonport last October, and nothing particular the matter with us. Now who are you?*"

"The *Mary of the Tower*, out of the Port of Rye on the day of Saint Anne, and only two men—"

A gasp interrupted him.

"*Out of* where?" that voice that so strangely moved Abel Keeling said unsteadily, while Bligh broke into groans of renewed rapture.

"Out of the Port of Rye, in the County of Sussex . . . nay, give ear, else I cannot make you hear me while this man's spirit and flesh wrestle so together! . . . Ahoy! Are you gone?" For the voices had become a low murmur, and the ship-shape had faded before Abel Keeling's eyes. Again and again he called. He wished to be informed of the disposition and economy of the wind-chamber. . . .

"The wind-chamber!" he called, in an agony lest the knowledge almost within his grasp should be lost. "I would know about the wind-chamber . . ."

Like an echo, there came back the words, uncomprehendingly uttered, "*The wind-chamber? . . .*"

" . . . that driveth the vessel—perchance 'tis not wind—a steel bow that is bent also conserveth force—the force you store, to move at will through calm and storm. . . ."

"*Can you make out what it's driving at?*"

"*Oh, we shall all wake up in a minute. . . .*"

"*Quiet, I have it; the engines; it wants to know about our engines.*

It'll be wanting to see our papers presently. Rye Port! . . . Well, no harm in humoring it; let's see what it can make of this. Ahoy there!" came the voice to Abel Keeling, a little strongly, as if a shifting wind carried it, and speaking faster and faster as it went on. *"Not wind, but steam; d'you hear? Steam, steam. Steam, in eight Yarrow water-tube boilers. S-t-e-a-m, steam. Got it? And we've twin-screw triple expansion engines, indicated horsepower four thousand, and we can do 430 revolutions per minute; savvy? Is there anything your phantomhood would like to know about our armament? . . ."*

Abel Keeling was muttering fretfully to himself. It annoyed him that words in his own vision should have no meaning for him. How did words come to him in a dream that he had no knowledge of when wide awake? The *Seapink*—that was the name of this ship; but a pink was long and narrow, low-carged and square-built aft. . . .

"And as for our armament," the voice with the tones that so profoundly troubled Abel Keeling's memory continued, *"we've two revolving Whitehead torpedo-tubes, three six-pounders on the upper deck, and that's a twelve-pounder forward there by the conning tower. I forgot to mention that we're nickel steel, with a coal capacity of sixty tons in most damnably placed bunkers, and that thirty and a quarter knots is about our top. Care to come aboard?"*

But the voice was speaking still more rapidly and feverishly, as if to fill a silence with no matter what, and the shape that was uttering it was straining forward anxiously over the rail.

"Ugh! But I'm glad this happened in the daylight," another voice was muttering.

"I wish I was sure it was happening at all. . . . Poor old spook!"

"I suppose it would keep its feet if her deck was quite vertical. Think she'll go down, or just melt?"

"Kind of go down . . . without wash . . ."

"Listen—here's the other one now—"

For Bligh was singing again:

For, Lord, Thou know'st our nature such
  If we great things obtain
And in the getting of the same
  Do feel no grief or pain,

We little do esteem thereof;
  But, hardly brought to pass,
A thousand times we do esteem
More than the other was

"But oh, look—look—look at the other! . . . Oh, I say, wasn't he a grand old boy! Look!"

For, transfiguring Abel Keeling's form as a prophet's form is transfigured in the instant of his rapture, flooding his brain with the white eureka-light of perfect knowledge, that for which he and his dream had been at a standstill had come. He knew her, this ship of the future, as if God's Frager had bitten her lines into his brain. He knew her as those already sinking into the grave know things, miraculously, completely, accepting Life's impossibilities with a nodded "Of course." From the ardent mouths of her eight furnaces to the last drip from her lubricators, from her bedplates to the breeches of her quick-firers, he knew her—read her gauges, thumbed her bearings, gave the ranges from her range-finders, and lived the life he lived who was in command of her. And he would not forget on the morrow, as he had forgotten on many morrows, for at last he had seen the water about his feet, and knew that there would be no morrow for him in this world. . . .

And even in that moment, with but a sand or two to run in his glass, indomitable, insatiable, dreaming dream on dream, he could not die until he knew more. He had two questions to ask, and a master-question; and but a moment remained. Sharply his voice rang out.

"Ho, there! . . . This ancient ship, the *Mary of the Tower,* cannot steam thirty and a quarter knots, but yet she can sail the waters. What more does your ship? Can she soar above them, as the fowls of the air soar?"

"Lord, he thinks we're an aeroplane! . . . No, she can't. . . ."

"And can you dive, even as the fishes of the deep?"

"No. . . . Those are submarines . . . we aren't a submarine. . . ."

But Abel Keeling waited for no more. He gave an exulting chuckle.

"Oho, oho—thirty knots, and but on the face of the waters—no more than that? Oho! . . . Now *my* ship, the ship I see as a mother sees a full-grown child she has but conceived—*my* ship I say—oho!—*my* ship. . . . Below there—trip that gun!"

The cry came suddenly and alertly, as a muffled sound came from below and an ominous tremor shook the galleon.

"By Jove, her guns are breaking loose below—that's her finish—"

"Trip that gun, and double-breech the others!" Abel Keeling's voice rang out, as if there had been any to obey him. He had braced himself within the belfry frame; and then in the middle of the next order his voice suddenly failed him. His ship-shape, that for the moment he had forgotten, rode once more before his eyes. This was the end, and his master-question, apprehension for the answer to which was now torturing his face and well-nigh bursting his heart, was still unasked.

"Ho—he that spoke with me—the master," he cried in a voice that ran high, "is he there?"

"Yes, yes!" came the other voice across the water, sick with suspense. *"Oh, be quick!"*

There was a moment in which hoarse cries from many voices, a heavy thud and rumble on wood, and a crash of timbers and a gurgle and splash were indescribably mingled; the gun under which Abel Keeling had lain had snapped her rotten breechings and plunged down the deck, carrying Bligh's unconscious form with it. The deck came up vertical, and for one instant longer Abel Keeling clung to the belfry.

"I cannot see your face," he screamed, "but meseems your voice is a voice I know. *What is your name?*"

In a torn sob the answer came across the water:

"*Keeling—Abel Keeling. . . . Oh, my God!*"

And Abel Keeling's cry of triumph, that mounted to a victorious "Huzza!" was lost in the downward plunge of the *Mary of the Tower*, that left the strait empty save for the sun's fiery blaze and the last smoke-like evaporation of the mists.

ON THE MOORS
by
W.F. HARVEY

Some aficionados of spectral fiction will argue, persuasively and perhaps validly, that W.F. Harvey is the author of the single finest supernatural story ever written. The story, of course, is "August Heat"—a masterpiece of mood, atmosphere, characterization, plot, and ultimate horror compressed into little more than two thousand words. The temptation to include it in these pages was considerable, but the plain fact is, "August Heat" has been so often anthologized that it is familiar to nearly every reader of macabre tales.

The decision, therefore, was to include "On the Moors" instead—a less well-known Harvey short story which contains some of the same elements as "August Heat" and which provides abundant chills in its own right. To the best of the editor's knowledge, this little nightmare has never before appeared in an American anthology. After you've read it, and perhaps felt the frisson *of its final page, I think you'll agree that the decision to present it here was a good one.*

William Fryer Harvey (1885–1937), a Yorkshire Quaker, was educated at Balliol College, Oxford, and later took his medical degree at Leeds. He served in the British Navy during the First World War, and was decorated in 1918 "for gallantry in saving life at sea"; but his lungs were damaged by oil fumes during his heroic act on board a destroyer, and for the remainder of his life he was an invalid. Among his writings are two novels, one for adults and one for children, two nonfiction books on Quaker themes, and a posthumous collection of criminous stories, The Arm of Mrs. Egan *(1952). But it is for his three volumes of ghost stories and uncanny tales—*Midnight House *(1910),* The Beast with Five Fingers *(1928), and* Moods and Tenses *(1933)—and of course for "August Heat," that he is best remembered.*

IT REALLY WAS MOST UNFORTUNATE.

Peggy had a temperature of nearly a hundred, and a pain in her side, and Mrs. Workington Bancroft knew that it was appendicitis. But there was no one whom she could send for the doctor.

James had gone with the jaunting-car to meet her husband who had at last managed to get away for a week's shooting.

Adolph she had sent to the Evershams, only half an hour before, with a note for Lady Eva.

The cook could not manage to walk, even if dinner could be served without her.

Kate, as usual, was not to be trusted.

There remained Miss Craig.

"Of course, you must see that Peggy is really ill," said she, as the governess came into the room, in answer to her summons. "The difficulty is, that there is absolutely no one whom I can send for the doctor." Mrs. Workington Bancroft paused; she was always willing that those beneath her should have the privilege of offering the services which it was her right to command.

"So, perhaps, Miss Craig," she went on, "you would not mind walking over to Tebbit's Farm. I hear there is a Liverpool doctor staying there. Of course I know nothing about him, but we must take the risk, and I expect he'll be only too glad to be earning something during his holiday. It's nearly four miles, I know, and I'd never dream of asking you if it was not that I dread appendicitis so."

"Very well," said Miss Craig, "I suppose I must go; but I don't know the way."

"Oh, you can't miss it," said Mrs. Workington Bancroft, in her anxiety temporarily forgiving the obvious unwillingness of her governess's consent.

"You follow the road across the moor for two miles, until you come to Redman's Cross. You turn to the left there, and follow a rough path that leads through a larch plantation. And Tebbit's farm lies just below you in the valley.

"And take Pontiff with you," she added, as the girl left the room. "There's absolutely nothing to be afraid of, but I expect you'll feel happier with the dog."

"Well, miss," said the cook, when Miss Craig went into the kitchen to get her boots, which had been drying by the fire; "of course she knows best, but I don't think it's right after all that's happened for the mistress to send you across the moors on a night like this. It's not as if the doctor could do anything for Miss Margaret if you do bring him. Every child is like that once in a while. He'll only say put her to bed, and she's there already."

"I don't see what there is to be afraid of, cook," said Miss Craig as she laced her boots, "unless you believe in ghosts."

"I'm not so sure about that. Anyhow I don't like sleeping in a bed where the sheets are too short for you to pull them over your head. But don't you be frightened, miss. It's my belief that their bark is worse than their bite."

But though Miss Craig amused herself for some minutes

by trying to imagine the bark of a ghost (a thing altogether different from the classical ghostly bark), she did not feel entirely at her ease.

She was naturally nervous, and living as she did in the hinterland of the servants' hall, she had heard vague details of true stories that were only myths in the drawing-room.

The very name of Redman's Cross sent a shiver through her; it must have been the place where that horrid murder was committed. She had forgotten the tale, though she remembered the name.

Her first disaster came soon enough.

Pontiff, who was naturally slow-witted, took more than five minutes to find out that it was only the governess he was escorting, but once the discovery had been made, he promptly turned tail, paying not the slightest heed to Miss Craig's feeble whistle. And then, to add to her discomfort, the rain came, not in heavy drops, but driving in sheets of thin spray that blotted out what few landmarks there were upon the moor.

They were very kind at Tebbit's farm. The doctor had gone back to Liverpoool the day before, but Mrs. Tebbit gave her hot milk and turf cakes, and offered her reluctant son to show Miss Craig a shorter path on to the moor, that avoided the larch wood.

He was a monosyllabic youth, but his presence was cheering, and she felt the night doubly black when he left her at the last gate.

She trudged on wearily. Her thoughts had already gone back to the almost exhausted theme of the bark of ghosts, when she heard steps on the road behind her that were at least material. Next minute the figure of a man appeared: Miss Craig was relieved to see that the stranger was a clergyman. He raised his hat. "I believe we are both going in the same direction," he said. "Perhaps I may have the pleasure of escorting you."

She thanked him. "It is rather weird at night," she went on, "and what with all the tales of ghosts and bogies that one hears from the country people, I've ended by being half afraid myself."

"I can understand your nervousness," he said, "especially on a night like this. I used at one time to feel the same, for my work often meant lonely walks across the moor to farms which were only reached by rough tracks difficult enough to find even in the daytime."

"And you never saw anything to frighten you—nothing immaterial I mean?"

"I can't really say that I did, but I had an experience eleven years ago which served as the turning-point in my life, and since you seem to be now in much the same state of mind as I was then in, I will tell it you.

"The time of year was late September. I had been over to Westondale to see an old woman who was dying, and then, just as I was about to start on my way home, word came to me of another of my parishioners who had been suddenly taken ill only that morning. It was after seven when at last I started. A farmer saw me on my way, turning back when I reached the moor road.

"The sunset the previous evening had been one of the most lovely I ever remember to have seen. The whole vault of heaven had been scattered with flakes of white cloud, tipped with rosy pink like the strewn petals of a full-blown rose.

"But that night all was changed. The sky was an absolutely dull slate colour, except in one corner of the west where a thin rift showed the last saffron tint of the sullen sunset. As I walked, stiff and footsore, my spirits sank. It must have been the marked contrast between the two evenings, the one so lovely, so full of promise (the corn was still out in the fields spoiling for fine weather), the other so gloomy, so sad with all the dead weight of autumn and winter days to come. And then added to this sense of heavy depression came another different feeling which I surprised myself by recognizing as fear.

"I did not know why I was afraid.

"The moors lay on either side of me, unbroken except for a straggling line of turf shooting-butts, that stood within a stone's throw of the road.

"The only sound I had heard for the last half hour was the cry of the startled grouse—Go back, go back, go back. But yet the feeling of fear was there, affecting a low centre of my brain through some little-used physical channel.

"I buttoned my coat closer, and tried to divert my thoughts by thinking of next Sunday's sermon.

"I had chosen to preach on Job. There is much in the old-fashioned notion of the book, apart from all the subtleties of the higher criticism, that appeals to country people; the loss of herds and crops, the breakup of the family. I would not have dared to speak, had not I too been a farmer; my own glebe land had been flooded three weeks before, and I suppose I stood to lose as much as any man in the parish. As I walked along the road repeating to myself the first chapter of the book, I stopped at the twelfth verse:

"'And the Lord said unto Satan: Behold, all that he hath is in thy power . . .'

"The thought of the bad harvest (and that is an awful thought in these valleys) vanished. I seemed to gaze into an ocean of infinite darkness.

"I had often used, with the Sunday glibness of the tired priest, whose duty it is to preach three sermons in one day, the old simile of the chess-board. God and the devil were the players: and we were helping one side or the other. But until that night I had not thought of the possibility of my being only a pawn in the game, that God might throw away that the game might be won.

"I had reached the place where we are now, I remember

it by that rough stone water-trough, when a man suddenly jumped up from the roadside. He had been seated on a heap of broken road metal.

" 'Which way are you going, guv'ner?' he said.

"I knew from the way he spoke that the man was a stranger. There are many at this time of the year who come up from the south, tramping northwards with the ripening corn. I told him my destination.

" 'We'll go along together,' he replied.

"It was too dark to see much of the man's face, but what little I made out was coarse and brutal.

"Then he began the half-menacing whine I knew so well— he had tramped miles that day, he had had no food since breakfast, and that was only a crust.

" 'Give us a copper,' he said, 'it's only for a night's lodging.'

"He was whittling away with a big clasp knife at an ash stake he had taken from some hedge."

The clergyman broke off.

"Are those the lights of your house?" he said. "We are nearer than I expected, but I shall have time to finish my story. I think I will, for you can run home in a couple of minutes, and I don't want you to be frightened when you are out on the moors again.

"As the man talked he seemed to have stepped out of the very background of my thoughts, his sordid tale, with the sad lies that hid a far sadder truth.

"He asked me the time.

"It was five minutes to nine. As I replaced my watch I glanced at his face. His teeth were clenched, and there was something in the gleam of his eyes that told me at once his purpose.

"Have you ever known how long a second is? For a third of a second I stood there facing him, filled with an over-whelming pity for myself and him; and then without a word of warning he was upon me. I felt nothing. A flash of lightning ran down my spine, I heard the dull crash of the ash stake, and then a very gentle patter like the sound of a far distant stream. For a minute I lay in perfect happiness watching the lights of the house as they increased in number until the whole heaven shone with twinkling lamps.

"I could not have had a more painless death."

Miss Craig looked up. The man was gone; she was alone on the moor.

She ran to the house, her teeth chattering, ran to the solid shadow that crossed and recrossed the kitchen blind.

As she entered the hall, the clock on the stairs struck the hour.

It was nine o'clock.

TfE CANTERUILLE GfOST
by
OSCAR WILDE

Once upon a time in England, there was a ghost who lived in a house called Canterville Chase. Now this ghost enjoyed a fine local reputation as being able (if he felt so inclined) to drive any man wild with terror. But then an American family named Otis went and bought Canterville Chase, and among the Otis brood were precocious twin boys who didn't understand the ethics of haunting. Nor did they understand the device traditionally used by a self-respecting ghost. The account of this clash between an English specter and turn-of-the-century American youth is something quite special—a blend of farce, satire, and things very curious indeed.

"The Canterville Ghost" has, for close to one hundred years, been amusing readers of spectral fiction who like their shudders tempered with chuckles. P.G. Wodehouse might have written it, and may even have wished he had. It has not been reprinted in a number of years, at least not to the editor's knowledge, and is long overdue for another appearance. The spirit, after all, is willing . . .

Dublin-born Oscar Wilde (1854–1900) was a writer whose work encompassed several categories: short stories, poetry, the novel, and the drama. His books include two collections of fairy stories, The Happy Prince and Other Tales *(1888) and* A House of Pomegranates *(1892), a collection of adult stories,* Lord Arthur Savile's Crime *(1891), and the well-known novel of moral decadence,* The Picture of Dorian Gray *(1891); among his famous plays are the comedies* Lady Windermere's Fan *(1892) and* The Importance of Being Earnest *(1895), and the drama* Salome *(1894). In 1895, at the height of his career, he was tried and convicted of sodomy—an offense which outraged the Victorian sensibilities of that era—and served two years at hard labor. It was while he was in prison that he wrote his two classic poems,* De Profundis *and* The Ballad of Reading Gaol. *He died in Paris of meningitis, bankrupt and spiritually broken—a tragic end to a brilliant literary career.*

I

WHEN MR. HIRAM B. OTIS, THE AMERICAN MINISTER, bought Canterville Chase, every one told him he was doing a very foolish thing, as there was no doubt at all that the place was haunted. Indeed, Lord Canterville himself, who was a man of the most punctilious honour, had felt it his duty to mention the fact to Mr. Otis when they came to discuss terms.

"We have not cared to live in the place ourselves," said Lord Canterville, "since my grand-aunt, the Dowager Duchess of Bolton, was frightened into a fit, from which she never really recovered, by two skeleton hands being placed on her shoulders as she was dressing for dinner, and I feel bound to tell you, Mr. Otis, that the ghost has been seen by several living members of my family, as well as by the rector of the parish, the Rev. Augustus Dampier, who is a Fellow of King's College, Cambridge. After the unfortunate accident to the

Duchess, none of our younger servants would stay with us, and Lady Canterville often got very little sleep at night, in consequence of the mysterious noises that came from the corridor and the library."

"My lord," answered the Minister, "I will take the furniture and the ghost at a valuation. I come from a modern country, where we have everything that money can buy; and with all our spry young fellows painting the Old World red, and carrying off your best actresses and primadonnas, I reckon that if there were such a thing as a ghost in Europe, we'd have it at home in a very short time in one of our public museums, or on the road as a show."

"I fear that the ghost exists," said Lord Canterville, smiling, "though it may have resisted the overtures of your enterprising impresarios. It has been well known for three centuries, since 1584 in fact, and always makes its appearance before the death of any member of our family."

"Well, so does the family doctor for that matter, Lord Canterville. But there is no such thing, sir, as a ghost, and I guess the laws of Nature are not going to be suspended for the British aristocracy."

"You are certainly very natural in America," answered Lord Canterville, who did not quite understand Mr. Otis's last observation, "and if you don't mind a ghost in the house, it is all right. Only you must remember I warned you."

A few weeks after this, the purchase was completed, and at the close of the season the Minister and his family went down to Canterville Chase. Mrs. Otis, who, as Miss Lucretia R. Tappan, of West 53rd Street, had been a celebrated New York belle, was now a very handsome, middle-aged woman, with fine eyes, and a superb profile. Many American ladies on leaving their native land adopt an appearnace of chronic ill-health, under the impression that it is a form of European refinement, but Mrs. Otis had never fallen into this error. She had a magnificent constitution, and a really wonderful amount of animal spirits. Indeed, in many respects, she was quite English, and was an excellent example of the fact that we have really everything in common with America nowadays, except, of course, language. Her eldest son, christened Washington by his parents in a moment of patriotism, which he never ceased to regret, was a fair-haired, rather good-looking young man, who had qualified himself for American diplomacy by leading the German at the Newport Casino for three successive seasons, and even in London was well known as an excellent dancer. Gardenias and the peerage were his only weaknesses. Otherwise he was extremely sensible. Miss Virginia E. Otis was a little girl of fifteen, lithe and lovely as a fawn, and with a fine freedom in her large blue eyes. She was a wonderful amazon, and had once raced old Lord Bilton on her pony twice round the park, winning by a length and a half, just in front of the Achilles statue, to the huge delight of the young Duke of Cheshire, who proposed for her on the spot, and was sent back to Eton that very night by his guardians, in floods of tears. After Virginia came the twins, who were usually called "The Stars and Stripes," as they were always getting swished. They were delightful boys, and with the exception of the worthy Minister the only true republicans of the family.

As Canterville Chase is seven miles from Ascot, the nearest railway station, Mr. Otis had telegraphed for a waggonette to meet them, and they started on their drive in high spirits. It was a lovely July evening, and the air was delicate with the scent of the pinewoods. Now and then they heard a wood pigeon brooding over its own sweet voice, or saw, deep in the rustling fern, the burnished breast of the pheasant. Little squirrels peered at them from the beech-trees as they went by, and the rabbits scudded away through the brushwood and over the mossy knolls, with their white tails in the air. As they entered the avenue of Canterville Chase, however, the sky became suddenly overcast with clouds, a curious stillness seemed to hold the atmosphere, a great flight of rooks passed silently over their heads, and, before they reached the house, some big drops of rain had fallen.

Standing on the steps to receive them was an old woman, neatly dressed in black silk, with a white cap and apron. This was Mrs. Umney, the housekeeper, whom Mrs. Otis, at Lady Canterville's earnest request, had consented to keep on in her former position. She made them each a low curtsey as they alighted, and said in a quaint, old-fashioned manner, "I bid you welcome to Canterville Chase." Following her, they passed through the fine Tudor hall into the library, a long, low room, panelled in black oak, at the end of which was a large stained-glass window. Here they found tea laid out for them, and, after taking off their wraps, they sat down and began to look round, while Mrs. Umney waited on them.

Suddenly Mrs. Otis caught sight of a dull red stain on the floor just by the fireplace and, quite unconscious of what it really signified, said to Mrs. Umney, "I am afraid something has been spilt there."

"Yes, madam," replied the old housekeeper in a low voice, "blood has been spilt on that spot."

"How horrid," cried Mrs. Otis; "I don't at all care for blood-stains in a sitting-room. It must be removed at once."

The old woman smiled, and answered in the same low, mysterious voice, "It is the blood of Lady Eleanore de Canterville, who was murdered on that very spot by her own husband, Sir Simon de Canterville, in 1575. Sir Simon survived her nine years, and disappeared suddenly under very mysterious circumstances. His body has never been discovered, but his guilty spirit still haunts the Chase. The blood-stain has been much admired by tourists and others, and cannot be removed."

"That is all nonsense," cried Washington Otis; "Pinkerton's Champion Stain Remover and Paragon Detergent will clean it up in no time," and before the terrified housekeeper could interfere he had fallen upon his knees, and was rapidly scouring the floor with a small stick of what looked like a black cosmetic. In a few moments no trace of the blood-stain could be seen.

"I knew Pinkerton would do it," he exclaimed triumphantly, as he looked round at his admiring family; but no sooner had he said these words than a terrible flash of lightning lit up the sombre room, a fearful peal of thunder made them all start to their feet, and Mrs. Umney fainted.

"What a monstrous climate!" said the American Minister calmly, as he lit a long cheroot. "I guess the old country is so over-populated that they have not enough decent weather for everybody. I have always been of opinion that emigration is the only thing for England."

"My dear Hiram," cried Mrs. Otis, "what can we do with a woman who faints?"

"Charge it to her like breakages," answered the Minister; "she won't faint after that"; and in a few moments Mrs. Umney certainly came to. There was no doubt, however, that she was extremely upset, and she sternly warned Mr. Otis to beware of some trouble coming to the house.

"I have seen things with my own eyes, sir," she said, "that would make any Christian's hair stand on end, and many and many a night I have not closed my eyes in sleep for the awful things that are done here." Mr. Otis, however, and his wife warmly assured the honest soul that they were not afraid of ghosts, and, after invoking the blessings of Providence on her new master and making arrangements for an increase of salary, the old housekeeper tottered off to her own room.

II

THE STORM RAGED FIERCELY ALL THAT NIGHT, BUT NOTHING of particular note occurred. The next morning, however, when they came down to breakfast, they found the terrible stain of blood once again on the floor. "I don't think it can be the fault of the Paragon Detergent," said Washington, "for I have tried it with everything. It must be the ghost." He accordingly rubbed out the stain a second time, but the second morning it appeared again. The third morning also it was there, though the library had been locked up at night by Mr. Otis himself, and the key carried upstairs. The whole family were now quite interested; Mr. Otis began to suspect that he had been too dogmatic in his denial of the existence of ghosts, Mrs. Otis expressed her intention of joining the Psychical Society, and Washington prepared a long letter to Messrs. Myers and Podmore on the subject of the Permanence of Sanguineous Stains when connected with Crime. That night all doubts about the objective existence of phantasmata were removed for ever.

The day had been warm and sunny; and, in the cool of the evening, the whole family went out for a drive. They did not return home till nine o'clock, when they had a light supper. The conversation in no way turned upon ghosts, so there were not even those primary conditions of receptive expectation which so often precede the presentation of psychical phenomena. The subjects discussed, as I have since learned from Mr. Otis, were merely such as form the ordinary conversation of cultured Americans of the better class, such as the immense superiority of Miss Fanny Davenport over Sarah Bernhardt as an actress; the difficulty of obtaining green corn, buckwheat cakes, and hominy, even in the best English houses; the importance of Boston in the development of the world-soul; the advantages of the baggage check system in railway travelling; and the sweetness of the New York accent as compared to the London drawl. No mention at all was made of the supernatural, nor was Sir Simon de Canterville alluded to in any way. At eleven o'clock the family retired, and by half-past all the lights were out. Some time after, Mr. Otis was awakened by a curious noise in the corridor, outside his room. It sounded like the clank of metal, and seemed to be coming nearer every moment. He got up at once, and struck a match, and looked at the time. It was exactly one o'clock. He was quite calm, and felt his pulse, which was not at all feverish. The strange noise still continued, and with it he heard distinctly the sound of foot-steps. He put on his slippers, took a small oblong phial out of his dressing-case, and opened the door. Right in front of him he saw, in the wan moonlight, an old man of terrible aspect. His eyes were as red burning coals; long grey hair fell over his shoulders in matted coils; his garments, which were of antique cut, were soiled and ragged, and from his wrists and ankles hung heavy manacles and rusty gyves.

"My dear sir," said Mr. Otis, "I really must insist on your oiling those chains, and have brought you for that purpose a small bottle of the Tammany Rising Sun Lubricator. It is said to be completely efficacious upon one application, and there are several testimonials to that effect on the wrapper from some of our most eminent native divines. I shall leave it here for you by the bedroom candles, and will be happy to supply you with more should you require it." With these words the United States Minister laid the bottle down on a marble table, and, closing his door, retired to rest.

For a moment the Canterville ghost stood quite motionless in natural indignation; then, dashing the bottle violently upon the polished floor, he fled down the corridor, uttering hollow groans, and emitting a ghastly green light. Just, however, as he reached the top of the great oak staircase, a door was flung open, two little white-robed figures appeared, and a large pillow whizzed past his head! There was evidently no time to be lost, so hastily adopting the Fourth Dimension of Space as a means of escape, he vanished through the wainscoting, and the house became quite quiet.

On reaching a small secret chamber in the left wing, he leaned up against a moonbeam to recover his breath, and began to try and realise his position. Never, in a brilliant and uninterrupted career of three hundred years, had he been so grossly insulted. He thought of the Dowager Duchess, whom he had frightened into a fit as she stood before the glass in her lace and diamonds; of the four housemaids, who had gone off into hysterics when he mereley grinned at them through the curtains of one of the spare bedrooms; of the rector of the parish, whose candle he had blown out as he was coming late one night from the library, and who had been under the care of Sir William Gull ever since, a perfect martyr to nervous disorders; and of old Madame de Tremouillac, who, having wakened up one morning early and seen a skeleton seated in an armchair by the fire reading her diary, had been confined to her bed for six weeks with an attack of brain fever, and, on her recovery, had become reconciled to the Church, and broken off her connection with that notorious sceptic Monsieur de Voltaire. He remembered the terrible night when the wicked Lord Canterville was found choking in his dressing-room, with the knave of diamonds halfway down his throat, and confessed, just before he died, that he had cheated Charles James Fox out of £50,000 at Crockford's by means of that very card, and swore that the ghost had made him swallow it. All his great achievements came back to him again, from the butler who had shot himself in the pantry because he had seen a green hand tapping at the window pane, to the beautiful Lady Stutfield, who was always obliged to wear a black velvet band round her throat to hide the mark of five fingers burnt upon her white skin, and who drowned herself at last in the carp-pond at the end of the King's Walk. With the enthusiastic

egotism of the true artist he went over his most celebrated
performances, and smiled bitterly to himself as he recalled
to mind his last appearnace as "Red Ruben, or the Strangled
Babe," his *début* as "Gaunt Gibeon, the Blood-sucker of Bexley
Moor," and the *furore* he had excited one lovely June evening
by merely playing nine-pins with his own bones upon the
lawn-tennis ground. And after all this, some wretched modern
Americans were to come and offer him the Rising Sun Lubricator, and throw pillows at his head! It was quite unbearable. Besides, no ghosts in history had ever been treated
in this manner. Accordingly, he determined to have vengeance, and remained till daylight in an attitude of deep thought.

III

THE NEXT MORNING WHEN THE OTIS FAMILY MET AT BREAK-
fast, they discussed the ghost at some length. The United
States Minister was naturally a little annoyed to find that
his present had not been accepted. "I have no wish," he said,
"to do the ghost any personal injury, and I must say that,
considering the length of time he has been in the house, I
don't think it is at all polite to throw pillows at him"—a very
just remark, at which, I am sorry to say, the twins burst into
shouts of laughter. "Upon the other hand," he continued,
"If he really declines to use the Rising Sun Lubricator, we
shall have to take his chains from him. It would be quite
impossible to sleep, with such a noise going on outside the
bedrooms."

For the rest of the week, however, they were undisturbed,
the only thing that excited any attention being the continual
renewal of the blood-stain on the library floor. This certainly
was very strange, as the door was always locked at night by
Mr. Otis, and the windows kept closely barred. The cha-

meleon-like colour, also, of the stain excited a good deal of comment. Some mornings it was a dull (almost Indian) red, then it would be vermilion, then a rich purple, and once when they came down for family prayers, according to the simple rites of the Free American Reformed Episcopalian Church, they found it a bright emerald-green. These kaleidoscopic changes naturally amused the party very much, and bets on the subject were freely made every evening. The only person who did not enter the joke was little Virginia, who, for some unexplained reason, was always a good deal distressed at the sight of the blood-stain, and very nearly cried the morning it was emerald-green.

The second appearance of the ghost was on Sunday night. Shortly after they had gone to bed they were suddenly alarmed by a fearful crash in the hall. Rushing downstairs, they found that a large suit of old armour had become detached from its stand, and had fallen on the floor, while, seated in a high-backed chair, was the Canterville ghost, rubbing his knees with an expression of acute agony on his face. The twins, having brought their pea-shooters with them, at once discharged two pellets on him, with that accuracy of aim which can only be attained by long and careful practice on a writing-master, while the United States Minister covered him with his revolver, and called upon him, in accordance with Californian etiquette, to hold up his hands! The ghost started up with a wild shriek of rage, and swept through them like a mist, extinguishing Washington Otis's candle as he passed, and so leaving them all in total darkness. On reaching the top of the staircase he recovered himself, and determined to give his celebrated peal of demoniac laughter. This he had on more than one occasion found extremely useful. It was said to have turned Lord Raker's wig grey in a single night, and had certainly made three of Lady Canterville's French governesses give warning before their month was up. He accordingly laughed his most horrible laugh,

till the old vaulted roof rang and rang again, but hardly
had the fearful echo died away when a door opened, and
Mrs. Otis came out in a light blue dressing-gown. "I am
afraid you are far from well," she said, "and have brought
you a bottle of Dr. Dobell's tincture. If it is indigestion, you
will find it a most excellent remedy." The ghost glared at
her in fury, and began at once to make preparations for
turning himself into a large black log, an accomplishment
for which he was justly renowned, and to which the family
doctor always attributed the permanent idiocy of Lord Canterville's uncle, the Hon. Thomas Horton. The sound of
approaching footsteps, however, made him hesitate in his
fell purpose, so he contented himself with becoming faintly
phosphorescent, and vanished with a deep churchyard groan,
just as the twins had come up to him.

On reaching his room he entirely broke down, and became
a prey to the most violent agitation. The vulgarity of the
twins, and the gross materialism of Mrs. Otis, were naturally
extremely annoying, but what really distressed him most
was, that he had been unable to wear the suit of mail. He
had hoped that even modern Americans would be thrilled
by the sight of a Spectre In Armour, if for no more sensible
reason, at least out of respect for their national poet Long-
fellow, over whose graceful and attractive poetry he himself
had whiled away many a weary hour when the Cantervilles
were up in town. Besides, it was his own suit. He had worn
it with great success at the Kenilworth tournament, and been
highly complimented on it by no less a person than the
Virgin Queen herself. Yet when he had put it on, he had
been completely overpowered by the weight of the huge
breastplate and steel casque, and had fallen heavily on the
stone pavement, barking both his knees severely, and bruising
the knuckles of his right hand.

For some days after this he was extremely ill, and hardly
stirred out of his room at all, except to keep the blood-stain

in proper repair. However, by taking great care of himself, he recovered, and resolved to make a third attempt to frighten the United States Minister and his family. He selected Friday, the 17th of August, for his appearance, and spent most of that day in looking over his wardrobe, ultimately deciding in favour of a large slouched hat with a red feather, a winding-sheet frilled at the wrists and neck, and a rusty dagger. Towards evening a violent storm of rain came on, and the wind was so high that all the windows and doors in the old house shook and rattled. In fact, it was just such weather as he loved. His plan of action was this. He was to make his way quietly to Washington Otis's room, gibber at him from the foot of the bed, and stab himself three times in the throat to the sound of slow music. He bore Washington a special grudge, being quite aware that it was he who was in the habit of removing the famous Canterville blood-stain, by means of Pinkerton's Paragon Detergent. Having reduced the reckless and foolhardy youth to a condition of abject terror, he was then to proceed to the room occupied by the United States Minister and his wife, and there to place a clammy hand on Mrs. Otis's forehead, while he hissed into her trembling husband's ear the awful secrets of the charnel-house. With regard to little Virginia, he had not quite made up his mind. She had never insulted him in any way, and was pretty and gentle. A few hollow groans from the wardrobe, he thought, would be more than sufficient, or, if that failed to wake her, he might grabble at the counterpane with palsy-twitching fingers. As for the twins, he was quite determined to teach them a lesson. The first thing to be done was, of course, to sit upon their chests, so as to produce the stifling sensation of nightmare. Then, as their beds were quite close to each other, to stand between them in the form of a green, icy-cold corpse, till they became paralysed with fear, and finally, to throw off the winding-sheet, and crawl round the room, with white bleached bones and one rolling eyeball, in the character of "Dumb Daniel, or the Suicide's Skeleton," a *rôle* in which he had on more than one occasion produced a great effect, and which he considered quite equal to his famous part of "Martin the Maniac, or the Masked Mystery."

At half-past ten he heard the family going to bed. For some time he was disturbed by wild shrieks of laughter from the twins, who, with the light-hearted gaiety of schoolboys, were evidently amusing themselves before they retired to rest, but at a quarter past eleven all was still, and, as midnight sounded, he sallied forth. The owl beat against the window panes, the raven croaked from the old yew-tree, and the wind wandered moaning round the house like a lost soul; but the Otis family slept unconscious of their doom, and high above the rain and storm he could hear the steady snoring of the Minister for the United States. He stepped stealthily out of the wainscoting, with an evil smile on his cruel, wrinkled mouth, and the moon hid her face in a cloud as he stole past the great oriel window, where his own arms and those of his murdered wife were blazoned in azure and gold. On and on he glided, like an evil shadow, the very darkness seeming to loathe him as he passed. Once he thought he heard something call, and stopped; but it was only the baying of a dog, from the Red Farm, and he went on, muttering strange sixteenth-century curses, and ever and anon brandishing the rusty dagger in the midnight air. Finally he reached the corner of the passage that led to luckless Washington's room. For a moment he paused there, the wind blowing his long grey locks about his head, and twisting into grotesque and fantastic folds the nameless horror of the dead man's shroud. Then the clock struck the quarter, and he felt the time was come. He chuckled to himself, and turned the corner; but no sooner had he done so, than, with a piteous wail of terror, he fell back, and hid his blanched face in his long, bony hands. Right in front of him was standing a horrible spectre, motionless as a carven image, and monstrous as a madman's dream! Its head was bald and burnished; its face round, and fat, and white; and hideous laughter seemed to have writhed its features into an eternal grin. From the eyes streamed rays of scarlet light, the mouth was a wide well of fire, and a hideous garment, like to his own, swathed with its silent snows the Titan form. On its breast was a placard with strange writing in antique characters, some scroll of shame it seemed, some record of wild sins, some awful calendar of crime, and, with its right hand, it bore aloft a falchion of gleaming steel.

Never having seen a ghost before, he naturally was terribly frightened, and, after a second hasty glance at the awful phantom, he fled back to his room, tripping up in his long winding-sheet as he sped down the corridor, and finally dropping the rusty dagger into the Minister's jack-boots, where it was found in the morning by the butler. Once in the privacy of his own apartment, he flung himself down on a small pallet-bed, and hid his face under the clothes. After a time, however, the brave old Canterville spirit asserted itself, and he determined to go and speak to the other ghost as soon as it was daylight. Accordingly, just as the dawn was touching the hills with silver, he returned towards the spot where he had first laid eyes on the grisly phantom, feeling that, after all, two ghosts were better than one, and that, by the aid of his new friend, he might safely grapple with the twins. On reaching the spot, however, a terrible sight met his gaze. Something had evidently happened to the spectre, for the light had entirely faded from its hollow eyes, the gleaming falchion had fallen from its hand, and it was leaning up against the wall in a strained and uncomfortable attitude. He rushed forward and seized it in his arms, when, to his horror, the head slipped off and rolled on the floor, the body assumed a recumbent posture, and he found himself clasping a white dimity bed-curtain, with a sweeping-brush,

a kitchen cleaver, and a hollow turnip lying at his feet!
Unable to understand this curious transformation, he clutched
the placard with feverish haste, and there in the grey morning
light, he read these fearful words:—

**Ye Otis Ghoste.
Ye Onlie True and Original Spook.
Beware of Ye Imitationes.
All others are Counterfeite.**

The whole thing flashed across him. He had been tricked,
foiled, and outwitted! The old Canterville look came into
his eyes; he ground his toothless gums together; and, rasing
his withered hands high above his head, swore, according
to the picturesque phraseology of the antique school, that
when Chanticleer had sounded twice his merry horn, deeds
of blood would be wrought, and Murder walk abroad with
silent feet.

Hardly had he finished this awful oath when, from the
red-tiled roof of a distant homestead, a cock crew. He laughed
a long, low, bitter laugh, and waited. Hour after hour he
waited, but the cock, for some strange reason, did not crow
again. Finally, at half-past seven, the arrival of the housemaids
made him give up his fearful vigil, and he stalked back to
his room, thinking of his vain hope and baffled purpose.
There he consulted several books of ancient chivalry, of
which he was exceedingly fond, and found that, on every
occasion on which his oath had been used, Chanticleer had
always crowed a second time. "Perdition seize the naughty
fowl," he muttered, "I have seen the day when, with my
stout spear, I would have run him through the gorge, and
made him crow for me an 'twere in death!" He then retired
to a comfortable lead coffin, and stayed there till evening.

IV

THE NEXT DAY THE GHOST WAS VERY WEAK AND TIRED. THE terrible excitement of the last four weeks was beginning to have its effect. His nerves were completely shattered, and he started at the slightest noise. For five days he kept his room, and at last made up his mind to give up the point of the blood-stain on the library floor. If the Otis family did not want it, they clearly did not deserve it. They were evidently people on a low, material plane of existence, and quite incapable of appreciating the symbolic value of sensuous phenomena. The question of phantasmic apparitions, and the development of astral bodies, was of course quite a different matter, and really not under his control. It was his solemn duty to appear in the corridor once a week, and to gibber from the large oriel window on the first and third Wednesday in every month, and he did not see how he could honourably escape from his obligations. It is quite true that his life had been very evil, but, upon the other hand, he was most conscientious in all things connected with the supernatural. For the next three Saturdays, accordingly, he traversed the corridor as usual between midnight and three o'clock, taking every possible precaution against being either heard or seen. He removed his boots, trod as lightly as possible on the old worm-eaten boards, wore a large black velvet cloak, and was careful to use the Rising Sun Lubricator for oiling his chains. I am bound to acknowledge that it was with a good deal of difficulty that he brought himself to adopt this last mode of protection. However, one night, while the family were at dinner, he slipped into Mr. Otis's bedroom and carried off the bottle. He felt a little humiliated at first, but afterwards was sensible enough to see that there was a great deal to be said for the invention, and, to a certain degree, it served his purpose. Still, in spite of everything, he was not left unmolested. Strings were continually being stretched across the corridor, over which he tripped in the dark, and on one occasion, while dressed for the part of "Black Isaac, or the Huntsman of Hogley Woods," he met with a severe fall, through treading on a butter-slide, which the twins had constructed from the entrance of the Tapestry Chamber to the top of the oak staircase. This last insult so enraged him, that he resolved to make one final effort to assert his dignity and social position, and determined to visit the insolent young Etonians the next night in his celebrated character of "Reckless Rupert, or the Headless Earl."

He had not appeared in this disguise for more than seventy years; in fact, not since he had so frightened pretty Lady Barbara Modish by means of it, that she suddenly broke off her engagement with the present Lord Canterville's grand-father, and ran away to Gretna Green with handsome Jack Castleton, declaring that nothing in the world would induce her to marry into a family that allowed such a horrible phantom to walk up and down the terrace at twilight. Poor Jack was afterwards shot in a duel by Lord Canterville on Wandsworth Common, and Lady Barbara died of a broken heart at Tunbridge Wells before the year was out, so, in every way, it had been a great success. It was, however, an extremely difficult "make-up," if I may use such a theatrical expression in connection with one of the greatest mysteries of the supernatural, or, to employ a more scientific term, the higher-natural world, and it took him fully three hours to make his preparations. At last everything was ready, and he was very pleased with his appearance. The big leather riding-boots that went with the dress were just a little too large for him, and he could only find one of the two horse-pistols, but, on the whole, he was quite satisfied, and at a quarter past one he glided out of the wainscoting and crept down the corridor. On reaching the room occupied by the twins, which I should mention was called the Blue Bed Chamber, on account of the colour of its hangings, he found the door just ajar. Wishing to make an effective entrance, he flung it wide open, when a heavy jug of water fell right down on him, wetting him to the skin, and just missing his left shoulder by a couple of inches. At the same moment he heard stifled shrieks of laughter proceeding from the four-post bed. The shock to his nervous system was so great that he fled back to his room as hard as he could go, and the next day he was laid up with a severe cold. The only thing that at all consoled him in the whole affair was the fact that he had not brought his head with him, for, had he done so, the consequences might have been very serious.

He now gave up all hope of ever frightening this rude American family, and contented himself, as a rule, with creeping about the passages in list slippers, with a thick red muffler round his throat for fear of draughts, and a small arquebuse, in case he should be attacked by the twins. The final blow he received occurred on the 19th of September. He had gone downstairs to the great entrance-hall, feeling sure that there, at any rate, he would be quite unmolested, and was amusing himself by making satirical remarks on the large Saroni photographs of the United States Minister and his wife, which had now taken the place of the Canterville family pictures. He was simply but neatly clad in a long shroud, spotted with churchyard mould, had tied up his jaw with a strip of yellow linen, and carried a small lantern and a sexton's spade. In fact, he was dressed for the character of "Jonas the Graveless, or the Corpse-Snatcher of Chertsey Barn," one of his most remarkable impersonations, and one which the Cantervilles had every reason to remember, as it was the real origin of their quarrel with their neighbour, Lord Rufford. It was about a quarter past two o'clock in the morning, and, as far as he could ascertain, no one was stirring. As he was strolling towards the library, however, to see if there were any traces left of the blood-stain, suddenly there leaped out on him from a dark corner two figures, who waved their arms wildly above their heads, and shrieked out "BOO!" in his ear.

Seized with a panic, which, under the circumstances, was only natural, he rushed for the staircase, but found Washington Otis waiting for him there with the big garden-syringe; and being thus hemmed in by his enemies on every side, and driven almost to bay, he vanished into the great iron stove, which, fortunately for him, was not lit, and had to make his way home through the flues and chimneys, arriving at his own room in a terrible state of dirt, disorder, and despair.

After this he was not seen again on any nocturnal expedition. The twins lay in wait for him on several occasions, and strewed the passages with nutshells every night to the great annoyance of their parents and the servants, but it was of no avail. It was quite evident that his feelings were so wounded that he would not appear. Mr. Otis consequently resumed his great work on the history of the Democratic Party, on which he had been engaged for some years; Mrs. Otis organized a wonderful clambake, which amazed the whole county; the boys took to lacrosse, euchre, poker, and other American national games; and Virginia rode about the lanes on her pony, accompanied by the young Duke of Cheshire, who had come to spend the last week of his holidays at Canterville Chase. It was generally assumed that the ghost had gone away, and, in fact, Mr. Otis wrote a letter to that effect to Lord Canterville, who, in reply, expressed his great pleasure at the news, and sent his best congratulations to the Minister's worthy wife.

The Otises, however, were deceived, for the ghost was still in the house, and though now almost an invalid, was by no means ready to let matters rest, particularly as he heard that among the guests was the young Duke of Cheshire, whose grand-uncle, Lord Francis Stilton, had once bet a hundred guineas with Colonel Carbury that he would play dice with the Canterville ghost, and was found the next morning lying on the floor of the cardroom in such a helpless paralytic state, that though he lived on to a great age, he was never able to say anything again but "Double Sixes." The story was well known at the time, though, of course, out of respect to the feelings of the two noble families, every attempt was made to hush it up; and a full account of all the circumstances connected with it will be found in the third volume of Lord Tattle's *Recollections of the Prince Regent and his Friends*. The ghost, then, was naturally very anxious to show that he had not lost his influence over the Stiltons, with whom, indeed, he was distantly connected, his own first cousin having been married *en secondes noces* to the Sieur de Bulkeley, from whom, as every one knows, the Dukes of Cheshire are lineally descended. Accordingly, he made arrangements for appearing to Virginia's little lover in his celebrated impersonation of "The Vampire Monk, or, the Bloodless Benedictine," a performance so horrible that when old Lady Startup saw it, which she did on one fatal New Year's Eve, in the year 1764, she went off into the most piercing shrieks, which culminated in violent apoplexy, and died in three days, after disinheriting the Cantervilles, who were her nearest relations, and leaving all her money to her London apothecary. At the last moment, however, his terror of the twins prevented his leaving his room, and the little Duke slept in peace under the great feathered canopy in the Royal Bedchamber, and dreamed of Virginia.

V

A FEW DAYS AFTER THIS, VIRGINIA AND HER CURLY-HAIRED cavalier went out riding on Brockley meadows, where she tore her habit so badly in getting through a hedge, that, on their return home, she made up her mind to go up by the back staircase so as not to be seen. As she was running past the Tapestry Chamber, the door of which happened to be open, she fancied she saw some one inside, and thinking it was her mother's maid, who sometimes used to bring her work there, looked in to ask her to mend her habit. To her immense surprise, however, it was the Canterville Ghost himself! He was sitting by the window, watching the ruined gold of the yellowing trees fly through the air, and the red leaves dancing madly down the long avenue. His head was leaning on his hand, and his whole attitude was one of extreme depression. Indeed, so forlorn, and so much out of repair did he look, that little Virginia, whose first idea had been to run away and lock herself in her room, was filled with pity, and determined to try and comfort him. So light was her footfall, and so deep his melancholy, that he was not aware of her presence till she spoke to him.

"I am so sorry for you," she said, "but my brothers are going back to Eton to-morrow and then, if you behave yourself, no one will annoy you."

"It is absurd asking me to behave myself," he answered, looking round in astonishment at the pretty little girl who had ventured to address him, "quite absurd. I must rattle my chains, and groan through keyholes, and walk about at night, if that is what you mean. It is my only reason for existing."

"It is no reason at all for existing, and you know you have been very wicked. Mrs. Umney told us, the first day we arrived here, that you had killed your wife."

"Well, I quite admit it," said the Ghost petulantly, "but it was a purely family matter, and concerned no one else."

"It is very wrong to kill any one," said Virginia, who at times had a sweet Puritan gravity, caught from some old New England ancestor.

"Oh, I hate the cheap severity of abstract ethics! My wife

was very plain, never had my ruffs properly starched, and knew nothing about cookery. Why, there was a buck I had shot in Hogley Woods, a magnificent pricket, and do you know how she had it sent up to table? However, it is no matter now, for it is all over, and I don't think it was very nice of her brothers to starve me to death, though I did kill her."

"Starve you to death? Oh, Mr. Ghost, I mean Sir Simon, are you hungry? I have a sandwich in my case. Would you like it?"

"No, thank you, I never eat anything now; but it is very kind of you, all the same, and you are much nicer than the rest of your horrid, rude, vulgar, dishonest family."

"Stop!" cried Virginia, stamping her foot, "it is you who are rude, and horrid, and vulgar, and as for dishonesty, you know you stole the paints out of my box to try and furbish up that ridiculous blood-stain in the library. First you took all my reds, including the vermilion, and I couldn't do any more sunsets, then you took the emerald-green and the chrome-yellow, and finally I had nothing left but indigo and Chinese white, and could only do moonlight scenes, which are always depressing to look at, and not at all easy to paint. I never told on you, though I was very much annoyed, and it was most ridiculous, the whole thing; for who ever heard of emerald-green blood?"

"Well, really," said the Ghost, rather meekly, "what was I to do? It is a very difficult thing to get real blood nowadays, and, as your brother began it all with his Paragon Detergent, I certainly saw no reason why I should not have your paints. As for colour, that is always a matter of taste: the Cantervilles have blue blood, for instance, the very bluest in England; but I know you Americans don't care for things of this kind."

"You know nothing about it, and the best thing you can do is to emigrate and improve your mind. My father will be only too happy to give you a free passage, and though

there is a heavy duty on spirits of every kind, there will be
no difficulty about the Custom House, as the officers are
all Democrats. Once in New York, you are sure to be a great
success. I know lots of people there who would give a hundred
thousand dollars to have a grandfather, and much more
than that to have a family Ghost."

"I don't think I should like America."

"I suppose because we have no ruins and no curiosities,"
said Virginia satirically.

"No ruins! no curiosities!" answered the Ghost; "you have
your navy and your manners."

"Good evening; I will go and ask papa to get the twins
an extra week's holiday."

"Please don't go, Miss Virginia," he cried; "I am so lonely
and so unhappy, and I really don't know what to do. I want
to go to sleep and I cannot."

"That's quite absurd! You have merely to go to bed and
blow out the candle. It is very difficult sometimes to keep
awake, especially at church, but there is no difficulty at all
about sleeping. Why, even babies know how to do that, and
they are not very clever."

"I have not slept for three hundred years," he said sadly,
and Virginia's beautiful blue eyes opened in wonder; "for
three hundred years I have not slept, and I am so tired."

Virginia grew quite grave, and her little lips trembled like
rose-leaves. She came towards him, and kneeling down at
his side, looked up into his old withered face.

"Poor, poor Ghost," she murmured; "have you no place
where you can sleep?"

"Far away beyond the pine-woods," he answered, in a low
dreamy voice, "there is a little garden. There the grass grows
long and deep, there are the great white stars of the hemlock
flower, there the nightingale sings all night long. All night
long he sings, and the cold, crystal moon looks down, and
the yew-tree spreads out its giant arms over the sleepers."

Virginia's eyes grew dim with tears, and she hid her face in her hands.

"You mean the Garden of Death," she whispered.

"Yes, Death. Death must be so beautiful. To lie in the soft brown earth, with the grasses waving above one's head, and listen to silence. To have no yesterday, and no to-morrow. To forget time, to forgive life, to be at peace. You can help me. You can open for me the portals of Death's house, for Love is always with you, and Love is stronger than Death is."

Virginia trembled, a cold shudder ran through her, and for a few moments there was silence. She felt as if she was in a terrible dream.

Then the Ghost spoke again, and his voice sounded like the sighing of the wind.

"Have you ever read the old prophecy on the library window?"

"Oh, often," cried the little girl, looking up; "I know it quite well. It is painted in curious black letters, and it is difficult to read. There are only six lines:

> *When a golden girl can win*
> *Prayer from out the lips of sin,*
> *When the barren almond bears,*
> *And a little child gives away its tears,*
> *Then shall all the house be still*
> *And peace come to Canterville.*

"But I don't know what they mean."

"They mean," he said sadly, "that you must weep with me for my sins, because I have no tears, and pray with me for my soul, because I have no faith, and then, if you have always been sweet, and good, and gentle, the Angel of Death will have mercy on me. You will see fearful shapes in darkness, and wicked voices will whisper in your ear, but they will not harm you, for against the purity of a little child the powers of Hell cannot prevail."

Virginia made no answer, and the Ghost wrung his hands in wild despair as he looked down at her bowed golden head. Suddenly she stood up, very pale, and with a strange light in her eyes. "I am not afraid," she said firmly, "and I will ask the Angel to have mercy on you."

He rose from his seat with a faint cry of joy, and taking her hand bent over it with old-fashioned grace and kissed it. His fingers were as cold as ice, and his lips burned like fire, but Virginia did not falter, as he led her across the dusky room. On the faded green tapestry were broidered little huntsmen. They blew their tasselled horns and with their tiny hands waved to her to go back. "Go back! little Virginia," they cried, "go back!" but the Ghost clutched her hand more tightly, and she shut her eyes against them. Horrible animals with lizard tails, and goggle eyes, blinked at her from the carven chimney-piece, and murmured "Beware! little Virginia, beware! we may never see you again," but the Ghost glided on more swiftly, and Virginia did not listen. When they reached the end of the room he stopped, and muttered some words she could not understand. She opened her eyes, and saw the wall slowly fading away like a mist, and a great black cavern in front of her. A bitter cold wind swept round them, and she felt something pulling at her dress. "Quick, quick," cried the Ghost, "or it will be too late," and, in a moment, the wainscoting had closed behind them, and the Tapestry Chamber was empty.

VI

ABOUT TEN MINUTES LATER, THE BELL RANG FOR TEA, AND, as Virginia did not come down, Mrs. Otis sent up one of the footmen to tell her. After a little time he returned and

said that he could not find Miss Virginia anywhere. As she
was in the habit of going out to the garden every evening
to get flowers for the dinner-table, Mrs. Otis was not at all
alarmed at first, but when six o'clock struck, and Virginia
did not appear, she became really agitated, and sent the
boys out to look for her, while she herself and Mr. Otis
searched every room in the house. At half-past six the boys
came back and said that they could find no trace of their
sister anywhere. They were all now in the greatest state of
excitement, and did not know what to do, when Mr. Otis
suddenly remembered that, some few days before, he had
given a band of gypsies permission to camp in the park. He
accordingly at once set off for Blackfell Hollow, where he
knew they were, accompanied by his eldest son and two of
the farm-servants. The little Duke of Cheshire, who was
perfectly frantic with anxiety, begged hard to be allowed to
go too, but Mr. Otis would not allow him, as he was afraid
there might be a scuffle. On arriving at the spot, however,
he found that the gypsies had gone, and it was evident that
their departure had been rather sudden, as the fire was still
burning, and some plates were lying on the grass. Having
sent off Washington and the two men to scour the district,
he ran home, and dispatched telegrams to all the police
inspectors in the county, telling them to look out for a little
girl who had been kidnapped by tramps or gypsies. He then
ordered his horse to be brought round, and, after insisting
on his wife and the three boys sitting down to dinner, rode
off down the Ascot Road with a groom. He had hardly,
however, gone a couple of miles when he heard somebody
galloping after him, and, looking round, saw the little Duke
coming up on his pony, with his face very flushed and no
hat. "I'm awfully sorry, Mr. Otis," gasped out the boy, "but
I can't eat any dinner as long as Virginia is lost. Please, don't
be angry with me; if you had let us be engaged last year,
there would never have been all this trouble. You won't

send me back, will you? I can't go! I won't go!"

The Minister could not help smiling at the handsome young scapegrace, and was a good deal touched at his devotion to Virginia, so leaning down from his horse, he patted him kindly on the shoulders, and said, "Well, Cecil, if you won't go back I suppose you must come with me, but I must get you a hat at Ascot."

"Oh, bother my hat! I want Virginia!" cried the little Duke, laughing, and they galloped on to the railway station. There Mr. Otis inquired of the station-master if any one answering the description of Viginia had been seen on the platform, but could get no news of her. The station-master, however, wired up and down the line, and assured him that a strict watch would be kept for her, and, after having bought a hat for the little Duke from a linen-draper, who was just putting up his shutters, Mr. Otis rode off to Bexley, a village about four miles away, which he was told was a well-known haunt of the gypsies, as there was a large common next to it. Here they roused up the rural policeman, but could get no information from him, and, after riding all over the common, they turned their horses' heads homewards, and reached the Chase about eleven o'clock, dead-tired and almost heart-broken. They found Washington and the twins waiting for them at the gate-house with lanterns, as the avenue was very dark. Not the slightest trace of Virginia had been discovered. The gypsies had been caught on Brockley meadows, but she was not with them, and they had explained their sudden departure by saying that they had mistaken the date of Chorton Fair, and had gone off in a hurry for fear they might be late. Indeed, they had been quite distressed at hearing of Virginia's disappearance, as they were very grateful to Mr. Otis for having allowed them to camp in his park, and four of their number had stayed behind to help in the search. The carp-pond had been dragged, and the whole Chase thoroughly gone over, but without any result. It was evident that, for that night at any rate, Virginia was lost to them; and it was in a state of the deepest depression that Mr. Otis and the boys walked up to the house, the groom following behind with the two horses and the pony. In the hall they found a group of frightened servants, and lying on a sofa in the library was poor Mrs. Otis, almost out of her mind with terror and anxiety, and having her forehead bathed with eau-de-cologne by the old housekeeper. Mr. Otis at once insisted on her having something to eat, and ordered up supper for the whole party. It was a melancholy meal, as hardly any one spoke, and even the twins were awe-struck and subdued, as they were very fond of their sister. When they had finished, Mr. Otis, in spite of the entreaties of the little Duke, ordered them all to bed, saying that nothing more could be done that night, and that he would telegraph in the morning to Scotland Yard for some detectives to be sent down immediately. Just as they were passing out of the dining-room, midnight began to boom from the clock tower, and when the last stroke sounded they heard a crash and a sudden shrill cry; a dreadful peal of thunder shook the house, a strain of unearthly music floated through the air, a panel at the top of the staircase flew back with a loud noise, and out on the landing, looking very pale and white, with a little casket in her hand, stepped Virginia. In a moment they had all rushed up to her. Mrs. Otis clasped her passionately in her arms, the Duke smothered her with violent kisses, and the twins executed a wild war-dance round the group.

"Good heavens! child, where have you been?" said Mr. Otis, rather angrily, thinking that she had been playing some foolish trick on them. "Cecil and I have been riding all over the country looking for you, and your mother has been frightened to death. You must never play these practical jokes any more."

"Except on the Ghost! except on the Ghost!" shrieked the twins, as they capered about.

"My own darling, thank God you are found; you must never leave my side again," murmured Mrs. Otis, as she kissed the trembling child, and smoothed the tangled gold of her hair.

"Papa," said Virginia quietly, "I have been with the Ghost. He is dead, and you must come and see him. He had been very wicked, but he was really sorry for all that he had done, and he gave me this box of beautiful jewels before he died."

The whole family gazed at her in mute amazement, but she was quite grave and serious; and, turning round, she led them through the opening in the wainscoting down a narrow secret corridor, Washington following with a lighted candle, which he had caught up from the table. Finally, they came to a great oak door, studded with rusty nails. When Virginia touched it, it swung back on its heavy hinges, and they found themselves in a little low room, with a vaulted ceiling, and one tiny grated window. Imbedded in the wall was a huge iron ring, and chained to it was a gaunt skeleton, that was stretched out at full length on the stone floor, and seemed to be trying to grasp with its long fleshless fingers an old-fashioned trencher and ewer, that were placed just out of its reach. The jug had evidently been once filled with water, as it was covered inside with green mould. There was nothing on the trencher but a pile of dust. Virginia knelt down beside the skeleton, and, holding her little hands together, began to pray silently, while the rest of the party looked on in wonder at the terrible tragedy whose secret was now disclosed to them.

"Hallo!" suddenly exclaimed one of the twins, who had been looking out of the window to try and discover in what wing of the house the room was situated. "Hallo! the old withered almond tree has blossomed. I can see the flowers plainly in the moonlight."

"God has forgiven him," said Virginia gravely, as she rose

to her feet, and a beautiful light seemed to illumine her face.

"What an angel you are!" cried the young Duke, and he put his arm round her neck and kissed her.

VII

FOUR DAYS AFTER THESE CURIOUS INCIDENTS A FUNERAL started from Canterville Chase at about eleven o'clock at night. The hearse was drawn by eight black horses, each of which carried on its head a great tuft of nodding ostrich-plumes, and the leaden coffin was covered by a rich purple pall, on which was embroidered in gold the Canterville coat-of-arms. By the side of the hearse and the coaches walked the servants with lighted torches, and the whole procession was wonderfully impressive. Lord Canterville was the chief mourner, having come up specially from Wales to attend the funeral, and sat in the first carriage along with little Virginia. Then came the United States Minister and his wife, then Washington and the three boys, and in the last carriage was Mrs. Umney. It was generally felt that, as she had been frightened by the ghost for more than fifty years of her life, she had a right to see the last of him. A deep grave had been dug in the corner of the churchyard, just under the old yew-tree, and the service was read in the most impressive manner by the Rev. Augustus Dampier. When the ceremony was over, the servants, according to an old custom observed in the Canterville family, extinguished their torches, and, as the coffin was being lowered into the grave, Virginia stepped forward and laid on it a large cross made of white and pink almond-blossoms. As she did so, the moon came out from behind a cloud, and flooded with its silent silver the little churchyard, and from a distant copse a nightingale began to sing. She thought of the ghost's description of the Garden of Death, her eyes became dim with tears, and she hardly spoke a word during the drive home.

The next morning, before Lord Canterville went up to town, Mr. Otis had an interview with him on the subject of the jewels the ghost had given to Virginia. They were perfectly magnificent, especially a certain ruby necklace with old Venetian setting, which was really a superb specimen of sixteenth-century work, and their value was so great that Mr. Otis felt considerable scruples about allowing his daughter to accept them.

"My lord," he said, "I know that in this country mortmain is held to apply to trinkets as well as to land, and it is quite clear to me that these jewels are, or should be, heirlooms in your family. I must beg you, accordingly, to take them to London with you, and to regard them simply as a portion of your property which has been restored to you under certain strange conditions. As for my daughter, she is merely a child, and has as yet, I am glad to say, but little interest in such appurtenances of idle luxury. I am also informed by Mrs. Otis, who, I may say, is no mean authority upon Art—having had the privilege of spending several winters in Boston when she was a girl—that these gems are of great monetary worth, and if offered for sale would fetch a tall price. Under these circumstances, Lord Canterville, I feel sure that you will recognize how impossible it would be for me to allow them to reamin in the possession of any member of my family; and, indeed, all such vain gauds and toys, however suitable or necessary to the dignity of the British aristocracy, would be completely out of place among those who have been brought up on the severe, and I believe immortal, principles of republican simplicity. Perhaps I should mention that Virginia is very anxious that you should allow her to retain the box as a memento of your unfortunate but misguided ancestor. As it is extremely old, and consequently a good deal out of repair, you may perhaps think fit to comply with her request. For my own part, I confess I am a good deal surprised to find a child of mine expressing sympathy with mediaevalism in any form, and can only account for it by the fact that Viginia was born in one of your London suburbs shortly after Mrs. Otis had returned from a trip to Athens."

Lord Canterville listened very gravely to the worthy Minister's speech, pulling his grey moustache now and then to hide an involuntary smile, and when Mr. Otis had ended he shook him cordially by the hand, and said, "My dear sir, your charming little daughter rendered my unlucky ancestor, Sir Simon, a very important service, and I and my family are much indebted to her for her marvellous courage and pluck. The jewels are clearly hers, and, egad, I believe that if I were heartless enough to take them from her, the wicked old fellow would be out of his grave in a fortnight, leading me the devil of a life. As for their being heirlooms, nothing is an heirloom that is not mentioned in a will or legal document, and the existence of these jewels has been quite unkown. I assure you I have no more claim on them than your butler, and when Miss Virginia grows up I daresay she will be pleased to have pretty things to wear. Besides, you forget, Mr. Otis, that you took the furniture and the ghost at a valuation, and anything that belonged to the ghost passed at once into your possession, as, whatever activity Sir Simon may have shown in the corridor at night, in point of law he was really dead, and you acquired his property by purchase."

Mr. Otis was a good deal distressed at Lord Canterville's refusal, and begged him to reconsider his decision, but the good-natured peer was quite firm, and finally induced the Minister to allow his daughter to retain the present the ghost had given her, and when, in the spring of 1890, the young Duchess of Cheshire was presented at the Queen's first drawing-room on the occasion of her marriage, her jewels were the universal theme of admiration. For Virginia received the coronet, which is the reward of all good little American girls, and was married to her boy-lover as soon as he came of age. They were both so charming, and they loved each other so much, that every one was delighted at the match, except the old Marchioness of Dumblton, who had tried to catch the Duke for one of her seven unmarried daughters, and had given no less than three expensive dinner-parties for that purpose, and, strange to say, Mr. Otis himself. Mr. Otis was extremely fond of the young Duke personally, but, theoretically, he objected to titles, and, to use his own words, "was not without apprehension lest, amid the enervating influences of a pleasure-loving aristocracy, the true principles of republican simplicity should be forgotten." His objections, however, were completely overruled, and I believe that when he walked up the aisle of St. George's, Hanover Square, with his daughter leaning on his arm, there was not a prouder man in the whole length and breadth of England.

The Duke and Duchess, after the honeymoon was over, went down to Canterville Chase, and on the day after their arrival they walked over in the afternoon to the lonely churchyard by the pinewoods. There had been a great deal of difficulty at first about the inscription on Sir Simon's tombstone, but finally it had been decided to engrave on it simply the initals of the old gentleman's name, and the verse from the library window. The Duchess had brought with her some lovely roses, which she strewed upon the grave, and after they had stood by it for some time they strolled into the ruined chancel of the old abbey. There the Duchess sat down on a fallen pillar, while her husband lay at her feet smoking a cigarette and looking up at her beautiful eyes. Suddenly he threw his cigarette away, took hold of her hand, and said to her, "Virginia, a wife should have no secrets from her husband."

"Dear Cecil! I have no secrets from you."

"Yes, you have," he answered, smiling, "you have never told me what happened to you when you were locked up with the ghost."

"I have never told any one, Cecil," said Virginia gravely.

"I know that, but you might tell me."

"Please don't ask me, Cecil, I cannot tell you. Poor Sir Simon! I owe him a great deal. Yes, don't laugh, Cecil, I really do. He made me see what Life is, and what Death signifies, and why Love is stronger than both."

The Duke rose and kissed his wife lovingly.

"You can have your secret as long as I have your heart," he murmured.

"You have always had that, Cecil."

"And you will tell our children some day, won't you?"

Virginia blushed.

PART II
CONTEMPORARY TALES

THE PANELLED ROOM
by
AUGUST DERLETH

Like the Bram Stoker tale, "The Panelled Room" is a good, old-fashioned haunted-house horror story. But the house here is not your typical, gloomy, isolated relic; it is simply a house, situated on Main Street in a town that might be yours. And the ghosts that haunt its panelled parlor room . . . well, as one of the characters explains, "Fifty years ago, come next month, Peter Mason killed his wife in that room and then he killed himself. They found them both the next day, she choked to death, and he hanging there. Sometimes you can see him hanging there yet—and her a-lying on the floor pale and white."

But that's not the most frightening thing about the panelled room. For the panels move on occasion, and when they do, terrible things have been known to happen. Terrible things . . .

Until his death in 1972, at the age of sixty-two, August Derleth was Wisconsin's foremost regional writer, having published an impressive number of fiction and nonfiction books about his home state. He was also the creator of Solar Pons, perhaps the most successful pastiche of Sherlock Holmes; and a lifelong student and

167

writer of macabre and supernatural fiction. In 1939, he founded
Arkham House—a publishing company which continues to specialize
in the prose and poety of such writers as H.P. Lovecraft. Derleth
wrote many spectral stories, most of which were originally published
in Weird Tales; *some of the best can be found in his collections,*
Lonesome Places *(1962) and* Mr. George and Other Odd
Persons *(1963), as by Stephen Grendon.*

WHEN FATHER BRAUMAN COULD NOT CHANGE MRS. GRANT'S
mind, Miss Barbara Allen, seeing him come down the steps
from the porch flung proudly across the face of the house
Mrs. Grant had taken, shaking his head dolefully, his lips
moving in silent speech, thought she would try. People said
that if Miss Barbara Allen could do nothing there was no
use trying longer. But it was necessary to do everything
possible to convince Mrs. Grant that the house on Main
Street was not a healthy place to live in, because of the things
that were whispered and sometimes openly said about it
since the murder some years back. So, after announcing her
intention to the town through her friends, Miss Barbara
Allen paid a visit to Mrs. Grant a week after that lady had
moved into the house on Main Street with her sister and
her sister's little daughter.

Her reception was not too cordial, and when she mentioned
the house and spoke about what people said of it, Mrs. Grant
put up her lorgnette and told the old lady that as she was
a Freethinker she didn't believe in such things.

"I'm a Freethinker, too, Mrs. Grant," said Miss Barbara,
"but I lived in this house once."

Mrs. Grant smiled politely and patiently and said, "Nothing
seems to have happened to you," her inference clear and
her manner no less so.

Miss Barbara blinked a little and said, "My sister died

here," announcing it rather, as if this fact alone were incontestable proof of the strange rumors current about the house in which they sat.

Mrs. Grant thought, How provincial! and raised her eyebrows a little. "Surely you don't think that this house had anything to do with that?" she asked, her voice more kind now.

The old lady was firm. "I know it did. If it wouldn't be for wanting to tell you, that being my duty, as I said to Elvira—that's my other sister—I'd never've set foot in this house again. My sister was found dead in the panelled room, the parlor—at least, it was our parlor."

"Heart attack, I suppose?"

Miss Barbara shook her head. "There was never anything the matter with Abby. She was just found dead. Old Doctor Brown, he said it was shock—a scare, most likely. That was after poor Abby began to see things in that room."

"What things?"

The old lady picked at her shawl and looked at Mrs. Grant over her spectacles, as if trying to discover from Mrs. Grant's features how much she had already been told. "Fifty years ago, come next month, Peter Mason killed his wife in that room and then he killed himself. They found them both the next day, she choked to death, and he hanging there. Sometimes you can see him hanging there yet—and her a-lying on the floor pale and white."

"Why, Miss Allen, that's a childish invention!"

Miss Barbara smiled faintly. "Almost my very words, when Abby and I took this house. But I've seen Peter Mason hanging, myself—and I've seen his wife there, too." There was an intensity in her voice, but no flicker of emotion disturbed her face.

Mrs. Grant leaned forward a little, saying, "Yes?", still polite, still patient, urging her visitor to continue, though she did not wish to hear more.

"He was hanging from the cross-beam over the bookcase—just like they found him when I was a little girl. You don't know what it is to walk into that room and see him there all unexpected—you don't know, yet. And to see her like that again—all crumpled up on the floor, her face twisted. I wouldn't want to be in your place for anything. I'd move out right away, this very minute!"

Mrs. Grant sighed, having heard the admonition many times since she had come to the town and taken the house. Miss Barbara Allen began to feel uncomfortable and rose presently to go, feeling that she had done what she could.

"Will you promise me something, Mrs. Grant?" she asked.

Mrs. Grant hesitated. "That can be almost anything," she said, feeling her position becoming intolerable and wanting this woman to go away.

Miss Barbara said, "It's nothing unreasonable. Promise me that when you see the panels moving in the parlor, in that room, you'll leave this house right away. There's a horror hanging over this house—and it may be too late to get away when you see the panels move."

Curiosity prompted Mrs. Grant to ask, "What do you mean, Miss Allen?"

"If you're staying, you'll see soon enough. But I hope you'll change your mind before then." Then she was gone, the door closing heavily behind her.

Mrs. Grant watched the old woman go down the outer steps, thinking, What a queer person! Then she turned away and went into the living-room, where she sat down, aware of the critical eye her sister turned on her.

"The usual thing, Irma," said Mrs. Grant. "We are to move right away."

The child in one corner of the room took up the words. "I like moving, mamma. When are we going to move?" She allowed her block building to tumble to the floor and jumped to her feet, clapping her hands.

"Do be quiet, Ellen," said her mother, fixing the child with her eyes while Mrs. Grant nodded stern but not unkind approval. "We aren't going to move, dear." Then she turned again to her older sister.

"But there's something new, this time," Mrs. Grant went on. "The panels in the parlor are said to move—that serpent design, I suppose Miss Allen meant."

Irma smiled. "An illusion, Lydia. Everyone knows that if you look at a design like that long enough, your eyes will seem to see a movement."

Mrs. Grant nodded, clasping her fingers and looking down at them in a moment of silent speculation. Presently she spoke again. "True, Irma. Still, there was something about Miss Allen that I didn't understand."

"What?"

"Why, I don't know. A peculiar earnestness—that's the best I can do by way of describing her attitude. She sat there telling me her story so simply, expecting me to believe every word of it. It was uncanny, Irma. I mean, she didn't look like the kind of woman who's very easily taken in by such things."

"I do believe the old lady's story has affected you," said Irma, not without impatience. "But I shan't let you fall under her spell. I declare, Lydia, you're white as a sheet, just thinking about it."

Mrs. Grant felt considerably better on coming down to breakfast next morning, for indeed Miss Allen's simple earnestness had insidiously destroyed her confident superiority the evening before. The prattle of Irma's child this unusually bright morning brought her mind away from Peter Mason and his unfortunate wife, and the unbelievable stories of weird hauntings that had been current since then.

In the afternoon Mrs. Grant let it be known that she would not welcome any more people, however well-intentioned, who came to warn her about the house. When she dropped this hint to her callers, she sensed immediately an air of restraint. Later, when she walked down Main Street at dusk, she felt a frightening air of waiting in the half-hidden faces peering out at her from behind the curtained windows of houses she passed.

In the evening she was afraid. With some reluctance, she said to her sister, "Really the house *is* beginning to oppress me," and when Irma said, "Nonsense, Lydia!" she was afraid to say more. She sat in comparative silence for the rest of the evening, an obvious air of unnatural restraint cloaking her. For this she could not entirely account, Miss Allen's story being already too far in the past to explain it.

Mrs. Grant's strange oppression grew. It crept upon her from all sides, day by day, and she felt it suddenly even when doing the most ordinary things: dusting the room, or rearranging the furniture, things she trusted no maid with doing. She could not understand this oppression's growing in, building itself stronger about and within her, but when fear found her she knew.

Ten days after Miss Barbara Allen's call, Mrs. Grant walked into the panelled room one evening and saw a man hanging in the shadows where the bookcase was—and a crumpled shape oddly darkening the floor near by. She fell back against the wall, but the thing was gone. She thought, It's nothing. There's nothing there at all. But it was two hours before she had convinced herself that she had seen nothing. When she came out of the parlor, Irma noticed her paleness.

"Well, I declare, Lydia, there's something the matter with you!" she exclaimed.

Mrs. Grant looked at her sister and knew she could not tell her, knew she could not face Irma's scornful skepticism. "I've got a terrible headache," she said.

Irma was surprised. "A headache—that's strange. You've never had one before, Lydia." She looked queerly at Mrs.

Grant for a moment before she said, "You'll find aspirin tablets in my purse. You'd better take one. But I can't understand your having a headache like this."

Mrs. Grant did not reply. Irma did not notice that Mrs. Grant went directly upstairs, avoiding the purse on the side table. In the night, Mrs. Grant's sleep was haunted by dreams of the panelled room and what she had seen there, and in her dreams there was no illusion.

After Mrs. Grant had seen the man hanging and the form huddled on the floor beneath four times, she steeled herself to speak to her sister, thinking that this was the only way, for it must come some time. "I've seen him," she said abruptly one day while the two of them sat at the table.

Irma put down her cup of coffee and looked at her sister with a frown on her forehead. "You've seen him," she said. "What do you mean? Who is it you've seen?"

"Why, Peter Mason—the man who killed his wife. And I've seen her, too." Mrs. Grant made a vague and uncertain gesture in the direction of the panelled room.

A sudden comprehension came to Irma, and a strange gleam began to grow in her eyes. Mrs. Grant did not understand, but Irma was thinking, If anything happens to her, I shall get everything. The thought had come to her with startling suddenness, but she made no attempt to beat it down. It would mean freedom for her . . . and Ellen. No more bending to Lydia's wish. With an effort she controlled her voice, for her abrupt excitement was beating in her. "You imagined it," she said calmly, but her fingers trembled as she took up a tea-cake.

"I think we *had* better give up this house," said Mrs. Grant.

Irma smiled in a superior fashion calculated to disarm her sister. "Nonsense, Lydia. I refuse to consider giving up this fine old house because of a few stories—like as not unfounded, my dear."

"But, Irma, *I have seen him!*" Her voice had become intense with the intensity of conviction that had grown in her during the past few days.

Irma stirred her coffee and said, "That is a peculiar arrangement of the shadows from the street-lamp, Lydia. I myself have got that impression several times—of someone hanging there. I had hoped you wouldn't see it because I knew you half believed those stories."

Mrs. Grant said "Oh," weakly, and Irma thought, *If anything should happen to her: if anything . . .*

Abruptly Irma pressed the temporary advantage she had gained. "I'll go into the parlor with you, Lydia. Then we'll see." She got up immediately and took her sister's arm.

If Irma noticed the shadow, she gave no sign, even when Mrs. Grant clutched her arm in fright. "There's nothing there, Lydia," she said, patting her sister's hand.

"Oh, you can't see him," breathed Mrs. Grant. "And now he's gone . . . he's gone."

Irma said, "You're tired, Lydia, dear."

Mrs. Grant stared at her sister in the semi-dusk and said, "I want to go away." Her voice was thick and rough. Her hands were shuddering.

"You must face what's worrying you, Lydia; that's the only way."

Mrs. Grant nodded and said, "Yes, I will." She did not notice the strange fixity of Irma's eyes.

Miss Barbara Allen called the next day. She sat in the living room, fixing Mrs. Grant with her eyes. She looked tired, yet there was a curious alertness about her. The two of them—Irma had not come into the room—talked of everything but the house. Mrs. Grant did not want to give the old lady a chance to say anything; so she spoke a great deal and repeated many things she had said once already. And then, in spite of her talking, there came a lull in the conversation, and Miss Barbara said what she had come to say.

"Why are you staying here, Mrs. Grant?"

Mrs. Grant asked, "What do you mean?" She had meant her voice to be polite and calm; but it was unsteady, alarmed. "I know you've seen him," said the old lady, dropping her voice. "And I had hoped you would leave when you saw— before the panels start moving. It's awful, when they start, unbearable. It works on your mind, Mrs. Grant."

"How did you know I had seen him, Miss Allen?"

The old lady said, "It's in your eyes, Mrs. Grant. I know what it is to see him, because I've seen him too—and her. And I remember Abby's eyes—waiting, always waiting, frightened."

Mrs. Grant made a nervous gesture with her hands as if seeking to brush the suggestion away like a tangible thing. "I've seen them both," she said, her words coming rapidly, "but it cannot be real, because Irma cannot see them."

Miss Barbara was obviously startled, for she jerked her head up and looked at her hostess as if she believed that Mrs. Grant was deliberately misleading her. Her eyes narrowed, her thin lips folded together, and abruptly she said, "Your sister lies!" her voice sharp and accusing.

Mrs. Grant was confused. "There's no reason why she should lie to me, Miss Allen."

"If your sister says she cannot see them, it's because she wants you to stay here for a very strong reason. Does she go often into the panelled room?" Mrs. Grant's sudden start, her widened eyes, answered the old lady; she went on. "Are you sure there is no reason for her wanting you to stay, Mrs. Grant? Perhaps it would be better for her . . . if something happened to you? I understand she's entirely dependent on you, and as she's very young yet, I don't suppose she'd like that. Seems to me it's your sister who's keeping you here, Mrs. Grant."

Mrs. Grant's confusion became even more evident. "I don't know," she said. "I really don't. Irma doesn't go into the parlor at all. And she wouldn't want anything to happen to me—I know she wouldn't. No, no, it's unthinkable, Miss Allen. I feel bound to resent such a suggestion."

But the old lady paid no attention. "I think you'd better leave the house right away, Mrs. Grant. Tomorrow is a day no one should be in this house, an anniversary. It was seventeen years ago tomorrow . . ."

At this moment Irma swept into the room, eyeing the old lady in cold hostility. Miss Allen nodded politely, but she rose to go immediately. When she left the house, the old lady's eyes were pleading with Mrs. Grant to follow.

That afternoon Mrs. Grant called on Miss Barbara Allen. She had dropped all pretense and began to talk frankly about the house, admitting her inability to understand Irma's liking for it, and her being unable to see the man hanging— and what lay below. Miss Barbara let her talk a while before she advanced the plan which she had been formulating. She outlined it patiently, urging it upon Mrs. Grant as a means with which to test her sister—and to punish her if anything should happen. After a while the two women went downtown to the local lawyer and Mrs. Grant made her will. In the evening Miss Barbara, having seen Mrs. Grant leave the house, made a short call on Irma.

"I don't know what you're up to," she said in her mild voice. "But I think you should know that Mrs. Grant has just made her will."

For a moment Irma was surprised. Then she drew herself together and said, "Really, Miss Allen, I don't understand." Her voice was edged and hostile.

"I think you do," the old lady went on, standing firmly before the younger woman. "I think you know as well as I do that Mrs. Grant should leave this house before anything happens—and I'm afraid something will happen."

"That's nonsense, Miss Allen, and you know it," Irma flung back. But her voice was not as firm as she would have liked, because she was thinking. Then something will happen, something will happen. . . .

The old lady disregarded this. "Mrs. Grant has put in her will that if anything happens to her here, if she is not gone tomorrow because you have kept her back, then you will get all she has—*provided you spend the rest of your life in this house!*"

Miss Barbara Allen went out of the house, and Irma stood in the dusk of the dimly lit room with her hands pressed to her breast. It was some moments before the full import of what the old lady had said broke in upon her, and then she thrust it blindly away, refusing to see it. It's not true, she told herself. But she looked at her little girl in growing fear. Something will happen tomorrow, she thought. Something must happen—afterward, we can go, Ellen and I.

Mrs. Grant got up early the next morning. She was definitely nervous and made little effort to hide it. At the breakfast table she said, "I must go away today. I can't stand this house any longer."

Irma steeled herself for combat. "Are you going to let children's tales and shadows affect you that way?" she demanded. Her voice was purposely very cold, and Mrs. Grant wavered in her resolve. Perhaps after all she *had* allowed herself to fall too easily a prey to unfounded fancies which her imaginative mind had lent support to by conjuring up suggestive hallucinations before her. And yet . . . Irma went on, "If you want, I shall send for a doctor. I can't help feeling that something's the matter with you. You've been acting so strangely of late, Lydia."

In the end, Mrs. Grant surrendered her resolve, so that when evening came, she was still in the house. Irma sat in the living room with her, waiting, wondering whether her sister would go into the parlor. In her own mind was forming a question of her right. But she crushed her conscience and said quickly, "Will you get my gold thimble from the parlor,

Lydia?" Her voice was casual, and her question suggested that she had already been in the parlor during the day.

Mrs. Grant looked at her sister, sitting calmly near her with folds of embroidery over her knees. She conquered the abrupt apprehension that had risen in her with patient effort, and presently she said, "Yes, I'll go," her voice as casual as Irma's.

She took a lamp and lit it, and went slowly toward the closed double doors leading into the panelled room. She opened them, and went into the room. A moment of breathless silence descended, hanging in the house. And then Irma heard a short, shrill scream of terror. She sat there half paralyzed, thinking of Miss Barbara's accusing eyes. Then she sprang up with a cry and ran toward the panelled room, her little girl following.

Mrs. Grant was standing in the middle of the room, pointing at the walls. Little choking sounds came from her throat, and her hands went up to tear at her high collar. Then before Irma could reach her, she fell in a heap on the floor. Irma came to her knees and caught up her sister's head.

"Lydia . . . Lydia" she moaned.

Even while she knelt there, she felt a horror such as she had never known, and she knew what it was that had stopped the beating of her sister's heart. She felt the brooding fear that came throbbing toward her from the walls, and she knew that unless she escaped, she too would be smothered and choked, this fear pressing in upon her with its icy hands until her life was gone. Her sister's collar came open, and Irma saw on her throat a faint line, red and bruised, as if the collar had strangled her. Irma's hands began to tremble, and her lips fell open and shut. She thought with sudden horror of Lydia's will, and as she strove to push away the thought, she heard Ellen's voice coming it seemed from very far away.

"Mamma, will they do it again?"

The child was standing near her, pointing at the panels of the walls. Irma put one hand up to her throat, and her voice, as she answered the child, was little more than whisper. "What?" she asked harshly. God, there's nothing, she thought. There's nothing.

The child continued to point at the panels, and she said, "I saw them move. I saw them."

There's nothing . . . There's nothing there at all. Irma began to sway, and then suddenly she reached out and began to strike the child unmercifully, striking blindly, until at last the child's crying brought her to her senses. She crouched there on her knees looking with unseeing eyes at the crying child and screamed at her. "*You didn't see anything! You didn't see anything! You didn't . . . You didn't . . . !*"

THE SKULL OF THE
MARQUIS DE SADE
by
ROBERT BLOCH

A large number of Robert Bloch's macabre stories have been adapted to film, including this tale. It was made into a chilling exercise in cinematic terror called The Skull *(1965), produced in England and starring Peter Cushing and Patrick Wymark. If you've seen it, it probably scared the pants off you. If you haven't seen it, the pages which follow will serve quite nicely, thank you.*

"The Skull of the Marquis de Sade" is for those who like nasty horror stories—tales that raise the hackles on the neck, curdle the blood, and disturb one's sleep. This account of a collector named Christopher Maitland, and what happens after he purchases the skull of the Prince of Pain, is definitely not for the squeamish. Let the reader beware. You've been warned . . .

Robert Bloch (born 1917) needs no introduction to aficionados of fantasy/horror fiction. The author of Psycho, *"Yours Truly, Jack the Ripper," and hundreds of other novels and stories has been frightening both the wary and the unwary for close to forty years. Few writers can equal him in conveying sheer terror. For all of that, I can tell you he's a nice and gentle man. But I can also tell*

180

you this: you wouldn't want to get trapped in one of his night-mares . . .

CHRISTOPHER MAITLAND SAT BACK IN HIS CHAIR BEFORE THE fireplace and fondled the binding of an old book. His thin face, modeled by the flickering firelight, bore a characteristic expression of scholarly preoccupation.

Maitland's intellectual curiosity was focused on the volume in his hands. Briefly, he was wondering if the human skin binding this book came from a man, a woman or a child.

He had been assured by the bookseller that this tome was bound in a portion of the skin of a woman, but Maitland, much as he desired to believe this, was by nature skeptical. Booksellers who deal in such *curiosa* are not overly reputable, as a rule, and Christopher Maitland's years of dealing with such people had done much to destroy his faith in their veracity.

Still, he hoped the story was true. It was nice to have a book bound in a woman's skin. It was nice to have a *crux ansata* fashioned from a thighbone; a collection of Dyack heads; a shriveled Hand of Glory stolen from a graveyard in Mainz. Maitland owned all of these items, and many more. For he was a collector of the unusual.

Maitland held the book up to the light and sought to distinguish pore-formation beneath the tanned surface of the binding. Women had finer pores than men, didn't they?

"Beg pardon, sir."

Maitland turned as Hume entered. "What is it?" he asked.

"That person is here again."

"Person?"

"Mr. Marco."

"Oh?" Maitland rose, ignoring the butler's almost grotesque expression of distaste. He suppressed a chuckle. Poor Hume didn't like Marco, or any of the raffish gentry who supplied Maitland with items for his collection. Hume didn't care for the collection itself, either—Maitland vividly remembered the old servant's squeamish trembling as he dusted off the case containing the mummy of the priest of Horus decapitated for sorcery.

"Marco, eh? Wonder what's up?" Maitland mused. "Well—better show him in."

Hume turned and left with a noticeable lack of enthusiasm. As for Maitland, his eagerness mounted. He ran his hand along the reticulated back of a jadeite *tao-tieh* and licked his lips with very much the same expression as adorned the face of the Chinese image of gluttony.

Old Marco was here. That meant something pretty special in the way of acquisitions. Perhaps Marco wasn't exactly the kind of chap one invited to the Club—but he had his uses. Where he laid hands on some of the things he offered for sale Maitland didn't know; he didn't much care. That was Marco's affair. The rarity of his offerings was what interested Christopher Maitland. If one wanted a book bound in human skin, old Marco was just the chap to get hold of it—if he had to do a bit of flaying and binding himself. Great character, old Marco!

"Mr. Marco, sir."

Hume withdrew, a sedate shadow, and Maitland waved his visitor forward.

Mr. Marco oozed into the room. The little man was fat, greasily so; his flesh lumped like the tallow coagulating about the guttering stump of a candle. His waxen pallor accentuated the simile. All that seemed needed was a wick to sprout from the bald ball of fat that served as Mr. Marco's head.

The fat man stared up at Maitland's lean face with what was meant to be an ingratiating smile. The smile oozed, too, and contributed to the aura of uncleanliness which seemed to surround Marco.

But Maitland was not conscious of these matters. His attention was focused on the curious bundle Marco carried under one arm—the large package, wrapped in prosaic butcher's paper which somehow contributed to its fascination for him.

Marco shifted the package gingerly as he removed his shoddy gray ulster. He did not ask permission to divest himself of the coat, nor did he wait for an invitation to be seated.

The fat little man merely made himself comfortable in one of the chairs before the fire, reached for Maitland's open cigar case, helped himself to a stogie, and lit it. The large round package bobbed up and down on his lap as his rotund stomach heaved convulsively.

Maitland stared at the package. Marco stared at Maitland. Maitland broke first.

"Well?" he asked.

The greasy smile expanded. Marco inhaled rapidly, then opened his mouth to emit a puff of smoke and a reply.

"I am sorry to come unannounced, Mr. Maitland. I hope I'm not intruding?"

"Never mind that," Maitland snapped. "What's in the package, Marco?"

Marco's smile expanded. "Something choice," he whispered. "Something tasty."

Maitland bent over the chair, his head outthrust to throw a vulpine shadow on the wall.

"What's in the package?" he repeated.

"You're my favorite client, Mr. Maitland. You know I never come to you unless I have something really rare. Well I have that, sir. I have that. You'd be surprised what this butcher's paper hides, although it's rather appropriate. Yes, appropriate it is!"

"Stop that infernal gabbling, man! What is in the package?"

Marco lifted the bundle from his lap. He turned it over gingerly, yet deliberately.

"Doesn't seem to be much," he purred. "Round. Heavy enough. Might be a medicine ball, eh? Or a beehive. I say, it could even be a head of cabbage. Yes, one might mistake it for a head of common cabbage. But it isn't. Oh no, it isn't. Intriguing problem, eh?"

If it was the little man's intention to goad Maitland into a fit of apoplexy, he almost succeeded.

"Open it up, damn you!" he shouted.

Marco shrugged, smiled, and scrabbled at the taped edges of the paper. Christopher Maitland was no longer the perfect gentleman, the perfect host. He was a collector, stripped of all pretenses—quivering eagerness incarnate. He hovered over Marco's shoulder as the butcher's paper came away in the fat man's pudgy fingers.

"Now!" Maitland breathed.

The paper fell to the floor. Resting in Marco's lap was a large, glittering silver ball of—tinfoil.

Marco began to strip the tinfoil away, unraveling it in silvery strands. Maitland gasped as he saw what emerged from the wrappings.

It was a human skull.

Maitland saw the horrid hemisphere gleaming ivory-white in the firelight—then, as Marco shifted it he saw the empty eye sockets and the gaping nasal aperture that would never know human breath. Maitland noted the even structure of the teeth, adherent to a well-formed jaw. Despite his instinctive repulsion, he was surprisingly observant.

It appeared to him that the skull was unusually small and delicate, remarkably well preserved despite a yellow tinge hinting of age. But Christopher Maitland was most impressed by one undeniable peculiarity. The skull was *different*, indeed.

This skull did not grin!

Through some peculiar formation or malformation of cheekbone in juxtaposition of jaws, the death's-head did not simulate a smile. The classic mockery of mirth attributed to all skulls was absent here.

The skull had a sober, serious look about it.

Maitland blinked and uttered a self-conscious cough. What was he doing, entertaining these idiotic fancies about a skull? It was ordinary enough. What was old Marco's game in bringing him such a silly object with so much solemn preamble?

Yes, what *was* Marco's game?

The little fat man held the skull up before the firelight, turning it from time to time with an impressive display of pride.

His smirk of self-satisfaction contrasted oddly with the sobriety set indelibly upon the skull's bony visage.

Maitland's puzzlement found expression at last. "What are you so smug about?" he demanded. "You bring me the skull of a woman or an adolescent youth—"

Marco's chuckle cut across his remark. "Exactly what the phrenologists said!" he wheezed.

"Damn the phrenologists, man! Tell me about this skull, if there's anything to tell."

Marco ignored him. He turned the skull over in his fat hands, with a gloating expression which repelled Maitland. "It may be small, but it's a beauty, isn't it?" the little man mused. "So delicately formed, and look—there's almost the illusion of a patina upon the surface."

"I'm not a paleontologist," Maitland snapped. "Nor a grave robber, either. You'd think we were Burke and Hare! Be reasonable, Marco—why should I want an ordinary skull?"

"Please, Mr. Maitland! What do you take me for? Do you think I would presume to insult your intelligence by bringing you an ordinary skull? Do you imagine I would ask a thousand pounds for the skull of a nobody?"

Maitland stepped back.

"A thousand pounds?" he shouted. "A thousand pounds for *that*?"

"And cheap at the price," Marco assured him. "You'll pay it gladly when you know the story."

"I wouldn't pay such a price for the skull of Napoleon," Maitland assured him. "Or Shakespeare, for that matter."

"You'll find that the owner of this skull tickles your fancy a bit more," Marco assured him.

"Enough of this. Let's have it, man!"

Marco faced him, one pudgy forefinger tapping the osseous brow of the death's-head.

"You see before you," he murmured, "the skull of Donatien Alphonse Francois, the Marquis de Sade."

II

GILES DE RETZ WAS A MONSTER. TORQUEMADA'S INQUISITORS exercised the diabolic ingenuity of the fiends they professed to exorcize. But it remained for the Marquis de Sade to epitomize the living lust for pain. His name symbolizes cruelty incarnate—the savagery men call "sadism."

Maitland knew de Sade's weird history, and mentally reviewed it.

The Count, or Marquis, de Sade was born in 1740, of distinguished Provencal lineage. He was a handsome youth when he joined his cavalry regiment in the Seven Years' War—a pale, delicate, blue-eyed man, whose foppish diffidence cloaked an evil perversity.

At the age of twenty-three he was imprisoned for a year as the result of a barbaric crime. Indeed, twenty-seven years of his subsequent life he spent in incarceration for his deeds— deeds which even today are only hinted at. His flagellations, his administration of outer drugs and his tortures of women have served to make his name infamous.

But de Sade was no common libertine with a primitive urge toward the infliction of suffering. He was, rather, the "philosopher of pain"—a keen scholar, a man of exquisite taste and breeding. He was wonderfully well-read, a disciplined thinker, a remarkable psychologist—and a sadist.

How the mighty Marquis would have squirmed had he envisioned the petty perversions which today bear his name! The tormenting of animals by ignorant peasants, the beating of children by hysteric attendants in institutions, the infliction of senseless cruelties by maniacs upon others or by others upon maniacs—all these matters are classified as "sadistic" today. And yet none of them are manifestations of de Sade's unnatural philosophy.

De Sade's concept of cruelty had in it nothing of concealment or deceit. He practiced his beliefs openly and wrote explicitly of such matters during his years in prison. For he was the Apostle of Pain, and his gospel was made known to all men in *Justine, Juliette, Aline et Valcour,* the curious *La Philosophie dans le Boudoir* and the utterly abominable *Les 120 Journées.*

And de Sade practiced what he preached. He was a lover of many women—a jealous lover, willing to share the embraces of his mistresses with but one rival. That rival was Death, and it is said that all women who knew de Sade's caresses came to prefer those of his rival, in the end.

Perhaps the tortures of the French Revolution were indirectly inspired by the philosophy of the Marquis—a philosophy that gained circulation throughout France following the publication of his notorious tomes.

When the guillotine arose in the public squares of the cities, de Sade emerged from his long series of imprisonments and walked abroad among men maddened at the sight of blood and suffering.

He was a gray, gentle little ghost—short, bald, mild-mannered and soft-spoken. He raised his voice only to save his aristocratic relatives from the knife. His public life was exemplary during these latter years.

But men still whispered of his private life. His interest in sorcery was rumored. It is said that to de Sade the shedding of blood was a sacrifice. And sacrifices made to certain things bring black boons. The screams of pain-maddened women are as prayer to the creatures of the Pit . . .

The Marquis was cunning. Years of confinement for his "offenses against society" had made him wary. He moved quite cautiously and took full advantage of the troubled times to conduct quiet and unostentatious burial services whenever he terminated an amour.

Caution did not suffice, in the end. An ill-chosen diatribe directed against Napoleon served as an excuse for the authorities. There were no civil charges; no farcical trial was perpetrated.

De Sade was simply shut up in Charenton as a common lunatic. The men who knew his crimes were too shocked to publicize them—and yet there was a satanic grandeur about the Marquis which somehow precluded destroying him outright. One does not think of assassinating Satan. But Satan chained—

Satan, chained, languished. A sick, half-blind old man who tore the petals from roses in a last gesture of demoniac destructiveness, the Marquis spent his declining days forgotten by all men. They preferred to forget, preferred to think him mad.

In 1814, he died. His books were banned, his memory desecrated, his deeds denied. But his name lived on—lives on as an eternal symbol of innate evil. . . .

Such was de Sade, as Christopher Maitland knew him. And as a collector of *curiosa*, the thought of possessing the veritable skull of the fabulous Marquis intrigued him.

He glanced up from revery, glanced at the unsmiling skull and the grinning Marco.

"A thousand pounds, you said?"

"Exactly," Marco nodded. "A most reasonable price, under the circumstances."

"Under what circumstances?" Maitland objected. "You bring me a skull. But what proof can you furnish me as to its authenticity? How did you come by this rather unusual *memento mori?*"

"Come, come, Mr. Maitland—please! You know me better than to question my source of supply. That is what I choose to call a trade secret, eh?"

"Very well. But I can't just take your word, Marco. To the best of my recollection, de Sade was buried when he died at Charenton, in 1814."

Marco's oozing grin expanded.

"Well, I can set you right about *that* point," he conceded. "Do you happen to have a copy of Ellis's *Studies* about? In the section entitled *Love and Pain* there is an item which may interest you."

Maitland secured the volume, and Marco riffled through the pages.

"Here!" he exclaimed triumphantly. "According to Ellis, the skull of the Marquis de Sade was exhumed and examined by a phrenologist. Phrenology was a popular pseudo-science in those days, eh? Chap wanted to see if the cranial formation indicated the Marquis was truly insane.

"It says he found the skull to be small and well formed, like a woman's. Exactly your remark, as you may recall!

"But the real point is this. The skull wasn't reinterred.

"It fell into the hands of a Dr. Londe, but around 1850 it was stolen by another physician, who took it to England. That is all Ellis knows of the matter. The rest I could tell— but it's better not to speak. Here is the skull of the Marquis de Sade, Mr. Maitland.

"Will you meet my offer?"

"A thousand pounds," Maitland sighed. "It's too much for a shoddy skull and a flimsy story."

"Well—let us say eight hundred, perhaps. A quick deal and no hard feelings?"

Maitland stared at Marco. Marco stared at Maitland. The skull stared at them both.

"Five hundred, then," Marco ventured. "Right now."

"You must be faking," Maitland said. "Otherwise you wouldn't be so anxious for a sale."

Marco's smile oozed off again. "On the contrary, sir. If I were trying to do you, I certainly wouldn't budge on my price. But I want to dispose of this skull quickly."

"Why?"

For the first time during the interview, fat little Marco hesitated. He twisted the skull between his hands and set it down on the table. It seemed to Maitland as if he avoided looking at it as he answered.

"I don't exactly know. It's just that I don't fancy owning such an item, really. Works on my imagination. Rot, isn't it?"

"Works on your imagination?"

"I get ideas that I'm being followed. Of course it's all nonsense, but—"

"You get ideas that you're followed by the police, no doubt," Maitland accused. "Because you stole the skull. Didn't you, Marco?"

Marco averted his gaze. "No," he mumbled. "It isn't that. But I don't like skulls—not my idea of ornaments, I assure you. Squeamish I am, a bit.

"Besides, you live in this big house here. You're safe. I live in Wapping now. Down on my luck at the moment and all that. I sell you the skull. You tuck it away here in your collection, look at it when you please—and the rest of the time it's out of sight, not bothering you. I'll be free of it knocking around in my humble diggings. Matter of fact, when I sell it, I'll vacate the premises to move to decent lodgings. That's why I want to be rid of it, really. For five hundred, cash in hand."

Maitland hesitated. "I must think it over," he declared. "Give me your address. Should I decide to purchase it, I'll be down tomorrow with the money. Fair enough?"

"Very well." Marco sighed. He produced a greasy stub of pencil and tore a bit of paper from the discarded wrappings on the floor.

"Here's the address," he said.

Maitland pocketed the slip as Marco commenced to enclose the skull in tinfoil once more. He worked quickly, as though eager to obscure the shining teeth and the yawning emptiness of the eye-sockets. He twisted the butcher's paper over the tinfoil, grasped his overcoat in one hand, and balanced the round bundle in the other.

"I'll be expecting you tomorrow," he said. "And by the way—be careful when you open the door. I've a police dog now, a savage brute. He'll tear you to pieces—or anyone else who tries to take the skull of the Marquis de Sade."

III

IT SEEMED TO MAITLAND THAT THEY HAD BOUND HIM TOO tightly. He knew that the masked men were about to whip him, but he could not understand why they had fastened his wrists with chains of steel.

Only when they held the metal scourges over the fire did he comprehend the reason—only when they raised the white-hot rods high above their heads did he realize why he was held so securely.

For at the fiery kiss of the lash Maitland did not flinch—

he convulsed. His body, seared by the hideous blow, described an arc. Bound by thongs, his hands would tear themselves free under the stimulus of the unbearable torment. But the steel chains held, and Maitland gritted his teeth as the two black-robed men flogged him with living fire.

The outlines of the dungeon blurred, and Maitland's pain blurred too. He sank down into a darkness broken only by the consciousness of rhythm—the rhythm of the savage, sizzling steel flails that descended upon his naked back.

When awareness returned, Maitland knew that the flogging was over. The silent, black-robed men in masks were bending over him, unfastening the shackles. They lifted him tenderly and led him gently across the dungeon floor to the great steel casket.

Casket? This was no casket. Caskets do not stand open and upended. Caskets do not bear upon their lids the raised, molded features of a woman's face.

Caskets are not spiked, inside.

Recognition was simultaneous with horror.

This was the Iron Maiden!

The masked men were strong. They dragged him forward, thrust him into the depths of the great metal matrix of torment. They fastened wrists and ankles with clamps. Maitland knew what was coming.

They would close the lid upon him. Then, by turning a crank, they would move the lid down—move it down as spikes drove in at his body. For the interior of the Iron Maiden was studded with cruel barbs, sharpened and lengthened with the cunning of the damned.

The longest spikes would pierce him first as the lid descended. These spikes were set so as to enter his wrists and ankles. He would hang there, crucified, as the lid continued its inexorable descent. Shorter spikes would next enter his thighs, shoulders and arms. Then, as he struggled, impaled in agony, the lid would press closer until the smallest spikes came close enough to penetrate his eyes, his throat, and—mercifully—his heart and brain.

Maitland screamed, but the sound served only to shatter his eardrums as they closed the lid. The rusty metal grated, and then came the harsher grating of the machinery. They were turning the crank, bringing the banks of spikes closer to his cringing body. . . .

Maitland waited, tensed in the darkness, for the first sharp kiss of the Iron Maiden.

Then, and then only, he realized that he was not *alone* here in the blackness.

There were no spikes set in the lid! Instead, a figure was pressed against the opposite iron surface. As the lid descended, it merely brought the figure closer to Maitland's body.

The figure did not move, or even breathe. It rested against the lid, and as the lid came forward Maitland felt the pressure of cold and alien flesh against his own. The arms and legs met his in unresponsive embrace, but still the lid pressed down, squeezing the lifeless form closer and closer. It was dark, but now Maitland could see the face that loomed scarcely an inch from his eyes. The face was white, phosphorescent. The face was—*not a face!*

And then, as the body gripped his body in blackness, as the head touched his head, as Maitland's lips pressed against the place where lips *should* be, he knew the ultimate horror.

The face that was *not* a face was the skull of the Marquis de Sade!

And the weight of charnel corruption stifled Maitland and he went down into darkness again with the obscene memory pursuing him to oblivion.

Even oblivion has an end, and once more Maitland woke. The masked men had released and were reviving him. He lay on a pallet and glanced toward the open doors of the Iron Maiden. He was oddly grateful to see that the interior was empty. No figure rested against the inside of the lid. Perhaps there had been no figure.

The torture played strange tricks on a man's mind. But it was needed now. He could tell that the solicitude of the masked ones was not assumed. They had subjected him to this ordeal for strange reasons, and he had come through unscathed.

They anointed his back, lifted him to his feet, led him from the dungeon. In the great corridor beyond, Maitland saw a mirror. They guided him up to it.

Had the torture changed him? For a moment Maitland feared to gaze into the glass.

But they held him before the mirror, and Maitland stared at his reflection—stared at his quivering body, on which was set the grim, unsmiling death's-head of the Marquis de Sade!

IV

MAITLAND TOLD NO ONE OF HIS DREAM, BUT HE LOST NO TIME in discussing Marco's visit and offer.

His confidant was an old friend and fellow-collector, Sir Fitzhugh Kissroy. Seated in Sir Fitzhugh's comfortable study the following afternoon, he quickly unburdened himself of all pertinent details.

Genial, red-bearded Kissroy heard him out in silence.

"Naturally, I want that skull," Maitland concluded. "But I can't understand why Marco is so anxious to dispose of it at once. And I'm considerably worried about its authenticity. So I was wondering—you're quite an expert, Fitzhugh. Would you be willing to visit Marco with me and examine the skull?"

Sir Fitzhugh chuckled and shook his head.

"There's no need to examine it," he declared. "I'm quite

sure the skull, as you describe it, is that of the Marquis de Sade. It's genuine enough."

Maitland gaped at him.

"How can you be so positive?" he asked.

Sir Fitzhugh beamed. "Because, my dear fellow—that skull was stolen from me!"

"What?"

"Quite so. About ten days ago, a prowler got into the library through the French windows facing the garden. None of the servants were aroused, and he made off with the skull in the night."

Maitland rose. "Incredible," he murmured. "But of course you'll come with me, now. We'll identify your property, confront old Marco with the facts, and recover the skull at once."

"Nothing of the sort," Sir Fitzhugh replied. "I'm just as glad the skull was stolen. And I advise you to leave it alone."

"I didn't report the theft to the police, and I have no intention of doing so. Because that skull is—unlucky."

"Unlucky?" Maitland peered at his host. "You, with your collection of cursed Egyptian mummies, tell me that? You've never taken any stock in such superstitious rubbish."

"Exactly. Therefore, when I tell you that I sincerely believe that skull is dangerous, you must have faith in my words."

Maitland pondered. He wondered if Sir Fitzhugh had experienced the same dreams that tormented his own sleep upon seeing the skull. Was there an associative aura about the relic? If so, it only added to the peculiar fascination exerted by the unsmiling skull of the Marquis de Sade.

"I don't understand you at all," he declared. "I should think you couldn't wait to lay hands on that skull."

"Perhaps I'm not the only one who can't wait," Sir Fitzhugh muttered.

"What are you getting at?"

"You know de Sade's history. You know the power of

morbid fascination such evil geniuses exert upon the imagination of men. You feel that fascination yourself; that's why you want the skull.

"But you're a normal man, Maitland. You want to *buy* the skull and keep it in your collection of *curiosa*. An abnormal man might not think of buying. He might think of stealing it—or even killing the owner to possess it. Particularly if he wanted to do more than merely own it; for example, he wanted to *worship* it."

Sir Fitzhugh's voice sank to a whisper as he continued, "I'm not trying to frighten you, my friend. But I know the history of that skull. During the last hundred years it has passed through the hands of many men. Some of them were collectors, and sane. Others were perverted members of secret cults—worshippers of pain, devotees of Black Magic. Men have died to gain that grisly relic, and other men have been—sacrificed to it.

"It came to me quite by chance, six months ago. A man like your friend Marco offered it to me. Not for a thousand pounds, or five hundred. He gave it to me as a gift, because he was afraid of it.

"Of course I laughed at his notions, just as you are probably laughing at mine now. But during the six months that the skull has remained in my hands, I've suffered.

"I've had queer dreams. Just staring at the unnatural, unsmiling grimace is enough to provoke nightmares. Didn't you sense an emanation from the thing? They said de Sade wasn't mad—and I believe them. He was far worse—he was *possessed*. There's something *unhuman* about that skull. Something that attracts others, living men whose skulls hide a bestial quality that is also unhuman or inhuman.

"And I've had more than my dreams to deal with. Phone calls came, and mysterious letters. Some of the servants had reported lurkers on the grounds at dusk."

"Probably ordinary thieves, like Marco, after a valuable object," Maitland commented.

"No," Sir Fitzhugh sighed. "Those unknown seekers did more than attempt to steal the skull. *They came into my house at night and adored it!*

"Oh, I'm quite positive about the matter, I assure you! I kept the skull in a glass case in the library. Often, when I came to see it in the morning, I found that it had been moved during the night.

"Yes, moved. Sometimes the case was smashed and the skull placed on the table. Once it was on the floor.

"Of course I checked up on the servants. Their alibis were perfect. It was the work of outsiders—outsiders who probably feared to possess the skull completely, yet needed access to it from time to time in order to practice some abominable and perverted rite.

"They came into my house, I tell you, and worshipped that filthy skull! And when it was stolen, I was glad—very glad.

"All I can say to you is, keep away from the whole business! Don't see this man Marco, and don't have anything to do with that accursed graveyard relic!"

Maitland nodded. "Very well," he said. "I am grateful to you for your warning."

He left Sir Fitzhugh shortly thereafter.

Half an hour later, he was climbing the stairs to Marco's dingy attic room.

V

HE CLIMBED THE STAIRS TO MARCO'S ROOM; CLIMBED THE creaking steps in the shabby Soho tenement and listened to the curiously muffled thumping of his own heartbeat.

But not for long. A sudden howl resounded from the landing above, and Maitland scrambled up the last few stairs in frantic haste.

The door of Marco's room was locked, but the sounds that issued from within stirred Maitland to desperate measures.

Sir Fitzhugh's warnings had prompted him to carry his service revolver on this errand; now he drew it and shattered the lock with a shot.

Maitland flung the door back against the wall as the howling reached the ultimate frenzied crescendo. He started into the room, then checked himself.

Something hurtled toward him from the floor beyond; something launched itself at his throat.

Maitland raised his revolver blindly and fired.

For a moment sound and vision blurred. When he recovered, he was half-kneeling on the floor before the threshold. A great shaggy form rested at his feet. Maitland recognized the carcass of a gigantic police dog.

Suddenly he remembered Marco's reference to the beast. So that explained it! The dog had howled and attacked. But—why?

Maitland rose and entered the sordid bedroom. Smoke still curled upward from the shots. He gazed again at the prone animal, noting the gleaming yellow fangs grimacing even in death. The he stared around at the shoddy furniture, the disordered bureau, the rumpled bed—

The rumpled bed on which Mr. Marco lay, his throat torn in a red rosary of death.

Maitland stared at the body of the little fat man and shuddered.

Then he saw the skull. It rested on the pillow near Marco's head, a grisly bedfellow that seemed to peer curiously at the corpse in ghastly *camaraderie*. Blood had spattered the hollow cheekbones, but even beneath this sanguinary stain Maitland could see the peculiar solemnity of the death's-head.

For the first time he fully sensed the aura of evil which clung to the skull of de Sade. It was palpable in this ravaged room, palpable as the presence of death itself. The skull seemed to glow with actual charnel phosphorescence.

Maitland knew now that his friend had spoken the truth. There *was* a dreadful magnetism inherent in this bony horror, a veritable Elixir of Death that worked and preyed upon the minds of men—and beasts.

It must have been that way. The dog, maddened by the urge to kill, had finally attacked Marco as he slept and destroyed him. Then it had sought to attack Maitland when he entered. And through it all the skull watched, watched and gloated just as de Sade would gloat had his pale blue eyes flickered in the shadowed sockets.

Somewhere within the cranium, perhaps, the shriveled remnants of his cruel brain were still attuned to terror. The magnetic force it focused had a compelling enchantment even in the face of what Maitland knew.

That is why Maitland, driven by a compulsion he could not wholly explain or seek to justify, stooped down and lifted the skull. He held it for a long moment in the classic pose of Hamlet.

Then he left the room, forever, carrying the death's-head in his arms.

Fear rode Maitland's shoulders as he hurried through the twilit streets. Fear whispered strangely in his ear, warning him to hurry, lest the body of Marco be discovered and the police pursue him. Fear prompted him to enter his own house by a side door and go directly to his rooms so that none would see the skull he concealed beneath his coat.

Fear was Maitland's companion all that evening. He sat there, staring at the skull on the table, and shivered with repulsion.

Sir Fitzhugh was right, he knew it. There *was* a damnable influence issuing from the skull and the black brain within.

It had caused Maitland to disregard the sensible warnings of his friend; it had caused Maitland to steal the skull itself from a dead man; it had caused him now to conceal himself in this lonely room.

He should call the authorities; he knew that. Better still, he should dispose of the skull. Give it away, throw it away, rid the earth of it forever. There was something puzzling about the cursed thing—something he didn't quite understand.

For, knowing these truths, he still desired to possess the skull of the Marquis de Sade. There was an evil enchantment here; the dormant baseness in every man's soul was aroused and responded to the loathsome lust which poured from the death's-head in waves.

He stared at the skull, shivered—yet he knew he would not give it up; could not. Nor had he the strength to destroy it. Perhaps possession would lead him to madness in the end. The skull would incite others to unspeakable excesses.

Maitland pondered and brooded, seeking a solution in the impassive object that confronted him with the stolidity of death.

It grew late. Maitland drank wine and paced the floor. He was weary. Perhaps in the morning he would think matters through and reach a logical, sane, conclusion.

Yes, he was upset. Sir Fitzhugh's outlandish hints had disturbed him; the gruesome events of the late afternoon preyed on his nerves.

No sense in giving way to foolish fancies about the skull of the mad Marquis . . . better to rest.

Maitland flung himself on the bed. He reached out for the switch and extinguished the light. The moon's rays slithered through the window and sought out the skull on the table, bathing it in eerie luminescence. Maitland stared once more at the jaws that should grin and did not.

Then he closed his eyes and willed himself to sleep. In the morning he'd call Sir Fitzhugh, make a clean breast of things, and give the skull over to the authorities.

Its evil career—real or imaginary—would come to an end. So be it.

Maitland sank into slumber. Before he dozed off he tried to focus his attention on something . . . something puzzling . . . an impression he'd received upon gazing at the body of the police dog in Marco's room. The way its fangs gleamed. Yes. That was it. There had been no blood on the muzzle of the police dog. Strange. For the police dog had bitten Marco's throat. No blood—how could that be?

Well, that problem was best left for morning too. . . .

It seemed to Maitland that as he slept, he dreamed. In his dream he opened his eyes and blinked in the bright moonlight. He stared at the table top and saw that the skull was no longer resting on its surface.

That was curious, too. No one had come into the room, or he would have been aroused.

If he had not been sure that he was dreaming, Maitland would have started up in terror when he saw the stream of moonlight on the floor—the stream of moonlight through which the skull was rolling.

It turned over and over again, its bony visage impassive as ever, and each revolution brought it closer to the bed.

Maitland's sleeping ears could almost hear the thump as the skull landed on the bare floor at the foot of the bed. Then began the grotesque process so typical of night fantasies. The skull climbed the side of the bed!

Its teeth gripped the dangling corner of a bed-sheet, and the death's-head literally whirled the sheet out and up, swinging it in an arc which landed the skull on the bed at Maitland's feet.

The illusion was so vivid he could feel the thud of its

impact against the mattress. Tactile sensation continued, and Maitland felt the skull rolling along up the covers. It came up to his waist, then approached his chest.

Maitland saw the bony features in the moonlight, scarcely six inches away from his neck. He felt a cold weight resting on his throat. The skull was moving now.

Then he realized the grip of utter nightmare and struggled to wake before the dream continued.

A scream rose in his throat—but never issued from it. For Maitland's throat was seized by champing teeth—teeth that bit into his neck with all the power of a moving human jawbone.

The skull tore at Maitland's jugular in cruel haste. There was a gasp, a gurgle and then no sound at all.

After a time, the skull righted itself on Maitland's chest. Maitland's chest no longer heaved with breathing, and the skull rested there with a curious simulation of satisfied repose.

The moonlight shone on the death's-head to reveal one very curious circumstance. It was a trivial thing, yet somehow fitting under the circumstances.

Reposing on the chest of the man it had killed, the skull of the Marquis de Sade was no longer impassive. Instead, its bony features bore a definite, unmistakably *sadistic* grin.

SILVER SPECTRE
by
JON L. BREEN

"Silver Spectre" is one of those stories with a little something for every reader. Not only is it a dandy ghost story, it is also a horseracing story, and a detective story. And it works equally well on all three levels.

It concerns a thoroughbred named Silver Spectre who broke his leg in the backstretch of a race on Blakemore Downs, in an apparent accident that also killed his jockey, and who was buried in the Downs' infield. Some said the horse's trainer, Stu Gallon, was to blame for what happened; those same people also said that the spectral gray stallion who subsequently and mysteriously came charging out of the fog during time trials was the ghost of Silver Spectre. Not many believed that. But then, how come a terrible tragedy befell Stu Gallon after the phantom horse's ride? And how come each time the phantom horse was seen to ride again, other tragedies plagued Gallon?

There are two answers to these questions, one natural and one supernatural. It's up to you to decide which one you want to believe . . .

Like this story, Jon L. Breen is a man who operates on three distinct levels: he is a college librarian, a fiction writer, and a mystery critic of considerable repute. His reviews of current mystery novels appear monthly in Ellery Queen's Mystery Magazine, *as well as in the* Wilson Library Bulletin; *his short stories, many of them parodies of the work of well-known writers in the genre, regularly grace the pages of* EQMM *and* Alfred Hitchcock's Mystery Magazine. *His first book,* What About Murder?, *a guide to books about mystery and detective fiction, appeared in 1981; his second, a collection of his fictional parodies,* Hair of the Sleuthhound, *was published earlier this year.*

Want to hear a ghost story? Come on, listen to this. The next drink's on me. You don't like ghost stories? Well, call it a detective story then, with yours truly as detective. I can't prove I was a detective, but then nobody can prove there was a ghost either. You don't like detective stories? Well, it's also a racing story—and I know you like racing, because you have today's program from Santa Anita sticking out of your jacket pocket. Pretty good, huh? I told you I was a detective.

I heard this story years ago, in a bar. It wasn't a sleazy joint like this one though. It was much cozier, sort of like a friendly English pub. It was back East, in a place called Blakemore Village, an Atlantic resort town. It doesn't exist any more—it hardly existed then. But there was a racetrack there, Blakemore Downs. It went bankrupt about the time racing was booming all over the country. The whole operation was snake-bit from the first, they say, though it managed to stay in business quite a few years. At the time I got to Blakemore Village, the wrecking ball was only a week or two away from that pretty grandstand. The track had been closed for a couple of years. My paper had assigned me to do a piece on the track—a nostalgia piece, they'd call it today.

I wasn't too thrilled with the assignment, but I always tried to do my best. In the middle of the day I went out and looked at the track. I talked to the caretaker, the only human being on the premises, an old ex-jockey named Billy Duff. He rode around the grounds on an aged gray gelding, the only horse left at a place where so many crashing hooves had thudded their way to glory or disaster. You can laugh all you want, but sportswriters had to write that way in the old days.

It turned out that nearly everything at the track was still intact. Even the jockey room had racks and racks of bright-colored silks hanging there. Everything was a little dusty and the infield was overgrown with weeds, but you had the idea they could have started racing tomorrow if there'd been any horses to race or any suckers to watch them. No offense, friend. I'm sure you're a scientific bettor and regularly show a profit on your investments. But I'm sure you'll agree that most of your brethren lack whatever sense they were born with.

I got what I could from Duff, but he was a close-mouthed old-timer without many stories to tell, and it began to look as if I'd be writing a dull piece. Over the forty years of Blakemore Downs' existence, some really fine horses had run there. But I wanted to turn in something more than just a walk through the old newspaper files and racing manuals.

That night I went into the local tavern, sat down at the bar, and ordered a drink. In those days, I did that for information, for color, not just because I wanted to drink away the evening. Now I don't have that excuse, but back then when I walked up to a bar I was working.

There were a few regulars sitting there shooting the breeze, and they were cordial to me. By that time in the history of Blakemore Village they weren't seeing many visitors and much of the conversation was devoted to figuring out why their town was dying. They were philosophical enough about it. Just one of those things—boom today, bomb tomorrow.

At a corner table, away from anyone else, was a gaunt and gloomy-faced man of about sixty. He didn't join in the conversation, but devoted himself to serious drinking. The bartender would provide him with a fresh drink periodically in response to some practically invisible signal, and the other regulars would cast a voyeuristic glance his way every so often.

Promptly at eight o'clock, Billy Duff came in for what was apparently a nightly quick one, something you could set your clock by. He was friendly enough but no more talkative than he had been with me that day at the track. He too cast an interested glance at the man at the corner table. Obviously, he knew him but he made no move to go over and say hello. I offered to buy Billy a drink but he assured me that one was his permanent limit, and he left at a quarter past eight.

I hung on, chatting with the regulars. I was enjoying the conviviality and had a hunch that if the man at the corner table ever got up and left the tavern an interesting story might come my way. It might or might not have any bearing on my story about Blakemore Downs—but by that time I didn't much care.

Sure enough, about ten o'clock, the man at the corner table lurched to his feet, made his way to the bar with wobbly dignity, wordlessly paid his tab, and made his way out the door.

As soon as he was out of earshot the bartender said, "Old Stu. I haven't seen him around here in years."

The other regulars nodded or grunted in uninformative agreement.

Finally I had to ask. "Who is he?"

"Stuart Gallon. He used to be a trainer of racehorses. He led the trainer standing at the Downs for years."

"He must be sorry to see the place torn down," I remarked.

One of the regulars snickered. "I don't know," he said.

I smiled. "Come on, you guys. There's a story to tell about this guy. So tell it."

"You may not be able to use it. It's sort of a ghost story," said the bartender.

I shrugged. "I don't believe in ghosts—but some of my readers might."

"Okay." The bartender looked over my shoulder toward the window with a slight smile. "Fog's rollin' in," he said. "Sometimes it gets so thick here you can't see your hand in front of your face."

"Save the atmosphere," I kidded. "Don't try to scare me. Just tell me the story, and I'll provide the whistling wind or the cold chill or whatever's called for when I write it up. And—" I added as an afterthought "—set up a round on me." I didn't want to lose the story, whatever it was.

"We do get a lot of fog here though," the bartender said. "It's one of the things that didn't do the Downs any good. Sometimes it would be so foggy in the afternoon they couldn't even do a full chart of the race. It'd just say 'fog' and give the positions at the finish. Along the backstretch, the jockeys could have been wrestling or shooting pool or kissing each other and nobody in the stands'd know it.

"But that's getting away from the story. Not too far though. The man who just left, Stu Gallon, was not well liked in these parts. Whether it was justified or not, I don't know."

"It was justified all right!" snapped one of the regulars, a smallish old man with leathery skin. Another ex-jockey? I wondered.

"I know you think so, Fred. All I know about it of my own knowledge is that he believed in racing his horses a lot. He thought a race wasn't much harder on a horse than a workout—and he might as well go for the money as just run 'em around the track for no reason. Some folks said that was inhumane, but I don't know."

Fred said heatedly, "It wasn't just that, Charley. A lot of good trainers believed in racing their horses a lot. But Stu Gallon was a hard man. He hated horses—that's the long and short of it. He'd race them when they weren't right and he'd take a whip to them if they looked cross-eyed at him. And he didn't treat people much better. I'd have gone over and punched him one tonight when he came in, but I guess he's been punished plenty already for what he did."

"Anyway," said Charley, the bartender, "for purposes of the story let's just say Stu Gallon was not a popular man around the racetrack. People who worked for him never seemed to stay long. But he was a successful trainer.

"Now about the best horse Stu Gallon ever trained was a gray stallion named Silver Spectre. Ever heard of him?"

I shook my head. And I knew most of the good horses in those days.

"It was thirty or more years ago, of course, and the Spectre never got to show what he could really do. But he was a good one—right, Fred?"

Fred nodded solemnly. "He could have been a great one. He was a beautiful thing too. His coat was nearly white, and that was a time when gray horses were a novelty on American tracks. I remember folks used to say that gray horses were bad luck, but I never bought that."

The bartender, who had established himself through the evening as the best raconteur of the group, took up the story again. "Well, Silver Spectre became a real favorite of the track patrons, for his style as much as for his color. He won four straight races at the Downs that year, beating a tougher field each time he went to the post. And every single time he'd enter the first turn at the rear of the field, and on the backstretch he'd sometimes be fifteen or twenty lengths behind the leader, but on the far turn he'd suddenly start to get himself in gear and make his move. As they turned into the stretch he'd be picking up his opposition one by one, and by the finish line he'd have his gray neck in front one way or another. He was a real crowd pleaser, I can tell you. I won some money on him in my day."

Fred allowed a suggestion of a smile to crease his grim face. "You were lucky, Charley. I just ate his dust."

"Well, came the week of the Blakemore Handicap—that was a real big race in those days. Horses used to ship in for it from all over the East. One year Equipoise was supposed to come—"

"And another year," Fred added, "Seabiscuit was supposed to come."

I laughed. "But who did come?"

"A lot of big horses came," said Fred. "It really was a big race."

"Sure it was," I said. "I remember."

They seem mollified. Charley went on. "Well, this particular year everybody was talking about Silver Spectre and whether he was good enough to challenge the great field that would be going to the post that Saturday. He'd beaten the best horses stabled on the grounds, but he hadn't yet faced any horses as good as some of the ones shipping in. I remember on Tuesday of that week there was a rumor going around that he had hurt himself in his stall and it was doubtful Stu Gallon would run him. All week it was touch and go. But on Saturday, sure enough, his name turned up in the entries.

"Well, the weather that day was typical of the kind of luck that dogged the Downs all the years it was in business—"

"Dogged this whole town, in fact," another of the regulars amended.

"That's right. The fog rolled in. The folks in the grandstand—I wasn't there, I had to work the bar that day—could only see the stretch run. Beyond the turns, around the backside, you couldn't see a thing. All in all it was a crummy day to have to run the Blakemore Handicap, but they had a big crowd just the same. And sure enough, when the bugler played 'Boots and Saddles,' there was Silver Spectre going to the post with Ike McCann on his back."

Fred tilted his glass in a suggestion of a toast. "A great rider," he said.

"Some of the folks that were there that day swear that Silver Spectre looked lame in the post parade."

"If it were now," Fred put in, "the vet would have scratched him on the spot. They weren't as careful in them days."

"Did you think he looked lame?" I asked Fred.

"I wasn't there—I had a mount in New York that day. I'm glad I missed it."

I looked around at the other regulars. "Were any of you there?"

None of them had been. I sighed. This was a second- or thirdhand story I was getting. And when was the ghost coming into it?

"I've seen pictures," said Charley. "And I know from the pictures that he had one foreleg wrapped going to the post— the right, I think. And we all know that any kind of front bandage makes a bettor wary. But to have just one leg bandaged! You might as well hang a sign reading UNSOUND around the horse's neck.

"It was a big field for the race—fifteen. They started from behind the webbing—that was before the days of the starting gate, you know. It was a mile-and-a-quarter race, so they went all the way down the homestretch once, in front of the crowd, then all the way around again. Silver Spectre broke with his field, but as usual he dropped quickly to the rear of the pack. He looked to be running okay though, and his fans were yelling encouragement to him and Ike McCann as the field passed the stands. If anything, the Spectre was closer to the pace than usual, even though all fourteen others had him beat going to the turn. Then the field swept past the clubhouse and out of sight into the fog."

Charley paused a beat for emphasis, then gave me the next bit dramatically.

"My friend, fifteen horses entered that fog, and only fourteen returned. It was much later before most of the spectators were to learn that Silver Spectre had gone down on the backstretch, his right foreleg broken. The vet put him down on the spot. What was worse, Ike McCann had fallen on his head, and after a couple of days in a coma he was dead too."

"It was a terrible tragedy," said Fred. "They buried Silver Spectre in the infield at the Downs. Ike's family had him buried in a regular cemetery but, knowing him, I think he'd have liked to buried alongside the Spectre. He loved that horse."

"And he hated Gallon," said Charley.

"Sure. The two emotions went together."

"Everybody figured Gallon ran the horse when he shouldn't have," said Charley.

"And everybody was right," said Fred. "He did."

"Up to then, Stu Gallon was unpopular only with people who knew him. Now he was hated by a world of horse lovers who had never met him. Stu Gallon had become the most despised man on the American turf."

A touch of hyperbole there, I thought. I'd never even heard of Stu Gallon until that evening.

"For a while at least," Charley went on, "it didn't seem to make that much difference to Gallon's career. As I say, he was a good trainer, nasty as he was, and his horses won their share of purses. But then things started to go bad for Stu Gallon. We ought to tell you about a certain morning in October, some thirty years back. It was during the morning training period out at the Downs, and it was pea-soup foggy. You were there, weren't you, Fred?"

The ex-rider nodded his head. "Yeah, I can give you this

part firsthand. It was a terrible morning, but the business of training horses went on as usual. The clockers had to keep a close watch on horses going on and off the track. They didn't want any expensive pieces of horseflesh running into each other in that treacherous fog. Oh, I guess they didn't want any of us jockeys getting ourselves killed either, but that wasn't uppermost.

"I remember I was sitting on a brown two-year-old filly. I don't remember her name—she wasn't much. We were at the gap on the backstretch where you could go from the stable area onto the track to work out. The ground crew had been renovating the track, so no one had been allowed to go out for several minutes. The filly's trainer and I were about to take her onto the track—the chief clocker had given us the nod—when all of a sudden this big gray stallion comes charging out of the fog, hell bent for leather. He was hugging the rail, and the boy on his back was pumping him for all he was worth. As he streaked past us, the chief clocker was sputtering about how he hadn't let any horse on the track and where the hell had the gray come from. He told his outrider to go after the horse and rider, but the outrider, who'd turned downright pale, said to him, 'Not me, boss. I ain't chasin' no ghosts.'

" 'Ghosts!' the clocker roared at him.

" 'Yeah, ghosts,' he said. 'You can laugh at me if you want, but that was Silver Spectre, with Ike McCann on his back.'

"We did laugh at him, but not for long. Because nobody ever found that gray horse or his rider. The only other interval on the track is on the front side where the horses come out in the afternoon, and there was a maintenance man working there who said no horse went through that interval all morning. So, as far as anybody could tell, that horse and rider didn't ever exist at all except along the backstretch rail from out of the soup and back into it.

"And it was that same morning that Stuart Gallon's little girl was drowned."

"Somebody drowned his daughter?" I asked.

"No, no, it was an accident," said Charley. "Hell—nobody, no matter how much they hated Stu, could have wanted a terrible thing like that to happen. It happened in the swimming pool at Gallon's hotel. It was a sad thing. The death of a child always is. And Stu Gallon was really devoted to her too. Nobody's all rotten, I guess. Gallon was only mostly rotten."

"Did you ever see the ghost again, Fred?" I asked.

"No, not me."

"He *was* seen again though," Charley said. "Several times. Always on foggy mornings. People I know have seen him—people who used to come in here."

I looked around at the gathered regulars. Again, no witnesses.

I think Charley sensed I was losing interest. He leaned across the bar and looked me in the eye. "And every time that gray phantom made his appearance something else terrible happened to Stu Gallon, as if Ike and the Spectre were getting their revenge from beyond the grave. The second time the ghost horse ran Stu Gallon's wife died. The very same day. Then his house burned down. Then he lost his job with Lakehills Stable and really went on the skids."

"I was surprised to see him in here tonight," said Fred.

"Yeah. He hasn't been in here in years."

I had a feeling I'd had enough for the evening, enough to drink and enough ghost story. Not that they'd scared me—I wondered if they were making it all up. As I swayed to my feet I asked Fred, "After all the terrible things that happened to him, did most people come to forgive him for the things he did in his earlier days?"

"Well, I never heard that his misfortunes made Stu Gallon

any nicer. And some of the things he did back when I knew him are the kind of things you just don't forgive."

I said good-night to the assembly, paid my bill, and made my way carefully through the fog back to Blakemore Village's last remaining excuse for a hotel. There I saw the former trainer, Stu Gallon, sitting in the lobby, just staring into space. He did seem to have an oddly haunted look in his eyes.

I have to confess, though, I slept well that night. No nightmares. And if I had had one, it probably would have been about confronting my editor without a good story.

I slept late into the morning, as is my custom. When I was out on the street at eleven, the fog had cleared and it was a bright, sunny day. I was debating whether to try to gather more material for my article or just go back to the city and do my best with what little I had. As I passed the tavern, Charley was just opening up. "You keep long hours," I said.

"It's my place and there's not enough business to hire anybody to help pour. You heard what happened at Blakemore Downs this morning?"

"No. Something happened and I missed it?"

"The town cop came by a few minutes ago and told me. Stu Gallon is dead. They found him out at the Downs. In the infield."

"What was he doing there?"

"The guys that found him are from the wrecking company that's going to tear the place down next week. They said he was lying on the grave of Silver Spectre. They say he had a shovel. It seems he was digging."

I must say that gave me more of a shiver, there in the bright sunlight, than anything I'd heard in the foggy, theatrical gloom of the night before.

"You know what I think?" said Charley. "I think Silver

Spectre and Ike McCann made one last appearance this morning."

And as I've thought about it over the years I think that's what happened too—in a manner of speaking.

Stuart Gallon died of a heart attack, they found. And it could have been brought on by the strain of his crazy digging. Or he could have been frightened to death by something he saw.

A ghost horse and rider coming at him out of the fog? Maybe.

But I thought of that old ex-jockey, Billy Duff, who took care of the place. And I thought of his old gray gelding, the only horse on the grounds. And I thought of that jockey room with the silks still hanging there ready to wear, surely including the silks worn by Ike McCann when he rode Silver Spectre. And I wondered if what scared Stu Gallon to death might not have been a flesh-and-blood man streaking out of the fog on a flesh-and-blood horse, participating in a quite deliberately deadly masquerade. It could have been an act of durable, burning hatred. Or it could have been an act of mercy.

Or it could have been a ghost.

DEATHLOVE
by
Bill Pronzini

Can love, no matter how warped it might be, transcend death? Can evil itself transcend death? These questions are the central theme of "Deathlove"—and the answers offered here might just disturb you a little. Might even frighten you a little.

It all depends on your attitude toward specters and horror stories. "Some authors excel and are successful in the descriptive passages that lay out for the reader all the terrors and horrors of monsters and the like," Charles Grant wrote when this story was first published, "[but] there are others who work on the principle that the less said the better—let the imagination do the heavy work, and nine times out of ten it will come up with a scene no author could ever produce on the printed page. In that sense, then, the last scene of 'Deathlove' is missing.

"Your move."

A native Californian, Bill Pronzini (born 1943) has been a full-time professional writer since 1969. He has published 25 novels, including the recent "novel of terror" from Arbor House, **Masques**; *one nonfiction book, a satirical study of the mystery genre called*

216

Gun In Cheek *(1982); and 250 short stories, articles, and essays.*
He has also edited or coedited sixteen anthologies, among them five
previous fantasy/horror chrestomathies, the latest of which was the
omnibus volume, The Arbor House Necropolis. *His hobbies*
include collecting old books and magazines, and trying to outwit
the Internal Revenue Service (legally, of course). He lives in San
Francisco.

I SIT HUNCHED FORWARD IN THE TAXI AS IT RUSHES THROUGH
the dark, empty streets of the city, and I feel exultant. It
will not be long now, Judith, my love; a few hours, then a
few weeks or a few short months until you and I are one.
Forever.

And the truck comes out of nowhere

And we come into the quiet residential area six blocks
from Lake Industrial Park. I lean forward and tell the driver
to stop at the next corner. A moment later I stand alone in
the darkness. The night wind is cold, and I turn up the
collar on my overcoat as I watch the taxi's taillights fade and
disappear. Then I begin to walk rapidly toward the park,
the fingers of my right hand touching the gun in my coat
pocket.

The industrial development is deserted when I arrive;
there is no sign of the night security patrols, which I know
make periodic checks of the area. I pause and look at my
watch: just past nine. Exactly right. I make my way to the
squat stone structure that houses McAnally's firm, the un-
imaginatively named Ajax Plumbling Supply Company. A
single light burns in the office, behind blind-covered front
windows—the only light in the abandoned park. As always

on Friday evenings, McAnally is working late and alone on the company books.

Stealthily I move to the rear of the building, to the shadowed parking area. Only one car is parked there: McAnally's, of course, one I know well. I have seen it every day for four years in the driveway of his house, diagonally across Mayflower Street from my own bachelor dwelling; and I have, in my capacity as insurance broker, written the policy on the vehicle.

I allow myself a small, relaxed smile as I walk some twenty yards distant, to the base of the high cyclone fence that rings the supply yard, and blend into the blackness there. All is progressing just as I have planned; I am confident that there will be no problems of any kind.

This isn't right, the truck

As I wait I concentrate on the visual image of Judith that lingers perpetually in my mind. Her long auburn hair, her gentle green eyes, her high cheekbones and her tiny ears and the miniature dimple in the center of her chin, the smooth sensous lines of her body. Judith smiling, Judith laughing, Judith in all her moods from pensive to gay to kittenish. How often do I dream of her? How often do I long to hold her in the warm silent hours of every night from now until eternity? Not often—always. There is no love greater than mine for her, and it is that love and the fulfillment of that love that is the very purpose of my existence.

"Soon now, Judith," I whisper in the cold silent hour of this night. "Soon . . ."

I do not have to wait long. Habitually precise as always, McAnally leaves the building at nine-thirty. I tense in anticipation, my fingers firm on the gun, as he crosses the darkened parking area. He reaches the car, but I wait until he begins to unlock it before I step out and approach him.

McAnally hears my footfalls and glances up in a jerky way, startled. I stop in front of him.

"Hello, Fred," I say.

Recognition smooths the nervous frown on his face. "Why— hello, Martin. You gave me a jolt, coming out of the darkness like that. What are you doing *here*, of all places?"

"Waiting for you."

"What on earth for?"

"Because I'm going to kill you."

He stares at me incredulously. "What did you say?"

"I'm going to kill you, Fred."

"Hey listen, that's not funny. Are you drunk?"

I take the gun out. "I'm both sober and deadly serious."

An abrupt mixture of fear and anger begins to shine in his eyes. "Martin, for God's sake, put that thing away. What's the matter with you? Why would you even think of killing *me?*"

"For love," I say.

"For what?"

"Love, pure and simple love. You're in the way, Fred; you stand between Judith and me, between our marriage. Does it all become clear now?"

"You—and Judith?"

I smile faintly.

"No!" McAnally says, and shakes his head in disbelief. "No, it's not true. My wife loves me, she's devoted to me. She'd never be a party to cold-blooded murder. . . ."

I am enjoying this; I smile again, enigmatically. "Have you ever wondered about the perfect murder, Fred? Whether or not there is such a thing? Well, I think there is—and in just a little while I'm going to prove it."

"This is . . . insane. You're insane, Martin!"

"Not at all. I'm merely in love. Of course, I do have my practical side as well. There's the fifty-thousand-dollar double-indemnity policy on your life, with my company, and that will take care of Judith's and my needs quite nicely once we're married. After a decent interval of mourning, naturally. We can't have the slightest shadow of suspicion cast on her good name, or on mine."

"You can't do this," McAnally says. "I won't *let* you do it!" And he makes a sudden jump forward, clawing at the gun.

But his fear and his anger destroy all coordination, and I move aside with calm ease and bring the barrel down on the side of his head. He falls moaning to the pavement. I hit him again, sharply; then I finish opening the car door, drag him onto the floor in back, and slip in under the wheel.

There is something wrong with all this

As I drive out of Lake Industrial, I am watchful for one of the night-patrol vehicles; but I see none, I see no one at all. Obvserving the speed limit, I follow the route that McAnally always takes to get home—a route that includes a one-mile stretch through Old Mill Canyon. The canyon road is little used since the construction of a bypassing freeway, but McAnally has long considered it a shortcut to the suburban development where we both live, and drives it invariably.

At the very top of the canyon road is a sharp curve, with a bluff wall on the left and a wide shoulder studded with red guardrail reflectors on the right. Beyond the rail is a sheer two-hundred-foot drop into the canyon below. There are no lights behind me as I take McAnally's car to the crest. From there I can see for perhaps a quarter mile past the curve, and that part of the road is also void of headlights.

I stop the car a hundred feet below the shoulder, hold a long breath. And then I press down hard on the accelerator and twist the wheel until the car is headed straight for the guardrail at the shoulder's edge. While the car is still on the road I brake sharply; the tires burn against the asphalt,

providing the skid marks that will confirm McAnally's death
as a tragic accident.

The truck

I manage to fight the car to a halt a dozen feet from the
guardrail. Then I rub sweat from my forehead, and reverse
to the road again. When I have set the emergency brake I
step out to make certain we are still alone. Once assured, I
pull the still-unconscious McAnally from the rear floor, prop
him behind the wheel, and wedge his foot against the accelerator pedal. The engine roars and the car begins to rock.
I grasp the release lever for the emergency brake, prepare
myself, jerk the brake off, and fling my body out of the
way.

The car hurtles forward. An edge of the open driver's
door slaps against my hip, knocking me down, but I am not
hurt. McAnnally's car crashes into the guardrail, splintering
it, and goes through; it seems to hang in space for a long
moment, amid a shower of woooden fragments, and then
plunges downward. The still darkness is filled with the thun-
derous rending of metal as the car bounces and rolls into
the canyon.

I go to the edge and look over. There is no fire, but I am
able to see the black outline of the wreckage far below. I
say softly, "I'm sorry, Fred. It's not that I hated you, or even
disliked you. It's just that you were in the way."

Then I turn, keeping to shadow along the side of the
deserted road, and begin the long three-mile walk home.

What is it that's so wrong

And late the following morning I stand on the porch of
the sprawling ranch-style home that now belongs only to

Judith, my Judith. I ring the bell, and my chest is constricted with excitement as I wait for her to answer.

Presently there are steps inside, and the door opens, and my love looks out at me. I stroke her with my eyes, stroke her hair and her sensuous body encased now in black widow's weeds, and the love I possess swells inside me until it is almost like physical pain.

"Hello, Judith," I say, and I make my voice grave. "I just heard about Fred, and of course I came right over."

Her grief-swollen mouth trembles. "Thank you," she says. "Thank you, Mr. Martin. It was such a terrible accident, so . . . so *unexpected.* I guess you know how devoted Fred and I were to each other; I feel lost and horribly alone without him."

Inside myself I smile. Poor Judith. She *is* shocked and sorrowed over McAnally's death—though her pain will not last long—for of course she knew nothing of my plans. Nor of my love, despite what I purposely led McAnally to believe; because of him, I could only worship her from afar. Until now. Until tomorrow and tomorrow and tomorrow.

"You're not alone," I say. "I'll always be here, Judith. Always . . ."

The truck!

I know what it is now, I know what is wrong.
None of this has actually happened.
It was planned to happen just this way, a thousand times I envisioned it just this way, it was so vivid in my mind as I rode in the taxi. But something else occurred, something interfered. The truck, the taxi—
There was an accident.
Yes, I remember it now: the taxi rushing through the dark, empty streets, and the truck coming out of nowhere, the truck coming through the red light at the intersection,

and the impact, and the spinning, and the pain. And then—
nothing.

Where am I?

Utter blackness. No pain, no feeling at all. Vague bodiless
sensation of floating, of drifting. Coma? Hospital? No,
something else, somewhere else. Thoughts, the sudden re-
membering, the bodiless drifting

and I am beginning to understand, I am beginning to
realize

that I was killed in that accident.

I'm dead.

Fred McAnally is alive and Alan Martin is dead. . . .

. . . and the door opens, and my love looks out at me. I
stroke her with my eyes, stroke her hair and her sensuous
body encased now in black widow's weeds, and the love I
possess swells inside me until it is almost like physical pain. . . .

But *am* I dead?

Even though I was killed in that accident, am I truly dead?

Increasing awareness now. If I were dead, I would no
longer *be*. There would be no perception, no memories, no
emotions, no vague sensation of drifting. I am alive; the
essence, the intellect, of Alan Martin survives.

Why?

And the answer comes: It is my love for Judith, the depth
and fervor of my love for her. Too strong even for death.
Transcending death. My love lives, therefore I live.

But again, where am I? A state of limbo? Or—

The Netherworld?

Yes. Drifting—spirit drifting. I *am* spirit.

The blackness is beginning to lighten somewhat, slowly,
becoming a soft, swirling gray; and as it does

my awareness continues to increase and I understand with
sudden joy that it will not be long before I am capable of

vision, of corporeality, of mobility through time and space. I will be able to penetrate the mortal world, re-enter it; even in death I will be able

to go to her, to bring my love to my love.

" . . . Judith, I'll always be here. Always . . ."

Oh yes, yes, I will go to her in the night, in the warmth and silence of a night when she is alone. . . .

And all at once—there is no temporality where I exist— I find myself standing in her bedroom, that place where I longed so often and so desperately to be. She is there, alone, wearing a pale blue dressing gown and sitting before her vanity mirror while she brushes her hair. Her face is radiant, smiling, and I know it is Friday night and she is waiting for McAnally. But I accept this, it does not disturb me. Nothing can disturb me now that I am in the presence of my love.

Her voice whispers in the stillness, counting each brush stroke. "Eighty-nine, ninety, ninety-one . . ." But she might be counting the minutes until we are together, and that is how I choose to hear her words. "Ninety-eight, ninety-nine, one hundred . . ."

Reflected in the vanity mirror, her beauty is so flawless that it is as if I am looking at a priceless painting framed eternally for my eyes alone. I no longer have a heart, but if I did it would be beating now like the muted thunder of surf. I no longer have loins, but if I did they would be aflame with the purity of my desire.

"One hundred and nineteen, one hundred and twenty . . ."

The need to be near her, to touch her, is exquisite. But how will she react when she sees me? I mustn't frighten her. And yet I cannot gaze on her any longer from a distance; it would be unbearable. I *must* go to her, I must.

Slowly I cross the room, watching her face in the mirror, preparing gentle words. But as I draw closer the image of myself that I expect to see behind hers does not materialize; there is no face in the mirror but Judith's. Then I am standing close to her, closer than I have ever been before—and still she is alone in the glass.

How is that possible? Is there something I do not yet understand?

"One hundred and forty-eight, one hundred and . . ."

Abruptly she stops counting, holding the brush against the silkiness of her hair. Her smile fades; small frown lines appear on her forehead.

"Judith," I whisper. "Judith."

She frowns with faint unease at the mirror, puts down the brush.

"I'm here, my love."

And I reach out with trembling fingers and touch the warmth and softness of her shoulder.

She shivers, as though it was not I but a sudden chill draft that caressed her. She turns, looks around the bedroom, and painfully I accept the truth: She can't see me, or hear me, or feel the gentle pressure of my hand. Perhaps it is because I am not strong enough yet. And perhaps . . .

Knowledge comes to me then, sharp and certain. Yes, of course: McAnally. He is still alive, he still stands between us—now like a wall erected between our two worlds, blocking out all perception.

McAnally. Always, always, it has been McAnally.

Judith rises from her chair, crosses to the window, and secures the lock. Then she sheds her dressing gown, and the silhouette of her body beneath the thin nightdress she wears fills me with rapture. I watch her shut off the lights, watch her get into bed ad lie with the coverlet pulled up to her chin.

After a time the rhythm of her breathing becomes regular. When I am sure she is asleep I walk to the bed and sit down beside her.

She stirs but does not open her eyes.

With great care I lift the coverlet. This is the moment I have ached for most, this is the moment that makes even my death inconsequential; I would die a thousand times for such a moment as this.

I take her in my arms.

She moans softly, shivers, tries to turn away in her sleep. But I hold her in a tender embrace. "Judith," I whisper in her ear, "it's all right. I'm growing stronger, and when I'm strong enough I'll find another way to kill Fred. A push as he starts down the basement steps, a falling object from the platform in the garage—I'll find a way. I will, I will."

She continues to make moaning sounds, but I hear them now as murmurs of love. I kiss the warm hollow of her throat, and my hand finds her breast, and in ecstasy I lie there with her, waiting. Waiting.

First, for McAnally.

But most of all for that time when my love will come awake and see and hear and feel me at last and forever, lying beside her in the warm silent hours of the night . . .

fISfi nIGfiT
by
JOE R. LANSDALE

The premise of "Fish Night," like the premise of a number of Joe Lansdale's other stories, is unique in macabre fiction. For the ghosts postulated here are not those of human beings, nor of animals, but of fish—extraordinary fish, in an extraordinary locale. Prehistoric creatures of the sea, all sizes and shapes, all the colors of the rainbow, swimming spectrally through a starlit night in a great southwestern desert.

How can that be possible? As the middle-aged protagonist explains to his young companion, "Millions and millions of years ago this desert was a sea bottom. Maybe even the birthplace of man . . . I read that in some science books. And I got to thinking this: If the ghosts of people who have lived can haunt houses, why can't the ghosts of creatures long dead haunt where they once lived, float about in a ghostly sea?"

What happens to these two men, stranded in the desert on "Fish Night," is strange and wonderful indeed . . .

A multi-talented young Texan, Joe R. Lansdale (born 1951) has begun to make a distinctive name for himself in the field of fantasy/

horror. His short stories have appeared in Twilight Zone Magazine, Charles L. *Grant's* Shadows *series, and several other volumes in this series of chrestomathies. He is equally at home in the mystery/ suspense and Western genres; his first novel,* Act of Love, *a chilling suspense tale about a modern Jack the Ripper, was critically acclaimed when it appeared last year, and he will have two Western novels published this year and next. At present he is working on his first macabre novel,* Night of the Goblins.

IT WAS A BLEACHED-BONE AFTERNOON WITH A CLOUDLESS SKY and a monstrous sun. The air trembled like a mass of gelatinous ectoplasm. No wind blew.

Through the swelter came a worn, black Plymouth, coughing and belching white smoke from beneath its hood. It wheezed twice, backfired loudly, died by the side of the road.

The driver got out and went around to the hood. He was a man in the hard winter years of life, with dead brown hair and a heavy belly riding his hips. His shirt was open to the navel, the sleeves rolled up past his elbows. The hair on his chest and arms was gray.

A younger man climbed out on the passenger side, went around front too. Yellow sweat-explosions stained the pits of his white shirt. An unfastened, striped tie was draped over his neck like a pet snake that had died in its sleep.

"Well?" the younger man asked.

The old man said nothing. He opened the hood. A calliope note of steam blew out from the radiator in a white puff, rose to the sky, turned clear.

"Damn," the old man said, and he kicked the bumper of the Plymouth as if he were kicking a foe in the teeth. He got little satisfaction out of the action, just a nasty scuff on his brown wingtip and a jar to his ankle that hurt like hell.

"Well?" the young man repeated.

"Well what? What do you think? Dead as the can opener trade this week. Deader. The radiator's chickenpocked with holes."

"Maybe someone will come by and give us a hand."

"Sure."

"A ride anyway."

"Keep thinking that, college boy."

"Someone is bound to come along," the young man said.

"Maybe. Maybe not. Who else takes these cutoffs? The main highway, that's where everyone is. Not this little no account shortcut." He finished by glaring at the young man.

"I didn't make you take it," the young man snapped. "It was on the map. I told you about it, that's all. You chose it. You're the one that decided to take it. It's not my fault. Besides, who'd have expected the car to die?"

"I did tell you to check the water in the radiator, didn't I? Wasn't that back as far as El Paso?"

"I checked. It had water then. I tell you, it's not my fault. You're the one that's done all the Arizona driving."

"Yeah, yeah," the old man said, as if this were something he didn't want to hear. He turned to look up the highway.

No cars. No trucks. Just heat waves and miles of empty concrete in sight.

They seated themselves on the hot ground with their backs to the car. That way it provided some shade—but not much. They sipped on a jug of lukewarm water from the Plymouth and spoke little until the sun fell down. By then they had both mellowed a bit. The heat had vacated the sands and the desert chill had settled in. Where the warmth had made the pair snappy, the cold drew them together.

The old man buttoned his shirt and rolled down his sleeves

while the young man rummaged a sweater out of the backseat. He put the sweater on, sat back down. "I'm sorry about this," he said suddenly.

"Wasn't your fault. Wasn't anyone's fault. I just get to yelling sometime, taking out the can-opener trade on everything but the can openers and myself. The days of the door-to-door salesman are gone, son."

"And I thought I was going to have an easy summer job," the young man said.

The old man laughed. "Bet you did. They talk a good line, don't they?"

"I'll say!"

"Make it sound like found money, but there ain't no found money, boy. Ain't nothing simple in this world. The company is the only one ever makes any money. We just get tireder and older with more holes in our shoes. If I had any sense I'd have quit years ago. All you got to make is this summer—"

"Maybe not that long."

"Well, this is all I know. Just town after town, motel after motel, house after house, looking at people through screen wire while they shake their heads No. Even the cockroaches at the sleazy motels begin to look like little fellows you've seen before, like maybe they're door-to-door peddlers that have to rent rooms too."

The young man chuckled. "You might have something there."

They sat quietly for a moment, welded in silence. Night had full grip on the desert now. A mammoth gold moon and billions of stars cast a whitish glow from eons away.

The wind picked up. The sand shifted, found new places to lie down. The undulations of it, slow and easy, were reminiscent of the midnight sea. The young man, who had crossed the Atlantic by ship once, said as much.

"The sea?" the old man replied. "Yes, yes, exactly like

that. I was thinking the same. That's part of the reason it bothers me. Part of why I was stirred up this afternoon. Wasn't just the heat doing it. There are memories of mine out here," he nodded at the desert, "and they're visiting me again."

The young man made a face. "I don't understand."

"You wouldn't. You shouldn't. You'd think I'm crazy."

"I already think you're crazy. So tell me."

The old man smiled. "All right, but don't you laugh."

"I won't."

A moment of silence moved in between them. Finally the old man said, "It's fish night, boy. Tonight's the full moon and this is the right part of the desert if memory serves me, and the feel is right—I mean, doesn't the night feel like it's made up of some soft fabric, that it's different from other nights, that it's like being inside a big dark bag, the sides sprinkled with glitter, a spotlight at the top, at the open mouth, to serve as a moon?"

"You lost me."

The old man sighed. "But it feels different. Right? You can feel it too, can't you?"

"I suppose. Sort of thought it was just the desert air. I've never camped out in the desert before, and I guess it is different."

"Different, all right. You see, this is the road I got stranded on twenty years back. I didn't know it at first, least not consciously. But down deep in my gut I must have known all along I was taking this road, tempting fate, offering it, as the football people say, an instant replay."

"I still don't understand about fish night. What do you mean, you were here before?"

"Not this exact spot, somewhere along in here. This was even less of a road back then than it is now. The Navajos were about the only ones who traveled it. My car conked out, like this one today, and I started walking instead of waiting. As I walked the fish came out. Swimming along in the starlight pretty as you please. Lots of them. All the colors of the rainbow. Small ones, big ones, thick ones, thin ones. Swam right up to me . . . *right through me!* Fish just as far as you could see. High up and low down to the ground.

"Hold on, boy. Don't start looking at me like that. Listen: You're a college boy, you know something about these things. I mean, about what was here before we were, before we crawled out of the sea and changed enough to call ourselves men. Weren't we once just slimy things, brothers to the things that swim?"

"I guess, but—"

"Millions and millions of years ago this desert was a sea bottom. Maybe even the birthplace of man. Who knows? I read that in some science books. And I got to thinking this: If the ghosts of people who have lived can haunt houses, why can't the ghosts of creatures long dead haunt where they once lived, float about in a ghostly sea?"

"Fish with a soul?"

"Don't go small-mind on me, boy. Look here: Some of the Indians I've talked to up North tell me about a thing they call the manitou. That's a spirit. They believe everything has one. Rocks, trees, you name it. Even if the rock wears to dust or the tree gets cut to lumber, the manitou of it is still around."

"Then why can't you see these fish all the time?"

"Why can't we see ghosts all the time? Why do some of us never see them? Time's not right, that's why. It's a precious situation, and I figure it's like some fancy time lock—like the banks use. The lock clicks open at the bank, and there's the money. Here it ticks open and we get the fish of a world long gone."

"Well, it's something to think about," the young man managed.

The old man grinned at him. "I don't blame you for

thinking what you're thinking. But this happened to me twenty years ago and I've never forgotten it. I saw those fish for a good hour before they disappeared. A Navajo came along in an old pickup right after and I bummed a ride into town with him. I told him what I'd seen. He just looked at me and grunted. But I could tell he knew what I was talking about. He'd seen it too, and probably not for the first time.

"I've heard that Navajos don't eat fish for some reason or another, and I bet it's the fish in the desert that keep them from it. Maybe they hold them sacred. And why not? It was like being in the presence of the Creator; like crawling back inside your mother and being unborn again, just kicking around in the liquids with no cares in the world."

"I don't know. That sounds sort of . . ."

"Fishy?" The old man laughed. "It does, it does. So this Navajo drove me to town. Next day I got my car fixed and went on. I've never taken that cutoff again—until today, and I think that was more than accident. My subconscious was driving me. That night scared me, boy, and I don't mind admitting it. But it was wonderful too, and I've never been able to get it out of my mind."

The young man didn't know what to say.

The old man looked at him and smiled. "I don't blame you," he said. "Not even a little bit. Maybe I am crazy."

They sat awhile longer with the desert night, and the old man took his false teeth out and poured some of the warm water on them to clean them of coffee and cigarette residue.

"I hope we don't need that water," the young man said.

"You're right. Stupid of me! We'll sleep awhile, start walking before daylight. It's not too far to the next town. Ten miles at best." He put his teeth back in. "We'll be just fine."

The young man nodded.

No fish came. They did not discuss it. They crawled inside

the car, the young man in the front seat, the old man in the back. They used their spare clothes to bundle under, to pad out the cold fingers of the night.

Near midnight the old man came awake suddenly and lay with his hands behind his head and looked up and out the window opposite him, studied the crisp desert sky.

And a fish swam by.

Long and lean and speckled with all the colors of the world, flicking its tail as if in good-bye. Then it was gone.

The old man sat up. Outside, all about, were the fish— all sizes, colors, and shapes.

"Hey, boy, wake up!"

The younger man moaned.

"Wake up!"

The young man, who had been resting face down on his arms, rolled over. "What's the matter? Time to go?"

"The fish."

"Not again."

"Look!"

The young man sat up. His mouth fell open. His eyes bloated. Around and around the car, faster and faster in whirls of dark color, swam all manner of fish.

"Well, I'll be . . . *How?*"

"I told you, I told you."

The old man reached for the door handle, but before he could pull it a fish swam lazily through the back window glass, swirled about the car, once, twice, passed through the old man's chest, whipped up and went out through the roof.

The old man cackled, jerked open the door. He bounced around beside the road. Leaped up to swat his hands through the spectral fish. "Like soap bubbles," he said. "No. Like smoke!"

The young man, his mouth still agape, opened his door and got out. Even high up he could see the fish. Strange fish, like nothing he'd ever seen pictures of or imagined. They flitted and skirted about like flashes of light.

As he looked up, he saw, nearing the moon, a big dark cloud. The only cloud in the sky. That cloud tied him to reality suddenly, and he thanked the heavens for it. Normal things still happened. The whole world had not gone insane.

After a moment the old man quit hopping among the fish and came out to lean on the car and hold his hand to his fluttering chest.

"Feel it, boy? Feel the presence of the sea? Doesn't it feel like the beating of your own mother's heart while you float inside the womb?"

And the younger man had to admit that he felt it, that inner rolling rhythm that is the tide of life and the pulsating heart of the sea.

"How?" the young man said. "Why?"

"The time lock, boy. The locks clicked open and the fish are free. Fish from a time before man was man. Before civilization started weighing us down. I know it's true. The truth's been in me all the time. It's in us all."

"It's like time travel," the young man said. "From the past to the future, they've come all that way."

"Yes, yes, that's it . . . Why, if they can come to our world, why can't we go to theirs? Release that spirit inside of us, tune into their time?"

"Now wait a minute . . ."

"My God, that's it! They're pure, boy, pure. Clean and free of civilization's trappings. That must be it! They're pure and we're not. We're weighted down with technology. These clothes. That car."

The old man started removing his clothes.

"Hey!" the young man said. "You'll freeze."

"If you're pure, if you're completely pure," the old man mumbled, "that's it . . . yeah, that's the key."

"You've gone crazy."

"I won't look at the car," the old man yelled, running across the sand, trailing the last of his clothes behind him. He bounced about the desert like a jackrabbit. "God, God, nothing is happening, nothing," he moaned. "This isn't my world. I'm of that world. I want to float free in the belly of the sea, away from can openers and cars and—"

The young man called the old man's name. The old man did not seem to hear.

"I want to leave here!" the old man yelled. Suddenly he was springing about again. "The teeth!" he yelled. "It's the teeth. Dentist, science, foo!" He punched a hand into his mouth, plucked the teeth free, tossed them over his shoulder.

Even as the teeth fell the old man rose. He began to stroke. To swim up and up and up, moving like a pale pink seal among the fish.

In the light of the moon the young man could see the pooched jaws of the old man, holding the last of the future's air. Up went the old man, up, up, up, swimming strong in the long-lost waters of a time gone by.

The young man began to strip off his own clothes. Maybe he could nab him, pull him down, put the clothes on him. Something . . . God, something. . . . But, what if *he* couldn't come back? And there were the fillings in his teeth, the metal rod in his back from a motorcycle accident. No, unlike the old man, this was his world and he was tied to it. There was nothing he could do.

A great shadow weaved in front of the moon, made a wriggling slat of darkness that caused the young man to let go of his shirt buttons and look up.

A black rocket of a shape moved through the invisible sea: a shark, the granddaddy of all sharks, the seed for all of man's fears of the deeps.

And it caught the old man in its mouth, began swimming upward toward the golden light of the moon. The old man dangled from the creature's mouth like a ragged rat from a house cat's jaws. Blood blossomed out of him, coiled darkly in the invisible sea.

The young man trembled. "Oh God," he said once.

Then along came that thick dark cloud, rolling across the face of the moon.

Momentary darkness.

And when the cloud passed there was light once again, and an empty sky.

No fish.

No shark.

And no old man.

Just the night, the moon and the stars.

DUST TO DUST
by
MARCIA MULLER

We know little about the realm of the supernatural, of course, and understand even less. We do know that it can intrude on the natural world, suddenly and without warning, and affect the lives of ordinary people; but the reasons why, even the exact nature of its intrusion, are sometimes inexplicable. And the results—

The results can be horrifying.

Take the strange series of events in "Dust to Dust," for example. The farthest thing from the narrator's mind when she embarks on the renovation of an old Victorian house in Phoenix is an encounter with the supernatural. But the workman she hires uncovers a walled-up nook, and the mummified body of a bird, under the staircase on the ground floor. And the photographs she subsequently takes, for a book on old houses she's preparing, reveal spectral images that may or may not be caused by the omnipresent dust. The horror, then, is just around the corner. Or more appropriately, waiting under the stairs . . .

Born in Detroit during World War II, Marcia Muller is a freelance writer and editorial consultant of considerable skill. She

*has published nonfiction articles, juvenile and adult stories, and
two mystery novels,* Edwin of the Iron Shoes *(1977) and* Ask
the Cards a Question *(1982), both of which feature a well-drawn
female private investigator named Sharon McCone. She lives in
San Francisco, where she is at work on a new McCone novel, as
well as a procedural mystery set in the Philippines.*

THE DUST WAS PARTICULARLY BAD ON MONDAY, JULY SIXTH.
It rose from the second floor where the demolition was
going on and hung in the dry air of the photo lab. The
trouble was, it didn't stay suspended. It settled on the formica
counter tops, in the stainless-steel sink, on the plastic I'd
covered the enlarger with. And worst of all, it settled on the
negatives drying in the supposedly airtight cabinet.

The second time I checked the negatives I gave up. They'd
have to be soaked for hours to get the dust out of the emulsion.
And when I rehung them they'd only be coated with the
stuff again.

I turned off the orange safelight and went into the studio.
A thick film of powder covered everything there too. I'd
had the foresight to put my cameras away, but somehow
the dust crept into the cupboards, through the leather cases
and onto the lenses themselves. The restoration project was
turning into a nightmare, and it had barely begun.

I crossed the studio to the Victorian's big front windows.
The city of Phoenix sprawled before me, skyscrapers shimmering in the heat. Camelback Mountain rose out of the
flat land to the right, and the oasis of Encanto Park beckoned
at the left. I could drive over there and sit under a tree by
the water. I could rent a paddlewheel boat. Anything to
escape the dry grit-laden heat.

But I had to work on the photos for the book.

And I couldn't work on them because I couldn't get the negatives to come out clear.

I leaned my forehead against the window frame, biting back my frustration.

"Jane!" My name echoed faintly from below. "Jane! Come down here!"

It was Roy, the workman I'd hired to demolish the rabbit warren of cubicles that had been constructed when the Victorian was turned into a rooming house in the thirties. The last time he'd shouted for me like that was because he'd discovered a stained-glass window preserved intact between two false walls. My spirits lifting, I hurried down the winding stairs.

The second floor was a wasteland heaped with debris. Walls leaned at crazy angles. Piles of smashed plaster blocked the hall. Rough beams and lath were exposed. The air was even worse down there—full of powder which caught in my nostrils and covered my clothing whenever I brushed against anything.

I called back to Roy, but his answering shout came from further below, in the front hall.

I descended the stairs into the gloom, keeping to the wall side because the bannister was missing. Roy stood, crowbar in hand, at the rear of the stairway. He was a tall, thin man with a pockmarked face and curly black hair, a drifter who had wandered into town willing to work cheap so long as no questions were asked about his past. Roy, along with his mongrel dog, now lived in his truck in my driveway. In spite of his odd appearance and stealthy comings and goings, I felt safer having him around while living in a half-demolished house.

Now he pushed up the goggles he wore to keep the plaster out of his eyes and waved the crowbar toward the stairs.

"Jane, I've really found something this time." His voice

trembled. Roy had a genuine enthusiasm for old houses, and this house in particular.

I hurried down the hall and looked under the stairs. The plaster-and-lath had been partially ripped off and tossed onto the floor. Behind it, I could see only darkness. The odor of dry rot wafted out of the opening.

Dammit, now there was debris in the downstairs hall too. "I thought I told you to finish the second floor before you started here."

"But take a look."

"I am. I see a mess."

"No, here. Take the flashlight. Look."

I took it and shone it through the hole. It illuminated gold-patterned wallpaper and wood paneling. My irritation vanished. "What is it, do you suppose?"

"I think it's what they call a 'cozy.' A place where they hung coats and ladies left their outside boots when they came calling." He shouldered past me. "Let's get a better look."

I backed off and watched as he tugged at the wall with the crowbar, the muscles in his back and arms straining. In minutes, he had ripped a larger section off. It crashed to the floor and when the dust cleared I shone the light once more.

It was a paneled nook with a bench and ornate brass hooks on the wall. "I think you're right—it's a cozy."

Roy attacked the wall once more and soon the opening was clear. He stepped inside, the leg of his jeans catching on a nail. "It's big enough for three people." His voice echoed in the empty space.

"Why do you think they sealed it up?" I asked.

"Fire regulations, when they converted to a rooming house. They . . . what's this?"

I leaned forward.

Roy turned, his hand outstretched. I looked at the object resting on his palm and recoiled.

"God!"

"Take it easy." He stepped out of the cozy. "It's only a dead bird."

It was small, probably a sparrow, and like the stained-glass window Roy had found the past week, perfectly preserved.

"Ugh!" I said. "How did it get in there?"

Roy stared at the small body in fascination. "It's probably been there since the wall was constructed. Died of hunger, or lack of air."

I shivered. "But it's not rotted."

"In this dry climate? It's like mummification. You could preserve a body for decades."

"Put it down. It's probably diseased."

He shrugged. "I doubt it." But he stepped back into the cozy and placed it on the bench. Then he motioned for the flashlight. "The wallpaper's in good shape. And the wood looks like golden oak. And . . . hello."

"Now what?"

He bent over and picked something up. "It's a comb, a mother-of-pearl comb like ladies wore in their hair." He held it out. The comb had long teeth to sweep up heavy tresses on a woman's head.

"This place never ceases to amaze me." I took it and brushed off the plaster dust. Plaster . . . "Roy, this wall couldn't have been put up in the thirties."

"Well the building permit shows the house was converted then."

"But the rest of the false walls are fireproof sheetrock, like regulations required. This one is plaster-and-lath. This cozy has been sealed off longer than that. Maybe since ladies wore this kind of comb."

"Maybe." His eyes lit up. "We've found an eighty-year-old bird mummy."

"I guess so." The comb fascinated me, as the bird had Roy. I stared at it.

"You should get shots of this for your book," Roy said.

"What?"

"Your book."

I shook my head, disoriented. Of course—the book. It was defraying the cost of the renovation, a photo essay on restoring one of Phoenix's grand old ladies.

"You haven't forgotten the book?" Roy's tone was mocking.

I shook my head again. "Roy, why did you break down this wall? When I told you to finish upstairs first?"

"Look, if you're pissed off about the mess . . ."

"No, I'm curious. Why?"

Now he looked confused. "I . . ."

"Yes?"

"I don't know."

"Don't know?"

He frowned, his pockmarked face twisting in concentration. "I really *don't* know. I had gone to the kitchen for a beer and I came through here and . . . I don't know."

I watched him thoughtfully, clutching the mother-of-pearl comb. "Okay," I finally said, "just don't start on a new area again without checking with me."

"Sorry. I'll clean up this mess."

"Not yet. Let me get some photos first." Still holding the comb, I went up to the studio to get a camera.

In the week that followed, Roy attacked the second floor with a vengeance and it began to take on its original floorplan. He made other discoveries—nothing as spectacular as the cozy, but interesting—old newspapers, coffee cans of a brand not sold in decades, a dirty pair of baby booties. I photographed each faithfully and assured my publisher that the work was going well.

It wasn't, though. As Roy worked, the dust increased and my frustration with the book project—not to mention the commercial jobs that were my bread and butter—deepened. The house, fortunately, was paid for, purchased with a bequest from my aunt, the only member of my family who didn't think it dreadful for a girl from Fairmont, West Virginia, to run off and become a photographer in a big western city. The money from the book, however, was what would make the house habitable, and the first part of the advance had already been eaten up. The only way I was going to squeeze more cash out of the publisher was to show him some progess, and so far I had made none of that.

Friday morning I told Roy to take the day off. Maybe I could get some work done if he wasn't raising clouds of dust. I spent the morning in the lab developing the rolls I'd shot that week, then went into the studio and looked over what prints I had ready to show to the publisher.

The exterior shots, taken before the demolition had begun, were fine. They showed a three-story structure with square bay windows and rough peeling paint. The fanlight over the front door had been broken and replaced with plywood, and much of the gingerbread trim was missing. All in all, she was a bedraggled old lady, but she would again be beautiful—if I could finish the damned book.

The early interior shots were not bad either. In fact, they evoked a nice sense of gloomy neglect. And the renovation of this floor, the attic, into studio and lab was well documented. It was with the second floor that my problems began.

At first the dust had been slight, and I hadn't noticed it on the negatives. As a result the prints were marred with white specks. In a couple of cases the dust had scratched the negatives while I'd handled them and the fine lines showed up in the pictures. Touching them up would be painstaking work but it could be done.

But now the dust had become more active, taken over. I was forced to soak and resoak the negatives. A few rolls of film had proven unsalvageable after repeated soakings. And, in losing them, I was losing documentation of a very important part of the renovation.

I went to the window and looked down at the driveway where Roy was sunning himself on the grass beside his truck. The mongrel dog lay next to a tire in the shade of the vehicle. Roy reached under there for one of his everpresent beers, swigged at it and set it back down.

How, I wondered, did he stand the heat? He took to it like a native, seemingly oblivious to the sun's glare. But then, maybe Roy *was* a native of the Sun Belt. What did I know of him, really?

Only that he was a tireless worker and his knowledge of old houses was invaluable to me. He unerringly sensed which were the original walls and which were false, what should be torn down and what should remain. He could tell whether a fixture was the real thing or merely a good copy. I could not have managed without him.

I shrugged off thoughts of my handyman and lifted my hair from my shoulders. It was wheat colored, heavy and, right now, uncomfortable. I pulled it on top of my head, looked around and spotted the mother-of-pearl comb we'd found in the cozy. It was small, designed to be worn as half of a pair on one side of the head. I secured the hair on my left with it, then pinned up the right side with one of the clips I used to hang negatives. Then I went into the darkroom.

The negatives were dry. I took one strip out of the cabinet and held it to the light. It seemed relatively clear. Perhaps, as long as the house wasn't disturbed, the dust ceased its silent takeover. I removed the other strips. Dammit, some were still spotty, especially those of the cozy and the objects we'd discovered in it. Those could be reshot, however. I decided to go ahead and make contact prints of the lot.

I cut the negatives into strips of six frames each, then inserted them in plastic holders. Shutting the door and turning on the safelight, I removed photographic paper from the small refrigerator, placed it and the negative holders under glass in the enlarger, and set my timer. Nine seconds at f/8 would do nicely.

When the first sheet of paper was exposed, I slipped it into the developer tray and watched, fascinated as I had been since the first time I'd done this, for the images to emerge. Yes, nine seconds had been right. I went to the enlarger and exposed the other negatives.

I moved the contact sheets along, developer to stop bath to fixer, then put them into the washing tray. Now I could open the door to the darkroom and let some air in. Even though Roy had insulated up here, it was still hot and close when I was working in the lab. I pinned my hair more securely on my head and took the contact sheets to the print dryer.

I scanned the sheets eagerly as they came off the roller. Most of the negatives had printed clearly and some of the shots were quite good. I should be able to assemble a decent selection for my editor with very little trouble. Relieved, I reached for the final sheet.

There were the pictures I had shot the day we'd discovered the cozy. They were different from the others. And different from past dust-damaged rolls. I picked up my magnifying loupe and took the sheet out into the light.

Somehow the dust had gotten to this set of negatives. Rather than leaving speckles, though, it had drifted like a sandstorm. It clustered in iridescent patches, as if an object had caught the light in a strange way. The effect was eerie; perhaps I could put it to use.

I circled the oddest-looking frames and went back into the darkroom, shutting the door securely. I selected the negative that corresponded to one circled on the sheet, routinely sprayed it with canned air for surface dirt and inserted it into the holder of the enlarger. Adjusting the height, I shone the light down through the negative, positioning the image within the paper guides.

Yes, I had something extremely odd here.

Quickly I snapped off the light, set the timer and slipped a piece of unexposed paper into the guides. The light came on again, the timer whirred and then all was silent and dark. I slid the paper into the developer tray and waited.

The image was of the cozy with the bird mummy resting on the bench. That would have been good enough, but the effect of the dust made it spectacular. Above the dead bird rose a white-gray shape, a second bird in flight, spiraling upward.

Like a ghost. The ghost of a trapped bird, finally freed.

I shivered.

Could I use something like this in the book? It was perfect. But what if my editor asked how I'd done it? Photography was not only art but science. You strove for images that evoked certain emotions. But you had dammed well better know how you got those images.

Don't worry about that now, I told myself. See what else is here.

I replaced the bird negative with another one and exposed it. The image emerged slowly in the developing tray: first the carved arch of the cozy, then the plaster-and-lath heaped on the floor, finally the shimmering figure of a man.

I leaned over the tray. Roy? A double exposure perhaps? It looked like Roy, yet it didn't. And I hadn't taken any pictures of him anyway. No, this was another effect created by the dust, a mere outline of a tall man in what appeared to be an old-fashioned frock coat.

The ghost of a man? That was silly. I didn't believe in such things. Not in *my* house.

Still, the photos had a wonderful eeriness. I could include them in the book, as a novelty chapter. I could write a little explanation about the dust.

And while on the subject of dust, wasn't it rising again? Had Roy begun work, even though I'd told him not to?

I crossed the studio to the window and looked down. No, he was still there by the truck, although he was now dappled by the shade of a nearby tree. The sun had moved; it was getting on toward midafternoon.

Back in the darkroom I continued to print from the dust-damaged group of negatives. Maybe I was becoming fanciful, or maybe the chemicals were getting to me after being cooped up in here all day, but I was seeing stranger and stranger images. One looked like a woman in a long, full-skirted dress, standing in the entrance to the cozy. In another the man was reaching out—maybe trying to catch the bird that had invaded his home?

Was it his home? Who were these people? What were they doing in my negatives?

As I worked the heat increased. I became aware of the dust which, with or without Roy's help, had again taken up its stealthy activity. It had a life all its own, as demonstrated by these photos. I began to worry that it would damage the prints before I could put them on the dryer.

The gritty air became suffocating. The clip that held my hair on the right side came loose and a lock hung hot and heavy against my neck. I put one last print on the dryer and went into the studio.

Dust lay on every surface again. What had caused it to rise? I went to the window and looked down. Roy was sitting on the bed of the truck with the mongrel, drinking another beer. Well, if he hadn't done anything, I was truly stumped.

Was I going to be plagued by dust throughout the restoration, whether work was going on or not?

I began to pace the studio, repinning my hair and securing the mother-of-pearl comb as I went. The eerie images had me more disturbed than I was willing to admit. And this dust . . . dammit, this *dust!*

Anger flaring, I headed down the stairs. I'd get to the bottom of this. There had to be a perfectly natural cause, and if I had to turn the house upside down I'd find it.

The air on the second floor was choking, but the dust seemed to rise from the first. I charged down the next flight of stairs, unheedful for the first time since I'd lived here of the missing bannister. The dust seemed thickest by the cozy. Maybe opening the wall had created a draft. I hurried back there.

A current of air, cooler than that in the hall, emanated from the cozy. I stepped inside and felt around with my hand. It came from a crack in the bench. A crack? I knelt to examine it. No, it wasn't a crack. It looked like the seat of the bench was designed to be lifted. Of course it was— there were hidden hinges which we'd missed when we first discovered it.

I grasped the edge of the bench and pulled. It was stuck. I tugged harder. Still it didn't give. Feeling along the seat, I found the nails that held it shut.

This called for Roy's strength. I went to the front door and called him. "Bring your crowbar. We're about to make another discovery."

He stood up in the bed of the truck and rummaged through his tools, then came toward me, crowbar in hand. "What now?"

"The cozy. That bench in there has a seat that raises. Some sort of woodbox, maybe."

Roy stopped inside the front door. "Now that you mention

it, I think you're right. It's not a woodbox, though. In the old days, ladies would change into house shoes from outdoor shoes when they came calling. The bench was to store them in."

"Well, it's going to be my woodbox. And I think it's what's making the dust move around so much. There's a draft coming from it." I led him back to the cozy. "How come you know so much about old houses anyway?"

He shrugged. "When you've torn up as many as I have, you learn fast. I've always had an affinity for Victorians. What do you want me to do here?"

"It's nailed shut. Pry it open."

"I might wreck the wood."

"Pry gently."

"I'll try."

I stepped back and let him at the bench. He worked carefully, loosening each nail with the point of the bar. It seemed to take a long time. Finally he turned.

"There. All the nails are out."

"Then open it."

"No, it's your discovery. You do it." He stepped back.

The draft was stronger now. I went up to the bench, then hesitated.

"Go on," Roy said. His voice shook with excitement.

My palms were sweaty. Grit stuck to them. I reached out and lifted the seat.

My sight was blurred by a duststorm like those on the negatives. Then it cleared. I leaned forward. Recoiled. A scream rose in my throat, but it came out a croak.

It was the lady of my photographs.

She lay on her back inside the bench. She wore a long, full-skirted dress of some beaded material. Her hands were crossed on her breasts. Like the bird mummy, she was perfectly preserved—even to the heavy wheat-colered hair, with the mother-of-pearl comb holding it up on the left side.

I put my hand to *my* wheat-colored hair. To *my* mother-of-pearl comb. Then, shaken, I turned to Roy.

He had raised the arm that held the crowbar—just like the man had had his hand raised in the last print, the one I'd forgotten to remove from the dryer. Roy's work shirt billowed out, resembling an old-fashioned frock coat. The look in his eyes was eerie.

And the dust was rising again . . .

CHAINED
by
BARRY N. MALZBERG

The spectral narrator of this delightful change of pace is none other than the ghost of Hamlet's father. The plot is . . . well, it defies synopsis; it has to be read to be properly savored. All that can be said is that the author's tongue was firmly in his cheek when he wrote it, and that it's quite funny in a macabre sort of way.

Shakespeare, one suspects, would have approved.

Barry N. Malzberg (born 1939) is one of those writers whose work engenders controversy. Readers, it seems, either love it or hate it; few have an indifferent reaction. But there can be little doubt that his talent is a special one, and that he has produced any number of stories and novels of power and literary merit. His credits include some eighty novels (four in collaboration with the editor of this chrestomathy), more than 250 short stories and essays, and the coeditorship of a dozen anthologies. His most recent books are The Arbor House Treasury of Mystery & Suspense, *coedited with Bill Pronzini and Martin H. Greenberg, a science fiction novel,* Cross of Fire, *and a deeply felt and much praised (and damned)*

commentary on the science fiction genre, Engines of the Night.
He makes his home in New Jersey.

SO FINALLY HE COMES, THE YOUNG FOOL, AND I LEAN FROM
the parapet and tell him everything. The poison in the ears.
The treachery. The lies. The huddling in incestuous bed
with Gertrude and the degree of corruption. The young
fool is shocked as well he should be and cries that revenge
will be terrible and swift. He departs with promises but I
have no hope. His record has always been high in potential,
low in performance. Sometimes I wondered if he could be
my issue and considering the evidence of later events perhaps
he was not. Gertrude was never to be trusted.

Nonetheless, I am granted no other alternative so I wait.
I wait and I wait as he waffles around, prays, flagellates
himself, mumbles about the possibility of sin, flirts with that
teasing, worthless bitch, Ophelia, who has no more sensibility
than a swan. Claudius continues to prosper. He wallows in
his office. He takes swift measure of Gertrude in incestuous
bed and preaches saintly office outside. It is all too much
to bear and when Hamlet desists from slaying him in the
corridor at prayer I feel my patience snap. It is not easy
existing in this difficult condition and there will be no peace,
absolutely no peace at all as long as these affairs continue.
Grumbling, furious, I drag myself to Gertrude's chambers
while he is berating her and brace him. His eyes become
round, shiny with disbelief but resolve fills his bearing. Responding to rustling behind the arras he draws his sword
and runs it through the curtain, disposing of that prating,
eavesdropping old fool, Polonius, father of the frivolous
bitch. His consternation is enormous but as nothing to mine.

It is at that precise moment—and not earlier, I want to

make it quite clear, not an instant earlier—that I finally lose all fatherly patience and resolve to take matters to a conclusion.

Claudius and I never got along. It was not only the matter of the succession, it was the corruption within him which I perceived from the first, the small cruelties, the weak, descending humiliation of a man who knew all his life that his older brother was the king not only in fact but spirit. He would spy on servants in the castle, set them at one another through small thefts, crush frogs in the moat, steal the jester's cap and bells; past all of these indignities, armored by my certainty and contempt I swept. Gertrude fell in love with me at once; she never paid any attention to Claudius whatsoever until, for reasons of state, I was distracted from our alliance and gave Claudius the opportunity to insinuate himself. I am sure of this. Still, with all of his vices and the deadly indications of his character I never realized until the moment that the warm fluid dripped deep into my ear, sickening me and causing me to shriek with pain so quickly terminated, I never realized until that moment how he hated me; I thought that the cruelties came from envy, the envy from admiration.

But when he poisoned me, sending me into this gray, chained Denmark of souls tormented and unavenged, I became quite angry and resolved to set the situation to right; the time was out of joint, as I reminded that snivelling Prince, and the obligation to correct it fell upon him.

Of course I should have looked more closely at Gertrude. If there is one quality which the unavenged netherworld grants it is ample time for recrimination and I should have known that the woman could never be trusted. Silly, frivolous bitches like Ophelia wear their hearts on their sleeves but Gertrude has not achieved her station without the exercise of cunning; it is possible that her relationship with Claudius preceded my murder. In fact it is possible that she put him up to it, that she gave him motive. "Just a little poison and I can be completely yours; you can be my little bloat king," she might have murmured to him. This state of passage brings the most terrible thoughts and suggestions; never have I hated these people as I hate them now. Murder unavenged leaves one in these endless corridors stalking, stalking, one does not really know where to turn, to whom to appeal, what to do to get *out* of this terrible state; I would never have turned to that hopeless conundrum I called my son if it had not been out of despair; if I had had the means I would have run Claudius through myself: why would I pace the battlements shouting in the wind for assistance if I were capable of anything on my own other than pleadings and prayer?

I was a just, a wise, a compassionate king; my wife was a slut, my son a disaster, my brother a traitor, nonetheless I brought to this domain a mild and sacrosanct order; it was only in this latter stage that I was driven to such extreme and destructive perceptions; to die and not be dead is—how can I put this?—extremely *embittering*. Without the Prince's task for evasion, flights of rhetoric, cheap, distracting and easily deterred lust I am left to confront, ah endlessly, that doomed and chained specter: myself.

So I present myself to Rosencrantz and Guildenstern, indistinguishable, jolly mercenaries with faces like smooth partitions to shield them from all reason. "I know who you are!" one of them says—I cannot tell them apart—and clutches the other. "We have heard all the reports."

"Enough of that," I say. "Throw him overboard. Then hasten back to Denmark and say that he was murdered by Polonius's legions. This will most distress Claudius and he will have no suspicions when you ask for a private conference to grant further important information. Get him alone in

quarters and *I* will run him through." Strictly speaking this
is a lie of course. I am blocked from direct action by the
conditions of the curse. Nonetheless it will at least mark a
beginning, some action at last, and it will keep me busy. The
paralysis of the Prince has leached into me. "I will pay you
well for your services," I say. "After all I am still a king. I
still have the court."

They stare at me with their impermeable faces. "You are
a ghost," one of them says. "How can you pay us?"

"I have grand mystical powers. Trust me."

"He is our schoolfellow," one points out thoughtfully. "We
owe him bonds of loyalty."

"He intends to kill you," I point out. "The orders are
already planted in your luggage."

"What an extremely treacherous court this must be."

"Oh, I can accede to that," I agree. "I can certainly agree
to that."

Their cooperation is gained—they are a submissive pair,
eager to please, with a deep faith in ghosts—but it does not
work out nonetheless; the Prince gets wind of some treachery
and speeds off the boat. Meanwhile the bumblers cannot
locate the damning orders in their own luggage. The situation
is hopelessly scrambled and upon our separate return to
the court I find out that Ophelia has further complicated
matters by drowning herself. Everyone seems to be done
away with in this tragic legend except the real culprit. At
chambers I confront the Prince who is drawing on his gloves,
adjusting his sword, mumbling about business which must
be swiftly attended to. "Oh," he says, looking at me with
dim and distracted countenance, "it's you again. That was
a really splendid production. You couldn't have possibly
done it better; I only wish that it had had better outcome.
Have you come for your purse? I'm sure that was settled."

I realize that in the dim light and because of his preoccupation he takes me for the Player King. My chains are not highly visible. "Yes, we have been paid," I say. "And the king has confessed all in your absence. He pleads for release."

"Then he shall have it." Hamlet looks at me shrewdly. "Your accent is different," he says. "Are you possibly an imposter?"

"Nothing is different," I say, "and everything is different. But only you can bring this to an end."

"I will not be intimidated," Hamlet says. His expression becomes sullen. "Get out of here before I run you through."

"You won't run anyone through. Nothing ever happens in your world until someone throws herself into a pond."

"Blackguard," he says. He draws his sword. "I will not accept that."

I laugh in his face and desert, leaving him there mumbling. The better part of apparition is disassembly through desire although there is, of course, always the pain.

I withdraw, sulkily, to observe subsequent events. I know that nothing can happen and yet I cannot abandon the prospect of hope. Anything is preferable to stumbling and clanking on the parapet. Amazingly many events do occur. Gertrude is poisoned. Claudius is run through. Hamlet himself, in consternation at his burst of activity, opens himself to a palpable hit. At the end, most astonishingly, Fortinbras blesses them all. I know better but offer no comment. Sometimes it is better to cultivate a posture of diffidence. Besides, I know now that it is only a brief matter of time until I am released from my chains.

Claudius joins me on the towers, puts an arm around me confidentially. "Not so soon, you fool," he says. "It isn't over yet." Gertrude, around a corner, winks. "Remember the three witches?" he says. "Remember Banquo's ghost? Now we'll have some real fun."

"Fun?" I say. "Real fun?"

Gertrude sweeps against me regally, her own chains clank-ing. "Absolutely," she says. "Just as soon as Lear gets on the heath, we can kick the hell out of him."

"We can make Caliban squirm a little too," Claudius says lovingly.

I feel the cool winds of the nether region tear through me like giggling knives.

Something sure as hell is rotten in the state of Denmark.

NIGHT-SIDE
by
JOYCE CAROL OATES

This disturbing and beautifully written story is not, on first glance, an inquiry into the validity of spiritualism; of trance mediums and seances, spirit guides and xenoglossis. Rather, it is an inquiry into the nature of death. And, even more profoundly, into the nature of life.

What happens after we die? Do we live on in a spirit world, or is the realm of the supernatural merely a way station on the soul's passage to someplace else? And what is it like on the "Night-Side"? The possible answers offered by Ms. Oates are guaranteed to make you uneasy, to make you ponder. And to disrupt your sleep for a night or two or three . . .

Joyce Carol Oates (born 1938) is one of the most loftily regarded (and prolific) of today's writers in the literary mainstream. She has published some twenty novels and 200 short stories; one of her novels, Them *(1969), was the recipient of the 1970 National Book Award, and another,* Expensive People *(1965), was a 1966 NBA finalist. Among her collections is* Night-Side *(1980), of which this is the title story—a gathering of the finest of her macabre*

tales. At present she is a professor of creative writing at Princeton
University, and with her husband, Raymond Smith, is the founder
and publisher of a small imprint, Windsor Press, devoted to the
publication of books of high literary merit.

6 February 1887. Quincy, Massachusetts. Montague House.
    Disturbing experience at Mrs. A——'s home yesterday
evening. Few theatrics—comfortable though rather pathet-
ically shabby surroundings—an only mildly sinister atmosphere (especially in contrast to the Walpurgis Night presented
by that shameless charlatan in Portsmouth: the Dwarf Eustace
who presumed to introduce me to Swedenborg himself, under
the erroneous impression that I am a member of the Church
of the New Jerusalem—*I!*). Nevertheless I came away disturbed, and my conversation with Dr. Moore afterward, at
dinner, though dispassionate and even, at times, a bit flippant,
did not settle my mind. Perry Moore is of course a hearty
materialist, an Aristotelian-Spencerian with a love of good
food and drink, and an appreciation of the more nonsensical
vagaries of life; when in his company I tend to support that
general view, as I do at the University as well—for there is
a terrific pull in my nature toward the gregarious that I
cannot resist. (That I do not wish to resist.) Once I am alone
with my thoughts, however, I am accursed with doubts about
my own position and nothing seems more precarious than
my intellectual "convictions."
    The more hardened members of our Society, like Perry
Moore, are apt to put the issue bluntly: Is Mrs. A—— of
Quincy a conscious or unconscious fraud? The conscious
frauds are relatively easy to deal with; once discovered, they
prefer to erase themselves from further consideration. The
unconscious frauds are not, in a sense, "frauds" at all. It
would certainly be difficult to prove criminal intention. Mrs.
A——, for instance, does not accept money or gifts so far as
we have been able to determine, and both Perry Moore and

I noted her courteous but firm refusal of the Judge's offer
to send her and her husband (presumably ailing?) on holiday
to England in the spring. She is a mild, self-effacing, rather
stocky woman in her mid-fifties who wears her hair parted
in the center, like several of my maiden aunts, and whose
sole item of adornment was an old-fashioned cameo brooch;
her black dress had the appearance of having been homemade,
though it was attractive enough, and freshly ironed. According
to the Society's records she has been a practicing medium
now for six years. Yet she lives, still, in an undistinguished
section of Quincy, in a neighborhood of modest frame dwell-
ings. The A——s' house is in fairly good condition, especially
considering the damage routinely done by our winters, and
the only room we saw, the parlor, is quite ordinary, with
overstuffed chairs and the usual cushions and a monstrous
horsehair sofa and, of course, the oaken table; the atmosphere
would have been so conventioanl as to have seemed disap-
pointing had not Mrs. A—— made an attempt to brighten
it, or perhaps to give it a glamourously occult air, by hanging
certain watercolors about the room. (She claims that the
watercolors were "done" by one of her contact spirits, a young
Iroquois girl who died in the seventeen seventies of smallpox.
They are touchingly garish—mandalas and triangles and
stylized eyeballs and even a transparent Cosmic Man with
Indian-black hair.)

At last night's sitting there were only three persons in
addition to Mrs. A——. Judge T—— of the New York State
Supreme Court (now retired); Dr. Moore; and I, Jarvis Williams. Dr. Moore and I came out from Cambridge under
the aegis of the Society for Psychical Research in order to
make a preliminary study of the kind of mediumship Mrs.
A—— affects. We did not bring a stenographer along this
time though Mrs. A—— indicated her willingness to have
the sitting transcribed; she struck me as being rather warmly
cooperative, and even interested in our formal procedures,
though Perry Moore remarked afterward at dinner that she
had struck him as "noticeably reluctant." She was, however,
flustered at the start of the séance and for a while it seemed

as if we and the Judge might have made the trip for nothing. (She kept waving her plump hands about like an embarrassed hostess, apologizing for the fact that the spirits were evidently in a "perverse uncommunicative mood tonight.")

She did go into trance eventually, however. The four of us were seated about the heavy round table from approximately 6:50 P.M. to 9 P.M. For nearly forty-five minutes Mrs. A—— made abortive attempts to contact her Chief Communicator and then slipped abruptly into trance (dramatically, in fact: her eyes rolled back in her head in a manner that alarmed me at first), and a personality named Webley appeared. "Webley's" voice appeared to be coming from several directions during the course of the sitting. At all times it was at least three yards from Mrs. A——; despite the semi-dark of the parlor I believe I could see the woman's mouth and throat clearly enough, and I could not detect any obvious signs of ventriloquism. (Perry Moore, who is more experienced than I in psychical research, and rather more casual about the whole phenomenon, claims he has witnessed feats of ventriloquism that would make poor Mrs. A—— look quite shabby in comparison.) "Webley's" voice was raw, singsong, peculiarly disturbing. At times it was shrill and at other times so faint as to be nearly inaudible. Something brattish about it. Exasperating. "Webley" took care to pronounce his final g's in a self-conscious manner, quite unlike Mrs. A——. (Which could be, of course, a deliberate ploy.)

This Webley is one of Mrs. A——'s most frequent manifesting spirits, though he is not the most reliable. Her Chief Communicator is a Scots patriarch who lived "in the time of Merlin" and who is evidently very wise; unfortunately he did not choose to appear yesterday evening. Instead, Webley presided. He is supposed to have died some seventy-five years ago at the age of nineteen in a house just up the street from the A——s'. He was either a butcher's helper or an apprentice tailor. He died in a fire—or by a "slow dreadful crippling disease"—or beneath a horse's hooves, in a freakish accident; during the course of the sitting he alluded self-pityingly to his death but seemed to have forgotten the exact

details. At the very end of the evening he addressed me
directly as Dr. Williams of Harvard University, saying that
since I had influential friends in Boston I could help him
with his career—it turned out he had written hundreds of
songs and poems and parables but none had been published;
would I please find a publisher for his work? Life had treated
him so unfairly. His talent—his genius—had been lost to
humanity. I had it within my power to help him, he claimed,
was I not *obliged* to help him . . . ? He then sang one of his
songs, which sounded to me like an old ballad; many of the
words were so shrill as to be unintelligible, but he sang it
just the same, repeating the verses in a haphazard order:

> *This ae nighte, this ae nighte,*
> *—Every nighte and alle,*
> *Fire and fleet and candle-lighte,*
> *And Christe receive thy saule.*

> *When thou from hence away art past,*
> *—Every nighte and alle,*
> *To Whinny-muir thou com'st at last:*
> *And Christe receive thy saule.*

> *From Brig o' Dread when thou may'st pass,*
> *—Every nighte and alle,*
> *The whinnes sall prick thee to the bare bane:*
> *And Christe receive thy saule.*

The elderly Judge T—— had come up from New York
City in order, as he earnestly put it, to "speak directly to his
deceased wife as he was never able to do while she was living";
but Webley treated the old gentleman in a high-handed,
cavalier manner, as if the occasion were not at all serious.
He kept saying, "Who is there tonight? *Who* is there? Let
them introduce themselves again—I don't *like* strangers! I
tell you I don't *like* strangers!" Though Mrs. A—— had informed us beforehand that we would witness no physical
phenomena, there were, from time to time, glimmerings of

light in the darkened room, hardly more than the tiny pul-
sations of light made by fireflies; and both Perry Moore and
I felt the table vibrating beneath our fingers. At about the
time when Webley gave way to the spirit of Judge T——'s
wife, the temperature in the room seemed to drop suddenly
and I remember being gripped by a sensation of panic—but
it lasted only an instant and I was soon myself again. (Dr.
Moore claimed not to have noticed any drop in temperature
and Judge T—— was so rattled after the sitting that it would
have been pointless to question him.)

The séance proper was similar to others I have attended.
A spirit—or voice—laid claim to being the late Mrs. T——;
this spirit addressed the survivor in a peculiarly intense,
urgent manner, so that it was rather embarrassing to be
present. Judge T—— was soon weeping. His deeply creased
face glistened with tears like a child's.

"Why Darrie! *Darrie!* Don't cry! Oh don't cry!" the spirit
said. "No one is dead, Darrie. There is no death. No death! . . .
Can you hear me, Darrie? Why are you so frightened? So
upset? No need, Darrie, no need! Grandfather and Lucy
and I are together here—happy together. Darrie, look up!
Be brave, my dear! My poor frightened dear! We never knew
each other, did we? My poor dear! My love! . . . I saw you
in a great transparent house, a great burning house; poor
Darrie, they told me you were ill, you were weak with fever;
all the rooms of the house were aflame and the staircase was
burnt to cinders, but there were figures walking up and
down, Darrie, great numbers of them, and you were among
them, dear, stumbling in your fright—so clumsy! Look up,
dear, and shade your eyes, and you will see me. Grandfather
helped me—did you know? Did I call out his name at the
end? My dear, my darling, it all happened so quickly—we
never knew each other, did we? Don't be hard on Annie!
Don't be cruel! Darrie? Why are you crying?" And gradually
the spirit voice grew fainter; or perhaps something went
wrong and the channels of communication were no longer
clear. There were repetitions, garbled phrases, meaningless
queries of "Dear? Dear?" that the Judge's replies did not

seem to placate. The spirit spoke of her gravesite, and of a trip to Italy taken many years before, and of a dead or unborn baby, and again of Annie—evidently Judge T——'s daughter; but the jumble of words did not always make sense and it was a great relief when Mrs. A—— suddenly woke from her trance.

Judge T—— rose from the table, greatly agitated. He wanted to call the spirit back; he had not asked her certain crucial questions; he had been overcome by emotion and had found it difficult to speak, to interrupt the spirit's monologue. But Mrs. A—— (who looked shockingly tired) told him the spirit would not return again that night and they must not make any attempt to call it back.

"The other world obeys its own laws," Mrs. A—— said in her small, rather reedy voice.

We left Mrs. A——'s home shortly after 9:00 P.M. I too was exhausted; I had not realized how absorbed I had been in the proceedings.

Judge T—— is also staying at Montague House, but he was too upset after the sitting to join us for dinner. He assured us, though, that the spirit was authentic—the voice had been his wife's, he was certain of it, he would stake his life on it. She had never called him "Darrie" during her lifetime, wasn't it odd that she called him "Darrie" now?—and was so concerned for him, so loving?—and concerned for their daughter as well? He was very moved. He had a great deal to think about. (Yes, he'd had a fever some weeks ago—a severe attack of bronchitis and a fever; in fact, he had not completely recovered.) What was extraordinary about the entire experience was the wisdom revealed: There is no death.

There is no death.

Dr. Moore and I dined heartily on roast crown of lamb, spring potatoes with peas, and buttered cabbage. We were served two kinds of bread—German rye and sour-cream rolls; the hotel's butter was superb; the wine excellent; the dessert—crepes with cream and toasted almonds—looked marvelous, though I had not any appetite for it. Dr. Moore was ravenously hungry. He talked as he ate, often punctuating his remarks with rich bursts of laughter. It was his opinion, of course, that the medium was a fraud—and not a very skillful fraud, either. In his fifteen years of amateur, intermittent investigations he had encountered far more skillful mediums. Even the notorious Eustace with his levitating table and hobgoblin chimes and shrieks was cleverer than Mrs. A——; one knew of course that Eustace was a cheat, but one was hard pressed to explain his method. Whereas Mrs. A—— was quite transparent.

Dr. Moore spoke for some time in his amiable, dogmatic way. He ordered brandy for both of us, though it was nearly midnight when we finished our dinner and I was anxious to get to bed. (I hoped to rise early and work on a lecture dealing with Kant's approach to the problem of Free Will, which I would be delivering in a few days.) But Dr. Moore enjoyed talking and seemed to have been invigorated by our experience at Mrs. A——'s.

At the age of forty-three Perry Moore is only four years my senior, but he has the air, in my presence at least, of being considerably older. He is a second cousin of my mother, a very successful physician with a bachelor's flat and office in Louisburg Square; his failure to marry, or his refusal, is one of Boston's perennial mysteries. Everyone agrees that he is learned, witty, charming, and extraordinarily intelligent. Striking rather than conventionally handsome, with a dark, lustrous beard and darkly bright eyes, he is an excellent amateur violinist, an enthusiastic sailor, and a lover of literature—his favorite writers are Fielding, Shakespeare, Horace, and Dante. He is, of course, the perfect investigator in spiritualist matters since he is detached from the phenomena he observes and yet he is indefatigably curious; he has a positive love, a mania, for facts. Like the true scientist he seeks facts that, assembled, may possibly give rise to hypotheses: he does not set out with a hypothesis in mind, like a sort of basket into which certain facts may be tossed, helter-skelter, while others are conveniently ignored. In all things he is an empiricist who accepts nothing on faith.

"If the woman is a fraud, then," I say hesitantly, "you believe she is a self-deluded fraud? And her spirits' information is gained by means of telepathy?"

"Telepathy indeed. There can be no other explanation," Dr. Moore says emphatically. "By some means not yet known to science . . . by some uncanny means she suppresses her conscious personality . . . and thereby releases other, secondary personalities that have the power of seizing upon others' thoughts and memories. It's done in a way not understood by science at the present time. But it will be understood eventually. Our investigations into the unconscious powers of the human mind are just beginning; we're on the threshold, really, of a new era."

"So she simply picks out of her clients' minds whatever they want to hear," I say slowly. "And from time to time she can even tease them a little—insult them, even: she can unloose a creature like that obnoxious Webley upon a person like Judge T—— without fear of being discovered. Telepathy. . . . Yes, that would explain a great deal. Very nearly everything we witnessed tonight."

"*Everything*, I should say," Dr. Moore says.

In the coach returning to Cambridge I set aside Kant and my lecture notes and read Sir Thomas Browne: *Light that makes all things seen, makes some things invisible. The greatest mystery of Religion is expressed by adumbration.*

19 March 1887. Cambridge. 11 P.M.

Walked ten miles this evening; must clear cobwebs from mind.

Unhealthy atmosphere. Claustrophobic. Last night's sitting in Quincy—a most unpleasant experience.

(Did not tell my wife what happened. Why is she so curious about the Spirit World?—about Perry Moore?)

My body craves more violent physical activity. In the summer, thank God, I will be able to swim in the ocean: the most strenuous and challenging of exercises.

Jotting down notes re the Quincy experience:

I. Fraud

Mrs. A——, possibly with accomplices, conspires to deceive: she does research into her clients' lives beforehand, possibly bribes servants. She is either a very skillful ventriloquist or works with someone who is. (Husband? Son? The husband is a retired cabinetmaker said to be in poor health; possibly consumptive. The son, married, lives in Waterbury.)

Her stated wish to avoid publicity and her declining of payment may simply be ploys; she may intend to make a great deal of money at some future time.

(Possibility of blackmail?—might be likely in cases similar to Perry Moore's.)

II. Non-fraud

Naturalistic

1. Telepathy. She reads minds of clients.
2. "Multiple personality" of medium. Aspects of her own buried psyche are released as her conscious personality is suppressed. These secondary beings are in mysterious rapport with the "secondary" personalities of the clients.

Spiritualistic

1. The controls are genuine communicators, intermediaries between our world and the world of the dead. These spirits give way to other spirits, who then speak through the medium; or
2. These spirits *influence* the medium, who relays their messages using her own vocabulary. Their personalities are then filtered through and limited by hers.

3. The spirits are not those of the deceased; they are perverse, willful spirits. (Perhaps demons? But there are no demons.)

III. Alternative hypothesis
Madness: the medium is mad, the clients are mad, even the detached, rationalist investigators are mad.

Yesterday evening at Mrs. A——'s home, the second sitting Perry Moore and I observed together, along with Miss Bradley, a stenographer from the Society, and two legitimate clients— a Brookline widow, Mrs. P——, and her daughter Clara, a handsome young woman in her early twenties. Mrs. A—— exactly as she appeared to us in February; possibly a little stouter. Wore black dress and cameo brooch. Served Lapsang tea, tiny sandwiches, and biscuits when we arrived shortly after 6 P.M. Seemed quite friendly to Perry, Miss Bradley, and me; fussed over us, like any hostess, chattered a bit about the cold spell. Mrs. P—— and her daughter arrived at six-thirty and the sitting began shortly thereafter.

Jarring from the very first. A babble of spirit voices. Mrs. A—— in trance, head flung back, mouth gaping, eyes rolled upward. Queer. Unnerving. I glanced at Dr. Moore but he seemed unperturbed, as always. The widow and her daughter, however, looked as frightened as I felt.

Why are we here, sitting around this table?

What do we believe we will discover?

What are the risks we face . . . ?

"Webley" appeared and disappeared in a matter of minutes. His shrill, raw, aggrieved voice was supplanted by that of a creature of indeterminate sex who babbled in Gaelic. This creature in turn was supplanted by a hoarse German, a man who identified himself as Felix; he spoke a curiously ungrammatical German. For some minutes he and two or three other spirits quarreled. (Each declared himself Mrs. A——'s Chief Communicator for the evening.) Small lights flickered in the semi-dark of the parlor and the table quivered beneath my fingers and I felt, or believed I felt, something brushing against me, touching the back of my head. I shuddered violently but regained my composure at once. An unidentified voice proclaimed in English that the Spirit of our Age was Mars: there would be a catastrophic war shortly and most of the world's population would be destroyed. All atheists would be destroyed. Mrs. A—— shook her head from side to side as if trying to wake. Webley appeared, crying "Hello? Hello? I can't see anyone! Who is there? Who has called me?" but was again supplanted by another spirit who shouted long strings of words in a foreign language. [Note: I discovered a few days later that this language was Walachian, a Romanian dialect. Of course Mrs. A——, whose ancestors are English, could not possibly have known Walachian, and I rather doubt that the woman has even heard of the Walachian people.]

The sitting continued in this chaotic way for some minutes. Mrs. P—— must have been quite disappointed, since she had wanted to be put in contact with her deceased husband. (She needed advice on whether or not to sell certain pieces of property.) Spirits babbled freely in English, German, Gaelic, French, even in Latin, and at one point Dr. Moore queried a spirit in Greek, but the spirit retreated at once as if not equal to Dr. Moore's wit. The atmosphere was alarming but at the same time rather manic; almost jocular. I found myself suppressing laughter. Something touched the back of my head and I shivered violently and broke into perspiration, but the experience was not altogether unpleasant; it would be very difficult for me to characterize it.

And then—

And then, suddenly, everything changed. There was complete calm. A spirit voice spoke gently out of a corner of the room, addressing Perry Moore by his first name in a slow, tentative, groping way. "Perry? Perry . . . ?" Dr. Moore jerked about in his seat. He was astonished; I could see by his expression that the voice belonged to someone he knew.

"Perry . . . ? This is Brandon. I've waited so long for you, Perry, how could you be so selfish? I forgave you. Long ago. You couldn't help your cruelty and I couldn't help my innocence. Perry? My glasses have been broken—I can't see. I've been afraid for so long, Perry, please have mercy on me! I can't bear it any longer. I didn't *know* what it would be like. There are crowds of people here, but we can't see one another, we don't know one another, we're strangers, there is a universe of strangers—I can't see anyone clearly— I've been lost for twenty years, Perry, I've been waiting for you for twenty years! You don't dare turn away again, Perry! Not again! Not after so long!"

Dr. Moore stumbled to his feet, knocking his chair aside. "No— Is it— I don't believe—"

"Perry? Perry? Don't abandon me again, Perry! Not again!"

"What is this?" Dr. Moore cried.

He was on his feet now; Mrs. A—— woke from her trance with a groan. The women from Brookline were very upset and I must admit that I was in a mild state of terror, my shirt and my underclothes drenched with perspiration.

The sitting was over. It was only seven-thirty.

"Brandon?" Dr. Moore cried. "Wait. Where are—? Brandon? Can you hear me? Where are you? Why did you do it, Brandon? Wait! Don't leave! Can't anyone call him back— Can't anyone help me—"

Mrs. A—— rose unsteadily. She tried to take Dr. Moore's hands in hers but he was too agitated.

"I heard only the very last words," she said. "They're always that way—so confused, so broken—the poor things— Oh, what a pity! It wasn't murder, was it? Not murder! Suicide—? I believe suicide is even worse for them! The poor broken things, they wake in the other world and are utterly, utterly lost—they have no guides, you see—no help in crossing over— They are completely alone for eternity—"

"Can't you call him back?" Dr. Moore asked wildly. He was peering into a corner of the parlor, slightly stooped, his face distorted as if he were staring into the sun. "Can't someone help me? . . . Brandon? Are you here? Are you here somewhere? For God's sake can't someone help!"

"Dr. Moore, please, the spirits are gone—the sitting is over for tonight—"

"You foolish old woman, leave me alone! Can't you see I—I—I must not lose him— Call him back, will you? I insist! I insist!"

"Dr. Moore, please— You mustn't shout—"

"I said call him back! At once! *Call him back!*"

Then he burst into tears. He stumbled against the table and hid his face in his hands and wept like a child; he wept as if his heart had been broken.

And so today I have been reliving the séance. Taking notes, trying to determine what happened. A brisk windy walk of ten miles. Head buzzing with ideas. Fraud? Deceit? Telepathy? Madness?

What a spectacle! Dr. Perry Moore calling after a spirit, begging it to return—and then crying, afterward, in front of four astonished witnesses.

Dr. Perry Moore of all people.

My dilemma: whether I should report last night's incident to Dr. Rowe, the president of the Society, or whether I should say nothing about it and request that Miss Bradley say nothing. It would be tragic if Perry's professional reputation were to be damaged by a single evening's misadventure; and before long all of Boston would be talking.

In his present state, however, he is likely to tell everyone about it himself.

At Montague House the poor man was unable to sleep. He would have kept me up all night had I had the stamina to endure his excitement.

There *are* spirits! There have always been spirits!

His entire life up to the present time has been misspent!

And of course, most important of all—there is no death!

He paced about my hotel room, pulling at his beard nervously. At times there were tears in his eyes. He seemed to want a response of some kind from me but whenever I started to speak he interrupted; he was not really listening.

"Now at last I know. I can't undo my knowledge," he said in a queer hoarse voice. "Amazing, isn't it, after so many years . . . so many wasted years. . . . Ignorance has been my lot, darkness . . . and a hideous complacency. My God, when I consider my deluded smugness! I am so ashamed, so ashamed. All along people like Mrs. A—— have been in contact with a world of such power . . . and people like me have been toiling in ignorance, accumulating material achievements, expending our energies in idiotic transient things. . . . But all that is changed now. Now I know. I *know.* There is no death, as the Spiritualists have always told us."

"But, Perry, don't you think— Isn't it possible that—"

"I *know,*" he said quietly. "It's as clear to me as if I had crossed over into that other world myself. Poor Brandon! He's no older now than he was *then.* The poor boy, the poor tragic soul! To think that he's still living after so many years. . . . Extraordinary. . . . It makes my head spin," he said slowly. For a moment he stood without speaking. He pulled at his beard, then absently touched his lips with his fingers, then wiped at his eyes. He seemed to have forgotten me. When he spoke again his voice was hollow, rather ghastly. He sounded drugged. "I . . . I had been thinking of him as . . . as dead, you know. As dead. Twenty years. Dead. And now, tonight, to be forced to realize that . . . that he isn't dead after all. . . . It was laudanum he took. I found him. His rooms on the third floor of Weld Hall. I found him. I had no real idea, none at all, not until I read the note . . . and of course I destroyed the note . . . I had to, you see: for his sake. For his sake more than mine. It was because he realized there could be no . . . no hope. . . . Yet he called me cruel! You heard him, Jarvis, didn't you? Cruel! I suppose I was. Was I? I don't know what to think. I must talk with him again. I . . . I don't know what to . . . what to think. I . . . ."

"You look awfully tired, Perry. It might be a good idea to go to bed," I said weakly.

". . . recognized his voice at once. Oh at once: no doubt. None. What a revelation! And my life so misspent. . . . Treating people's *bodies.* Absurd. I know now that nothing matters except that other world . . . nothing matters except our dead, our beloved dead . . . who are *not dead.* What a colossal revelation . . . ! Why, it will change the entire course of history.

It will alter men's minds throughout the world. You were there, Jarvis, so you understand. You were a witness. . . ."

"But—"

"You'll bear witness to the truth of what I am saying?"

He stared at me, smiling. His eyes were bright and threaded with blood.

I tried to explain to him as courteously and sympathetically as possible that his experience at Mrs. A——'s was not substantially different from the experiences many people have had at séances. "And always in the past psychical researchers have taken the position—"

"You were *there*," he said angrily. "You heard Brandon's voice as clearly as I did. Don't deny it!"

"—have taken the position that—that the phenomenon can be partly explained by the telepathic powers of the medium—"

"That was Brandon's *voice*," Perry said. "I felt his presence, I tell you! *His*. Mrs. A—— had nothing to do with it—nothing at all. I feel as if . . . as if I could call Brandon back by myself. . . . I feel his presence even now. Close about me. He isn't dead, you see; no one is dead, there's a universe of . . . of people who are not dead. . . . Parents, grandparents, sisters, brothers, everyone . . . everyone. . . . How can you deny, Jarvis, the evidence of your own senses? You were there with me tonight and you know as well as I do. . . ."

"Perry, I don't *know*. I did hear a voice, yes, but we've heard voices before at other sittings, haven't we? There are always voices. There are always 'spirits.' The Society has taken the position that the spirits could be real, of course, but that there are other hypotheses that are perhaps more likely—"

"Other hypotheses indeed!" Perry said irritably. "You're like a man with his eyes shut tight who refuses to open them out of sheer cowardice. Like the cardinals refusing to look through Galileo's telescope! And you have pretensions of being a man of learning, of science. . . . Why, we've got to destroy all the records we've made so far; they're a slander on the world of the spirits. Thank God we didn't file a report yet on Mrs. A——! It would be so embarrassing to be forced to call it back. . . ."

"Perry, please. Don't be angry. I want only to remind you of the fact that we've been present at other sittings, haven't we?—and we've witnessed others responding emotionally to certain phenomena. Judge T——, for instance. He was convinced he'd spoken with his wife. But you must remember, don't you, that you and I were not at all convinced . . . ? It seemed to us more likely that Mrs. A—— is able, through extrasensory powers we don't quite understand, to read the minds of her clients, and then to project certain voices out into the room so that it sounds as if they are coming from other people. . . . You even said, Perry, that she wasn't a very skillful ventriloquist. You said—"

"What does it matter what, in my ignorance, I said?" he cried. "Isn't it enough that I've been humiliated? That my entire life has been turned about? Must you insult me as well—sitting there so smugly and insulting *me*? I think I can make claim to being someone whom you might respect."

And so I assured him that I did respect him. And he walked about the room, wiping at his eyes, greatly agitated. He spoke again of his friend, Brandon Gould, and of his own ignorance, and of the important mission we must undertake to inform men and women of the true state of affairs. I tried to talk with him, to reason with him, but it was hopeless. He scarcely listened to me.

" . . . must inform the world . . . crucial truth. . . . There is no death, you see. Never was. Changes civilization, changes the course of history. Jarvis?" he said groggily. "You see? *There is no death.*"

25 March 1887. Cambridge.

Disquieting rumors re Perry Moore. Heard today at the University that one of Dr. Moore's patients (a brother-in-law of Dean Barker) was extremely offended by his behavior during a consultation last week. Talk of his having been drunk—which I find incredible. If the poor man appeared to be excitable and not his customary self, it was not because he was *drunk*, surely.

Another far-fetched tale told me by my wife, who heard it from her sister Maude: Perry Moore went to church (St. Aidan's Episcopal Church on Mount Street) for the first time in a decade, sat alone, began muttering and laughing during the sermon, and finally got to his feet and walked out, creating quite a stir. *What delusions! What delusions!*—he was said to have muttered.

I fear for the poor man's sanity.

31 March 1887. Cambridge. 4 A.M.

Sleepless night. Dreamed of swimming . . . swimming in the ocean . . . enjoying myself as usual when suddenly the water turns thick . . . turns to mud. Hideous! Indescribably awful. I was swimming nude in the ocean, by moonlight, I believe, ecstatically happy, entirely alone, when the water turned to mud. . . . Vile, disgusting mud; faintly warm; sucking at my body. Legs, thighs, torso, arms. Horrible. Woke in terror. Drenched with perspiration: pajamas wet. One of the most frightening nightmares of my adulthood.

A message from Perry Moore came yesterday just before dinner. Would I like to join him in visiting Mrs. A—— sometime soon, in early April perhaps, on a noninvestigative basis . . . ? He is uncertain now of the morality of our "investigating" Mrs. A—— or any other medium.

4 April 1887. Cambridge.

Spent the afternoon from two to five at William James's home on Irving Street, talking with Professor James of the inexplicable phenomenon of consciousness. He is robust as always, rather irreverent, supremely confident in a way I find enviable; rather like Perry Moore before his conversion. (Extraordinary eyes—so piercing, quick, playful; a graying beard liberally threaded with white; close-cropped graying hair; a large, curving, impressive forehead; a manner intelligent and graceful and at the same time rough-edged, as if he anticipates or perhaps even hopes for recalcitration in his listeners.) We both find conclusive the ideas set forth in Binét's *Alterations of Personality* . . . unsettling as these ideas may be to the rationalist position. James speaks of a *peculiarity* in the constitution of human nature: that is, the fact that we inhabit not only our ego-consciousness but a wide field of psychological experience (most clearly represented by the phenomenon of memory, which no one can adequately explain) over which we have no control whatsoever. In fact, we are not generally aware of this field of consciousness.

We inhabit a lighted sphere, then; and about us is a vast penumbra of memories, reflections, feelings, and stray uncoordinated thoughts that "belong" to us theoretically, but that do not seem to be part of our conscious identity. (I was too timid to ask Professor James whether it might be the case that we do not inevitably own these aspects of the personality—that such phenomena belong as much to the objective world as to our subjective selves.) It is quite possible that there is an element of some indeterminate kind: oceanic, timeless, and living, against which the individual being constructs temporary barriers as part of an ongoing process of unique, particularized survival; like the ocean itself, which appears to separate islands that are in fact not "islands" at all, but aspects of the earth firmly joined together below the surface of the water. Our lives, then, resemble these islands. . . . All this is no more than a possibility, Professor James and I agreed.

James is acquainted, of course, with Perry Moore. But he declined to speak on the subject of the poor man's increasingly eccentric behavior when I alluded to it. (It may be that he knows even more about the situation than I do—he enjoys a multitude of acquaintances in Cambridge and Boston.) I brought our conversation round several times to the possibility of the *naturalness* of the conversion experience in terms of the individual's evolution of self, no matter how his family, his colleagues, and society in general viewed it, and Professor James appeared to agree; at least he did not emphatically disagree. He maintains a healthy skepticism, of course, regarding Spiritualist claims, and all evangelical and enthusiastic religious movements, though he is, at the same time, a highly articulate foe of the "rationalist" position and he believes that psychical research of the kind some of us are attempting will eventually unearth riches—revealing aspects of the human psyche otherwise closed to our scrutiny.

"The fearful thing," James said, "is that we are at all times vulnerable to incursions from the 'other side' of the personality. . . . We cannot determine the nature of the total personality simply because much of it, perhaps most, is hidden from us. . . . When we are invaded, then, we are overwhelmed and surrender immediately. Emotionally charged intuitions, hunches, guesses, even ideas may be the least aggressive of these incursions; but there are visual and auditory hallucinations, and forms of automatic behavior not controlled by the conscious mind. . . . Ah, you're thinking I am simply describing insanity?"

I stared at him, quite surprised.

"No. Not at all. Not at all," I said at once.

Reading through my grandfather's journals, begun in East Anglia many years before my birth. Another world then. Another language, now lost to us. *Man is sinful by nature. God's justice takes precedence over His mercy.* The dogma of Original Sin: something brutish about the innocence of that belief. And yet consoling. . . .

Fearful of sleep since my dreams are so troubled now. The voices of impudent spirits (Immanuel Kant himself come to chide me for having made too much of his categories—!), stray shouts and whispers I cannot decipher, the faces of my own beloved dead hovering near, like carnival masks, insubstantial and possibly fraudulent. Impatient with my wife, who questions me too closely on these personal matters; annoyed from time to time, in the evenings especially, by the silliness of the children. (The eldest is twelve now and should know better.) Dreading to receive another lengthy letter—sermon, really—from Perry Moore re his "new position," and yet perversely hoping one will come soon.

I must know.

(Must know *what* . . . ?)

I must know.

10 April 1887. Boston. St. Aidan's Episcopal Church.

Funeral service this morning for Perry Moore; dead at forty-three.

17 April 1887. Seven Hills, New Hampshire.

A weekend retreat. No talk. No need to think.

Visiting with a former associate, author of numerous books. Cartesian specialist. Elderly. Partly deaf. Extraordinarily kind to me. (Did not ask about the Department or about my work.) Intensely interested in animal behavior now, in observation primarily; fascinated with the phenomenon of hibernation.

He leaves me alone for hours. He sees something in my face I cannot see myself.

The old consolations of a cruel but just God: ludicrous today.

In the nineteenth century we live free of God. We live in the illusion of freedom-of-God.

Dozing off in the guest room of this old farmhouse and then waking abruptly. *Is someone here? Is someone here?* My voice queer, hushed, childlike. *Please: is someone here?*

Silence.

Query: Is the penumbra outside consciousness all that was ever meant by "God"?

Query: Is inevitability all that was ever meant by "God"?

God—the body of fate we inhabit, then; no more and no less.

God pulled Perry down into the body of fate: into Himself.
(Or Itself.) As Professor James might say, Dr. Moore was
"vulnerable" to an assault from the other side.

At any rate he is dead. They buried him last Saturday.

25 April 1887. Cambridge.

Shelves of books. The sanctity of books. Kant, Plato, Scho-
penhauer, Descartes, Hume, Hegel, Spinoza. The others.
All. Nietzsche, Spencer, Leibnitz (on whom I did a torturous
Master's thesis). Plotinus. Swedenborg. *The Transactions of the
American Society for Psychical Research.* Voltaire. Locke. Rous-
seau. And Berkeley: the good Bishop adrift in a dream.

An etching by Halbrech above my desk, The Thames 1801.
Water too black. Inky-black. Thick with mud . . . ? Filthy
water in any case.

Perry's essay, forty-five scribbled pages, "The Challenge
of the Future." Given to me several weeks ago by Dr. Rowe,
who feared rejecting it for the *Transactions* but could not, of
course, accept it. I can read only a few pages at a time, then
push it aside, too moved to continue. Frightened also.

The man had gone insane.

Died insane.

Personality broken: broken bits of intellect.

His argument passionate and disjointed, with no pretense
of objectivity. Where some weeks ago he had taken the stand
that it was immoral to investigate the Spirit World, now he
took the stand that it was imperative we do so. We are on
the brink of a new age . . . new knowledge of the universe . . .
comparable to the stormy transitional period between the
Ptolemaic and the Copernican theories of the universe. . . .
More experiments required. Money. Donations. Subsidies
by private institutions. All psychological research must be
channeled into a systematic study of the Spirit World and
the ways by which we can communicate with that world.
Mediums like Mrs. A—— must be brought to centers of
learning like Harvard and treated with the respect their

genius deserves. Their value to civilization is, after all, beyond estimation. They must be rescued from arduous and routine lives where their genius is drained off into vulgar pursuits . . . they must be rescued from a clientele that is mainly concerned with being put into contact with deceased relatives for utterly trivial, self-serving reasons. Men of learning must realize the gravity of the situation. Otherwise we will fail, we will stagger beneath the burden, we will be defeated, ignobly, and it will remain for the twentieth century to discover the existence of the Spirit Universe that surrounds the Material Universe, and to determine the exact ways by which one world is related to another.

Perry Moore died of a stroke on the eighth of April; died instantaneously on the steps of the Bedford Club shortly after 2 P.M. Passers-by saw a very excited, red-faced gentleman with an open collar push his way through a small gathering at the top of the steps—and then suddenly fall, as if shot down.

In death he looked like quite another person: his features sharp, the nose especially pointed. Hardly the handsome Perry Moore everyone had known.

He had come to a meeting of the Society, though it was suggested by Dr. Rowe and by others (including myself) that he stay away. Of course he came to argue. To present his "new position." To insult the other members. (He was contemptuous of a rather poorly organized paper on the medium Miss E—— of Salem, a young woman who works with objects like rings, articles of clothing, locks of hair, et cetera; and quite angry with the evidence presented by a young geologist that would seem to discredit, once and for all, the claims of Eustace of Portsmouth. He interrupted a third paper, calling the reader a "bigot" and an "ignorant fool.")

Fortunately the incident did not find its way into any of the papers. The press, misunderstanding (deliberately and maliciously) the Society's attitude toward Spiritualism, delights in ridiculing our efforts.

There were respectful obituaries. A fine eulogy prepared

by Reverend Tyler of St. Aidan's. Other tributes. *A tragic loss. . . . Mourned by all who knew him. . . .* (I stammered and could not speak. I cannot speak of him, of it, even now. Am I mourning, am I aggrieved? Or merely shocked? Terrified?) Relatives and friends and associates glossed over his behavior these past few months and settled upon an earlier Perry Moore, eminently sane, a distinguished physician and man of letters. I did not disagree, I merely acquiesced; I could not make any claim to have really known the man.

And so he has died, and so he is dead. . . .

Shortly after the funeral I went away to New Hampshire for a few days. But I can barely remember that period of time now. I sleep poorly. I yearn for summer, for a drastic change of climate, of scene. It was unwise for me to take up the responsibility of psychical research, fascinated though I am by it; my classes and lectures at the University demand most of my energy.

How quickly he died, and so young: so relatively young.

No history of high blood pressure, it is said.

At the end he was arguing with everyone, however. His personality had completely changed. He was rude, impetuous, even rather profane; even poorly groomed. (Rising to challenge the first of the papers, he revealed a shirtfront that appeared to be stained.) Some claimed he had been drinking all along, for years. Was it possible . . . ? (He had clearly enjoyed the wine and brandy in Quincy that evening, but I would not have said he was intemperate.) Rumors, fanciful tales, outright lies, slander. . . . It is painful, the vulnerability death brings.

Bigots, he called us. Ignorant fools. Unbelievers—atheists—traitors to the Spirit World—heretics. Heretics! I believe he looked directly at me as he pushed his way out of the meeting room: his eyes glaring, his face dangerously flushed, no recognition in his stare.

After his death, it is said, books continue to arrive at his home from England and Europe. He spent a small fortune on obscure, out-of-print volumes—commentaries on the Kabbala, on Plotinus, medieval alchemical texts, books on astrology, witchcraft, the metaphysics of death. Occult cosmologies. Egyptian, Indian, and Chinese "wisdom." Blake, Swedenborg, Cozad. *The Tibetan Book of the Dead.* Datsky's *Lunar Mysteries.* His estate is in chaos because he left not one but several wills, the most recent made out only a day before his death, merely a few lines scribbled on scrap paper, without witnesses. The family will contest, of course. Since in this will he left his money and property to an obscure woman living in Quincy, Massachusetts, and since he was obviously not in his right mind at the time, they would be foolish indeed not to contest.

Days have passed since his sudden death. Days continue to pass. At times I am seized by a sort of quick, cold panic; at other times I am inclined to think the entire situation has been exaggerated. In one mood I vow to myself that I will never again pursue psychical research because it is simply too dangerous. In another mood I vow I will never again pursue it because it is a waste of time and my own work, my own career, must come first.

Heretics, he called us. Looking straight at me.

Still, he was mad. And is not to be blamed for the vagaries of madness.

19 June 1887. Boston.

Luncheon with Dr. Rowe, Miss Madeleine van der Post, young Lucas Matthewson; turned over my personal records and notes re the mediums Dr. Moore and I visited. (Destroyed jottings of a private nature.) Miss van der Post and Matthewson will be taking over my responsibilities. Both are young, quick-witted, alert, with a certain ironic play about their features; rather like Dr. Moore in his prime. Matthewson is a former seminary student now teaching physics at the Boston University. They questioned me about Perry Moore, but I avoided answering frankly. Asked if we were close, I said *No.* Asked if I had heard a bizarre tale making the rounds of Boston salons—that a spirit claiming to be Perry Moore has intruded upon a number of séances in the area—I said honestly that I had not; and I did not care to hear about it.

Spinoza: *I will analyze the actions and appetites of men as if it were a question of lines, of planes, and of solids.*

It is in this direction, I believe, that we must move. Away from the phantasmal, the vaporous, the unclear; toward lines, planes, and solids.

Sanity.

8 July 1887. Mount Desert Island, Maine.

Very early this morning, before dawn, dreamed of Perry Moore: a babbling, gesticulating spirit, bearded, bright-eyed, obviously mad. Jarvis? Jarvis? Don't deny me! he cried. I am so . . . so bereft. . . .

Paralyzed, I faced him: neither awake nor asleep. His words were not really *words* so much as unvoiced thoughts. I heard them in my own voice; a terrible raw itching at the back of my throat yearned to articulate the man's grief.

Perry?

You don't dare deny me! Not now!

He drew near and I could not escape. The dream shifted, lost its clarity. Someone was shouting at me. Very angry, he was, and baffled—as if drunk—or ill—or injured.

Perry? I can't hear you—

—our dinner at Montague House, do you remember? Lamb, it was. And crepes with almond for dessert. You remember! You remember! You can't deny me! We were both nonbelievers then, both abysmally ignorant—you can't deny me!

(I was mute with fear or with cunning.)

—that idiot Rowe, how humiliated he will be! All of them! All of you! The entire rationalist bias, the—the conspiracy of—of fools—bigots— In a few years—In a few short years— Jarvis, where are you? Why can't I see you? Where have you gone? —My eyes can't focus: will someone help me? I seem to have lost my way. Who is here? Who am I talking with? You remember me, don't you?

(He brushed near me, blinking helplessly. His mouth was a hole torn into his pale ravaged flesh.)

Where are you? Where is everyone? I thought it would be crowded here but—but there's no one— I am forgetting so much! My name—what was my name? Can't see. Can't remember. Something very important—something very important I must accomplish—can't remember— Why is there no God? No one here? No one in control? We drift this way and that way, we come to no rest, there are no landmarks—no way of judging—everything is confused—disjointed— Is someone listening? Would you read to me, please? Would you read to me?—anything!—that speech of Hamlet's—*To be or not*—a sonnet of Shakespeare's—any sonnet, anything—*That time of year thou may in me behold*—is that it?—is that how it begins? *Bare ruin'd choirs where the sweet birds once sang.* How does it go? Won't you tell me? I'm lost—there's nothing here to see, to touch—isn't anyone listening? I thought there was someone nearby, a friend: isn't anyone here?

(I stood paralyzed, mute with caution: he passed by.)

—*When in the chronicle of wasted time—the wide world dreaming of things to come*—is anyone listening?—can anyone help?—I am forgetting so much—my name, my life—my life's work—to penetrate the mysteries—the veil—to do justice to the universe of—of what—what I had intended?—am I in my place of repose now, have I come home? Why is it so empty here? Why is no one in control? My eyes—my head—mind broken and blown about—slivers—shards—annihilating all that's made to a—a green thought—a green shade—Shakespeare? Plato? Pascal? Will someone read me Pascal again? I seem to have lost my way—I am being blown about—Jarvis, was it? My dear young friend Jarvis? But I've forgotten your last name—I've forgotten so much—

(I wanted to reach out to touch him—but could not move, could not wake. The back of my throat ached with sorrow. Silent! Silent! I could not utter a word.)

—my papers, my journal—twenty years—a key somewhere

hidden—where?—ah yes: the bottom drawer of my desk—
do you hear?—my desk—house—Louisburg Square—the key
is hidden there—wrapped in a linen handkerchief—the
strongbox is—the locked box is—hidden—my brother Edward's house—attic—trunk—steamer trunk—initials R. W.
M.—Father's trunk, you see—strongbox hidden inside—my
secret journals—life's work—physical and spiritual wisdom—
must not be lost—are you listening?—is anyone listening? I
am forgetting so much, my mind is in shreds—but if you
could locate the journal and read it to me—if you could
salvage it—me—I would be so very grateful—I would forgive
you anything, all of you— Is anyone there? Jarvis? Brandon?
No one? —My journal, my soul: will you salvage it? Will—
      (He stumbled away and I was alone again.)
      Perry—?
But it was too late: I awoke drenched with perspiration.

      Nightmare.
      Must forget.

      Best to rise early, before the others. Mount Desert Island
lovely in July. Our lodge on a hill above the beach. No spirits
here: wind from the northeast, perpetual fresh air, perpetual
waves. Best to rise early and run along the beach and plunge
into the chilly water.
      Clear the cobwebs from one's mind.
      How beautiful the sky, the ocean, the sunrise!
      No spirits here on Mount Desert Island. Swimming: skillful
exertion of arms and legs. Head turned this way, that way.
Eyes half shut. The surprise of the cold rough waves. One
yearns almost to slip out of one's human skin at such times . . . !
Crude blatant beauty of Maine. Ocean. Muscular exertion
of body. How alive I am, how living, how invulnerable; what
a triumph in my every breath. . . .
      Everything slips from my mind except the present moment.
I am living. I am alive, I am immortal. Must not weaken:
must not sink. Drowning? No. Impossible. Life is the only

reality. It is not extinction that awaits but a hideous dreamlike state, a perpetual groping, blundering—far worse than extinction—incomprehensible: so it is life we must cling to, arm over arm, swimming, conquering the element that sustains us.

Jarvis? someone cried. *Please hear me—*

How exquisite life is, the turbulent joy of life contained in flesh! I heard nothing except the triumphant waves splashing about me. I swam for nearly an hour. Was reluctant to come ashore for breakfast, though our breakfasts are always pleasant rowdy sessions: my wife and my brother's wife and our seven children thrown together for the month of July. Three boys, four girls: noise, bustle, health, no shadows, no spirits. No time to think. Again and again I shall emerge from the surf, face and hair and body streaming water, exhausted but jubilant, triumphant. Again and again the children will call out to me, excited, from the dayside of the world that they inhabit.

I will not investigate Dr. Moore's strongbox and his secret journal; I will not even think about doing so. The wind blows words away. The surf is hypnotic. I will not remember this morning's dream once I sit down to breakfast with the family. I will not clutch my wife's wrist and say *We must not die! We dare not die!*—for that would only frighten and offend her.

Jarvis? she is calling at this very moment.

And I say *Yes—? Yes, I'll be there at once.*

BIBLIOGRAPHY

NONFICTION

Carrington, Hereward and Nandor Fodor. *Haunted People.* New York: Dutton, 1951.

Cohen, Daniel. *Real Ghosts.* New York: Dodd, Mead, 1977.

Creighton, Helen. *Blue Nose Ghosts.* Toronto: Ryerson Press, 1957.

Doyle, Sir Arthur Conan. *The Case for Spirit Photography* (with others). New York: Doran, 1923.

———. *A Debate on Spiritualism.* Girard, Kansas: Haldeman Julius, 1922.

———. *The Edge of the Unknown.* New York: Putnam, 1930.

———. *The History of Spiritualism.* 2 vols. New York: Doran, 1926.

———. *The New Revelation: or, What is Spiritualism?* New York: Doran, 1918.

———. *Psychic Experiences.* New York: Putnam, 1925.

———. *Spiritualism and Rationalism.* London: Hodder & Stoughton, 1920.

———. *The Vital Message.* New York: Doran, 1919.

289

———. *The Wanderings of a Spiritualist*. New York: Doran, 1921.

Holzer, Hans. *The Ghost Hunter*. Indianapolis: Bobbs-Merrill, 1965.

———. *The Ghost Hunter's Strangest Cases*. New York: Ace Books, 1975.

———. *Lively Ghosts of Ireland*. Indianapolis: Bobbs-Merrill, 1967.

———. *Yankee Ghosts*. New York: Ace Books, 1966.

Leslie, Shane. *Shane Leslie's Ghost Book*. New York: Sheed and Ward, 1956.

Lovecraft, H.P. *Supernatural Horror in Literature*. New York: Dover Books, 1973 (reprint of 1927 limited edition).

May, Antoinette. *Haunted Ladies*. San Francisco: Chronicle Books, 1975.

Meyers, F.W.H. *Human Personality and Its Survival of Bodily Death*. New York: circa 1900.

O'Donnell, Elliott. *Ghosts of London*. New York: Dutton, 1933.

———. *Some Haunted Houses of England and Wales*. London: 1908.

Penzoldt, Peter. *The Supernatural in Fiction*. London: Peter Nevill, 1952.

Playfair, Guy Lyon. *This House is Haunted*. New York: Stein & Day, 1980.

Reynolds, James. *Ghosts in American Houses*. New York: Farrar, Straus, 1954.

———. *Ghosts in Irish Houses*. New York: Farrar, Straus, 1955.

———. *More Ghosts in Irish Houses*. New York: Farrar, Straus, 1956.

Rhine, J.B. *Parapsychology, Frontier Science of the Mind*. New York: 1957.

———. *The Reach of the Mind*. New York: 1947.

Smith, Susy. *Ghosts Around the World*. New York: World, 1970.

———. *Haunted Houses for the Millions*. New York: Bell, 1967.

———. *Prominent American Ghosts*. New York: World, 1967.

Stirling, N.M.W. *Ghosts Vivisected*. New York: Citadel Press, 1958.

Sullivan, Jack. *Elegant Nightmares: The English Ghost Story from LeFanu to Blackwood*. Athens, Ohio: Ohio University Press, 1978.

Tackaberry, Andrew. *Famous Ghosts, Phantoms and Poltergeists for the Millions*. New York: Bell, 1966.

Tweedale, Violet. *Found Dead and Other True Ghost Stories*. London: Herbert Jenkins, 1928.

Tyrell, G.N.M. *Apparitions*. New York: Collier Books, 1963.

Walker, Danton (ed). *I Believe in Ghosts*. New York: Taplinger, 1969 (revised edition of book first published in 1956 under the title *Spooks Deluxe*).

Webb, Richard. *Great Ghosts of the West*. Los Angeles: Nash Pub. Co., 1971.

NOVELS

Acton, Frances. *My Haunted House*. Edinburgh: Nimmo's Popular Tales, 1866.

Alexander, Evelyn. *The Heart of a Monk*. London: John Long, 1910.

Ashton, Helen. *Belinda Grove*. London: Gollancz, 1932.

Atherton, Mary. *Whispers*. London: Hurst & Blackett, 1929.

Barrie, J.M. *Farewell, Miss Julie Logan*. London: Times Pub. Corp., 1931.

Bennett, Arnold. *The Ghost*. London: Catto & Windus, 1907.

Beraud, Henry. *The Wood of the Hanging Templar*. New York: Macmillan, 1930.

Berrow, Norman. *Ghost House*. New York: St. Martin's Press, 1980 (revised edition of novel first published in England in 1940).

Blyth, James. *My Haunted Home*. London: Aldine, 1914.

Bourdillion, F.W. *Nephele*. London: Redway, 1896.

Bozman, E.F. *The Traveler's Return*. London: Dent, 1938.

Brahms, Caryl and S.J. Simon. *No Nightingales*. London: Michael Joseph, 1944.

Bulwer-Lytton, Edward George. *The Haunted and the Haunters*, in *Tales from Blackwood*, First Series, Vol. X. London: Blackwood, 1860.

Clewes, Winston. *Sweet River in the Morning*. New York: Appleton-Century, 1946.

Crawford, F. Marion. *Man Overboard*. New York: Macmillan, 1903.

———. *The Upper Berth*. London: Unwin, 1894 (novella).

Dane, Clemence. *The Babyons*. London: Heinemann, 1921.

DeFelitta, Frank. *The Entity*. New York: Putnam, 1978.

Echard, Margaret. *The Dark Fantastic*. New York: Doubleday, 1947.

Gautier, Theophile. *Spirite: A Fantasy*. New York: Appleton, 1877.

Golding, Louis. *Honey for the Ghost.* London: Hutchinson, 1949.

Groom, Arthur. *The Ghost of Gordon Gregory.* London: Peter Lunn, 1946.

Hichens, Robert S. *Harps in the Wind.* London: Cassell, 1945.

Hocking, Joseph. *The Everlasting Arms.* London: Hodder & Stoughton, 1920.

————. *The Tenant of Cromlech Cottage.* London: Ward Lock, 1927.

Howells, William Dean. *The Seen and Unseen at Stratford-on-Avon.* New York: Harper, 1914.

Irwin, Inez H. *Out in the Air.* New York: Harcourt Brace, 1921.

Jackson, Shirley. *The Haunting of Hill House.* New York: Viking Press, 1959.

James, Henry. *The Turn of the Screw.* London: Heinemann, 1898.

King, Stephen. *The Shining.* New York: Doubleday, 1977.

Kroll, Harry Harrison. *The Ghosts of Slave Driver's Bend.* Indianapolis: Bobbs-Merrill, 1937.

LeFanu, J. Sheridan. *A Strange Adventure in the Life of Miss Laura Mildmay.* London: Home & Van Thal, 1947.

Lowndes, Marie Belloc. *From Out the Vasty Deep.* London: Hutchinson, 1920.

Macardle, Dorothy. *Uneasy Freehold.* London: Peter Davies, 1941.

McNally, Claire. *Ghost House.* New York: Bantam Books, 1979.

Mann, Jack. *Nightmare Farm.* London: Wright & Brown, 1937.

Marasco, Robert. *Burnt Offerings.* New York: Delacorte, 1973.

Marsh, Richard. *Tom Ossington's Ghost.* London: J. Bowden, 1898.

Matheson, Richard. *Hell House.* New York: Viking Press, 1971.

Meade, L.T. *Belinda Treherne.* London: John Long, 1910.

Metcalfe, John. *Brenner's Boy.* London: White Owl Press, 1932.

Murphy, James. *The Haunted Church.* London: Spencer & Blackett, 1889.

O'Connor, William D. *The Ghost.* New York: Putnam, 1867.

Owen, Frank. *Rare Earth.* New York: Lantern Press, 1931.

Pendered, Mary L. *The Uncanny House.* London: Hutchinson, 1927.

Reynolds, G.W.M. *The Pixy; or the Unbaptized Child.* London: John Dicks, 1848.

Riddell, Mrs. J.J. *The Disappearance of Mr. Jeremiah Redworth.* London: Routledge, 1878.

————. *Fairy Water.* London: Routledge, 1873.

———. *The Uninhabited House and The Haunted River*. London: Routledge, 1883.

Russell, Ray. *Incubus*. New York: Morrow, 1976.

Sand, George. *The Naiaid; A Ghost Story*. New York: W.R. Jenkins, 1892.

Smith, Mark. *Moonlamp*. New York: Knopf, 1976.

Smith, Thorne. *Topper; An Improbable Adventure*. New York: McBride, 1926.

———. *Topper Takes a Trip*. New York: Doubleday, 1932.

Spencer, R.E. *The Lady Who Came to Stay*. New York: Knopf, 1931.

Straub, Peter. *Ghost Story*. New York: Coward, McCann, 1979.

———. *If You Could See Me Now*. New York: Coward, McCann, 1977.

———. *Julia*. New York: Coward, McCann, 1975.

Strong, L.A.G. *The Jealous Ghost*. London: Gollancz, 1931.

Thayer, Tiffany. *One-Man Show*. New York: Messner, 1937.

Tracy, Louis. *The House 'round the Corner*. London: Ward Lock, 1914.

Trollope, Frances E. *Black Spirits and White*. London: Bentley, 1877.

Tweedale, Violet. *The House of the Other World*. London: John Long, 1913.

Wilde, Oscar. *The Canterville Ghost*. Boston: J.W. Luce, 1906 (novelette).

ANTHOLOGIES AND COLLECTIONS

Aickman, Robert. *Cold Hand in Mine*. New York: Scribner's, 1975.

Anonymous. *Avon Ghost Reader*. New York: Avon Books, 1946.

———. *A Century of Ghost Stories*. London: Hutchinson, 1936.

———. *Fifty Years of Ghost Stories*. London: Hutchinson, 1935.

———. *Ghost Stories and Other Queer Tales*. London: Pearson, 1931.

———. *Ghost Stories and Presentiments*. London: Redway, 1888.

———. *Ghost Stories*. London: R. Ackermann, 1823.

———. *Ghosts and Things*. New York: Berkely Books, 1962.

———. *Modern Ghosts*. New York: Harper, 1890.

———. *Nightmares*. London: Philip Allan, 1933.

————. *Powers of Darkness*. London: Philip Allan, 1934.

————. *Quakes*. London: Philip Allan, 1933.

————. *Shivers*. London: Philip Allan, 1932.

————. *Twenty-Five Great Ghost Stories*. New York: Avon Books, 1943.

Asquith, Cynthia (ed). *The Ghost Book*. 3 vols. New York: Beagle Books, 1970–1971 (reprints of 1927 editions).

Baker, Betty (ed). *Great Ghost Stories of the Old West*. New York: Four Winds Press, 1968.

Benson, E.F. *More Spook Stories*. London: Hutchinson, 1934.

————. *The Room in the Tower*. London: Mills & Boon, 1912.

————. *Spook Stories*. London: Hutchinson, 1928.

————. *Visible and Invisible*. New York: Doran, 1923.

Bierce, Ambrose. *Can Such Things Be?* Washington, D.C.: Neale, 1903.

Blackwood, Algernon. *Best Ghost Stories of Algernon Blackwood*. Ed. E.F. Bleiler. New York: Dover Books, 1964.

————. *John Silence, Physician Extraordinary*. London: John Backer, 1969 (reprint of 1908 edition).

————. *Tales of the Mysterious and the Macabre*. 2 vols. London: Spring Books, 1967.

Bowen, Marjorie. *Kecksies and Other Twilight Tales*. Sauk City, WI: Arkham House, 1973.

Campbell, Ramsey. *Demons by Daylight*. Sauk City, WI: Arkham House, 1973.

————. *The Height of the Scream*. Sauk City, WI: Arkham House, 1967.

Cerf, Bennett (ed). *Famous Ghost Stories*. New York: Random House, 1944.

Chambers, Robert W. *The King in Yellow*. New York: Dover Books, 1970.

Collier, John. *The John Collier Reader*. New York: Knopf, 1972.

Collins, Wilkie. *Tales of Terror and the Supernatural*. New York: Dover Books, 1972.

Crawford, F. Marion. *Wandering Ghosts*. London: Unwin, 1911.

Dare, M.P. *Unholy Relics*. London: Edward Arnold, 1947.

Davenport, Basil (ed). Tales to be Told in the Dark. New York: Dodd, Mead, 1953.

De la Mare, Walter. *The Connoisseur and Other Stories.* New York: Knopf, 1926.

———. *Eight Tales.* Sauk City, WI: Arkham House, 1971.

———. *On the Edge.* London: Faber, 1930.

———. *The Riddle and Other Tales.* New York: Knopf, 1930.

Derleth, August. *Lonesome Places.* Sauk City, WI: Arkham House, 1962.

Doyle, Sir Arthur Conan. *Tales of Terror and Mystery.* New York: Doubleday, 1977.

Fraser, Phyllis and Herbert Wise. *Great Tales of Terror and the Supernatural.* New York: Modern Library, 1944.

Grendon, Stephen (August Derleth). *Mr. George and Other Odd Persons.* Sauk City, WI: Arkham House, 1963.

Hartley, L.P. *The Killing Bottle.* New York: Putnam, 1932.

———. *Night Fears.* New York: Putnam, 1924.

———. *The Traveling Grave and Other Stories.* Sauk City, WI: Arkham House, 1948.

Harvey, W.F. *The Beast with Five Fingers and Other Tales.* New York: Dutton, 1948.

———. *Midnight House and Other Tales.* London: Dent, 1910.

———. *Midnight Tales.* London: Dent, 1946.

———. *Moods and Tenses.* London: Dent, 1933.

Heard, H.F. *The Great Fog and Other Weird Tales.* New York: Vanguard, 1944.

Hodgson, William Hope. *Carnacki the Ghost Finder.* Sauk City, WI: Arkham House, 1947.

———. *Deep Waters.* Sauk City, WI: Arkham House, 1967.

Jackson, Shirley. *The Lottery.* New York: Avon Books, 1969.

James, Henry. *Ghostly Tales of Henry James.* Ed. Leon Edel. New York: Grosset & Dunlap, 1949.

———. *Stories of the Supernatural.* Ed. Leon Edel. New York: Taplinger, 1970.

James, M.R. *Best Ghost Stories of M.R. James.* New York: World, 1944.

———. *Ghost Stories of an Antiquary.* New York: Dover Books, 1971 (reprint of 1904 edition).

———. *More Ghost Stories of an Antiquary.* London: Edward Arnold, 1911.

———. *A Thin Ghost and Others.* New York: Longmans, Green, 1919.

———. *A Warning to the Curious and Other Ghost Stories.* London: Edward Arnold, 1925.

Jerome, Jerome K. *Told After Supper.* Philadelphia: 1891.

Kipling, Rudyard. *Phantoms and Fantasies.* New York: Doubleday, 1965.

Laing, Alexander. *The Haunted Omnibus.* New York: Farrar & Rinehart, 1937 (reprinted as *Great Ghost Stories of the World,* Blue Ribbon Books, 1941).

Lamb, Hugh (ed). *Return from the Grave.* New York: Taplinger, 1976.

———. *Victorian Nightmares.* London: W.H. Allen, 1977.

LeFanu, J. Sheridan. *Best Ghost Stories.* Ed. E.F. Bleiler. New York: Dover Books, 1964.

———. *Ghost Stories and Mysteries.* Ed. E.F. Bleiler. New York: Dover Books, 1975.

Lofts, Norah. *Hauntings: Is There Anybody There?* New York: Doubleday, 1965.

Lovecraft, H.P. *Dagon and Other Macabre Tales.* Sauk City, WI: Arkham House, 1965.

———. *The Haunter of the Dark.* Sauk City, WI: Arkham House, 1963.

———. *The Horror in the Museum and Other Revisions.* Sauk City, WI: Arkham House, 1970.

Machen, Arthur. *Tales of Horror and the Supernatural.* 2 vols. New York: Pinnacle Books, 1971 (reprint of 1949 editions).

Manley, Seon and Gogo Lewis (eds). *Christmas Ghosts.* New York: Doubleday, 1978.

Mazzeo, Henry (ed). *Hauntings: Tales of the Supernatural.* New York: Doubleday, 1968.

Molin, Charles (ed). *Ghosts, Spooks & Specters.* New York: David White, 1967.

Moskowitz, Sam and Alden H. Norton (eds). *Ghostly by Gaslight.* New York: Pyramid, 1971.

Onions, Oliver. *Collected Ghost Stories.* New York: Dover Books, 1971.

———. *Widdershins.* London: Nicholson & Watson, 1911.

Quiller-Couch, Arthur. *Old Fires and Profitable Ghosts*. New York: Scribner's, 1900.

——. *Two Sides of the Face: Midnight Tales*. New York: Scribner's, 1903.

——. *The White Wolf and Other Fireside Tales*. New York: Scribner's, 1902.

Riddell, Mrs. J.H. *The Collected Ghost Stories*. Ed. E.F. Bleiler. New York: Dover Books, 1977.

Sinclair, May. *Uncanny Stories*. New York: Macmillan, 1923.

Singer, Kurt (ed). *Kurt Singer's Ghost Omnibus*. New York: Leisure Books, 1971.

Stern, Philip Van Doren (ed). *The Pocket Book of Great Ghost Stories*. New York: Pocket Books, 1942.

Stoker, Bram. *The Bram Stoker Bedside Companion*. New York: Taplinger, 1973.

Summers, Montague (ed). *The Supernatural Omnibus*. London: Gollancz, 1931.

——. *Victorian Ghost Stories*. London: Simkin Marshall, 1934.

Wakefield, H.R. *The Clock Strikes Twelve*. Sauk City, WI: Arkham House, 1946.

——. *Ghost Stories*. London: Jonathan Cape, 1932.

——. *A Ghostly Company*. London: Jonathan Cape, 1936.

——. *Others Who Returned*. New York: Appleton, 1929.

——. *Strayers from Sheol*. Sauk City, WI: Arkham House, 1961.

——. *They Return at Evening*. New York: Appleton, 1928.

Walpole, Hugh. *All Soul's Night*. New York: Doubleday, Doran, 1933.

Wharton, Edith. *The Ghost Stories of Edith Wharton*. New York: Scribner's, 1973.

FILMS

Burnt Offerings (1976). Oliver Reed, Karen Black, Burgess Meredith. Based on the novel by Robert Marasco.

Canterville Ghost, The (1944). Charles Laughton, Margaret O'Brien, William Gargan, Robert Young. Based on the story by Oscar Wilde.

Don't Look Now (1973). Donald Sutherland, Julie Christie.

The Fog (1980). Adrienne Barbeau, John Houseman, Jamie Lee Curtis.

Ghost and Mrs. Muir, The (1947). Rex Harrison, Gene Tierney.

Ghost Goes West, The (1936). Robert Donat, Jean Parker, Elsa Lanchester.

Ghost Story (1981). Fred Astaire, Melvyn Douglas, Douglas Fairbanks, Jr., John Houseman. Based on the novel by Peter Straub.

Ghosts—Italian Style (Italian, 1969). Sophia Loren, Vittorio Gassman.

Haunting, The (1963). Julie Harris, Claire Bloom, Richard Johnson. Based on the novel *The Haunting of Hill House* by Shirley Jackson.

Hold That Ghost (1942). Bud Abbott, Lou Costello, Martha Raye.

House That Wouldn't Die, The (1970). Barbara Stanwyck, Richard Egan.

Innocents, The (1962). Deborah Kerr, Michael Redgrave, Peter Wyngarde. Based on Henry James's *The Turn of the Screw*.

Legend of Hell House, The (1973). Pamela Franklin, Clive Revill, Roddy McDowall. Based on the novel *Hell House* by Richard Matheson.

Shining, The (1980). Jack Nicholson, Shelley Duval. Based on the novel by Stephen King.

Skull, The (1965). Peter Cushing, Patrick Wymark. Based on the story "The Skull of the Marquis de Sade" by Robert Bloch.

Spectre (Made-for-TV, 1977). Robert Culp, Gig Young. Produced in England by Gene Roddenberry.

Spectre, The (1964). Barbara Steele.

Spirit is Willing, The (1967). Sid Caesar, Vera Miles, John McGiver.

Thirteen Ghosts (1980). Charles Herbert, Jo Morrow. Directed by William Castle.

Topper (1937). Cary Grant, Roland Young, Constance Bennett. Based on the novel by Thorne Smith.

Topper Returns (1941). Roland Young, Joan Blondell, Dennis O'Keefe.

Topper Takes a Trip (1938). Roland Young, Constance Bennett. Based on the novel by Thorne Smith.

Uninvited, The (1944). Ray Milland, Ruth Hussey, Donald Crisp.

Unseen, The (1945). Joel McCrea, Gail Russell, Herbert Marshall.